"They've captured two prisoners, a female
and a wounded male."

"I know that."

"Humph. Well, did you know he's a dragon shifter? And
the girl is the Norveshki princess."

The Woodsman stiffened. "King Silas's sister?"

"Exactly. The heir to the throne. I heard the general has already sent a message to Silas. A trade. His sister and the
dragon shifter in exchange for Gwennore."

So the brave and beautiful soldier was a princess. And she
was in grave danger. "We have to rescue her."

The priest's eyes widened. "We do?"

"Aye. I have a plan."

"Of course you do," Father Kit muttered.

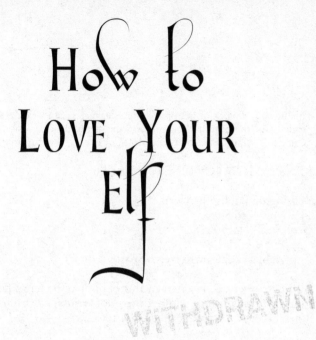

How to Love Your Elf

kerrelyn
SPARKS

KENSINGTON BOOKS
www.kensingtonbooks.com

KENSINGTON BOOKS are published by

Kensington Publishing Corp.
119 West 40th Street
New York, NY 10018

All Kensington titles, imprints, and distributed lines are available at special quantity discounts for bulk purchases for sales promotion, premiums, fund-raising, educational, or institutional use.

Special book excerpts or customized printings can also be created to fit specific needs. For details, write or phone the office of the Kensington Sales Manager: Kensington Publishing Corp., 119 West 40th Street, New York, NY 10018. Attn. Sales Department. Phone: 1-800-221-2647.

Kensington and the K logo Reg. U.S. Pat. & TM Off.

ISBN-13: 978-1-4967-3005-3 (ebook)
ISBN-10: 1-4967-3005-4 (ebook)
Kensington Electronic Edition: March 2020

ISBN-13: 978-1-4967-3004-6
ISBN-10: 1-4967-3004-6
First Kensington Trade Paperback Printing: March 2020

10 9 8 7 6 5 4 3 2 1

Printed in the United States of America

*In memory of my mother,
who passed away while I was writing this story.
She was always happy as long as she had a
good book to read.
All the stories in the universe
are open to you now.*

Acknowledgments

First of all, I always want to thank my readers, for without you, my writing career would have ended years ago. Thank you for continuing to embrace this series! If you would like to experience Aerthlan for yourself, please visit my website at www.kerrelynsparks.com, where you will find a map that allows you to travel about the magical world!

Secondly, I would like to thank Alicia Condon and the great folks at Kensington Publishing for taking on the last two books of the series. It is a pleasure working with you! Also, a big thank-you to my agent, Michelle Grajkowski of Three Seas, for always being there.

And lastly, many thanks to those who support me on the home front: my best friends and critique partners, MJ Selle and Sandra Weider; my father, Les; my children; and my all-time best friend/husband/chief accountant/road manager/personal hero, Don. Love you all so very much!

Prologue

In another time on another world called Aerthlan, there are five kingdoms. Four of the kingdoms extend across a vast continent. The fifth kingdom consists of two islands in the Great Western Ocean. These are the Isles of Moon and Mist. There is only one inhabitant on the small Isle of Mist—the Seer.

Twice a year, one of the two moons of Aerthlan eclipses the other, or as the people call it, embrace. Any child born when the moons embrace will be gifted with a magical power. These children are called the Embraced, and traditionally, the kings on the mainland have sought to kill them. Some of the Embraced infants are sent secretly to the Isle of Moon, where they will be safe.

For many years, the Seer predicted continuous war and destruction across the four mainland kingdoms. But not anymore. Now he claims a wave of change is sweeping across Aerthlan—a change that will bring peace to a world that has known violence for too long. And it is happening because of five young women from the fifth kingdom—Luciana, Brigitta, Gwennore, Sorcha, and Maeve.

The women were hidden away as infants on the Isle of Moon, and there, they grew up as sisters. They knew not where they had been born, nor if they had any family. They only knew each one of them was Embraced.

Chapter 1

Sorcha lunged into an attack, but with a swift kick, her opponent knocked the weapon from her hand.

"Ouch." Sorcha rubbed her wrist as the dagger clattered onto the wooden floor of the castle roof. "That hurt." She aimed an injured look at her cousin.

Annika waved a dismissive hand. "If this was a real battle, I would have stabbed you a dozen times by now. *Then* you could complain about being hurt."

"I don't think she could," Dimitri muttered. "She'd already be dead."

"Oh, thanks. My confidence is now soaring." Sorcha shot him an annoyed look, but he merely shrugged.

"Pick up the knife," Annika said as she widened her stance. She was dressed in the brown breeches and green shirt of the Norveshki army uniform. For this lesson, she'd loaned Sorcha one of her spare uniforms. "We'll try again."

"Must we?" Sorcha motioned to the assortment of weapons that lay scattered upon the wide planks of wood, weathered gray from years of exposure to sun, rain, and snow. "You've disarmed me ten times in a row. I'm obviously not any good at this."

"Obviously," Dimitri agreed, ignoring the face she made at him. "But the king ordered us to teach you self-defense, so we must persevere."

"Don't worry," Annika assured her. "You just need practice. I was bad, too, when I first started."

"Not this bad," Dimitri grumbled.

Sorcha whipped a dagger off the floor. "Can I stab him, please?"

Annika's mouth twitched. "You don't want Dimitri for a sparring partner. He would break some of your bones."

He stiffened with an affronted look. "I would never injure Her Highness."

Sorcha groaned at the title she wasn't yet accustomed to. Life had been so much simpler at the Convent of the Two Moons, where she'd grown up with her adopted sisters. There had been no fancy titles, no uncomfortable gowns or pinching headdresses to wear, no long, boring banquets to endure, and no need to learn how to defend herself. "I'm not sure I could actually plunge a knife into somebody."

Dimitri gave her a stern look. "If an assassin is trying to kill you, then you must."

"Is it really that dangerous now?" Sorcha asked. "Didn't Silas sign a truce with Woodwyn?" Her brother, Silas Dravenko, the new king of Norveshka, was doing his best to live peacefully with the elves on his border.

"We can't trust the elves to abide by the truce." Dimitri scowled as he folded his arms over his wide chest. "Besides, danger could come in many forms. The Chameleon could make himself look like someone you know and take you completely by surprise."

Sorcha groaned. That much was true. In the past few years, the Chameleon had proven himself a formidable enemy. Not only was he a gifted shifter, but he was a vicious murderer. And he had proved impossible to catch, since no one knew what he really looked like.

"I bet we haven't seen the last of him," Annika muttered. "We foiled his plan to take over Norveshka, so he's probably looking for revenge."

"And we also have the Circle of Five to worry about," Dimitri added. "We're fairly certain they're in league with the Chameleon, but we don't know who the members are, so danger could strike at any time."

"Exactly," Annika agreed with her husband, then turned to Sorcha. "If the Circle wants to conquer Norveshka, they could target you since you're the heir to the throne."

"You're an heir, too," Sorcha muttered. Her cousin was currently second in line.

"I can defend myself. You can't." With a sigh, Annika planted her hands on her hips. "If a man attacks you, just remember this: Stomp on his feet. Go for his eyes. Then kick him in the balls."

Dimitri winced. "She wouldn't have to resort to that if you taught her how to properly wield a knife."

Sorcha snorted. "You sound like you'd rather be stabbed than emasculated."

Dimitri shrugged. "A man has his priorities."

"So does a woman," Annika declared. "We do what we must in order to survive." She smiled sweetly at her newly wedded husband. "Perhaps you would help me demonstrate?"

Dimitri's eyes narrowed.

Sorcha suppressed a grin. "That's right. I need to know exactly where to kick."

When Annika crooked her fingers at her husband, he arched a brow.

"If you attack me," he said softly as he took a step toward her, "I will be forced to retaliate in a manner that you might consider overly . . . aggressive."

Annika lifted her chin with a defiant look, even though a blush was sweeping across her cheeks. "I can handle whatever you dish out."

He stepped closer. "Are you sure? You have yet to experience the full extent of my . . . wrath."

Annika bit her lip. "Try me."

When he leaned forward to whisper something in her ear, her blush flared red-hot.

Ick. Sorcha grimaced. *Newlyweds.* At any second, she expected them to pounce on each other. "Don't mind me. I'll just throw myself off the nearest turret, shall I?"

Annika nodded. "That sounds lovely . . ." Her voice faded as Dimitri stroked a finger down her cheek.

With a groan, Sorcha turned away to give them privacy. Not that they needed it. Her two instructors had forgotten she was there. And if this wasn't bad enough, she had to endure the same sort of behavior from Gwennore. She and Silas kept disappearing to their suite of rooms. Even in the middle of the day. They'd been married for six whole weeks. Weren't they tired of each other by now?

Sorcha glanced back, and sure enough, Annika and Dimitri were kissing. A pang reverberated through her heart as she looked away. A small part of her was worried she would never find the gloriously passionate kind of love that her cousin and older sisters were enjoying.

But a much larger part of her was afraid that she would. And it would be an utter disaster.

At the convent, she'd grown up loving her adopted sisters and the nuns who had raised them with kindness. Love there had been soft and comforting. Easy and natural. But that safe cocoon had been ripped to shreds the day Luciana had left to face the unknown.

For the first time, Sorcha had found herself floundering in a deep well of fear, a fear so profound she'd had trouble eating or sleeping. After a few weeks, they'd learned that Luciana had found her true love, but by then, Sorcha had felt physically ill. She'd hid it well, concealing her pain and distress behind a facade of anger and strength.

Life had become peaceful for a short while, but then, the notorious pirate, Rupert, had kidnapped Brigitta in the middle of the Great Western Ocean. Once again, Sorcha's fear for a loved one had consumed her.

Brigitta had fallen in love with her kidnapper, so Sorcha had tried to relax in the following three peaceful years. But then something dreadful had happened. The sister closest to her heart, Gwennore, had been snatched up by a dragon and taken off to Norveshka. There, Gwen had learned that she was half elf and half Norveshki, two peoples who were constantly at war.

Even though Gwennore was now happily married to Silas, the new king of Norveshka, all these events served to reconfirm something Sorcha had suspected about herself for over three years now. When she loved, she loved too desperately. She loved without reason. She couldn't be practical like Luciana, trusting like Brigitta, or clever like Gwennore. When her loved ones were in danger, she was overwhelmed with a sense of helplessness. Love didn't make her strong as it did her sisters.

Sure, she could put on a good show of being fierce. If someone was rude to her sisters, she had no problem cursing or threatening the offender. This had most people fooled into thinking she was strong, but deep inside she knew she was weak. Whenever her sisters had been in danger, she'd been unable to help them. And that had nearly killed her.

The best solution, as far as she could see, was never to allow anyone else into the small group of those she loved. Recently, she'd had to include her newly found brother and cousin, but that was where she drew the line. No one else would be given entry into her heart.

Unfortunately, her older sisters were so happy in their marriages that they wanted her to experience the same sort of marital bliss. And, just as unfortunately, now that everyone knew she was the Norveshki princess, suitors were swarming around like a pack of greedy rodents.

Noblemen from Norveshka as well as the nearby king-doms of Eberon and Tourin had made offers for her hand. She'd turned them all down. There had been a few Norveshki courtiers who had been reluctant to take *no* for an answer, so she'd finally resorted to publicly slapping each one of them in the Great Hall. Now, the courtiers were spreading the word that the princess was a volatile creature with a temper as fiery as her red hair.

Her hands curled into fists as she wandered over to the battlements. She was on the roof of the southern wing of Draven Castle, where Annika had insisted they would have enough room for a proper self-defense class. Now that the truce with Woodwyn was in place, Annika's medical skills were no longer needed at the Norveshki army camp.

In spite of the truce, the elves remained encamped just south of the Vorus River. So Silas had no choice but to keep his army close to the border in case the elves suddenly de-cided to restart the war that had gone on for over two years.

Sorcha propped her elbows on the stone battlement and leaned forward to gaze at the garden below. It was a shame she couldn't turn into a dragon like her brother. Then she would be tempted to simply fly away. Or breathe fire on any-one who threatened her sisters.

Oh, how she missed them! Her sisters had come for Gwen's wedding and coronation six weeks ago, but a month ago they had left. Brigitta and her husband, Rupert, had gone back to Tourin. Luciana and her husband, Leo, had returned to Eberon, and Maeve had gone with them. The youngest sister liked being close to the Ebe River, where she could shift into a seal every month when the moons were full.

When they were all here, they had talked and laughed into the wee hours of the morning. They'd also played the Game of Stones to predict Sorcha's future.

The number five, the colors white and lavender—those were the stones Luciana had selected for Sorcha. They had suspected the five referred to the mysterious Circle of Five, who wanted to take over the world. No one was quite sure who the Five were, but they figured the Chameleon and the power-hungry priest, Lord Morris, were two of them.

As for the colors, white and lavender, none of Sorcha's sisters had wanted to state the obvious. They only had to look at Gwennore's white-blond hair and lavender eyes to predict that Sorcha was fated to meet an elf.

Ha! Ridiculous. No way would she ever fall for an elf. The white and lavender had to signify something else. White teeth? That would be nice. Maybe he would give her lavender flowers. Or his clothes would smell of lavender. Not that it mattered, for she had decided never to fall in love.

A movement in the distance dragged her away from her thoughts. A group of horsemen was headed north, along the Norva River toward the village of Dreshka. The men in the back were holding flags aloft, one white, one dark, the material stirring slightly in the constant breeze that swept down the river valley from the surrounding mountains.

Perhaps the men were merchants? Sorcha knew from her visits to the village that different shops used different flags to indicate what type of goods they were selling. And this group of men had several mules packed with parcels.

As they came closer, she was able to count ten men. Six were dressed in the uniforms of the Norveshki army. They seemed to be escorting the other four men, who all wore hooded cloaks.

A stronger breeze whipped down the river valley, causing the flags to unfurl for a few seconds. Sorcha's breath caught as she realized the white flag had a golden sun in the middle. All four mainland kingdoms worshipped the sun, calling it the Light, an all-powerful male god that reflected their male-dominated society. This flag, with a sun in the center, meant these men were requesting a peaceful parlay. They were probably official envoys.

But from where? Brigitta and her husband usually sent messages by carrier pigeon, and Luciana and her husband sent Brody. Since his Embraced power was the ability to shift into any animal, Brody was able to reach them quickly when he took on the form of an eagle.

That left Woodwyn.

Elves. Sorcha grew tense. Was the elf predicted by the Telling Stones on his way to meet her? Good goddesses, she hoped not. She shook her head, trying to convince herself that these men couldn't possibly be from Woodwyn. The elves never ventured this far away from their homeland.

Only once had she encountered any. A few months ago, three elfin envoys had crossed the border to the nearby Eberoni encampment, and there, they had demanded the return of their princess, Gwennore.

At first Sorcha had been struck by their handsome looks and elegant demeanor, but their snooty attitude had quickly annoyed her. And when Brody had overheard them calling Gwen a half-breed and a pawn, Sorcha had realized that beneath their pretty exterior, they were ugly, two-faced bastards. Luciana and Leo had been relieved that Gwen was far away at Draven Castle, so they'd been able to send the nasty elves back home empty-handed.

Now, as Sorcha watched the approaching horsemen, she focused on the four men wearing dark cloaks, their heads hidden with hoods. Who would wear a hooded cloak in the summertime? Maybe an elf, who was hiding his pointed ears so no one would know who he was?

After all, most people here hated elves. The Norveshki had lost too many loved ones in the war with Woodwyn. That would explain why this group had a military escort.

Her gaze narrowed on the second flag. Brown. The flag of Woodwyn boasted a tall green tree on a brown background. A strong gust of wind whistled down the river valley, unfurling the flags once again and blowing the hoods off two of the men. Sorcha gasped. They had white-blond hair, just like Gwennore. And the brown flag had a green tree in the middle.

She jumped when a horn suddenly blasted from the southeastern tower. The guard there was alerting the castle.

"What is it?" Dimitri demanded as he and Annika dashed toward her.

"Elves." Sorcha motioned toward the horsemen as, once again, fear for a loved one clawed its way into her heart. "What if they insist on taking Gwennore?"

Annika frowned. "They can't have her. She's our queen."

Dimitri waved a dismissive hand. "They just want to talk. We've known about them since they crossed the border two days ago."

Annika's mouth dropped open. "And you never thought to share that with me?"

"Well, I . . . I'd better tell Silas that they're here." Dimitri ran to the stairwell.

"I'm not forgetting this," Annika yelled as he disappeared from view. "I can't believe he didn't tell me."

Sorcha huffed. "I didn't know, either. You would think Silas would keep us informed of this sort of thing. After all, we're his heirs."

"Men," Annika muttered.

"Well, I'm relieved you can still get mad. I was afraid marriage had turned you into a meek lamb."

Annika snorted, then pressed against the battlements to study the elves. "The two in front have the white-blond hair of the River Elves, so they must hail from the area around the Wyn River. They could be from Wyndelas Palace, where the king of Woodwyn lives."

"That would be Gwen's grandfather?" Sorcha asked.

"We believe so," Annika replied. "When Dimitri's uncle

went to Woodwyn as an envoy, we think he may have had an affair with the king's daughter, and Gwennore was the result. Since she's half Norveshki and our queen, there's no way we'll let these envoys take her."

Sorcha watched as Dimitri and a group of soldiers strode from the southern gate to meet the elves. "Where do you think Silas and Gwen will talk to them?"

"The Great Hall, most probably."

"Then, let's go." Sorcha headed for the stairwell.

"Wait a minute." Annika scooped a dagger off the floor and slid it into her boot. "They won't allow us in there."

"But I have to know what's going on. I have to . . ." The fear in Sorcha's heart tightened painfully. Good goddesses, she was so sick of feeling useless whenever her sisters were in danger. "I refuse to be left out!"

Annika's eyes lit up. "The minstrels' balcony. I know a secret way in."

They could hide there and hear every word. Sorcha ran to the stairs. "Let's go!"

Sorcha was grateful she was wearing a shirt and breeches as she sprawled on the wooden floor of the minstrels' balcony at the far end of the Great Hall. The balcony was usually accessed by a staircase in the Great Hall, but Annika had shown her a hidden staircase that originated in a nearby waiting room.

After blowing out the candle they'd used to light the dark stairway, Sorcha and Annika had hurriedly closed the balcony's thick, velvet curtains. Now, they were lying on the floor, peeking under the curtain's hem and between the wooden slats of the balustrade.

The afternoon sun was streaming through the long westward-facing windows, illuminating the large, rectangular room and cooling it with a mountain breeze, but up here in the balcony with the curtains drawn, it was dark. And hot.

"What's taking them so long?" Sorcha adjusted the belt buckle that was digging into her stomach.

"Silas and Gwen must be putting on their finest clothes. And they probably sent for their crowns," Annika whispered. "They'll make the elves wait."

Sorcha wrinkled her nose. She hoped the elves had been told to wait outside in the courtyard, where it tended to get hot and stuffy at this time of day. "We're Silas's heirs," she grumbled. "He should have invited us to this meeting. I'll be letting him know how aggravated I—"

"Sorcha." Annika sounded impatient. "You're still too naïve. I guess it comes from growing up in a convent. But this is strategy."

"What do you mean?"

"Silas doesn't want the elves to know what his heirs look like. It will keep us from becoming easy targets."

"Oh." Sorcha swallowed hard. Her cousin had a point. If she was going to be useful, she needed to be smarter. And stronger. And if she was going to survive as the heir to the throne, she would have to be wary and suspicious of almost everybody. Completely the opposite from the convent. "I'm glad I have you, Annika."

Her cousin gave her shoulder a squeeze, then lifted the curtains a bit more to peer down into the room.

The curtain and floor were dusty and made Sorcha's nose twitch. "I'm afraid I'll sneeze."

"Don't you dare." Annika handed her a handkerchief. "Here, hold this against your mouth and nose."

Sorcha pressed the lavender-scented cloth to her nose as a creaking noise reverberated below. The doors were being opened. Footsteps sounded on the stone floor and a low voice spoke in Norveshki. It was Dimitri, giving orders. Only two elves had been allowed in, the two with white-blond hair. The other two, who had been tasked with carrying the flags, were most probably servants.

Sorcha couldn't tell much about the elves as they crossed the hall, since she was seeing them from the back. With their hooded cloaks gone, their fancy clothes were now revealed— blue velvet tunics over cream-colored silk shirts and cream-colored leather breeches. That had to be hot, she thought, although they didn't show any sign of discomfort. They were tall, as tall as Dimitri, but whereas he moved like a wildcat stalking his prey, the elves were as smooth as a pair of swans gliding across a cool lake.

Dimitri instructed them to stop a good six feet away from the dais and to move to the left. They set down two parcels encased in blue silk, then stood, facing Dimitri.

Now that Sorcha had a side view of them, she could see they were not the same envoys who had come to the Eberoni camp. But they were equally as handsome, damn them.

Hopefully, the Telling Stones had not referred to either of these men. One was shorter and looked quite a bit older than the other with strands of silver gleaming in his hair. Sorcha glowered at the younger and taller elf. He was as pretty as Gwennore. She was tempted to run down there and mess up his hair.

They were just too perfect. No wrinkles in their elegant clothes, even after a long journey. Not a single smudge on their flawless complexions. Like Gwennore, these elves had black eyebrows, which made a stunning contrast to their white-blond hair that fell to their shoulder blades like silk curtains. Side braids kept their hair back from their noble brows, which were decorated with circlets of gold.

The elves had no weapons on them, so they must have been disarmed before entering the Great Hall. But they didn't seem at all intimidated by Dimitri, who glared at them with a hand resting on the hilt of his sword. Another sheath was strapped to his thigh, the jeweled, golden handle of a vicious dagger clearly on display.

"You are in Norveshka, so you will be expected to speak Norveshki," Dimitri announced.

The elves gave him a bland look, then the older one spoke quietly in perfect Norveshki, "We did not come to speak to you."

Sorcha gritted her teeth. Arrogant bastards.

The door creaked again and more footsteps sounded. She pressed her face against the railing and spotted Silas and Gwennore, walking arm in arm toward the dais, followed by Aleksi Marenko, a captain in the army, who was as fiercely armed as Dimitri.

Sorcha couldn't help but smile at how radiant Gwen looked in her sparkling gold gown. Silas was quite dashing in his army uniform. They were both wearing their newly crafted crowns.

They stopped briefly in front of the elves, giving them a slight nod of their heads. At least the elves were well mannered enough to bow. But it seemed to Sorcha that they were bowing more to Gwennore than to Silas.

Her brother helped his wife step up on the dais; then they both took their seats on the gold, jewel-encrusted thrones. Aleksi positioned himself next to Gwennore's throne, where he eyed the elves with suspicion.

"Your Majesties." Dimitri bowed to Gwen and Silas, then added, "General Caladras and his son, Colonel Griffin Caladras, extend greetings from King Rendelf of Woodwyn."

Silas gave the elves another nod. "I bid you welcome to Norveshka."

The elves bowed slightly, and then the general spoke. "His Majesty, King Rendelf, asked me to congratulate you on his behalf. He was quite impressed by your quick and successful ascension to the throne."

Silas's eyes narrowed.

Sorcha winced. Silas wouldn't have become king if his older brother hadn't been killed by the Chameleon. Since a spy had been caught trying to cross into Woodwyn, it was very possible that the Chameleon had been working with the elves. Silas even suspected the Chameleon might be an elf.

"Thank you," Silas replied curtly. "I trust your king wishes to continue the truce between our two countries?"

"Of course." The general motioned to Gwennore. "We would also like to congratulate you on your marriage to our beloved princess, Gwennore."

Sorcha wadded the handkerchief in her fist. Beloved, her ass. The general had to know that Gwen had been rejected as a babe and shipped off to the convent.

Gwennore looked tense but was doing a good job of keeping her face blank.

"Our Majesty, King Rendelf, has sent a wedding gift. We hope it meets with your approval." General Caladras untied the knot at the top of the bigger parcel, then let the blue silk fall into a puddle around an ornate box of carved wood inlaid with pearl.

As the general opened the lid, Dimitri stepped close to check what was in the box. Then he stepped back, his hand tightening on the hilt of his sword till his knuckles turned white.

The general lifted out a sculpture, carved entirely of wood. "Not to sound overly boastful, but I believe this piece proves that the craftsmen of Woodwyn are the best in all Aerthlan. It is magnificent, yes?"

It was an exquisite dragon, delicately carved and polished to a lustrous gleam. A pair of sparkling rubies marked its eyes.

Sorcha swallowed hard, and next to her, Annika hissed in a quick breath. Was this genuinely a present, or were the elves hinting that they knew the true nature of the Norveshki dragons?

As a member of the royal family, Sorcha had been told the secret, that a few male descendants of the Three Cursed Clans were capable of shifting into dragons. Silas, Aleksi, and Dimitri could, along with about a dozen others. For centuries, it had been Norveshka's most closely guarded secret.

The three dragon shifters below grew very still.

Silas's mouth thinned; then he nodded. "It is, indeed, a work of art. Thank you."

"I'm delighted you're pleased." The general's voice dripped with sarcasm as he returned the dragon to its box. He unwrapped the smaller parcel to reveal a small flat box of polished wood. "And this one is for our very own Princess Gwennore."

"She is a queen," Silas corrected him. "*Our* queen."

"Of course." The general opened the box to display the contents. "Woodwyn also has the best silversmiths. This necklace was made especially for you, Your Majesty."

"It's quite beautiful. Thank you." Gwennore accepted the open box.

"It was designed by your own mother," the general continued, and Gwen's hands flinched slightly. "She is thrilled at the prospect of seeing her beloved daughter once again."

"Who is her mother?" Silas asked.

"You didn't know?" The general exchanged a smirk with his son. "Princess Jenetta, of course."

"How would we know who she was?" Gwennore asked quietly. "She sent me away when I was two months old."

"And it broke her heart!" The general placed a hand on his chest. "She was a victim, too, in that dreadful mess. Not only was she forced to part with you, but she was sentenced to seven years of solitude in the white tower."

Gwennore grew pale. "My . . . mother was punished?"

"Yes. But now that Princess Jenetta is heir to the throne, His Majesty greatly regrets his decision. He no longer blames his daughter. She simply fell prey to the seduction of that insidious foreigner, Lord Tolenko."

Annika hissed in another breath at this blatant insult to Dimitri's uncle.

With a muttered curse, Dimitri took a step forward, but Silas lifted a hand to stop him.

Gwennore's cheeks flushed as she snapped the jewelry box shut. "Do not insult my father. It is bad enough that he met an untimely death while in your country."

"I understand." The general bowed hastily. "Your loyalty to your father is commendable." He removed a letter from his tunic. "I hope it will not deter you from reading this letter. Your mother wrote it."

Gwennore accepted the letter, her face growing pale once again. "I will look at it later."

"Of course." The general nodded. "Your mother and grandfather are extremely eager to see you. His Majesty is not well, I'm afraid, so if you would please visit them at Wyndelas Palace—"

"Too far," Silas interrupted.

"We would make sure she was comfortable on the journey," the general told him. "After all, she is our princess."

"It is too far," Silas repeated, leaning forward. "I cannot allow our queen to venture that far into what was enemy territory only a few weeks ago."

The general stiffened. "Surely you are not suggesting we would do harm to our own beloved princess."

"We will be happy to meet Her Majesty's family at the border," Silas said.

The general sighed. "As I said, King Rendelf is not well. His health is too precarious at the moment to undertake such a long journey."

"My wife is not up to a long journey, either," Silas countered. "She is now carrying our future heir."

Sorcha gasped. Gwennore was with child? And this was how she found out? Annika nudged her, and Sorcha winced, now realizing that Gwen's gaze had shot up to the balcony for a brief second. Elves had notoriously good hearing, and even though her gasp had been muffled by the handkerchief, Gwen had still heard. Even the younger elfin colonel turned his head slightly.

Gwen coughed as if to draw their attention to her. "What you fail to understand, General, is that I have no desire to meet my grandfather, not when he had my father executed and my mother imprisoned."

The general's hands fisted for a few seconds before he relaxed them. "Then we will meet you at the border."

"Excellent." Silas stood. "We will make arrangements. As for now, no doubt you wish to rest after your long journey."

He and Gwen stepped off the dais and, followed by Aleksi, they sauntered across the room and out the door.

"I will escort you to your rooms," Dimitri told the elves.

"If you don't mind, we're extremely parched after our long journey," the general murmured. "Would you be so kind as to bring us some wine?"

Dimitri's back stiffened at being treated like a servant. "There are refreshments in your rooms, but since you're unable to endure your discomfort for a few more minutes, I will have a servant tend to you in the waiting room." He motioned toward the door. "This way."

The general and his son followed Dimitri out the door.

After the door slammed shut, Sorcha scrambled to her feet.

"What an ass," Annika muttered. "Did you hear how he talked to my husband?"

"Come on. We have to hurry." Sorcha used her gift as one of the Embraced, snapping her fingers to make a flame and light the candle. Then holding up the candlestick, she slipped quietly down the secret staircase.

"We can't leave this way," Annika whispered as she followed behind her. "We'll end up in the waiting room where the elves will be."

"We're not leaving." Sorcha reached the ground floor and held a finger to her lips to warn her cousin not to talk.

Annika joined her next to the exit, and Sorcha quietly set down the candlestick and blew out the flame. Then she pressed an ear to the thick canvas that served as a hidden door.

The waiting room was small, its walls covered with wooden paneling. Numerous paintings of former kings and queens lined the walls, and one portrait, a large floor-length one, had a hidden latch, so that it opened like a door. With just the canvas separating Sorcha from the waiting room, she could hear every word said inside.

"A servant will attend to you soon," Dimitri announced. "A guard will remain outside this door, so please make yourselves comfortable." The door was shut firmly.

"Comfortable?" the colonel grumbled in Elfish. "In this dark and dreary little room? No windows, just these hideous portraits to look at."

"Indeed," the general agreed. "The artists here are definitely inferior to what we're accustomed to."

"Look at this monstrosity." The younger elf's voice sounded very near, and Sorcha guessed he was standing only a foot away from her. "I guess these barbarians think the bigger the better."

"I suppose so," the father murmured. From his footsteps, he seemed to be pacing about the room.

"Did you see how many jewels they crammed onto those gaudy thrones? It took all my willpower not to wrench the princess off—"

"Watch what you say, Griffin," the general interrupted. "The walls could have ears."

The colonel was silent for a moment. "I think I did hear someone up in the minstrels' loft." He knocked on the paneling. "This seems solid enough, though. Besides, I don't think any of these barbarians understand Elfish."

Sorcha smirked. *Think again, bastard.*

Griffin pounded a fist harder on the paneling. "It's bloody unfair! The princess was promised to me!"

"Relax," the general grumbled. "We must remain patient. So far, the plan has worked well."

"Not well enough," Griffin whined. "It's bad enough I have to take that half-breed after she's already been bedded, but now she's with child!"

"Calm yourself," his father growled. "A babe is not difficult to get rid of. It is her freakish husband that will be the problem."

Sorcha pressed a hand against her mouth to keep from making a sound.

The door creaked open, and a servant murmured in Norveshki, "Excuse me, my lords, I have brought your refreshments."

"Pour me a cup and be quick about it," the general ordered in the same language. "Then take us to our rooms."

"Yes, my lords."

After a few minutes, footsteps clumped on the wooden floor and the door closed.

Sorcha held her breath for a minute longer, making sure the elves were truly gone.

"Did you understand what they were saying?" Annika whispered in the dark.

"Yes." Sorcha inhaled deeply. The elves planned to capture Gwen and murder her brother. "When Silas and Gwen travel to the border, we must go with them."

"All right," Annika agreed.

Sorcha pressed her fingers to her thumbs, making two circles that signified the twin moons. *Goddesses, hear my vow. I will not stand by, feeling helpless once again, when my loved ones are in danger. Never again.*

Chapter 2

"Are you all right?" Sorcha asked Gwen as she pressed a hand to her stomach.

"Are you feeling nauseated again?" Annika asked.

It was two weeks later, and Gwen was now certain that she was, indeed, with child. "I'm fine. A little nervous, that's all." She touched the silver necklace she was wearing. The gift from her mother. "After twenty-one years, I'm finally meeting my mother."

"I'm sure everything will go well," Sorcha said, even though she was nervous, too.

The three women were alone, sitting around a camp table inside the royal tent, just north of the Vorus River, which served as a boundary between Norveshka and Woodwyn. The meeting had been set for this evening at sunset. Gwen, Silas, and a dozen guards were to walk halfway across the nearby bridge. Gwen's mother, along with General Caladras and a few guards, would meet them there.

Annika patted Gwen's hand. "It'll be fine. There's not enough room on the bridge for an actual battle."

Gwennore winced, and Sorcha shot her cousin an annoyed look. "That's not helpful."

Annika scowled back at her. "You're the one who told us what the general and his son said. Obviously, we cannot trust those two."

"I don't. I don't trust any of those elves." After all, it was a well-known fact that the elves had a nasty habit of attacking villages in Eberon and Norveshka for no apparent reason other than a vicious desire to maim innocent people and destroy their homes. Sorcha leaned forward, her elbows on the table. "But I do trust my brother. He's not going to let them kidnap Gwen."

"If they try something, it will be the end of the truce," Annika muttered. "We'll be at war again."

"Enough." Gwen rubbed her stomach. "I want to have positive thoughts about today."

"Of course. Sorry." Sorcha exchanged a sheepish look with her cousin.

After hearing the general's conversation with his son, Sorcha had quickly passed on the information to Silas and Gwen. Then, with newly inspired determination, she'd joined the army and spent the last two weeks laboring hard to learn her combat skills. She was now battered and bruised, but fairly adept at defending herself.

She and Annika had been named Queen Gwennore's official ladies-in-waiting, but in reality, they were her bodyguards. Even now, they were both in uniform with daggers strapped to their thighs and hidden in their boots.

"I don't care what Silas says," Sorcha told Gwen. "I'm going on that bridge with you."

Annika nodded. "Me, too."

Gwen's eyes glimmered with tears as she looked at them. "What would I do without you two?"

Sorcha sighed. Gwen seemed to cry over nothing these days.

"When I think about how much Silas and I love each other and how much we want this baby"—Gwen looked down at her belly—"I can't imagine the pain and hardship my mother went through. The man she loved was executed. Her new-born baby was ripped from her arms and sent away. Then she was locked in a tower for seven years. How does someone survive that much cruelty?"

Sorcha wasn't sure how to respond, for she wasn't convinced the sad story was even true. Granted, she had very little experience with elves, but from what she did know of them, it seemed abundantly clear that they could not be trusted. "We only have the general's word that your mother suffered," she began quietly, but Gwen shook her head.

"My mother explained everything." Gwen reached across the table to open the jeweled keepsake box that she had brought with her on the journey. "It's all in here." She removed the letter her mother had written.

"May I?" Sorcha extended a hand.

Gwen paused a minute, then passed her the letter. "It's in Elfish, but you should be able to understand it."

Sorcha unfolded the paper and quickly scanned the contents. It did, indeed, chronicle a tragic story as Gwen's mother described the heart-wrenching pain of being separated from her baby, and how she'd spent the last twenty-one years missing her daughter and praying daily for her safety and wellbeing.

Gwen watched her carefully. "What do you think?"

Sorcha hesitated. Knowing Gwen as well as she did, she figured her sister had focused on the words and their meaning. But Sorcha had always been better at artwork than composition. She leaned back in her chair and eyed the letter from the viewpoint of an artist.

The script was elegant and flowing. Bold and carefree. Not what she would expect from someone who had been imprisoned or suffered for many years. It made her suspicious, but then again, she could be letting her distrust of elves color her interpretation.

She knew all too well that she and her sisters had grown up with the pain of having been abandoned as wee babes. Fortunately for Sorcha, she'd learned several months ago that her mother had sent her away to protect her from a curse and a plague. Knowing that her mother had always loved her meant the world to Sorcha.

Of course Gwennore wanted the same for herself. Who wouldn't? The hopeful look on her face tugged painfully at Sorcha's heart. It would be petty to let her suspicions spoil what might turn out to be a beautiful and joyful reunion.

She folded the letter and handed it back. "It seems sincere."

"I think so, too." With a smile, Gwen returned the letter to her keepsake box.

Please don't let her be hurt, Sorcha prayed to the twin moon goddesses.

"Your Majesty?" Aleksi's voice called from the entrance to the tent. "Permission to enter?"

"Yes," Gwennore responded.

Sorcha rose to her feet, worried that something had gone wrong with the plan, but to her surprise, the captain entered with his arms filled with flowers.

He bowed his head, his nose bumping into a bouquet of yellow and orange blossoms. "Your Majesty, my ladies, I . . . I . . . ah . . . ahchoo!"

Petals flew at Gwen's face, and she sat back.

"Is this a new method of attack?" Sorcha asked wryly.

"Forgive me." Aleksi bowed his head again. "Where can I put . . . ahchoo!"

"For Light's sake, get your nose out of them." Jumping to her feet, Annika grabbed the now-bedraggled flowers and dumped them on the table.

Gwennore smiled at the captain. "Since Annika and I are both happily married, I can only assume that you intend Princess Sorcha to be the recipient of your lovely gift?"

Aleksi's eyes widened, and Sorcha groaned inwardly. Gwen

was still trying her hand at matchmaking. As fond as Sorcha was of Aleksi, he had always seemed like an older brother to her. Much the same as Brody.

Aleksi shifted his weight as he shot an awkward look at Sorcha. "Well, if Her Highness wants some flowers—"

"I don't," Sorcha grumbled.

Gwen gave Sorcha a disapproving glance at her refusal to cooperate. "Surely there is something that Aleksi could do that would impress you."

Sorcha thought about it, then smiled. "I'd like to go for another flight." He'd taken her for a dragon ride once, and she'd loved it.

He grinned. "We can do that."

"Excellent." Gwen exchanged a knowing smirk with Annika.

Sorcha rolled her eyes. No doubt the two of them thought romance was in the air. Aleksi was a handsome young man, but he could never pierce the defenses of her locked up and closely guarded heart. No man could. "So why did you bring all these flowers?"

"They're for Her Majesty," Aleksi explained. "A group of women and their husbands came from Vorushka and asked me to deliver the flowers to the queen. The women are all with child now, and they and their husbands asked me to convey their gratitude."

Gwennore rose to her feet, her eyes wide. "The tonic worked?"

"Yes!" Annika punched the air with her fist. "We did it!"

With a happy squeal, Gwen hugged Annika; then Sorcha embraced them both. The tonic, invented by Gwen and Annika, had been made in hopes of reversing the effects of a plague that had rendered most Norveshki women infertile.

"Congratulations," Aleksi said, grinning at them.

"Oh." Annika stepped back, releasing Gwen. "You should rest. You were nauseated before."

Gwen shook her head. "I feel much better now." She snatched up some flowers and tossed them in the air. "This is going to be a wonderful day!"

With a laugh, Sorcha tossed more flowers in the air. Petals rained down on them, landing on their hair and shoulders.

Aleksi grabbed a bunch of flowers to join them just as Silas and Dimitri marched into the tent. He immediately stood at attention, along with Annika and Sorcha, but when he thumped his fist to his chest in salute, he crushed the flowers against his leather breastplate. "Ahchoo!"

Silas gave him a wry look, then glanced at the women.

Gwennore beamed at him. "We can explain."

Sorcha brushed the petals off her long braid of hair. "A bunch of grateful women gave the flowers to Aleksi. They're with child now."

Dimitri looked askance at Aleksi. "You dog."

"What?" Aleksi's face turned red. "I didn't . . ."

Gwennore laughed. "The tonic worked, Silas. Women are getting pregnant."

"By their husbands," Aleksi added, and Dimitri snorted.

"That is good news," Silas said, and Sorcha wondered why his strained smile didn't reach his eyes.

"Is something wrong?" she asked.

He withdrew a letter from beneath his leather vest. "This message was secretly passed to one of our guards on the bridge. I couldn't read it, since my Elfish is very limited, but I recognized the name at the bottom. Princess Jenetta."

"My mother." Gwennore grabbed the letter and unfolded it.

Sorcha peered over her shoulder to read the contents.

"She wants to meet us in secret an hour before sunset," Gwennore translated.

"An hour before the meeting on the bridge?" Dimitri asked.

"Yes." Gwennore continued, "My mother says we can't trust the general and his son."

Sorcha snorted. "We already knew that."

"But she's admitting it's true?" Annika asked.

Gwennore nodded. "She wants a secret meeting in order to assure our safety. She says three miles east of here, the river is only a foot deep and we can cross easily on horseback. She will have refreshments for us in a tent about a mile south of the river."

Silas stiffened. "That's in Woodwyn."

"She's trying to lure us across the border," Aleksi muttered.

Dimitri nodded. "It could be a trap."

"No." Gwen dropped the letter on the table. "According to my mother, the trap was supposed to happen on the bridge. This is her way of keeping us safe."

Sorcha grabbed the paper and read it once again. Gwennore's interpretation seemed to be correct, but suspicion gnawed at her gut.

"Aleksi, fly over the elfin encampment, then go three miles east to where the princess is setting up her tent," Silas ordered. "See if any soldiers are moving toward the new meeting point."

"Yes, Your Majesty." Aleksi saluted and hurried from the tent so he could shift into a dragon.

"You don't trust my mother," Gwen said with a hurt voice.

Silas winced. "I can't risk losing you."

"But why would she cause me any harm?" Gwen argued. "She's heir to the Woodwyn throne. How could she possibly benefit by hurting me?" When Silas was silent for a moment, Gwen pressed harder. "Since she's going to be the queen of Woodwyn, shouldn't we try to have a good relationship with her?"

With a frown, Silas dragged a hand through his hair.

"Shouldn't my mother know she's going to have a grandchild?" Gwennore pleaded with tears in her eyes. "Please,

Silas. I just want to see her for a few minutes. Isn't there some way we can do this?"

Silas shifted his weight. "If Aleksi doesn't spot any elfin soldiers around your mother's tent, we could try crossing the river. But we would need several troops of soldiers with us."

Dimitri gritted his teeth. "We can't do that. It would be seen as an invasion. They would have every right to attack us."

"We would carry white flags of truce," Gwennore suggested, then motioned to the message, written by her mother. "And we'll take this letter with us, since it clearly invites us into the country."

"The general will attack first and ask questions later," Annika muttered.

"If the general is still expecting to meet us on the bridge at sunset, he won't be anywhere close to this secret meeting," Gwennore insisted. "Please, I want to do this."

Silas sighed, and Sorcha knew he was going to cave in. It was too hard for him to refuse his wife anything.

"If you do it, then I'm going, too," Sorcha declared.

"Me, too," Annika added. "We're her official bodyguards. It's our duty to protect her."

Silas gave the women a wry look. "You're going to insist on doing this, aren't you?" When they all nodded, he let out a groan. "Fine, but I'll have Lieutenant Kashenko go in first with an entire troop. And we'll have another troop behind us. At the first sign of trouble, I'll shift and fly Gwennore back across the border. Dimitri, you will shift and take Annika. Aleksi will take Sorcha. As long as we stay close to the border, we can be back in Norveshka in just a minute or two."

Dimitri nodded. "That should work."

Sorcha took a deep breath and exchanged a look with her cousin. They were going! But even as excited as she was, there was something about the plan that didn't seem right.

"Be ready to leave within a half hour," Silas told them. "I'll have Kashenko ready the troops."

As he and Dimitri ducked under the low entrance to the tent, Sorcha realized what was bothering her and rushed forward to stop her brother.

"Silas," she whispered, touching his sleeve. "If we come under attack and you and the others have to shift, the elfin army will see you. They'll know your secret."

He nodded. "It's a risk we'll have to take in order to keep you safe. Besides, I have a feeling it's no longer a secret. The Chameleon probably told them. That gift they gave us was a strong hint."

The carved dragon with the ruby eyes. Sorcha winced.

"It will be all right." Silas gave her a smile and a pat on the shoulder. "Trust me."

She smiled back, but her smile faded as he rushed after Dimitri. What if Gwen's mother had orchestrated this meeting to make it look as if she was trustworthy when in actuality, she wasn't? The elves not only wanted to kidnap Gwen, but they wanted to be rid of Silas. What if this was a trap designed to achieve both ends?

Perched high on a thick branch of an oak tree, the Woodsman scanned the elfin army encampment on the flat plain below. His spy had sent him a message late last night that the camp would be empty and easily infiltrated this afternoon. And so, he and his men were now hidden on a high ridge overlooking the camp.

To the north, farther than he could see, the Vorus River marked the boundary with Norveshka. How long would the truce last this time? Not long if that bastard, General Caladras, had his way.

The Woodsman turned his attention back to the elfin camp below and spotted several guards standing stiffly at attention in front of officer tents. He wasn't the only one interested in the camp today. On his way here, he'd spied one of the Norveshki dragons flying overhead.

It was gone now, and the camp was quiet. Too quiet. And too still.

A flash caught his eye, and he spotted his spy, Tarrant, emerging from the thick forest on the east side of the camp and holding up a mirror to reflect the sun's rays. Three quick flashes, the signal that meant it was safe for the Woodsman and his band to make their move.

Safe? With all the guards there?

As if Tarrant knew what he would be thinking, the spy ran toward the nearest guard and pulled off the helmet to reveal a straw dummy underneath. The Woodsman snorted. The guards were all fake, but at a distance, they certainly looked real. They'd fooled him. They'd probably fooled the dragon. Removing a mirror from his pocket, he signaled his position up on the ridge.

As Tarrant headed in his direction, the Woodsman slipped to the bottom branch of the oak tree, then jumped, landing neatly on the spongy, moss-covered ground. He made the soft hooting sound of an owl, and several of his men emerged from their hiding places behind trees. Dressed just like the Woodsman, with brown breeches, dark green tunics, and brown hooded cloaks, they blended in well with the forest. They waited silently as the rest of his troop led the horses through the woods to join them.

"Don't get greedy and take more than you can carry," the Woodsman warned them softly. "We follow the plan, go straight to the supply tents, help ourselves, and get out. Once the horses are packed, take them down Norus Creek for a while so you can't be traced, then take the goods to Drudaelen Castle before heading back to Haven. You two—" He looked at two of the youngest in the group, Ronan and Colwyn. "You know what to do."

"Yes, sir!" The two young men glanced at each other, excitement glittering in their eyes.

The Woodsman winced inwardly. He hated endangering any of his men, but when the elfin army discovered they had been robbed, they would send out search parties. If these two didn't succeed in leading them astray, then the people at Drudaelen Castle and Haven could be in danger. "Just because you've outsmarted them in the past, it doesn't mean you can afford to be lax. Keep your wits about you. If they capture you, they will torture you. They'll want to know the location of Haven."

Their faces sobered. Both had family in the hidden village.

The Woodsman placed a hand on each of their shoulders. "Do as you were trained, and you'll be fine."

"Don't worry, Captain." Colwyn smiled. "We'll lead them into Whistler's Bog. We grew up near there, so no one knows the bog better than we."

The Woodsman squeezed their shoulders, then let go. "If something goes wrong, tell a Living Oak, and it will let me know. We'll come for you. We never leave men behind."

The rest of his followers murmured their agreement; then they all headed down the ridge.

Tarrant met them at the edge of the camp. "There's no one here, so help yourselves." He pointed out the supply tents, and the Woodsman's band quickly took the horses over, then set to work, relieving the army of most of their food supplies.

"How are my mother and sister?" Tarrant asked as he walked alongside the Woodsman.

"Good. They're happily settled in Haven and send their love." He wasn't sure he should mention that Tarrant's thirteen-year-old sister was smitten with Colwyn.

"Thank you, sir." Tarrant bowed his head. After the army had ransacked a local village, they'd burned it to the ground, leaving his family without a home.

As the Woodsman glanced around the camp, memories

from his childhood flooded his mind. Some were good. Some horrific. He shook those thoughts away and stopped in front of an officer's tent, much like the one he had shared with his father and his father's squire so many years ago. In front of the tent stood a straw dummy decked out in full uniform. "Why did Caladras go to so much trouble to make it look like the army is here?"

"He wanted to fool the Norveshki," Tarrant explained. "He's planning an attack a few miles east of here where the Vorus River is shallow. That's where I was. We were ordered to move last night in the dark, and we've been hiding there since before dawn. I managed to sneak away to meet you—"

"Is Caladras planning to invade Norveshka?" the Woodsman asked.

Tarrant shook his head. "I don't think so. He has the army about two miles south of the border, hiding in the forest on both sides of a road."

"So it's a trap? Who is the target?"

Tarrant dragged a hand through his long, brown hair. "I'm not sure. The officers don't tell us foot soldiers everything."

"Tell me what you do know."

Tarrant pointed in the direction of the river. "There's a bridge over there, and that's where the king and queen of Norveshka were supposed to meet the general and Princess Jenetta at sunset."

The Woodsman stiffened. "The princess is here?"

Tarrant nodded. "I heard she came to see her long-lost daughter, who's the queen of Norveshka now."

Gwennore. The Woodsman took a deep breath. His informants had told him about the latest events in Norveshka, but he wasn't sure what Princess Jenetta and General Caladras were up to. Was the princess trying to lure Gwennore and King Silas across the border?

"But the meeting on the bridge was canceled," Tarrant continued. "Now the princess has set up a tent—"

"Dammit." Gwennore was in trouble. The Woodsman whistled for one of his men to bring him a horse. "I need to go there."

Tarrant gasped. "Captain, you can't! The place is swarming with soldiers, and you have a price on your head."

Father Kit, the band's resident priest, jogged over to them, leading a horse. "What's wrong?"

Tarrant grabbed the reins with a mutinous look. "I can't let him go. It's suicidal."

"Caladras has laid a trap for the king and queen of Norveshka," the Woodsman explained as he swung into the saddle. "I have to stop it."

"By yourself?" Father Kit frowned at him. "It's too dangerous. You're too valuable to—"

"Enough! And you, let go." The Woodsman yanked the reins from Tarrant's grip. "Father, make sure everyone gets away safely. I'll see you later in Haven."

Father Kit shook his head. "I'm staying. Halfric will, too, until we know you're safe." He pointed at the ridge. "We'll wait for you there tonight."

The Woodsman gritted his teeth. He didn't have time to deal with the stubborn priest now. "Fine, but whatever you do, don't get caught." He urged the horse into a fast gallop, headed east for the forest.

How could he keep Gwennore from falling into a trap? Dammit, he needed a plan. She was a member of the royal family, so she might be able to communicate with trees.

Living Oaks, he called to them. *Are you able to converse with the elfin queen of Norveshka?*

She cannot hear us, one replied.

She is not as gifted as you, another said. *Her abilities are limited.*

Damn. He leaned forward, encouraging the horse to run faster. They cleared the camp, then headed into the woods. As the forest grew thicker and the terrain more hilly, he was forced to slow his pace. Frustration gnawed at his normally calm determination. What if he didn't reach her in time?

I have heard her talk to the Kings of the Forest, another oak told him.

Renewed hope lightened his heart, and he called to the giant redwoods. *Great Kings, hear my plea. Can you pass on a message to Queen Gwennore?*

The silence of the forest bore down on him, and he worried that the Kings hadn't heard. The trees surrounding him were beech, ash, and oak. No redwoods in sight.

What is your message, Woodsman? A faint reply filtered into his head. The Kings might be far away, but they had heard him.

Thank you. Will you tell Gwennore to remain in Norveshka? She must not venture into Woodwyn. The elfin army has set a trap for her!

We will tell her, the Kings replied.

Too late, a Living Oak whispered in his head. *She and her husband have crossed the river.*

Too late, the Woodsman repeated to himself, as he rushed forward. The trap would soon be sprung.

Chapter 3

The plan was working, Sorcha thought as her horse plodded across a narrow sandbar in the Vorus River, then splashed into water less than a foot deep. Ahead of her, Lieutenant Kashenko led a dozen men on horseback, their shields and spears ready, as they ventured onto the river's southern bank into the country of Woodwyn. In the center of his troop, a soldier held up a white flag with a golden sun in the center.

No elves in sight.

Silas motioned for the rest of the entourage to move forward. He and Gwennore rode in the middle with Annika and Dimitri to their right. Sorcha was on the left, between Silas and Aleksi, dressed much the same as they, in brown leather breeches and breastplate, dark green shirt with a matching cape attached to the shoulders. Her sword rested against her hip, and as the late afternoon sun gleamed off her brass helmet, she could swear her head was being cooked.

But there was no help for it. Silas had insisted that she and Annika dress the same as the male soldiers. Since everyone knew his heirs were female, he feared they would be targeted if this was a trap.

They reached the Woodwyn shore, followed by a dozen cavalrymen. After traveling south across a grassy plain for about a mile, they spotted a narrow road flanked by a thick forest. Far down the road, a lone tent waited for them.

Sorcha eyed the thick forest. A perfect setting for an ambush. Apparently her brother shared her suspicion, for he called the group to a halt.

"We should turn back." Silas gave his wife an apologetic look. "I'm sorry."

Gwennore nodded, then suddenly flinched, her eyes growing wide. "The Kings of the Forest say it's a trap!"

"Shields up!" Silas yelled. "Retreat!"

But as soon as the troop in front raised their shields to form a barrier, a barrage of arrows shot from the woods. Most arrows plunked off the metal shields, but a few flew over the top of the barrier and wounded some soldiers.

"Shift!" Silas ordered as he jumped off his horse. Dimitri and Aleksi also dismounted, so they could shift into dragons.

An arrow hit Sorcha's horse, and with a shriek, it reared up on its hind legs. She plummeted to the ground, her head knocking hard against the brass helmet. For a few seconds she saw stars, but when she refocused, she realized her horse's flailing hooves were about to crash down on top of her. With a cry, she rolled to the side. The horse landed with a thud, then crumpled to its knees.

Poor horse. Sorcha's heart raced. She had no horse now, but surely Aleksi would get her out of here. She spotted Silas already in dragon form with Gwennore in his tight grip. As he rose into the air, a barrage of arrows and spears sped toward him. He retaliated with a burst of fire that incinerated all the weapons.

As soon as Silas took off for Norveshka, Dimitri shot into the air in dragon form with Annika riding on his back.

Sorcha scrambled to her feet and spotted elfin soldiers streaming from the forest into the road. Their battle cry echoed in her ears. Their swords gleamed in the afternoon sun.

Dimitri shot flames at them, forcing them back. The grass surface of the road caught fire, forming a barrier between the elves and the Norveshki.

"Retreat!" Lieutenant Kashenko yelled.

Dimitri flew off with Annika while soldiers spurred their horses into a gallop toward the river. Sorcha ran to the side to keep from being trampled. Everything was happening so fast. Where was Aleksi?

She froze in shock as a mass of elfin soldiers charged from the long length of the forest. Holy goddesses, there were hundreds of them! The front line of archers stopped and took aim with their bows and arrows.

"Sorcha!" Aleksi was on foot, looking frantically for her. He'd torn off his breastplate and shirt to make it easier to shift.

"I'm here!" She ran toward him.

He dashed toward her, his skin turning a greenish black as he started to shift. Just a few feet away from her, he halted suddenly with a jerk. His skin faded to its natural color as he fell to his knees, an arrow embedded in his back.

"Aleksi!" *No!* He wouldn't be able to shift now. She looked frantically around her. Her horse was down. The white flag of truce lay on the ground, trampled. Aleksi's horse! She sprinted toward it, grabbed the reins, and led it to him. "We'll ride back. Hurry! Get on!"

With his teeth gritted against the pain, he rose to his feet. "You get on first."

She mounted, then extended a hand to help pull him up. But to her surprise, he slapped the horse's rump to make it run.

"No!" She pulled hard at the reins, desperate to stop the animal. It bucked, threatening to toss her off. A few cavalrymen raced past her toward the river. Dammit. It had been a big mistake, dressing like the other soldiers. They didn't realize who she was. Or how new she was to all this.

"I need help!" she yelled as she forced her horse to turn back toward Aleksi. With a surge of panic, she realized the elfin army was moving in fast.

"Dammit, Sorcha!" Aleksi stumbled toward her. "Get out of here!"

She jumped off the horse. "Not without you!" She grabbed his arm.

His eyes widened, and he swung her around, using himself as a shield as more arrows came at them. His body jerked as one thudded into his shoulder.

"No!" Sorcha wailed as he crumpled to his knees.

"Go," he whispered.

How could she leave him? "Dammit, Aleksi." She tried to pull him up, but his eyes flickered shut and he slumped to the ground. Had he fainted or . . . ?

"Your Highness?" Lieutenant Kashenko rode up beside her.

"Help me!" She struggled to lift Aleksi, and the lieutenant leaped off his horse.

Another soldier stopped and dismounted. With dismay, she realized they were the only ones left. All the other soldiers had done as ordered and retreated to Norveshka.

And the elfin army was getting too close.

"Guard us while I lift the captain," Lieutenant Kashenko ordered the other soldier as he leaned over to pick up Aleksi.

The soldier pulled his sword from its sheath, then abruptly turned toward them and plunged the sword into the lieutenant's back.

Sorcha gasped as Lieutenant Kashenko fell to his knees. The soldier pushed on the sword, shoving the blade all the way through the lieutenant's chest till it erupted through his leather breastplate, coated with blood.

She stumbled back, struggling to breathe. The lieutenant collapsed on his side. Blood spilled from his mouth, and he coughed, a nasty gurgling sound. His gaze wandered toward Sorcha, then stopped.

Dead. She looked in horror at his glassy, sightless eyes. *Dead.* Two weeks of training had not prepared her for this. How could anything prepare her for this?

Her sight grew hazy. Her heart thudded in her ears, drowning out all sound. Her mind spun in circles, unable to focus.

Something squeezed her ankle hard, and she blinked. Aleksi had grabbed her boot. Aleksi. He was still alive. And he needed her.

She pulled her sword and pointed it at the soldier. "Traitor! Put the captain on that horse before I run you through!"

The traitor smirked. "Go ahead and try. There will be more like me. The Circle of Five is everywhere. And you'll never know who to trust."

"Drop your sword!" a voice called out in Elfish.

Shock slithered icy cold down her spine. Elfin soldiers had surrounded her. *Goddesses, help me!* She glanced at the poor lieutenant who had died trying to help her. Her mind threatened to retreat once more into a haze, but she shook off the numbness. *Keep your wits about you.* Whenever her loved ones were in danger, she'd always put up a strong front. She'd have to do it again. This time for herself.

She kept her sword aimed at the traitor and announced in Norveshki with a voice she hoped sounded masculine, "You will release me and this wounded soldier. If we don't make it across the border, the king will retaliate with his full force."

"Oh, I'm so scared," a mocking voice replied in Norveshki.

The elfin soldiers moved aside as a tall man in an officer's uniform sauntered toward her. She stiffened with recognition. Colonel Griffin Caladras, the one who thought Gwennore had been promised to him.

"Drop your sword," he ordered, still speaking Norveshki. When she hesitated, he lifted a hand, and two of his archers aimed arrows at Aleksi, only a few inches from his head.

She released the sword, letting it fall to the ground.

Griffin's mouth twisted with a smirk. "I know why you're so desperate to save him. I saw him start to shift. He's one of those damned dragons, isn't he?"

"He is," the traitor confirmed. "He's Captain Aleksi Marenko, close friend to King Silas."

Sorcha clenched her fists. She scanned the traitor's features, mentally drawing his portrait so she could remember his face.

Griffin smiled. "Good work, Paxell."

The traitor beamed at the compliment, then pointed at Sorcha. "She's even more valuable."

"*She?*" Griffin's eyes narrowed as he looked her over. "By the Light, you're right. That uniform doesn't quite hide all the curves."

"She's the—" Paxell began, but Griffin lifted a hand to stop him.

"Don't tell me." He moved closer to Sorcha. "She's my prisoner. She will speak when I tell her to. Do whatever I tell her to. Understand, wench?"

She glared at him.

"Take off your helmet. I want to see my new property."

Sorcha looked away, ignoring him.

He motioned to a soldier behind her, and a gloved hand gripped her shoulder and shoved her to her knees. Another soldier grabbed at the cheek guards of her helmet.

She knocked his hands away. "No one touches me."

"Bitch," the soldier growled in Elfish.

She started to call him a bastard, then bit her lip. It might be wise to keep her knowledge of Elfish a secret. If only she could keep her identity a secret, but no doubt the traitor was eager to let the elves know that they'd captured the heir to the Norveshki throne.

The best she could do was beat him to the punch. She removed her helmet, and her long braid of red hair slipped down her back. "I am—" She stopped, taken aback by the disgusted look on the colonel's face.

"By the Light," Griffin muttered in Elfish. "Don't tell me the barbarians consider this pretty."

Several soldiers snickered.

Asshole. Sorcha kept her face blank so they wouldn't know that she understood all their snide comments about the unfortunate freckles on her face or the upturned nose that reminded them of a pig.

The traitor, Paxell, seemed to understand them, for he waved his hands to get their attention as he announced in broken Elfish. "She . . . still valuable! She . . . princess!"

The chuckles and comments halted immediately.

"The princess?" Griffin stepped closer to Sorcha and asked in Elfish, "Are you the king's sister?"

She ignored him. Still on her knees, she grabbed onto her thighs, digging her fingers into the leather breeches. She had to stay sharp. Focused.

"Maybe she doesn't know Elfish," a soldier mumbled.

Griffin used the flat edge of his sword to lift Sorcha's chin. "Prisoner," he growled in Norveshki. "Tell me who you are."

She was about to answer when a deep voice in the distance cursed in Elfish.

"Dammit! You call yourselves soldiers?" General Caladras shoved an archer to the ground as he marched toward them.

The colonel and his group of soldiers quickly moved out of the general's way and saluted.

General Caladras glowered at them. "We outnumbered them by hundreds, and this is all you have to show for it? Two prisoners and one dead officer?"

Griffin bowed his head. "The Norveshki began their retreat before they reached the woods, sir. We were unable to spring the trap as planned."

"There should be more casualties!" the general roared.

"We could chase after them," a soldier suggested. "Try to kill some more as they cross the river."

Griffin waved a dismissive hand. "I already ordered a troop to go after them."

"Are you incompetent fools?" the general growled at them.

"How can you shoot hundreds of arrows and miss?" He kicked at the fallen arrows and spears that littered the ground. "What the . . ." He leaned over to grab a handful of arrows. "These are broken."

Sorcha's eyes widened. The wooden shafts of the arrows had been cleanly broken in two. She glanced at the ground around her and spotted more arrows and spears, all with broken wooden shafts.

"The Woodsman!" the general shouted. "He's here! Quickly, scour the forest and find him! I want his head!"

The Woodsman? Sorcha watched as elfin soldiers mounted their horses and charged toward the forest. Was there someone out there who was on her side?

"So whom did you capture?" the general asked his son, and Griffin smirked.

"A dragon shifter. And this." Griffin pointed his sword at Sorcha and switched to Norveshki. "She was about to tell us her name."

She lifted her chin. "I am Princess Sorcha. And if you don't return this wounded soldier and myself immediately, my brother will retaliate with the full force of his army and his war dragons. Your army will be destroyed." She motioned to the burning grassy area, where elfin soldiers were desperately trying to keep the fire from spreading to the forest. "The dragons will set your country ablaze till nothing is left but ashes."

Griffin snorted. "She hasn't quite realized she's a prisoner."

General Caladras arched a brow as he looked her over. "So she's the heir to the throne?" He slowly smiled. "I will gladly return you, Your Highness. As soon as your brother gives us Gwennore."

Sorcha swallowed hard. They expected Silas to trade his wife for his sister? Poor Silas. This was going to kill him. "He will never give you Gwennore."

The general chuckled. "He won't have to. I suspect our

foolishly brave and loyal Princess Gwennore will come voluntarily in order to save you."

Sorcha's breath caught. Good goddesses, that was true. Gwennore would sneak away on her own if she thought it was the only way to save her adopted sister. "Silas will never let her go."

"That would be a shame." Griffin shrugged. "Because then we'll have to kill you."

Sorcha gripped her thighs hard as panic threatened to consume her. Her gaze wandered toward Lieutenant Kashenko. *Don't go into shock again.* Her gaze flitted to Aleksi, who looked unconscious. Blood still seeped from his wounds. He would not be able to save her. And if she didn't manage to save him, he would die.

She had to do it. She had to rescue Aleksi. And save herself before Gwennore tried to do it. But how?

"Tie them up and throw them in the cages," Griffin ordered in Elfish.

As one of the soldiers made a grab for Sorcha, she knocked his hands away.

"You won't like what happens when you don't cooperate," Griffin muttered in Norveshki as he stalked toward her, lifting his sword.

She raised her hands to defend herself, but two soldiers seized her arms to hold her still. With the hilt of his sword, Griffin knocked her hard on the head.

Pain exploded as she collapsed next to Aleksi. Then everything turned black.

Chapter 4

Sorcha woke slowly to a dull pounding in her head. She blinked, wondering why she couldn't see well; then her befuddled mind realized that night had fallen.

She gasped, coming fully awake as the afternoon's terrible events flashed through her mind. *Escape.* That was what she needed to do.

Furtively, she glanced around, willing her eyes to adjust quickly to the dark. She was lying on her left side, her cheek against cool grass. A few feet in front of her was a line of round wooden poles. She shifted slightly for a different view and realized with a start that her hands were tied. Her feet, also.

About five feet away from her feet was another row of wooden poles. A gate with a lock on it. She glanced up. More wooden beams crisscrossed the top. She was in a wooden cage. The night was clear, the two moons gleaming half full, surrounded by a million stars.

Not far away, she spotted campfires. Tents and a few soldiers. She was on the border of the elfin army camp. Should she pretend she was still unconscious? Where was Aleksi?

She quietly rolled onto her back, turning her head to the right.

Another cage. Some twenty or thirty yards away. She squinted, barely making out a man's body lying on the ground.

"So you're awake," a man's voice grumbled in Elfish.

She froze, wondering if she should pretend to fall back asleep. Probably too late for that now. But it might be a good idea to continue her pretense of not understanding Elfish. She might hear something useful.

The guard sauntered up to the cage to look at her. "I heard you're a princess. The colonel said we have to keep you alive. For a while." He chuckled.

Another elfin asshole. She sat up slowly, ignoring the pain in her head as she looked around. Behind her cage, she spotted the jagged silhouettes of tall trees. She was not far from the forest.

"Hey, I'm talking to you!" The guard rattled something against the cage, and she glanced his way. "I bet you're hungry. Hell, we all are, but some thieving bastards wiped out our supplies. All we have left is some stale bread and some casks of wine. Guess the casks were too heavy for the bastards to carry off."

Someone had robbed the army camp? Sorcha smiled to herself. The elves deserved any rotten thing that happened to them. It was hard to see her guard in the dark, but he seemed like an older, heavyset man. His hair was a dark color, not whitish-blond, so he had to be one of the Wood Elves.

He turned a wooden plate sideways to slip it between two poles, and she realized that was what he'd used to rattle her cage. He threw the plate, and it hit the ground, rolling on its edge before wobbling and falling flat not far from her feet. Then he tossed a small loaf of bread that landed on the grass a few inches from the plate.

"Oops. Missed." He stepped back with a chuckle.

Sorcha lifted her tied wrists and spoke in Norveshki, "If you expect me to eat, untie me."

With a smirk, the guard responded in Elfish, "I can guess what you're saying, and it's not going to happen."

"Hey." Another soldier approached, holding two pewter tankards. "It looks like this is dinner."

"More wine?" The guard grabbed one of the tankards and took a big gulp. "Those damned thieves."

"I know. I'm so hungry." The soldier took a long drink, then wiped his mouth with his hand. "The general sent out six hunting parties."

"Good. I hope they bag a few deer."

The soldier snorted. "Idiot. They're not hunting for food. They're trying to catch the thieves."

"Oh, right." The guard rubbed his ample belly and belched. "So is there any bread left?"

"I wish." The soldier drank some more wine.

"Damn." The guard glanced at the small loaf he'd thrown at Sorcha. "I shouldn't have wasted that on her."

"So she's awake?" The soldier stepped close to the cage to peer at her. "She doesn't look like a princess."

"I know." The guard gave her an annoyed look. "She just sits there, staring at us. Too dumb to understand a word we're saying. So does the general know who robbed us?"

The soldier shrugged and took another drink from his tankard. "He thinks it was the Woodsman and his gang."

The guard snorted. "He would. He thinks the Woodsman is the cause of every foul thing that happens."

"Aye. If he smelled a fart, he would think the Woodsman did it."

The two men laughed and finished off their drinks. The guard stumbled a bit, then caught one of the poles to steady himself.

With only wine and no food, they were getting drunk, Sorcha realized. This might work in her favor and help her escape. But who was this Woodsman that General Caladras hated so much? Had he actually broken all those arrows and spears during the battle? The general had sent out search parties, but apparently, they had not caught the man. Whoever he was, he was probably long gone.

The guard yawned. "Don't forget to relieve me in a few

hours. I didn't get any sleep last night, what with us moving to that new site to lay the trap."

"None of us got any sleep," the other soldier mumbled, casting a sour look at Sorcha. "Don't worry about her. She can't go anywhere. And the other one is too weak to do anything."

The guard glanced over at Aleksi. "Aye, he might not live through the night."

Aleksi, stay alive. Sorcha slumped down on the ground, hoping to look like someone who had given up all hope. With any luck, her guard and the other soldiers would fall into a drunken slumber. And then, she could make her move. Thank the goddesses she had a weapon no one could take from her.

Her Embraced gift of fire had been frowned upon at the convent, especially after she'd burned down the kitchen in a horrendous accident that had come close to killing one of the nuns. She'd been only eight years old at the time, eager to experiment with the new talent she'd discovered. But after the accident, Mother Ginessa had forbidden her to use the gift, declaring it too destructive and dangerous.

Sorcha had agreed, for the realization that she could have killed someone had terrified her. From then on, she'd only used her gift on rare occasions when no other source of fire had been readily available.

But now, her gift could save her. And Aleksi. With her tied hands, she made the sign of the moons. *Goddesses be with me while I make my escape.*

"Where were you?" the Woodsman whispered as Father Kit approached him on the ridge. The priest was holding a rusty old army lantern to light his way. "Where did you get that—Oh, don't tell me you were captured."

The priest shrugged. "I was captured."

"Dammit, Fa—"

"Don't fuss at me. It was your fault." The priest held up a hand when the Woodsman started to object. "It's true. They figured out you were here and scoured the forest, searching for you. That's when they found me. Or rather, I let them find me. They were getting too close to the copse where the horses were hidden, so I led them away."

The Woodsman sighed. As soon as he'd realized that General Caladras was sending out search parties for him, he'd asked the Living Oaks to hide his friends and their horses. When it came to keeping himself safe, he could always evade capture by remaining high in the trees. "You should have stayed hidden with the horses."

"Don't worry. I gave them the usual story, that I'm a poor itinerant priest from Eberon, traveling about the world to spread the joy and peace of enlightenment."

The Woodsman snorted. Father Kit had been using that same story since he'd fled Eberon eighteen years ago. His version of enlightenment usually entailed lightening a person's pockets.

"They gave me some wine. Excellent wine. And they even apologized for not having any food to give me." Father Kit chuckled. "I tried so hard not to laugh that my eyes watered, and they thought I was crying for them. Then they gave me more wine and asked me to lead them in prayer. Guess what I had to pray for."

"I wouldn't know." With a wave of his hand, the Woodsman moved the tree branches that were hiding the horses.

"I beseeched the Light to help them catch the thieves who stole their food. I had to pray for your capture, too. They're really looking forward to torturing you."

The Woodsman gave him a wry look. "I can only hope the Light gave up on you years ago."

The priest shrugged. "I figure the Light is all-knowing, so he knows when I'm kidding. Oh!" His eyes lit up. "Guess what! They're laying bets on how the general will decide to execute you. Drawing and quartering is in first place. Apparently, they hate your guts so much, they want to see them up close."

"I'm touched." The Woodsman led the three horses out of their hiding place.

"Hanging was second place." The priest shook his head with a disapproving frown. "Sorely lacking in imagination, that one, but a few of the others were more interesting. Like suffocating you in the mud of Whistler's Bog or chaining you to a lightning rod—"

"Enough. We need to go before someone wins the wager. Where is Liz?"

Father Kit grimaced at the name he didn't approve of. "He's around here somewhere. You know he would never get caught."

True, the Woodsman thought. Liz, short for Lizard, had an unusual gift as one of the Embraced. He could manipulate colors and camouflage himself so well, he could be standing six feet away right now and they wouldn't know it. That made him an excellent spy. And unfortunately, an even better thief.

After eluding the elfin army until nightfall, the Woodsman had finally made it back to the ridge, only to discover the horses were there and the priest and Liz were not. While he'd waited for their return, he'd discovered the cages where the army was holding two Norveshki prisoners. Even though it would be dangerous, his instincts were urging him to rescue them.

"Oh, there was something else I heard," Father Kit said as he gathered the reins to his horse. "They've captured two prisoners, a female and a wounded male."

"I know that."

"Humph. Well, did you know he's a dragon shifter? And the girl is the Norveshki princess."

The Woodsman stiffened. "King Silas's sister?"

"Exactly. The heir to the throne. I heard the general has already sent a message to Silas. A trade. His sister and the dragon shifter in exchange for Gwennore."

Holy shit. The Woodsman paced away a few steps. He'd checked on the prisoners only a minute ago. The man had appeared unconscious, the young woman asleep. So she was Princess Sorcha.

He'd watched the battle that afternoon from a spot high up in a tree. From there, he'd been able to use his Embraced power to break the elves' arrows and spears. And he'd caught a glimpse of Gwennore before her husband had shifted into a dragon and flown off with her. A second dragon had escaped with a female soldier, and he had assumed she was the princess. With most of the Norveshki troops retreating as fast as they could, he'd witnessed one brave soldier who had returned to rescue an injured comrade.

He'd been impressed. The soldier followed the same philosophy that he did—never leave a man behind. Unfortunately, there had been nothing he could do to help when that soldier had ended up captured. Frustration had clawed at him. And then shock had nearly caused him to fall out of the tree, for the soldier had turned out to be a woman. A beautiful woman. Intrigued, he'd made sure to learn where she and her companion were being held.

So the brave and beautiful soldier was a princess. And she was in grave danger. "We have to rescue her."

The priest's eyes widened. "We do?"

"Aye. I have a plan."

"Of course you do," Father Kit muttered.

"The cages are about half a mile west of here. Whistle for Liz to return, then bring your horses to meet me there. Stay hidden on the ridge." The Woodsman mounted his horse and rode through the forest to the place where he'd spied the cages earlier. Luckily, they were on the edge of the camp, not far from the ridge lined with trees.

He tied off his horse, then adjusted his brown cloak, pulling the hood far over his head. Leaning against a large oak tree, he studied the two cages. Light from the twin moons and a million stars allowed him to see the two prisoners. No movement from the injured dragon shifter. The lone guard was slumped over, snoring while he slept. The young woman appeared to be sleeping, too.

So she was Sorcha. King Silas's sister. Adopted sister of the queens of Eberon, Tourin, and Norveshka. General Caladras might think it a smart move to trade her for Gwennore, but he was inviting the wrath of the other mainland countries. No doubt Silas and the other kings would want to declare war. But the general was probably threatening to kill Sorcha and the dragon shifter if the other countries attacked.

Sorcha's friends and family had to be worried sick. The Woodsman called out mentally to the giant redwoods, *Great Kings, hear my plea.*

The redwoods responded quickly. *We hear you, Woodsman.*

The Living Oaks chimed in with several voices. *Be careful. The forests are teeming with soldiers looking for you.*

They believe they are stealthy, but they are clumsy and foolish.

True, the redwoods agreed. *They are disturbing the silence of the night.*

My apologies, the Woodsman replied. *Great Kings, could you pass another message to Gwennore? Please tell her that I will rescue Princess Sorcha and the dragon shifter. They will be under my protection until I can safely deliver them to the border. This I vow as a man of honor.*

We will do as you ask.

Thank you, Great Kings. And Living Oaks, please keep me apprised of the location of the soldiers as we make our escape.

We will watch over you. As usual.

Thank you. The Woodsman rested a hand on the oak tree

that was sheltering him. While others might feel only rough bark, he could feel the pulse of the tree's living spirit. *You are always there for me.*

Until we become one, the Living Oaks whispered back, their voices drifting away with the night breeze.

The Woodsman shifted his attention back to the princess's cage. It was made of wood, so he'd have no trouble slicing a few poles in two. The hard part would be removing her without waking the guard. If he simply walked into her cage and grabbed her, she might struggle or scream.

He started forward, then froze when all of a sudden, she sat up. Her head turned from one side to the other. Then slowly and quietly, she scooted herself to the back of the cage. What on Aerthlan was she up to?

The guard snuffled in his sleep and rolled onto his side.

The Woodsman slipped back into the shadow of the oak tree, eager to see what she would do next.

She swiveled around on her rear until she faced him, her back to the guard. Then with a snap of her fingers, a flame appeared.

What the hell? The Woodsman's mouth fell open. Somehow she was holding fire on her fingertips without burning herself. The flames ate through the ropes encircling her wrists; then she quickly rolled her hands on the ground to extinguish the fire.

She had to be Embraced and fire was her gift. Or maybe her gift came from being part of a family of fire-breathing dragon shifters. Was she a dragon, too? No, he doubted it. He'd never heard of a female dragon. And if she were a dragon, she would have flown away by herself. She wouldn't have needed to wait for the man in the other cage to shift.

Whatever the truth was about her, one thing was certain— she was surprising the hell out of him. He would have to make adjustments to his plan.

After glancing over her shoulder at the still-sleeping guard, she positioned her tied feet in front of herself and stretched the rope taut. Another snap of her fingers, and the rope caught fire.

As she pulled her legs apart, a section of flaming rope fell onto the grass, which caught fire.

Damn! The Woodsman stepped forward. He'd better get her out of there before she was trapped inside a burning cage.

Using the end of her cape, she quickly smothered the fire.

With a sigh of relief, he moved back into the shadow.

She inched forward on her knees and grabbed hold of the wooden poles. Was she intending to burn her way out? That would be dangerous. Quickly, he swiped his hand, using his Embraced power to slice through the two poles she was holding. She fell forward as the poles gave way and ended up on all fours, halfway out of the cage.

After a quick, frantic look around, she eased out of the cage. She ran, then scrambled up the ridge and through the trees, not far from where he was hiding. In the small clearing, she leaned over, her hands on her knees while she breathed heavily.

Now that she was closer, he could see her golden red hair. He'd marveled at it earlier when she'd been captured and it had gleamed like fire in the afternoon sun. His mouth curled up. The color seemed fitting, considering her gift of fire. And he'd never realized before how appealing a woman could look in tight leather breeches. *Damn.*

She straightened and took a deep breath as if to calm her nerves. "Aleksi," she whispered.

Was that the dragon shifter? Did she intend to rescue him? She was gutsy, he had to admit, but too unpredictable. He would feel much more comfortable if they were following his plan. Stepping out of the shadows, he whispered in Elfish, "I'm here to help you."

She spun toward him with a gasp.

"Shh." He held a finger to his mouth. "We don't want to wake the guard."

When he moved closer, she lashed out an arm to strike him across the chest, then stomped on his foot.

"Ow. What the—?" He caught her by the wrist as she tried to jam her fingers into his eyes. Her knee came up, aimed for his groin, and he quickly grabbed her thigh and jerked it to the side.

She lost her balance, starting to fall backward, so he released her wrist to catch her, wrapping his arm around her waist to pull her forward. With a thump, she collided against his chest.

"Are you all right?" His knowledge of Norveshki was limited, but that was something he knew how to say.

She glanced up at him, her eyes growing wide.

Green eyes. As green as the newly unfurled leaves of an oak tree in spring. *Sorcha.* His hand flinched, still gripping her thigh. She was different. With her face turned up to look at him, the moon shone off her luminous skin, and a million stars sparkled in her eyes.

She was incredible. Unique. Her beauty paired with her brave fighting spirit made a combination that took his breath away. How long could he hold her in his arms?

"Who are you?" she whispered in Norveshki.

"I am the Woodsman."

Chapter 5

He has a beautiful mouth.

Sorcha blinked. What was she thinking? "Who . . . what . . . ?" Good goddesses, her mind was racing so fast, she didn't know what to think or say.

So this tall man in a hooded cloak was the Woodsman? Had he actually broken all those arrows and spears? Had he robbed the army camp? How had he eluded capture with so many soldiers hunting for him? Well, for one thing, he was fast. He'd been very quick to avoid her knee.

She pushed at his chest. "Let me go."

He released her at once, and she stumbled back. With a start, she realized that when she'd attacked him, he hadn't retaliated. In fact, he'd saved her from falling by pulling her against his chest. A chest that had felt as solid as the giant redwoods Gwennore liked to talk to.

But was he friend or foe? He'd spoken to her in Norveshki, but his accent proved that it wasn't his native tongue. So was he an elf?

Oh, dear goddesses! What if he was *her* elf, the one predicted by the Telling Stones? If he was, then she needed to get away from him as quickly as possible. She peered up at him to see whether he had lavender-blue eyes or white-blond hair, but she couldn't tell with that hood covering most of his head. All she could see in the dark was a sharp jawline and

chin that looked like they could have been chiseled from marble. And his beautifully shaped mouth.

Don't think about that. How long was he planning to just
stand there and stare at her? "I . . ." She cleared her throat
and continued in Norveshki, "You're not planning to turn
me in, are you? After all, you want to avoid the army, too,
right?"

There was a pause while she wondered if he'd understood
her. Should she go ahead and speak to him in Elfish? Was the
rest of his face as beautiful as his mouth? *Stop wasting time
thinking about that.*

"I will help you," he replied in Norveshki.

He had a nice voice, deep and soothing. But could she
trust a complete stranger? A light in the distance interrupted
her thoughts. It was moving through the trees, coming
straight toward them. An army search party!

"Hurry!" She grabbed the Woodsman's arm and pulled
him behind a large oak tree. Was the shadow enough to hide
them? His brown cloak blended in well with the tree, so she
tugged the edge of it up to cover herself as she huddled
against his broad chest.

"What—?" he began, but she stopped him by resting a finger against his mouth.

"Soldiers," she whispered. Then she realized she was
touching his lips and jerked her hand away.

He turned her so her back was to the tree, then placed his
hands on the wide tree trunk, pinning her between his arms.
What was he doing? Her heart thundered in her ears as he
leaned closer. She opened her mouth to object, but she didn't
dare make a sound, not with enemy soldiers nearby. Holy
goddesses, if her heart pounded any harder than this, they
might hear her.

His voice feathered against her ear as he whispered in Elfish,
"Are you so brave, you're trying to protect me?"

A shiver skittered across her skin. Why was she reacting like this? It had to be alarm. After all, he spoke Elfish as if it was his native language. And she knew all too well that she could never trust an elf.

The light grew closer, illuminating the clearing on the other side of the tree. The Woodsman leaned to the left as if he was planning to peer around the tree, and she quickly placed her hand against his face to shove him back into the shadow.

Oh, damn, she'd touched him again. She yanked her hand away, but he caught it and peered closely at her fingers.

He brushed his thumb over her fingertips. "You make fire without getting burned," he whispered in Elfish.

He'd seen her make her escape. She pulled her hand away.

A soft hooting sound came from behind them, and the Woodsman stepped out of the shadow.

"Father—" he began in Elfish, but another voice interrupted him in the same language.

"Oh, there you are. Have you rescued the princess?"

Sorcha stiffened. They knew who she was.

The Woodsman glanced at her, then motioned for her to join him.

She peeked around the tree and spotted a large man dismounting from his horse. A young man, who appeared close to the age of twenty, was holding a lantern and the reins of a second horse. They were dressed the same as the Woodsman, but their hoods were resting on their shoulders. She blinked. They weren't elves!

She stepped into the clearing. "Norveshki?"

The father shook his head. "Eberoni."

"Oh!" Sorcha clasped her hands together. She could talk to them in Eberoni! "I grew up on the Isle of Moon, so Eberoni is my native language. Although I do have a wee bit of an accent."

The father smiled. "It's a relief that we can talk to you."

He motioned to the young man beside him. "We come from the village of Mt. Baedan."

"I've been there." Sorcha smiled back. Since these men were from Eberon, she might be able to trust them.

"You're the Norveshki princess, then?" the father asked.

"She doesn't look like a princess," the youth muttered, and the father elbowed him in the ribs.

"Mind your manners, son."

So was this a family? Sorcha wondered. A father and two sons from Eberon?

"I am Father Kit." The older man introduced himself with a small bow. "And this is Halfric."

"But everyone calls me Liz," the young man added.

"How do ye do?" Sorcha murmured as she tried to figure things out. The older man was not their father after all, but a priest?

"You're not a Lizard," Father Kit hissed under his breath. "Use the name I gave you as a babe."

Liz grimaced. "I hate that name."

"Humph." The priest lifted his chin. "Halfric is considered a noble name in Eberon."

"What's so great about Eberon?" Liz grumbled. "We had to leave."

"Enough!" the Woodsman growled in Elfish. "Liz, you weren't at the meeting place when you were supposed to be."

The young man winced, then replied in the same language, "It was just too easy, Captain. Most of the army is out looking for you and the rest of our group, and the few soldiers who were left behind are in a drunken stupor. Look what I brought for us!" He held the lantern up to display the goods that were tied to the second horse. Several dozen quivers filled with arrows and another dozen bundles of spears.

The Woodsman stiffened. "You raided their armory? Did I not make my orders clear? You were to take only food."

"But this means fewer weapons they can use on us," Liz argued. "And don't we need weapons for the rebel—"

"Shh." The Woodsman glanced at Sorcha, and she innocently studied her boots as if she hadn't understood a word.

Rebellion? Was that what the young man had almost said? What was this Woodsman up to? It seemed clear now that he and his men were a group of thieves from Eberon. Brigands who invaded a neighboring country to steal and cause trouble. She didn't dare trust them after all.

"I don't want you taking risks like that again," the Woodsman ordered in Elfish. "This is my fight, not yours."

"But we're all with you, Captain!" Liz insisted.

The Woodsman lifted a hand to stop him. "We'll discuss it later. We've wasted enough time for now." He turned to Sorcha and switched to the Eberoni language. "We need to be going. I'll fetch your friend. Then you can ride with me."

She stepped back. "I-I'm not going with you."

The Woodsman seemed taken aback for a few seconds. "But I am here to help you. I have a plan."

Liz smirked. "The Woodsman always has a plan."

Sorcha shook her head. "I can manage quite well on my own, thank you. Norveshka's only about a mile to the north." She pointed to the right.

The Woodsman's sigh sounded exasperated. "That's south."

"Whatever." She glared at him. "Once the sun comes up, I'll know which direction to go."

He stepped closer to her. "Before the sun rises, you need to be far away from here. Once they realize you've escaped, there will be soldiers hunting for you all along the Norveshki border." He motioned toward the second cage. "Were you planning to leave your comrade behind?"

"Of course not." She lifted her chin. "I broke out of my cage. I can break Aleksi out, too."

"With fire? If you set the cage on fire, it could wake up the soldiers. And how will you save an unconscious man? Can you carry him out of a burning cage? Can you carry him to the border? It's actually ten miles from here."

She gritted her teeth. Blast him, he was making good points, but she didn't want to admit it. "I won't set the cage on fire. I can control what I do."

"Really?" He nabbed the edge of her cape and showed her the area that had burned away when she'd used it to smother flames. "Is this what you call control?"

She yanked the cape from his grip. "Ye're too pushy."

"I'm in a hurry because we're wasting too much time. Will you let your friend bleed to death while we talk?"

Now he was just making her angry. "I know I need help, but do ye expect me to trust a bunch of bandits?"

He stiffened.

"Your Highness." Father Kit approached her. "I give you my word as a priest that the Woodsman is an honorable man."

"Honor among thieves?" she shot back, then instantly regretted her words. The Woodsman had stepped away, his beautiful mouth compressed to a thin line. She'd hurt him, but dammit, hadn't she spoken the truth?

"I'm sorry," she murmured, then darted through the trees to the cage that held Aleksi.

Why did it upset her that she'd hurt his feelings? She didn't even know the man. What the hell was a Woodsman, anyway? True, if he hadn't broken all those arrows and spears during the battle, more Norveshki soldiers and horses would have been killed. But was that enough reason to trust him? He was still a thief. What if he was planning to hold her hostage and demand a ransom?

As terrible as that thought was, she had to admit it was still better than letting the elfin army use her to coerce Silas into handing over Gwennore. If she left with the Woodsman, would it keep Gwennore safe? Would it be better for Aleksi?

At the edge of the woods, she stopped and scanned the area. The lone guard was still asleep, and the rest of the camp quiet. Her heart squeezed at the sight of Aleksi lying so still in his cage, and in that instant, she knew she had to do whatever gave him the best chance at survival. Even if that meant accepting help from the Woodsman.

Quickly, she dashed toward his cage. "Aleksi," she whispered in Norveshki. "Can you hear me?"

No response. He lay there on his stomach, his eyes closed, his face pale, an arrow still in his back and another in his shoulder. Those damned elves hadn't even bothered to treat him.

"I'll get you out." She grabbed onto two wooden poles and gave them a shake. They didn't budge. Odd, the poles on her cage had given away so easily. It was too odd, she realized now. At the time she'd been so frantic to escape, she hadn't questioned her good fortune.

She studied the cage, looking for some sort of binding that she could burn. Damn. The cage was nailed together. She had no choice but to set a few poles on fire.

With a snap, she made a small flame. The fire flickered and grew as she moved it toward a wooden pole. Her hand was safe, but she knew from experience that the rest of her could burn. There was still a scar on her shoulder where a beam had collapsed on her years ago during the kitchen fire. The fire had spread so quickly. She and Sister Colleen had barely made it out in time. Goddesses help her, she would never be able to live with herself if she trapped Aleksi inside a burning cage.

A hand suddenly grabbed her wrist.

She flinched. The Woodsman! Relief flooded through her. For a terrifying second, she'd thought an elfin soldier had caught her.

But she really needed to be more careful. She hadn't even heard the Woodsman sneak up on her.

Her flame wavered as he brought it slowly toward him, and for a few seconds, his face was illuminated with a flickering golden light as if he were an angel. Her breath caught.

High cheekbones as sharp as a blade. Dark eyebrows. His gaze was lowered as he looked down at her hand, his eyelids fringed with thick, dark lashes.

He sucked in a breath, then pursed his lips as if he were going to kiss her. And her heart stopped. He was far too beautiful for a man. And yet, he was undeniably male. A second later, he blew the flame out, and his face was gone.

In the darkness, she could feel the firm grip of his hand against her skin. She could hear his soft breathing and sense him looking at her. And somehow, it felt like the entire world had shrunk to only this small place in time and space where she was alone with him.

"Sorcha," he whispered in Eberoni. "You can trust me."

She stared at him, stunned. He knew her name. And he hadn't given up on her.

"Here." He placed her hands onto two poles. "Hold tight." He grabbed a third pole with his right hand, then with his left he made a slicing motion across the top of the cage and then across the bottom.

The poles were loose! She gripped them harder to keep them from falling into the cage on top of Aleksi.

The Woodsman set the third pole on the ground outside the cage, then relieved her of the two she was holding.

"How—?" she asked as he quietly placed her poles on the ground.

"Woodsman." He cut a fourth pole and set it down with the others. "The opening should be wide enough now."

With a gasp, she realized the poles from her cage hadn't simply given away. He had broken them. "Ye . . . ye helped me escape."

"Yes." He stepped into the cage.

"Why? Why are ye helping us?"

He ignored her as he kneeled beside Aleksi. With a swipe of a finger, he snapped off the wooden arrow shafts close to the skin.

"How do ye do that?" She'd never seen a power like this before. "Are ye Embraced? Or just strange?" She bit her lip.

He glanced at her, but in the dark she couldn't tell if he was offended. "Both. And you?"

"Both, I suppose." Her cheeks grew warm. Apparently, one of her strange powers was the ability to insert her foot in her mouth.

He lifted Aleksi, placed him on his shoulder, then straightened. "Let's go."

He'd made it look so easy. Sorcha winced inwardly. She would never have been able to carry Aleksi like that. "I needed yer help after all."

He paused at the opening in the cage and looked at her.

She couldn't see his eyes, but she felt uncomfortably aware that he was studying her. "Thank you for not giving up on me."

"You're welcome."

Why was he still staring at her? Did she have dirt or drool on her face? She quickly wiped her cheek. Her hot skin could only mean she was blushing. Dammit. "My brother will gladly reward you for our safe return."

His stare continued. "You think I'm doing this for money?"

"I didn't mean it like that. But if ye were forced to steal food, then you and your people must be in need—"

"You know nothing about me." He stalked toward the ridge, carrying Aleksi as if he weighed no more than a sack of potatoes.

She groaned. Had she insulted him again? It was true that she didn't know him, but did it matter? Soon she would be across the border and then she would never have to deal with him again. *Then you'll never know him,* she thought with a twinge of regret.

Dammit. The man was making her too curious. And too nervous. Even now, she shivered when she recalled that moment when he'd blown out her flame. Why was he having such a strong effect on her? He was an outlaw from Eberon, not the elf who was predicted by the Telling Stones.

Stay focused, she reminded herself as she strode toward the woods. Her goal right now was to get Aleksi and herself across the border as quickly as possible. The Woodsman had helped her so far, so she had to trust that he would continue to do so.

But was she making a mistake by trusting him? Had she stepped out of a frying pan and into a fire? She took a deep breath. Fire was the one thing she could handle.

Chapter 6

After tying the injured dragon shifter across the saddle of the second horse, the Woodsman realized that Sorcha had not yet returned to the clearing. Dammit, was she making a run for the border? Would she do something that reckless and impulsive?

Yes, she might. As far as he could tell, she was as unpredictable as the fire she claimed to control.

"Finish up here and be ready to go," he told Father Kit and Liz. As they rearranged the stolen weapons around the injured man, he strode across the clearing.

Living Oaks, do you know where—? He stopped his mental question when Sorcha emerged from behind some trees.

Relief flooded him. Thank the Light she hadn't run away on her own. But why the hell was he worrying so much about this woman? She had nothing to do with his life. She had no part in his plan for revenge.

It didn't matter how brave or beautiful she was. Or how much his heart had raced when he'd blown out her flame. This was a temporary snag in his plans. An interesting diversion. Nothing more.

He crossed his arms over his chest. "What took you so long?" he grumbled in Eberoni.

She avoided looking at him as she wandered over to the horses. "I needed to relieve myself."

"Ah." He nodded. "Good. We have a long ride ahead of us, and I don't want to make any unnecessary stops."

She turned toward him with a wary look. "What do ye mean long ride? Ye said it was only ten miles to the border."

"I'll explain as we go." He motioned for Father Kit and Liz to leave. The priest had already mounted the third horse, while Liz remained on foot, leading the second horse, which carried the injured dragon shifter. As they headed into the forest, the Woodsman continued, "One of my skills is the ability to communicate with trees, especially the—"

"What are they doing?" Sorcha pointed at the others. "Didn't ye say that way was south? They're going the wrong direction!"

"Keep your voice down."

"Are ye kidnapping us? Taking us prisoner?" She planted her fists on her hips. "I won't have it! Ye'll return Aleksi to me at once!" She dashed after the others, but he caught her by the arms to stop her. "Let go!"

"No yelling," he growled as he pinned her flailing arms. Dammit, she was like wildfire, jumping to wrong conclusions.

"Release me." She stomped on his foot, but he knew her routine from the last attack and grabbed her knee the second she raised it.

"Do you have something against my groin?" He pulled her close, and she gasped as she collided with his chest. "Will you listen to me now?" Damn, but his heart raced whenever she looked up at him with her wide green eyes.

Her gaze lingered on his mouth for a few seconds before she turned her head.

Dammit, why did she keep focusing on his mouth? It made him think about kissing her. *Don't do it!* He released her and stepped back. "Now that you've calmed down, we can quietly discuss my plan."

She huffed. "Who says I'm calm?"

"One can only hope."

She gave him an incredulous look. "Ye've abducted my friend!"

"No. We're taking him to a healer south of—"

"No!" She pointed at the others, who could barely be seen now. "Call them back. I want to take him to Gwen and Annika. They're excellent healers, and they're close by."

"No. We cannot cross the Norveshki border."

"Of course we can. Stop telling me no!"

"No," he growled. "The Living Oaks told me—"

"I don't care what a bunch of trees are saying."

He gritted his teeth. This woman made it damned hard to retain his usual calm demeanor. "Trees don't lie. The only place shallow enough for us to cross the river is where the battle took place earlier. The Living Oaks have warned me that the area is swarming with soldiers. The army will never anticipate that you would actually flee southward farther into Woodwyn, so that is our best course of action. Now, enough time has been wasted, so mount up. We need to go."

Father Kit had taken the lantern with him, but there was enough light from the twin moons and a million stars to see that her pretty face was scowling at him.

"I said *now*." He gave her a little shove toward the horse, and she spun around to face him.

"Ye're being pushy again."

He stepped closer to her. "It's not pushiness. It's decisiveness."

"Ye shoved me."

"Excuse me, Princess, for being in a hurry to save your life."

She narrowed her eyes. "Don't call me princess."

"Are you going to argue with me until they discover you're missing?"

"Are ye going to make all the decisions without consulting me? Who put you in charge?"

With a groan of frustration, he walked over to his horse and nabbed the reins. In Elfish, he muttered under his breath, "I don't know whether to kidnap her or kiss her."

When she gave a small gasp, he glanced back at her. Had she understood him? This wasn't the first time he thought he'd caught a reaction. And how did she know that he and his men had robbed the army if she didn't understand Elfish?

She turned away, studying her boots. "I don't mean to argue. It's just that I'm trying to do what's best for Aleksi. And I suddenly find myself in a position where I have to trust you, and I'm not at all sure that I can—"

"I will prove that I am trustworthy."

She kicked at the ground. "Are ye sure it's not safe to cross the border?"

"I'm sure. Most of the army is roaming about searching for us."

"It's *you* they're looking for." She lifted her chin. "I might be safer away from you."

He scoffed. "On your own, you'll wander around lost until you're caught. Do you think they'll let you go? Will they try to save your friend's life?"

She winced.

"Your best chance for escape is with us. But if we go north, we'll most likely be captured. You would probably survive since they consider you useful. The rest of us would be executed, including your friend."

She glanced at him with a look of alarm. "Then I will do as ye say."

Was that all it took? The minute she realized that others were in danger, she was willing to cooperate. "Thank you." He gave her a small smile, and her gaze shifted once again to his mouth.

Damn. If she didn't stop staring at him like that, he was going to give in to temptation. And that would be a disaster. Because even though she was brave and beautiful, she was completely wrong.

Her fiery temperament was a threat to his normal coolheaded demeanor. Already he felt seared at the edges. He would deliver her as quickly as possible to the Eberoni border. She would be safe with the king and queen there. And she would be far away from him.

That's what he needed. Distance.

As she mounted easily and gracefully, swinging one of her long legs over the saddle, his breath caught in his throat. Distance? He was going to have to share the saddle with her. Her hair would brush against his chin. Each time she inhaled, he would feel it. Her well-rounded rump in those tight leather breeches would press against his groin.

Just the thought made him react. Dammit. He'd better get himself under control before it became obvious.

"How do ye wish to mount?" she asked. "Do ye want to be in front or behind?"

Now she was torturing him. "Behind." He slid a booted foot into the stirrup and hefted himself into the saddle.

She stiffened as their bodies came into contact. When she attempted to wiggle forward, it caused her legs to rub against his thighs.

"Be still." He wrapped an arm around her, holding her steady as he urged the horse into a quick walk.

She grasped the saddle horn and hunched forward.

"That will give you a backache." He pulled her back against his chest.

Beneath his arm, he felt her rib cage expanding with each quick breath. She was nervous, dammit, but what could he do? If he tried to console her with soft words and a gentle touch, she would probably think he was molesting her. She already considered him a thief with no honor.

He ought to tell her the truth, but dammit, why should he have to explain himself? Why should he care what she thought? She was completely wrong for him. Even her gift was an utter disaster. While his Embraced power relied on wood, her power destroyed wood.

Just how dangerous was she? "Can you make a flame with both hands or only your right one?" he asked.

"My right hand has a much stronger flame. The left one tends to fizzle out, but that might be from lack of practice."

"I see." He transferred the reins to his left hand and took her right hand in his.

"What are ye doing?" She attempted to pull her hand away, but he held tight.

"We're going into a dense forest. I can't have you accidentally starting a fire."

She scoffed. "That's ridiculous. I don't accidentally snap my fingers."

He laced his fingers with hers. "Now you won't be able to."

She yanked her hand away. "Ye don't trust me at all, do you?"

"As much as you trust me."

She turned her head to look at him, and her hair brushed against his chin.

He leaned back to sever the contact.

With a huff, she faced front. "I am fully aware of how dangerous my gift can be. That's why I rarely use it. I live with the fear that I might hurt someone."

He winced. Why was he being rude? He'd seen her endanger herself to save her friend, so he knew she had a good heart. And he knew she wouldn't actually try to burn down the forest.

He lowered his right hand, accidentally brushing against her leg before resting his hand on his own thigh. Dammit. Would she think he'd done that on purpose?

Had he? Since when did he not have complete control over

his own movements? He winced when she leaned forward in a futile attempt to put some space between them.

She held on to the saddle horn. "So ye said ye have a plan?"

"Yes." He nodded. "It's imperative to always have a plan. First we go to Drudaelen Castle. I'll ask the physician to meet us there. She'll take good care of your friend."

"She?"

"Yes. And once you and your friend have rested a bit, we'll move on to the village of Haven. The army doesn't know where Haven is, so you'll be safe there while your friend recuperates."

"It's like a secret hideout?"

"Yes."

"I see." She took a deep breath and seemed to relax a bit.

They rode in silence for a while, weaving through the trees. In the dark, he could hear her soft breathing, feel the motion of the horse and their bodies swaying together. *Don't think about how good she feels between your thighs.*

He turned his attention to the forest around them. His night vision was better than most, but even when he couldn't see well, he could sense where the trees were. He also had a good sense of direction, made even better because the Living Oaks would let him know if he veered off course.

For now, he had better alert the physician so she would be ready. Thankfully, Morghen could also communicate with trees. *Living Oaks, will you pass a message to Morghen? I'm bringing an injured man to Drudaelen Castle. Can she meet us there? We should arrive tomorrow by noon.*

We will do as you ask, Woodsman.

Thank—His mental conversation screeched to a halt as his horse climbed a steep hill and Sorcha fell back against his chest. Should he wrap an arm around her to hold her steady? Would she object to being held in his arms?

"Actually, I was a bit frightened when I thought I would

have to set Aleksi's cage on fire," she whispered. "It was a great relief when ye stopped me."

He took a deep breath. *Don't talk to her. Don't hold her. Don't get closer to her.*

She turned her head to look at him, and the feel of her hair was like silk against his skin. How easy it would be to cradle her head in the curve of his neck.

He took another deep breath, and the scent of her hair was sweet. She must use a soap made with honeysuckle. "I watched the battle earlier from high up in a tree." Oh hell, why was he talking?

"Ye broke a bunch of arrows and spears," she murmured.

"Yes." He leaned forward to breathe in more of the honeysuckle scent. "Before the battle, I asked the redwoods to warn Queen Gwennore about the trap."

Sorcha gasped, turning toward him so suddenly that her temple brushed against his mouth.

He sat back.

"That was you? Oh!" She pressed her knuckles briefly against her lips. "I just had a wonderful idea! Could ye ask the redwoods to tell Gwennore that I'm safe?"

"I already did. I told her I would return you to your family."

"Oh, thank you!" She beamed up at him, and his heart skipped a beat. Still grinning, she faced front. "Gwen and Silas will be so relieved. Thank you."

He was hopelessly attracted to her, he realized with a wince. Attracted to a woman who could easily start a forest fire. And if that wasn't bad enough, she was a princess from another country. Dammit. She was probably betrothed for some stupid political purpose. Or perhaps her brother would have mercy on her and let her marry for love.

A startling thought jumped into his mind. If she hadn't gone back to rescue the dragon shifter, she would have escaped. She could be safe at home now, but she'd turned back to save the dragon. Even now, she was determined to save him.

Dammit, what brave young woman wouldn't be attracted to a dragon? Was she in love with the wounded warrior?

Good. Then she won't be interested in you. He gritted his teeth. Crap. "The . . . uh . . . injured soldier . . ."

She glanced up at him. "Aleksi?"

"Yes. He's a . . . dragon, isn't he?"

She sighed. "So ye know about the shifters."

"Yes. Are you . . . ?" *Don't ask if she's betrothed, you fool.* "You seem to care a lot about him."

She nodded. "Of course. He's one of my brother's best friends. I consider him a good friend, too."

"And . . . nothing more?"

She stiffened and her hands tightened around the saddle horn.

Damn. Now she knew what he was really asking. As time stretched on, the air around them felt heavy, the silence deafening.

"After you've rested a few days in Haven, I'll take you across the border into Eberon," he said to fill the awkward silence. "That will be fine with you, right?"

"Yes." She nodded. "Queen Luciana is like a sister to me."

"Good. It should take about two days to cross the Haunted Woods—"

"Haunted?" She glanced back at him. "Ye mean with ghosts?"

"Something like that."

They descended a hill and came across Norus Creek. He let the horse splash along the creek for a while. This waterway flowed northward, eventually merging with the Vorus River, which served as a boundary between Woodwyn and Norveshka. Streams located in the south flowed into the Wyn River, where the River Elves lived and Wyndelas Palace was situated.

Although the River Elves had been the dominant power in Woodwyn for several centuries, the Wood Elves had begun to resent their rule. And well they should since the River Elves had started abusing their power, forcing too many Wood Elves into the army so they could fight wars for no apparent reason.

The Woodsman's grip on the reins tightened. He knew the reason, and it never failed to anger him.

He took a deep breath and the scent of honeysuckle filled his head, giving him an odd sensation of comfort. Damn, but this woman was a distraction. *A sweet one*, an inner voice taunted him.

They left the creek, climbed a bank, then descended through a dark forest until they emerged onto a narrow road. The light of the twin moons gleamed brightly, making it easier to see. A few tendrils of Sorcha's hair had escaped her braid and were curling along her brow and the slender nape of her neck. They looked so soft. And her little ears were sweetly rounded, just like the rest of her. *Don't think about that.*

A short distance ahead, he spotted Father Kit's lantern. He and Sorcha would soon catch up. That meant his time alone with her was almost over.

"While I was watching the battle, I saw something amazing," he said softly. "The Norveshki soldiers were retreating as fast as they could, but I spotted a fallen soldier. Then I saw another soldier who turned back to save him. And I thought to myself—here's a soldier like me, who refuses to leave a man behind. Here's a soldier who knows the true meaning of honor, bravery, and loyalty."

She tilted her head up to look at him. "Ye thought all that?"

He nodded. "You asked earlier why I was helping you. That is why. That soldier was you."

Tears glistened in her eyes. "That has to be the most beautiful compliment I've ever received."

Was she going to cry? Damn. He should have kept his mouth shut. One thing was for sure—he needed to get her to

Eberon as fast as possible. The more time he spent with her, the more his self-control went up in smoke. He'd worked too hard and waited too long to complete his quest of vengeance. He couldn't let anything stop him now.

Thankfully, she managed to blink away the tears. But then her gaze drifted to his mouth once again. *Oh, hell.*

"Sorcha," he whispered. "Do you mean to tempt me?"

With a gasp, she faced front. "No! No, of course not."

Of course not, he thought ruefully. Was he the only one feeling the air around them sizzle with heat?

Ahead of them, the injured man let out a moan.

"Aleksi!" Sorcha cried. "He's awake! Let me down!"

The Woodsman pulled his horse to a stop, and she scrambled to the ground without even waiting for him to dismount.

She dashed to her friend, talking to him in Norveshki. "Aleksi, are you all right? I'm so glad you woke up! I was terribly worried!"

With a silent groan, the Woodsman realized he must be the only one feeling it.

This unfortunate longing.

Chapter 7

Accompanied by six of her personal guards, Princess Jenetta stormed toward General Caladras's tent. Incompetence. Failure. By the Light, someone was going to pay for this.

"Wait here," she growled at her men, then waved the general's guards aside. "Move."

The general's guards, all four of them, continued to block the entrance.

How dare these fools treat her like this? "Don't you know who I am? Or do *my* guards need to explain it to you?"

The four men exchanged looks. No matter what their orders, they knew they couldn't lay a hand on the future queen. Bowing their heads, they acknowledged defeat and stepped out of her way.

She gave the nearest one a shove as she strode into the tent. "Your guards are impertinent, General. I expect you to have them whipped."

"For following orders?" Caladras stepped into the flickering light cast by the one candlestick on his dark wooden desk. "They were told not to let anyone in."

"I am not anyone."

"Of course, Your Highness. How kind of you to stop by."

His sarcastic tone only added fuel to her rage. "Is it true what I heard? The Norveshki princess and dragon have escaped?" When the general didn't answer quickly enough, she jabbed a finger in his direction. "Why are you even here?

Shouldn't you be with the search parties? First you failed to deliver my daughter, and now you've lost the prisoners! How many failures can you incur in one day?"

There was just enough light to see his jaw clench as he suppressed his anger. "Don't push me, Princess. You still need our help."

Our? She stiffened when she spotted movement in the dark shadows behind the general.

"Your Highness." A man stepped forward, wearing a hooded cloak of rich maroon velvet. As he pushed the hood off his head, the light from the candlestick gleamed off the gold and jeweled rings adorning his spindly fingers.

It was Lord Morris, former head priest and chief counsel to the king of Eberon. Jenetta opened her mouth to greet him, but stopped when another man moved slightly forward. Shrouded in a black cloak, he even wore dark gloves to cover his hands. Still half in shadow, he declined to remove his hood.

The Chameleon. A chill prickled her skin as she stared at the dark hole in the hood where his face should be. As far as she knew, no one had ever seen what he really looked like. She turned away, not wanting him to sense how uneasy she felt in his presence.

Her gaze landed on the desk, where a brass pitcher of wine rested along with three goblets. Only three, one for each of these members of the Circle of Five. No wonder the general had ordered his guards not to let anyone in. The Circle of Five was holding a secret meeting in the middle of the night.

And she had not been invited.

Her anger rushed back, and she welcomed it for it made her feel stronger. More daring. Soon she would be queen, and she would make these men pay for not giving her the respect she deserved.

She pasted a wry smile on her face. "You must be getting

old and forgetful, my dear general. It's not like you to hold an important meeting without inviting me."

"Forgive me," he muttered as he filled a goblet with wine, then offered it to her.

She took a sip. "So tell me. How did the princess manage to escape with an unconscious dragon shifter?"

Caladras sighed. "The wooden poles of the cages were sliced neatly through. I believe the Woodsman has them. He also broke most of our arrows and spears during the ambush."

The Woodsman. Jenetta scoffed. She was sick of hearing about this mysterious man. "So you're telling me that *one* Embraced creature was able to disrupt the ambush and take our prisoners? How can one man wreak so much havoc? You should have killed him months ago!"

"I have every available man looking for him." Caladras poured wine into the last two goblets. "There's no need for you to be concerned. We'll find him and the missing prisoners."

Her hand tightened around the goblet. "How can I not be concerned? What did you do to the guard who lost the prisoners? I hope you had him executed."

"He was whipped," Caladras replied. "We can't afford to lose any soldiers. We'll need them in case the Woodsman attacks."

Did the Woodsman have an army? A trickle of alarm slithered through her. Was this man going to be a threat to her gaining the throne? "How many followers does he have?"

"I'm not sure." Caladras handed a goblet to Lord Morris. "Isn't that why you're here, my lord?"

"Aye." Morris took a sip of wine. "I came to collect information from all the priests in Woodwyn who work for me."

His spies. Jenetta set her goblet down with a clunk. "Is that all you offer the Circle of Five? A network of spies? I have spies, too. I should be in the Circle."

Lord Morris arched a brow at her. "Then it wouldn't be a Circle of *Five*, would it?"

She gritted her teeth. "I see only three people here. Who are the other two?"

Morris smirked. "You have to be in the Circle to know their identities. And you're not."

"Is it because I'm a woman? Do you consider me weak?"

"We know how ruthless you can be," Caladras muttered.

She narrowed her eyes. They thought she was a mere pawn for them to use, the bastards. *Disrespect.* She'd dealt with it all her life. But not for much longer. "Woodwyn will be mine. Soon. Remember that."

"And you should remember that you promised Gwennore to my son," Caladras told her. "It was the price you agreed to in order to procure my help."

Yes, he'd helped her. But she'd done her share of the dirty work. Even so, he wouldn't have helped her if she hadn't promised her daughter to his son. The general wanted Griffin to be king someday.

She snorted. Griffin would have to wait, for she intended to be queen for a long time.

A sudden thought jumped into her mind, so chilling that it caused a shiver to skitter down her spine. What if Caladras was planning to kill her after his son married Gwennore and became the heir?

She made sure her face remained blank while her mind raced. How could she stay alive? She would have to become queen before the wedding occurred. Then she could kill the general first. Yes, this made perfect sense. After all, he knew her secrets. It was simply too dangerous to keep him alive. As soon as she was crowned, she would declare him a traitor and have him executed.

"I look forward to the wedding." She smiled at the general. "I hope you can capture Gwennore soon."

"We will." The general offered the last goblet to the

Chameleon, but the shrouded figure refused it with a slight wave of a gloved hand.

"I'll be so happy to see my daughter again," Jenetta said with what she hoped sounded like wistful longing. "Do you have a plan?"

Caladras drank from the goblet himself, then set it on the desk. "We have a spy in the Norveshki army. A good one. He killed one of their lieutenants today. I sent him back tonight, roughed up, so it would look like he'd fought with our soldiers in order to escape. Paxell will lure Gwennore away from their camp, knock her unconscious, and deliver her to us."

Jenetta nodded. "I hope it will work."

"It will." Caladras motioned toward the tent entrance. "Now, if you will excuse us, we have other matters to discuss."

They were dismissing her? *Disrespect.* Anger surged inside her once again, so hot she could no longer contain it. "You think you don't need me? Why? Because you're so wonderfully efficient in getting things done? I thought you were supposed to have taken over Eberon, Tourin, and Norveshka by now. Years have gone by, and you have absolutely nothing to show for it. You only have Woodwyn on your side because of me."

Lord Morris slammed his goblet onto the table. "Our plans wouldn't have failed if those damned Embraced men hadn't gotten in our way. That beast, Leo, cost us Eberon, and the accursed pirate, Rupert, made us lose Tourin."

"You're forgetting the contributions of their Embraced wives," Jenetta muttered. So like these men to belittle the accomplishments of women. She pointed at the Chameleon. "You have your own Embraced creature. Why has he failed in every mission you've sent him on?"

The Chameleon moved forward so quickly, she hardly saw him until his arm shot out and he gripped her neck with a gloved hand. "I have killed three kings," he growled in a raspy voice. "I would have no problem killing a princess."

She sucked in a shaky breath. His grip wasn't tight enough to completely cut off her air supply, but she knew, at any second, his hand could close like a vise.

"Back off, Chameleon," Caladras said softly. "We need her."

"Do we?" The Chameleon released her and shoved back his hood.

She gasped. He looked just like her.

"Do you think you can't be replaced?" he asked in a higher-pitched voice that sounded much like hers.

"You monster," she whispered as she stepped back. "Stay away from me."

He smirked at her, still wearing her face.

Damn him. She lifted her chin. "I suggest you use your bizarre gift to track down the mysterious Woodsman. Or perhaps you don't care if another Embraced creature destroys all of your plans?"

The Chameleon pulled the hood back over his head until his face was once again shrouded in darkness. "I will discover where the Woodsman and his followers are hiding. I will not fail again."

"Good." Jenetta gave him a regal nod, then turned to the other men. "You would do well to remember that I have spies of my own. And no aversion to murder. If you want my continued support, you will treat me with respect."

"Yes, Your Highness," Caladras murmured, and Morris bowed his head.

With a swish of her skirts, Jenetta strode from the tent. *Don't show any weakness*, she told herself as she hurried to her tent.

The whispering of the trees grew louder as she approached the edge of the camp where her tent was located.

We know what you did.

Murderer.

Slayer of innocent children.

Shut up! she mentally hissed at the trees. It was one of the unfortunate consequences of being a member of the royal family. She'd always been able to hear the Kings of the Forest and the Living Oaks.

There had been a time when she'd been grateful for their company. For seven long years she'd been imprisoned in the white tower, and the trees had kept her from dying of loneliness. They had been her only friends.

But no more! By the Light, she loathed just thinking about how weak and pathetic she had been back then. Now she was strong. She didn't need the company of trees. Not when she would soon be queen, and every elf would have to bow down to her. Anyone who had ever looked down on her would pay for it!

We know what you did.

Murderer.

Slayer of innocent children.

Stop it! she mentally screamed.

We told Gwennore about your trap.

"You dare to betray me!" she growled.

"No, Your Highness!" her lead guard, Durban, exclaimed, and all six of her guards fell to one knee, their heads bowed. "We would never betray you."

The men thought she'd been talking to them. Jenetta gave them a regal nod. "Then I will trust you to keep your word."

"Yes, Your Highness," they murmured, their heads still bowed.

"We leave for Wyndelas Palace at dawn. Have everything ready to go." She turned and marched into her tent.

Once she was back at Wyndelas, she could take matters into her own hands. The king was becoming weaker every day, and she would play the role of the dutiful daughter who was frantically using all of her medical knowledge to keep her father alive.

But alas, the poor man would pass away in just a few days. She would make sure of that.

Before a week was gone, she would be queen. Then she could have General Caladras and his son executed for treason. Once she had the army under her control, she would be safe. There would be no one in all of Woodwyn who could threaten her.

And there would be an added bonus, she realized with a smile. With the general gone, there would be a vacant spot in the Circle of Five. Soon, that spot would be hers, and the whole world would acknowledge her power.

Chapter 8

"Are you feeling better now?" Sorcha asked as Aleksi drank some water from a leather flagon that Father Kit had given him.

Aleksi gave her a wry look that questioned her intelligence.

"I guess you're in pain," she muttered.

"What was your clue?" He wiped his mouth with the back of his hand. "Oh, could it be the two arrowheads stuck in my back?"

Sorcha sighed. Aleksi was in a foul mood after waking to find himself strapped belly-down across a saddle, traveling to an unknown location in the company of three strangers he didn't trust. Now, he was standing beside her on the road, firing questions at her in Norveshki so their conversation would be private. So far, he hadn't been too pleased with her answers.

"What the hell is a Woodsman?" he growled.

A pushy guy who annoyed her but still made her heart race? Sorcha winced. She couldn't say that. The owner of the most beautiful male face she'd ever seen? That was even worse. His last words kept tumbling through her thoughts, making it hard to focus. *Do you mean to tempt me?* Good goddesses, when he'd said that, she'd nearly fallen out of the saddle.

The Woodsman was currently standing next to his horse, and even though she was trying to ignore him, his presence made her feel on edge. She couldn't tell what he was thinking or how much he could understand of her conversation in Norveshki. He seemed tense and impatient, though, for he kept glancing in the direction of the army encampment.

"He's Embraced," she whispered to Aleksi. "He's able to talk to trees. And break things. Wooden things."

Aleksi scoffed. "Isn't that special?" He slanted a dubious look at their travel companions. "You still haven't explained why three men from Eberon are helping us escape the elfin army. What's in it for them? Why were they even in the vicinity of the army?"

Sorcha shifted her weight. This might not be a good time to admit that the Woodsman and his men were a bunch of bandits. She was still having trouble accepting that, herself.

"And why the hell are we headed that way?" Aleksi pointed down the road. "That's south."

Damn, how come everyone knew that but her? "They're taking you to a physician."

"So they say." Aleksi grimaced. "If only I'd been wounded in an arm or leg. Then I would still be able to shift. But with my back injuries, I can't sprout my wings."

"I know." She touched his arm. "You were injured while protecting me. I'm both grateful and sorry."

He waved a dismissive hand. "I've had worse injuries than this. But really, you should have left when I told you to. If these people find out you're the princess—"

"They already know."

"*What?*" Aleksi shouted.

The Woodsman spun toward them. "Do not yell at her again," he warned in Eberoni.

Aleksi huffed, then whispered in Norveshki, "Why is he acting like your protector? That's *my* job." He leaned close to her. "He's not interested in you, is he?"

Her heart did a little leap. Was he? She couldn't be sure. "I don't know."

Aleksi frowned. "As soon as I can manage it, I'll shift and fly you out of here. Don't let them know that I'm a dragon—"

"They already know."

"*What?*" Aleksi bellowed.

"Enough!" The Woodsman stalked toward them. "Your time is up," he announced in Eberoni. "We're leaving now."

"Who put him in charge?" Aleksi grumbled.

"Tell me about it," Sorcha muttered.

"Now," the Woodsman ground out.

"Fine," Aleksi answered in Eberoni. "But first, I need to know one thing. Why are you helping us?"

Sorcha tensed, worried that the Woodsman would confess to admiring her bravery and sense of honor. The compliment had touched her heart, but it had felt like such a private moment, she didn't want to share it with anyone else.

After a pause, the Woodsman answered, "We rescued you because it was the right thing to do. The army was not going to treat your wounds. No doubt they were hoping you would die so there would be one less war dragon for them to worry about."

Aleksi stiffened, but remained silent.

The Woodsman motioned to Sorcha. "Her Highness was also in grave danger. General Caladras sent a message to your king, threatening to kill Sorcha if the king didn't hand over Gwennore."

"How do you know all this?" Aleksi asked.

"I know. Now let's be on our way." The Woodsman extended a hand toward Sorcha.

Aleksi pulled her back. "She'll ride with me, Tree Man."

"Woodsman." He flexed his hand before dropping it by his side. "It would be best for her to ride with me. Neither of you know where we are going."

"We don't need to know," Aleksi argued. "We can follow you."

"You are in a weakened state. If you lose consciousness

again, you could fall off your horse and further injure yourself. Her Highness would not be able to catch you as Liz could." The Woodsman extended his hand once more. "Sorcha?"

Her breath caught. Somehow it felt as if he was asking for more than a mere ride on a horse.

As she hesitated, she looked at his face, but could only see his beautiful mouth and feel his gaze focused intently on her. And still, he kept reaching for her, not giving up as the seconds ticked by.

She felt drawn to him, she realized. Intrigued. Attracted, which made no sense at all. She rested her fingers against his, and instantly, his hand tightened around them.

What have I done? she wondered with a touch of alarm.

He exhaled slowly, and the soft sigh reverberated through her, causing a shocking realization. If he was that relieved, it could only mean he had been worried that she would reject him.

Good goddesses, did he truly care about her?

Sorcha sat stiffly in the saddle, wondering what on Aerthlan was happening to her. She should be more concerned about her and Aleksi's safety, but instead, she was becoming obsessed with this mysterious Woodsman.

"You must be exhausted," he murmured, his voice soft against her ear. "We've been riding for over an hour. You can lean against me and sleep, if you like."

As if she could when her heart was pounding and her nerves were on edge. And it didn't help that Aleksi was glaring at them from his seat behind Liz. "How much farther is it?"

"We'll reach Drudaelen Castle tomorrow. But in a few minutes, we'll arrive at the village of Northwood."

She glanced back at him. "Is there someone there who could help Aleksi?"

He shook his head. "It's a ghost town."

Ghosts? Sorcha suppressed a shudder. It was a shame her sister Luciana wasn't here, since she could see and talk to the dead. A pang tightened Sorcha's chest. Oh, how she missed her sisters! This was the first night she'd ever been parted from all four of them. They would know exactly what to say to reassure her and calm her nerves.

Had Gwennore heard the message from the giant redwoods? Were carrier pigeons already taking the news to her other sisters? When they learned what was happening, they would be worried sick.

But how strange was this? In the past, it had always been her sisters who were in danger, and Sorcha who had been left to feel desperate and helpless. In fact, it was her worry for Gwennore's safety that had caused her to stumble into this dangerous situation.

Sorcha's thoughts turned to her sister Brigitta, who loved to create what the nuns teasingly referred to as overly dramatic stories. For months now, Gwennore had been playing the role of heroine, but with a small shock, Sorcha realized this was no longer her sister's story. Her own overly dramatic tale had begun.

She groaned inwardly. This was not something she had ever wanted to happen. Did this mean she would meet the elf predicted by the Telling Stones? If so, then why was she experiencing this odd attraction to the Woodsman?

Dammit, she didn't want to be attracted to anyone. *Why should you be?* Surely, she could control her own feelings.

As they rounded a bend, her attention turned to an old stone cottage. Blackened stone walls and a crumbling chimney were all that remained. The roof had burned away, and black holes marked where the door and windows had been.

She winced. It looked too much like the kitchen she'd accidentally burned down. But where the nuns had rebuilt the kitchen, this cottage had been abandoned to the elements. Green moss and ivy were slowly taking over.

More burned cottages came into view. The light of Father Kit's lantern flickered eerily across the skeletal remains of what had once been a vibrant community built around a village green. On the north side of the green, a slightly charred chapel of Enlightenment sat, its wooden spire still reaching for the heavens. Next to the chapel was a large, stone well. In the center of the village green, a few stone benches surrounded a sandbox and a children's swing.

Sorcha's heart sank. What had become of the children? "What happened here?"

"The villagers lost everything, but they survived," the Woodsman replied. "Most went to live with relatives, but those who had nowhere to take refuge went to Haven."

Father Kit dismounted close to the well and set the lantern on the ground next to a stone trough. "We should water the horses and refill our flagons."

The Woodsman dismounted, then waited while Sorcha swung down. When the horse suddenly moved, she lost her balance, and he caught her by the arms to steady her.

"Goodness." She wondered why the horse was acting so skittish. "Do ye think it's sensing a ghost nearby?" She looked up at the Woodsman, who was silently studying her.

Once again, the air between them felt hotter, almost sizzling with energy. Her gaze drifted to his beautiful mouth, and his grip on her arms tightened ever so slightly.

Aleksi cleared his throat, signaling his disapproval.

She stepped back. "Excuse me."

Without a word, the Woodsman turned and strode toward the center of the village green.

"Was it something I said?" she muttered.

Father Kit chuckled as he lifted a wooden bucket of water from the well. "More likely, it's something one of the Living Oaks said. He can hear them better if he's not listening to us. They're keeping him apprised as to the whereabouts of all the search parties." He poured the water into the trough, and the horses gathered around to drink.

Aleksi frowned as he folded his arms across his bare chest.

"Why has the army sent out search parties? Are they aware that the princess and I have escaped?"

Father Kit shrugged. "I wouldn't know about that."

"We're the ones they're looking for," Liz boasted as he raised another bucketful of water from the well.

"Why?" Aleksi asked. "What did you do?"

Sorcha winced. "Ye must be cold without yer shirt." She draped her cloak around Aleksi's shoulders.

He gave her a wry look. "Are you trying to change the subject?"

Father Kit filled his flagon with water. "The search parties are looking for us—the Woodsman and his followers. Most will have made it safely to Haven by now."

"What is Haven?" Aleksi demanded.

"Our hideout." Liz grinned. "The army doesn't know where it is."

Aleksi narrowed his eyes. "And why do you need a hideout?"

"Shouldn't we be going now?" Sorcha asked, and Aleksi shot her an annoyed look.

"Did no one tell you, son?" Father Kit jammed the cork back into his flagon. "While the elfin soldiers were away, luring you into a trap, our band was stealing their food supplies."

"You're *thieves*?" Aleksi shouted.

With a wince, Sorcha slanted a glance at the Woodsman. No doubt, he had heard Aleksi, for he was now facing them, his fists clenched at his sides.

She turned to Aleksi. "Would ye have preferred to stay with the army? The elves were going to let you die. I couldn't carry you to the border, so we were damned lucky these men offered to help."

Aleksi dragged a hand through his long black hair. "But how can we trust a band of thieves? How do we know they didn't rob this village and set it on fire?"

"What?" Father Kit huffed. "Of all the—I'll have you know that we are men of honor. It was the army who destroyed this village."

"The elfin army attacked its own people?" Aleksi scoffed. "You expect me to believe that?"

"It's true!" Liz cried. "Whenever the army runs out of supplies, they raid the neighboring villages. The people here objected, so the army locked them up in the chapel and stole all their food and livestock."

Father Kit nodded. "And then, to teach them a lesson, the army set their houses on fire."

Sorcha grimaced. "That's terrible!"

Aleksi looked unconvinced. "I know the elfin army attacks villages in Eberon and Norveshka, but why would they treat their own people like that?"

Father Kit shrugged. "This is not the only village to have suffered the same fate. Every community within fifty miles of the army encampment has been destroyed. That is why the people left this place. There was no point in starting over as long as the army was close by."

"I believe it," Sorcha muttered. "I know for a fact that General Caladras and his son are a pair of bastards."

"All right," Aleksi conceded. "I'll agree with that. But why did your band steal food from the army?"

Liz huffed. "They stole it first. They raided Drudaelen Castle two days ago, and there was nothing Lord Daelen could do about it. If you defy the army, they can label you a traitor and hang you on the spot."

Sorcha stiffened when she realized what the Woodsman and his men were actually doing. "Ye're returning the goods to the original owners."

Father Kit nodded. "The Woodsman told all the villages in northern Woodwyn to comply with the army's demands so they wouldn't get hurt or lose their homes. Then we raid the army and return the stolen goods. If we didn't help them, the villagers could starve to death."

"Damn," Aleksi murmured.

He's not a thief. Sorcha pressed a hand to her chest. He was risking his life to help people. She turned and saw him stalking toward them, strength and determination in each stride. He was fearless and beautiful. A hero.

Dear goddesses, how would she resist him?

He stopped in front of them. "We are in danger. A search party is approaching, closing in fast."

She gasped.

"A total of six soldiers," the Woodsman continued. "Less than a mile away."

Six? We're outnumbered, she thought with a growing sense of panic. "We need to go!"

"No." The Woodsman shook his head. "We can't have them following us to Drudaelen."

"So we're going to fight?" Aleksi asked.

"What?" Sorcha gave him an incredulous look. "Ye're not in any condition to fight."

"There will be no fighting," the Woodsman declared. "I have a plan."

Liz smirked. "He always has a plan."

"Father Kit, take the horses into the woods," the Woodsman ordered. "I have asked the Living Oaks to hide you."

"Right away, Captain." The priest gathered up the reins and led the horses away.

Liz picked up the lantern. "And the rest of us?"

The Woodsman pointed at the ruins of a cottage on the far side of the village green. "Sorcha and Aleksi will hide there."

Aleksi scoffed. "I'm not hiding."

The Woodsman turned toward him. "You will remain with the princess in order to protect her. Isn't that your job?"

Aleksi sighed. "Fine."

"That's the plan?" Sorcha frowned. "What if the soldiers decide to search all the cottages?"

"That won't happen. Liz and I are going to make them run away." The Woodsman motioned to the abandoned buildings around them. "The elfin army believes this is a ghost town. We'll simply confirm that. And scare the hell out of them. Are you ready, Liz?"

The young man grinned. "This is going to be fun!"

Chapter 9

In the abandoned cottage, Sorcha set the lantern down next to the crumbling fireplace, then dashed over to an open window partially covered with a flowering vine.

"We need to blow out that lantern before the soldiers arrive," Aleksi warned her.

"I know." She peered out the window, but Liz and the Woodsman were nowhere to be seen. What were they up to? What if they failed to frighten away the search party?

A sliver of fear crept up her spine, threatening to erupt into full panic. What if the soldiers came to this cottage? She had no weapon on her. The bloody elves had taken her sword and the dagger from her boot.

A loud cracking sound made her jump. She spun around and discovered Aleksi had ripped the leg off an old chair.

He practiced swinging it like a club. "I'll clobber anyone coming in and breathe fire on them. Don't worry, Sorcha. I'll protect you."

She winced. "I hope it doesn't come to that." She peered out the window. "I don't see anything yet."

He joined her at the window, his face brushing close to the flowering vine. "I wonder what ah . . . ah . . ."

Sorcha quickly grabbed the edge of her cape and leaned toward him to muffle the sound of his sneeze.

"Ahchoo!"

She winced. Goddesses help them. If Aleksi sneezed again

once the soldiers arrived, they would hear him. They would come running, ready to attack.

"What are you doing?" the Woodsman asked from the cottage's rear doorway.

With a squeal, Sorcha jumped back. "Oh, good goddesses." She pressed a hand to her chest. "Ye gave me a fright. I didn't hear you come in."

"How could you hear anything over that sneeze?" the Woodsman asked drily.

"It won't happen again. I'll stay away from the flowers." Aleksi moved back toward the broken chair. "Shall I break off a leg for you, too, Tree Man?"

"Woodsman," he muttered. With a flick of his hand, he sliced off another chair leg. "We won't be needing any weapons, but you can offer that to Sorcha, if it will make her less jumpy."

She huffed. "I'm not jumpy."

The corner of the Woodsman's mouth curled up.

So he thought she was amusing? She lifted her chin. "I know how to protect myself."

"Are you planning to knee them?" His smile widened. "At least *my* groin will be safe now."

"Ha! Who says I'm done with your groin?"

He tilted his head. "So you have plans?"

"No! I—" Dear goddesses, what was she saying?

"Humph." Aleksi glared at the Woodsman and took another practice swing with his club.

"Where is Liz?" Sorcha tried desperately to change the subject. After all, there was no hole for her to crawl into.

The Woodsman seemed as calm as ever, completely unruffled by Aleksi's show of strength. "He's in the cottage next door, undressing, so he can use his Embraced power once the search party arrives."

"So he's a shifter?" Aleksi set his club down on a rickety table. "Holy Light, does he change into a lizard?"

"No." The Woodsman shook his head. "His body reflects the colors around him, so he appears invisible."

"Oh, that's why ye call him Liz," Sorcha said. "He changes color like a lizard."

"Aye." The Woodsman held up a hand. "The search party is almost here. From now on, we must remain quiet." He bent over the lantern and blew out the flame.

The room became dark, and Sorcha's nerves tensed once again. *Get a grip. There's no need to be afraid.*

Who was she kidding? She made the sign of the moons, beseeching the goddesses to keep them safe. Then she inched back to the window.

The Woodsman joined her, and when he bent a stem of the flowering vine so he could look out, she nudged a few leaves to the side so she could also see. The village green was empty, but visible thanks to the light of the twin moons. Across the green, the chapel appeared a ghostly gray.

Her hand shook, causing the leaves to tremble, so she let go. "How much longer till they arrive?"

"A minute or two," the Woodsman whispered.

She shuddered. The thought of being captured again was too much to bear. The Woodsman's words sifted through her mind once again. She would survive capture, but he and his friends would be executed. Aleksi would probably die, too. "I'll be so relieved when we get out of this awful country."

"Woodwyn is not that bad," the Woodsman muttered.

"Of course, it is. It's full of nasty elves."

The stem snapped in the Woodsman's hand, and he tossed it on the ground. "Not all elves are bad."

She snorted. "I've never met one that wasn't an arrogant, two-faced bastard."

"Enough! What did you not understand about remaining quiet?"

"They're not here yet."

He leaned toward her. "Not another word."

She huffed. "Pushy—" She stiffened when he pressed a finger against her lips. The rascal. How could she object to his touch when she had to remain quiet?

He ran his fingertip across her bottom lip, and with a gasp, she stepped back out of his reach. Her heart pounded, but he simply turned and gazed calmly out the window.

How could he stay so cool under pressure? Was he even human? She was tempted to knee him in the groin just to see if he reacted like a man. *Fool. You know good and well he's a man. A beautiful man.* But he had an annoying habit of being right too often. And he knew it. That was probably why he felt entitled to be pushy.

She squared her shoulders. Whenever he pushed, she would simply push back. Refusing to be intimidated, she moved close to him, so she could look out the window, too.

After a minute that seemed to stretch into an eternity, she finally heard the pounding of horse hooves. She leaned forward so she could see out the hole the Woodsman had made in the tangle of branches. He angled his shoulders sideways so she could get closer, then hissed in a breath when she accidentally trampled on his foot.

"Sor—" She started to apologize, then clamped her mouth shut before he could touch her lips again. *Focus*, she told herself as she concentrated on the village green.

The six horsemen came into view. Three in front, three in back. The ones on each side were carrying torches, making a total of four. They rode into the village, scanning their surroundings as they went.

"Don't they say this place is haunted?" The voice of one soldier filtered across the green.

Another soldier chuckled. "Why are you talking so loud?"

"I heard that if you're loud, you can scare off the ghosts," the first one replied.

"Don't be ridiculous," the soldier in the center said with

an air of authority. "There's no such thing as ghosts." He dismounted. "Let's water our horses, then take a look around."

"Aye, Captain." The other soldiers dismounted.

"Whoooooo," a plaintive voice called from across the green.

That had to be Liz, Sorcha thought.

"Whoooooo," the voice repeated in a high pitch.

A soldier whirled around, holding his torch out like a weapon. "What was that?"

"It's just an owl," the captain growled. "Stop acting like you're—"

"Whoooo—who are you?" Liz said in a singsong voice. Then one of the swings in the center of the green began to rise into the air.

"What the hell?" a soldier shouted.

"It—it's just the wind," the captain stuttered.

"No! It's a ghost!"

Liz let out a high-pitched cackle as he released the swing and it swung back and forth.

"It's a child ghost!"

"That's the worst kind!"

"Why? What do they do?"

"They—they poke you. And bite!"

"Stop being ridiculous," the captain ordered.

A pail in the sandbox lifted and poured out some sand.

"Ack!" The soldiers huddled together. "Captain, we need to go!"

"What kind of soldiers are you?" The captain shoved away a few who had been clinging to him. "You let a dead child scare you? Now, you, haul up a bucket of water. And you two, check out that chapel. The Woodsman could be hiding inside."

"There could be more ghosts inside!"

"Go!" the captain bellowed.

Two soldiers holding torches eased slowly up the steps to

the chapel. The wooden doors creaked as they pulled them open. Then they inched inside.

"How dare you return to our village?" Liz called out in a creepy voice.

The two men in the chapel spun around with horrified expressions, and just then, the Woodsman caused the doors to shut in their faces. The men screamed.

"Stop that nonsense." The captain marched up the steps and attempted to open the doors. The Woodsman held up a hand, keeping the doors shut.

"Help us!" the trapped soldiers cried.

Another soldier ran up the steps to help the captain. As they yanked on the door handles, the horses suddenly reared up, crying out with frightened neighing. Sorcha figured Liz must have swatted them on their rumps.

Just as the captain and his comrade gave the doors a mighty heave, the Woodsman released his hold. The doors were flung open, and the two men fell backward, tumbling down the stairs.

The trapped soldiers dashed from the chapel. "We need to get out of here!" The flames of their torches flickered as their arms shook with fear.

"Ack!" One of the fallen soldiers scrambled to his feet. "Something just grabbed my ankle!"

The soldier at the well lifted a bucketful of water over the trough. The Woodsman waved a hand, and the bucket split in two, splashing water all over the soldier's breeches.

"The ghosts are attacking us!"

"Captain, we need to go!"

The captain hesitated, then said, "If anyone asks, we searched this entire village, and no one was here. Understand?"

"Aye, Captain!" The men struggled to mount their nervously prancing horses.

The Woodsman made a slicing motion with his hand, and a loud cracking sound thundered across the green.

"Retreat!" the captain yelled.

The top half of the chapel spire broke off and plummeted toward the soldiers, pointed side down.

"Run away!" With the pounding of hooves and a cloud of dust, the search party thundered down the road, headed back to the army encampment. The spire landed on the ground with a loud thud, then shattered into a dozen pieces.

The Woodsman waved a hand, and the trees lining the road began to thrash back and forth. Pinecones flew from branches, pelting the soldiers, who cried out in fear as they made their escape.

"Run away!"

Sorcha stifled a laugh as she turned toward the Woodsman. "That was brilliant! I love it!"

There was a pause in which she felt him studying her. And then she realized how close she was standing to him. Goodness, she even had a hand resting on his chest.

With a small gasp, she lifted her palm, but he grabbed her hand and pressed it back against him.

"Have I earned your trust now?" he whispered.

Her heart gave a small leap. *Yes.* After all, this was a man who risked his life to return food to beleaguered villagers. And his heart was pounding beneath the palm of her hand.

Aleksi cleared his throat. "Can we go now? In case you've forgotten, I still have two arrowheads in my back."

Sorcha stepped away, pulling her hand free. "I haven't forgotten." With a snap of her fingers, she made a flame and hurried toward the lantern to light it once more. In the flickering light, she could see Aleksi's face, pale and drawn with pain.

"We should be on our way." The Woodsman strode toward the front doorway, keeping his head turned away from the light.

"We did it!" an excited voice called from the doorway. "Those soldiers nearly pissed their breeches!"

With a gasp, Sorcha held up the lantern. "Liz? I can't see you at all."

"Good work." The Woodsman seemed to be shaking Liz's hand.

"Yes, thank you." Sorcha extended her hand to the same place and stiffened when she grasped something firm but invisible. "Oh, my."

"That's not my hand," Liz muttered.

With a squeak, she let go.

Liz burst into laughter. "I was kidding!"

"Enough!" the Woodsman growled. "Go get dressed."

"Aye, Captain!" The sound of snickers and footsteps headed toward the cottage next door.

"My apologies, Your Highness." The Woodsman bowed his head, then strode stiffly across the village green.

Sorcha smiled to herself. Had he been insulted on her behalf? Goddesses help her, the man was too . . . endearing.

It was almost noon the next day when Sorcha spotted a castle perched on a flat plateau in the distance. For the last few hours, she'd barely been able to keep her eyes open. Exhausted, she'd sagged against the Woodsman's chest. No doubt she would have fallen off the horse if his strong arm hadn't been wrapped around her. He had encouraged her to take a nap, but the thought of sleeping in his arms seemed far too intimate.

But now she rallied what little energy she had left and examined the castle before her. The sun glistened off the numerous helmets of soldiers lined up along the outer wall that skirted the perimeter of the plateau. The wall had a hexagonal shape with a round turret set in each of the six angles. The stone was a cream color, gleaming almost golden in the sunlight. Inside the wall, a large keep stretched several floors high and boasted six more towers, each one topped with a cone-shaped roof and a pennant flapping in the breeze that swept down from the surrounding foothills.

"Is that where we're going?" she asked.

"Aye. Drudaelen Castle," the Woodsman replied.

She suppressed a shiver at the sound of his deep voice so close to her ear. It was wrong of her, she knew, to lean against him like this, but she was so damned tired, and this felt so good. Safe, but at the same time dangerous, for she tingled with a heightened awareness of his every move. His every breath. She wanted it to go on forever.

No, she corrected herself. She needed it to end.

"They're expecting us," he continued. "Morghen has brought her herbs and instruments from Haven and is ready to take care of your comrade."

She glanced over at Aleksi. His eyes were closed, his jaw clenched, his skin glistening with sweat. Was he running a fever? "He's not doing well."

"I know, but don't worry. Morghen is an excellent healer. She used to be the royal physician at Wyndelas Palace."

Used to be? Had she made a mistake that had caused her dismissal? "Why did she leave?"

"She didn't do anything wrong, if that's what you're thinking. I've warned her the patient is a dragon shifter."

"What?" Sorcha stiffened and glanced back at him. "Ye shouldn't have—"

"I wanted her to be careful with his back. That is where his wings are located, right?"

"Yes, but . . ."

"She can be trusted. Don't worry."

Sorcha sighed. Could she trust an elfin physician? "Ye've been talking to her? How?"

"Morghen also has the ability to communicate with trees, so I've been passing messages to her. I told her who you are, too."

Sorcha winced.

"She'll tell Lord Daelen and his family," the Woodsman continued. "But most of the castle folk will simply think you and Aleksi are soldiers. If they knew your true identities, it would cause too much excitement, and the news might leak back to the army. Then the general would retaliate by attacking the castle."

Sorcha glanced back at him. "I don't want anyone to be in danger because of us."

"I know." His mouth curled up in a slight smile. "We'll warn the castle folk not to talk about the Norveshki soldiers. They'll comply when they realize the danger." He pointed at the castle. "They're sending an escort for us."

A group of four horsemen had emerged from the front gate and were headed down the winding road from the plateau. Their spears looked long and deadly.

She swallowed hard. Soon she would be surrounded by armed elves and then she would be trapped in an elfin castle. "Are ye sure these elves are friendly? They're not going to hold us prisoner?"

He snorted. "You think they're . . . how did you put it? Arrogant, two-faced bastards?"

She winced. "I'll have to hope these elves are different."

"That's big of you."

She shot him an annoyed look.

His mouth twitched. "You have my word that they'll take good care of you and Aleksi." He leaned closer. "You trust me now, don't you?"

Her heart squeezed. "I want to." But at the same time, she didn't want to. She didn't want to fall for this man.

As the escort approached, she sat forward so they wouldn't see her leaning against the Woodsman.

"Woodsman," the leader greeted them in Elfish and bowed his head.

The other elfin soldiers also bowed their heads, and Sorcha realized they were paying respect to the Woodsman. They were handsome men, all with the reddish-brown hair of the Wood Elves. Their uniforms were blue and green, the same color as the pennants flying from the castle towers.

"This is Marius, captain of the guard of Drudaelen Castle." The Woodsman introduced the leader in Eberoni.

"How do ye do?" Sorcha nodded at Marius, then smiled at the other escorts. "Thank you for yer help." When they didn't respond, she figured they didn't understand Eberoni. But they were giving her and Aleksi curious looks.

The Woodsman switched to Elfish as he addressed the soldiers. "The army had taken these soldiers prisoner, so we rescued them. Word of their presence here should not leak beyond the castle, or the army could retaliate."

"We understand." Marius motioned for the escort to turn their horses around and lead the newcomers back to the castle. He drew his horse up alongside the Woodsman and Sorcha. "Last night, the castle folk gathered in the bailey to cheer on your followers when they arrived. Everyone was willing to wait up all night for your return, but Lord Daelen encouraged them to go home and sleep."

"That's good," the Woodsman replied. "I don't want to draw any attention to our guests. If the injured man is able to move tomorrow morning, we'll go on to Haven."

Sorcha bit her lip. Should she admit that she understood what they were saying? Thankfully, they stopped talking, so she focused her attention on the soldiers in front of her. Their blue breeches and shirts were made of fine linen, their vests made of leather that somehow had been dyed green. On the back of each vest, a tree had been tooled into the leather and a swirling design edged the neckline and bottom hem.

Then she noticed that the bridles of their horses were also made of green leather, decorated with silver buckles and a blue silk tassel. Why, even their spears boasted blue and green silk tassels close to the blade. At the opposite end, the wood was carved with more swirling designs.

As they approached the castle, she noted the same swirling design had been carved into the stone surrounding the front gate. The guards up on the battlements were all dressed in blue and green with ornate silver helmets.

She snorted. Leave it to the warmongering elves to turn weapons and uniforms into works of art.

Growing up at the convent with her sisters, Sorcha had been the one who excelled in doing illustrations for the books that the nuns transcribed. Drawing and painting were her specialties, but she had great admiration for all sorts of craftsmanship. Even though it irked her now, she grudgingly had to admit that the elves were truly talented when it came to making beautiful things.

As their horses passed through the front gate, she leaned forward for a closer view of the castle keep. The ground floor was thick and formidable, no doubt for defense purposes, but as her gaze lifted to the higher floors and towers, she spotted exquisitely carved windows and balconies. It was the most beautiful castle she'd ever seen. Whereas Draven Castle had always struck her as stark and prosaic, this place was bright and whimsical.

When they came to a stop, the Woodsman slid neatly off the horse, then stood by while Sorcha dismounted.

"Thank—" She stopped talking to the Woodsman when she spotted Aleksi leaning precariously to the side, about to tumble off the horse. "Aleksi!" She dashed toward him.

Liz and Father Kit caught him and helped him dismount.

"I'll take him to the healer." Father Kit wrapped an arm around the dragon shifter and led him toward a stone building next to the stable.

The building's door flew open and two women hurried

toward them—an older elfin woman with silver hair and a younger woman, who looked like Liz with her sandy-blond hair and blue eyes.

The Woodsman motioned to the older woman. "Sorcha, this is Morghen," he said in Eberoni.

Morghen gave the Woodsman a quick perusal as she approached them. "I'm glad to see you're all right. You had us all worried when you didn't arrive with the others." She stopped in front of them and spoke quietly in Eberoni to Sorcha. "I'm pleased to meet you, Your Highness."

"Please call me Sorcha." She extended a hand.

Morghen clasped it in both of hers and gave Sorcha an assessing look. "You have strength about you, an inner fire that burns brightly."

"Oh?" Sorcha glanced at the Woodsman with surprise. Had he told this woman about her gift of fire?

His mouth curled up. "Morghen can sense things that the normal person cannot."

"Aye." With a smile, Morghen squeezed Sorcha's hand. "You'll do. You'll do quite nicely."

"Do what?" Sorcha asked.

"Now don't you worry, dear. I'll take good care of your friend." Morghen dashed back to the building, where Father Kit was dragging a stumbling Aleksi through the doorway.

For an older woman, she was certainly full of energy, Sorcha thought. "What did she mean that I'll do?"

The Woodsman shrugged. "Morghen has a way of seeing the future sometimes, but she never explains what she sees."

"Hal!" The younger woman's shout drew Sorcha's attention. "I was so worried about you!"

"I'm fine, Hallie." Liz gave her a hug. "You know I would never get captured, right?"

She swatted his chest. "That doesn't mean I don't worry about you."

Liz grinned, then turned to Sorcha. "This is my sister, Hallie."

Sorcha smiled at the young woman. "I figured as much. Ye resemble each other quite a bit."

She nodded. "That's because we're twins."

"Oh." Sorcha looked the two of them over. Since Liz was Embraced, then his sister had to be, too. Did she have the same gift that he had, or was hers different?

Sorcha also knew from her eldest sister, Luciana, that not long ago, it had been dangerous to be born a twin in Eberon. Traditionally, the mainland countries had always worshipped the Light, and any worship of the twin moon goddesses had been strictly forbidden and punishable by death. Since it was believed that the twin moons caused the birth of twins, those infants were considered evil.

Being born Embraced was also deemed evil, since it only happened when the twin moons embraced. If a child was born both a twin and Embraced, then he or she was twice as dangerous and quickly condemned to death.

Luckily, now that Luciana and Leo were ruling Eberon, those old practices were no longer allowed. But Liz and his sister, Hallie, looked about eighteen years old. When they were born, the old ways had flourished. Lord Morris had been head priest then, and Sorcha shuddered at the thought of how many innocent children had died because of him.

"It must have been dangerous for you in Eberon," she told the twins.

Liz nodded. "That's why Father Kit brought us here."

Hallie leaned closer and whispered, "Is it true? The injured man is a dragon?" When Sorcha nodded, she pressed a hand to her chest. "That is so amazing. Well, I'd better go. Nice to meet you!" She ran inside and shut the door behind her.

Liz smiled at her proudly. "She's learning how to be a physician. Morghen says she has talent."

"That's wonderful." Sorcha's attention was drawn to a

conversation the Woodsman was having with Marius next to the horses.

"Hide these weapons in the catacombs with the other ones," the Woodsman ordered in Elfish.

"Aye, my lord." Marius called some soldiers over, and they began unloading the weapons.

"Are these for the rebellion?" one of the soldiers whispered and Marius hushed him.

Rebellion? Sorcha narrowed her eyes on the Woodsman. What was he up to? And why had Marius referred to him as a lord?

"There you are!" a woman's voice called from the keep.

"Bronnie." The Woodsman strode toward the keep, where an elfin woman and little girl were descending the stairs.

Sorcha's breath caught. The woman was as beautiful as Gwennore. Tall, slim, and elegant, she rushed toward the Woodsman, but didn't appear hurried since her every move was so graceful. Her hair was the rich reddish-brown of the Wood Elves, her skin flawless. The little girl was so pretty, Sorcha suspected she was the woman's daughter.

"That's Lady Bronwen and her daughter, Helen," Liz explained.

Sorcha's mouth fell open when the Woodsman gathered the woman in his arms for a hug. Good goddesses, were they married? Was that why the soldier had called the Woodsman a lord? Her heart plummeted at the thought. No, surely not. Surely, he wouldn't have touched her lips or whispered in her ear if he was a married man.

Had she imagined the attraction between her and the Woodsman? No, it was real. At least on her part. Her heart sank even more when he picked up the little girl. Without hesitation, the girl flung her arms around the Woodsman's neck. Was she his daughter? "They—they seem very close."

"Well, they're family," Liz said. "The Woodsman and Lady Bronwen are cousins."

"They're not married?"

Liz snorted. "That's Lady Bronwen's husband there. Lord Aiden." He pointed at an elfin man descending the steps from the keep. "Well, I'm starving. See you later." He dashed off to the kitchen.

Not married. Sorcha pressed a hand to her chest as she exhaled with relief. The Woodsman was not married. But wait . . . if the Woodsman was a cousin to an elfin woman . . .

With a laugh, the little girl shoved the Woodsman's hood off his head.

Sorcha stumbled back with a gasp. Oh, dear goddesses! The Woodsman was an elf.

Chapter 10

He didn't know whether to be amused or angry. With his superior hearing, the Woodsman had heard Sorcha's gasp. And he had to admit that the look of utter shock on her face was amusing. Just as he started to smile, her expression suddenly changed.

"Oh, my," Bronwen whispered. "Why does she look so horrified?"

His smile withered away, and anger took over. "She just realized I'm what she calls an arrogant, two-faced bast—"

"Stop!" Bronwen interrupted him. With her head, she motioned toward her daughter while flashing him a pointed look.

He winced. With his normally calm demeanor, he never cursed in front of children. But then normally, he never felt this aggravated. He scowled at Sorcha. What did she have against elves? Had she trusted him only because she'd thought he was Eberoni? Would she reject him now? Hate him, even though he'd rescued her?

Damn! He put a screeching halt to those thoughts. Why should he care what she thought? In a week, she'd be gone from his life forever. And that would be for the best, because she was completely wrong for him.

"How can you have two faces?" Helen asked, her chubby little hands on his cheeks as she studied him. "I see only one face, and it looks really mad."

"Is something wrong?" Bronwen touched his shoulder. "Were you injured?"

"I'm fine. Perfectly fine." He gave them a strained smile, but Bronwen's eyes narrowed suspiciously.

"What's a bast?" Helen asked, and her mother groaned.

"Never mind about that." He set the three-year-old on her feet, and she ran toward Lord Aiden, who had just reached the foot of the stairs.

"Daddy! Cousin Woody has two faces! And he's a bast! What's a bast?"

"What?" Aiden picked her up with a confused look.

Bronwen leaned close to the Woodsman and whispered, "So who called you a bastard?"

When he angled his head toward Sorcha, Bronwen snorted. "Good for her. I've been wanting to call you that for years."

"Why am I not surprised?"

"So what did you do?" Bronwen smirked. "Let me guess. You were too bossy."

"Not at all." Sorcha had used the word *pushy.* "I was simply decisive. It's a mark of good leadership."

Bronwen rolled her eyes. "I know this will come as a shock to you, but not everyone wants to be led."

"Especially women," Aiden muttered as he approached, and Bronwen switched her glare to her husband. He quickly added, "But I love strong-willed females. I have two." He glanced at his daughter with a wry look. "I'm outnumbered."

"Daddy, I want to see the horses," Helen demanded.

Aiden sighed. "In a little while."

The Woodsman snorted. Whenever he married, he would make sure his future wife and children knew who was in command. Sorcha's words from earlier that afternoon flitted through his mind: *Are ye going to make all the decisions without consulting me? Who put you in charge?*

At the time, he'd been taken aback. No one in Haven or

Drudaelen Castle had ever challenged his authority. In his frustration, he hadn't known whether to kidnap her or kiss her. But he'd decided to rise to her challenge. For some strange reason, the prospect of proving himself and earning her trust had greatly appealed to him. So, when he had chased off the search party, and she'd said she loved it, he'd felt as if he'd accomplished something enormous. She'd even called it brilliant.

And in that moment, he had realized which one he wanted to do. *Kiss her.*

By the Light, he'd become some sort of fool. He had no time for this now. And how many times did he have to tell himself that she was wrong for him? Hell, she didn't even like elves. She'd called them nasty.

He glanced at her and discovered she was easing her way toward the building where Aleksi was. She looked mortified now, her face downcast and her cheeks almost as red as her hair as she surreptitiously inched across the courtyard. His mouth twitched. She must be hoping no one would notice her escape.

He called out in Eberoni, "Sorcha, wait."

She halted with a wince.

Yes, you've been caught. He smirked. "I'd like to introduce you to Lord Aiden and Lady Bronwen. And their daughter, Helen."

Sorcha glanced shyly at his family and curtsied.

"Did you say my name?" Helen asked in Elfish as they walked toward Sorcha. She twisted in her father's arms for a better view of their guest. "Why is she wearing breeches like a man? She looks different. She's not an elf, is she?"

"Shh," Bronwen hushed the little girl.

"Why is her hair so red?" Helen continued. "And her face is red, too. How can she be so red?"

"Let's go look at the horses," Aiden muttered as he carried the little girl to the stables.

With a wince, Bronwen leaned close to the Woodsman. "The princess doesn't understand us, does she?"

He was wondering that, himself. He watched Sorcha carefully as he said in Elfish, "Some might find her looks unusual, but I think she's beautiful." Was that a flinch? Had her blush just turned a darker shade? "I want to take her to my bed."

With a gasp, Sorcha stumbled back, her green eyes growing wide.

"Cousin!" Bronwen gave him an astounded look.

"Ha!" The Woodsman stepped toward Sorcha and pointed a finger at her. "I knew it. You do understand Elfish."

"I . . . maybe a little," she sputtered in Elfish. She lifted her chin. "Did you say that horrible thing just to get a reaction from me?"

He stepped closer and lowered his voice. "Was it that horrible?"

"Of course! It was—oh!" She blinked, then another look of horror crossed her face. "This is terrible. Your eyes are lavender!"

Terrible? He scoffed. "That's not unusual among us arrogant, two-faced—"

"But thank the goddesses!" She pressed a hand against her chest. "Your hair is completely wrong."

"What?" He gave her an incredulous look. "You're judging me by my hair now?"

"No, no." She waved her hands in denial. "There's nothing wrong with you. Nothing at all." She wrinkled her nose as she brushed an errant curl off her brow. "Actually, the problem is quite the opposite. We traveled for hours and scared off a search party, and your hair and face and clothes still look *perfect*! Do you have any idea how aggravating that is?"

He tilted his head. He'd gone from terrible to perfect? This woman was as unpredictable as wildfire.

Suddenly, she lunged toward him and splayed her hands into his hair.

He stiffened. "What are you doing?" He felt her hands swirling around madly.

She stepped back, frowning as she muttered in Norveshki, "Dammit. He's still handsome."

Handsome? His knowledge of Norveshki was limited, but he could have sworn that was what she said. Why would she say that if she thought elves were nasty? By the Light, this woman made no sense at all. No wonder he was not in his right mind when he was around her.

He reached up and winced at the rat's nest of hair on his head. "What the hell?"

Bronwen grinned as she extended a hand toward Sorcha. "Please allow me to welcome you to Drudaelen Castle. We're delighted you're here."

"Thank you, my lady." Sorcha took her hand. "And I must thank you for taking care of my friend, too. We are greatly in your debt."

"I'm the one who rescued you," the Woodsman mumbled.

"It must have been terrifying when the army captured you." Bronwen wrapped an arm around Sorcha's shoulders. "But don't worry. You'll be safe here."

"You're very kind." Sorcha's eyes glimmered with tears. "You remind me of my adopted sister, Gwennore."

"You must miss her."

Sorcha nodded. "I'd never spent the night away from all my sisters before."

"We'll take good care of you." Bronwen led her toward the castle keep. "I have a hot bath and meal ready for you, Your Highness."

"Oh, thank you. And please call me Sorcha."

The Woodsman watched as the two women headed up the stairs, arm in arm, as if they were old friends. "Where's my thank-you?" He shoved back a lock of hair that had been hanging in his face ever since Sorcha's strange attack. Why was she ignoring him if she thought he was handsome?

Aiden sauntered up to him, giving him a curious look, while his daughter pranced about. "Is there something going on between you and the princess?"

"No!" With a scoff, he shook his head. "No, no, of course not."

Aiden's mouth curled up. "One *no* would have sufficed."

Helen yanked on her father's breeches. "Daddy, who's a princess?"

"You are. And I believe it's time for your lunch." Aiden picked her up and gave her a kiss on the cheek. He turned back to the Woodsman. "Lord Daelen wants to see you. He would have come down to greet you, but his leg is hurting again."

The Woodsman nodded as a twinge of guilt needled him. "He's in his bedchamber?"

"Aye." Aiden carried his daughter toward the keep. "See you later."

The Woodsman watched as Sorcha disappeared inside the keep with his cousin. She definitely spoke more than a little Elfish. He thought back over all the time he'd spent with her, trying to recall if anything had been said that she shouldn't have heard.

Why had she pretended not to understand Elfish? She was definitely a sneaky one. Unpredictable. Surprising. A challenge.

His mouth tilted up. He'd always enjoyed a challenge.

"My lord." The guard greeted the Woodsman with a small bow, then opened the door to Lord Daelen's bedchamber.

As the Woodsman strode inside, he spotted the man who had been like a father to him for the past fourteen years. Lord Bowen Daelen was sitting in front of a dwindling fire in the hearth, his leg propped up on a cushioned footstool, a goblet of wine in his hand.

He was growing old, the Woodsman thought, as he noted the abundance of gray in his uncle's formerly reddish-brown hair. His cousin Bronwen was concerned that her father was drinking too much, but the Woodsman suspected it was his uncle's way of dealing with too much pain. The wound from fourteen years ago had never healed properly, leaving him barely able to walk. But on horseback, Lord Bowen Daelen was still a formidable warrior.

"You wanted to see me, Uncle?"

Lord Daelen glanced up. "Oh, there you are. We were worried about you." He set his goblet on the nearby table and lifted his stiff leg off the footstool.

"There's no need to get up." The Woodsman rushed forward.

"And there's no need to treat me like an invalid." Lord Daelen struggled to stand. "I get enough of that from Bronnie." His eyes narrowed as the Woodsman stopped in front of him. "What happened? Did you get into a skirmish with the army?"

"No, I handled everything from a distance." The Woodsman refilled his uncle's goblet with wine. "They never saw me."

"Then why is your hair sticking up like that?"

With a wince, the Woodsman smoothed down his hair. "That's a long story." He filled a second goblet and took a gulp of wine.

"Humph." Lord Daelen resettled in his chair. "Well, we were worried when you didn't arrive with the others. Your men said you'd gone off to stop an ambush. A noble act, I'm sure, but I wish you wouldn't take risks like that. All our plans will come to naught if you're captured as a thief."

"I understand." The Woodsman sat in the chair across from his uncle and watched as the older man hefted his injured leg back onto the footstool.

Once again, the Woodsman felt a twinge of guilt. His uncle had been wounded while trying to save him, his father, and his father's squire. The Woodsman had survived. His father and the young squire hadn't. "Maybe Morghen could give you a tonic for the pain."

"She did." Lord Daelen motioned to a glass flask on the nearby table. "It makes me drowsy, though, and I didn't want to sleep until I knew you were all right."

"I'm always careful. You trained me well."

With a small smile, Lord Daelen turned his gaze to the fire in the hearth. "Your father would be proud of you."

The Woodsman's grip tightened around his goblet. It was hard to think of his father without recalling the last day he'd seen him. The day he'd witnessed his father and squire being murdered. He shoved that memory aside. "I take it all the foodstuffs arrived safely?"

Lord Daelen nodded. "We hid most of the goods in the catacombs. The rest I told your men to take to Haven."

"Thank you."

"No, thank you. My people would have gone hungry if you hadn't returned our supplies." Lord Daelen sat forward. "Is it true what Morghen told me? You rescued a dragon shifter and the Norveshki princess?"

"I would have rescued them regardless of their—"

"I know that, but is it true?" When the Woodsman nodded, Lord Daelen sat back with a grin. "That was a brilliant move on your part! Imagine how much stronger our forces will be once we have a dragon on our side."

"He's wounded."

"But he'll get better, right? And the Norveshki princess—after we return her, her brother will be indebted to us. He might loan us more dragons."

The Woodsman winced. "I don't intend to use her or the dragon's present misfortune for my own personal gain."

"Why not?" Lord Daelen gave him an incredulous look. "We need all the help we can get."

"We have many followers, all across the country. And we have the weapons I designed. Besides, if our plan goes well, there will be no need for violence. We certainly wouldn't need any fire-breathing dragons."

"Yes, but if we can get King Silas's support—"

"No." The Woodsman shook his head. "The people of Woodwyn have hated the Norveshki and their dragons for centuries. If they learn that I have allied myself with them, they could lose their trust in me."

"Humph." Lord Daelen sat back, frowning. "I'm not sure about that."

"I've already sent word to Gwennore, promising to return the dragon and the princess."

Lord Daelen's brows rose. "How did you send a message to Gwennore?"

"It turns out that she can hear the Kings of the Forest, so I let her know about the rescue."

"Hmm." Lord Daelen drummed his fingers on the arms of his chair. "So, she inherited some of the abilities of the royal family. This is excellent. King Silas will already know that he's indebted to you."

"Uncle—"

"Hear me out. I received news this morning from our man in Wyndelas Palace. The king has read the letters from the Earl of Whistlyn and me, in which we explained your true identity and the truth behind the deaths in the royal family. The good news is that Rendelf believes us, and now he's eager to meet you."

The Woodsman took a deep breath. The years of planning and hard training were finally coming to fruition. "That *is* good news." Once the king was onboard with the plan, the transfer of power could go smoothly.

Lord Daelen winced. "There's bad news, too. Rendelf has taken to his bed and is not expected to recover. He certainly won't if that bitch, Princess Jenetta, has her way. So, we have to move quickly now."

The Woodsman nodded. "I agree." The success of Plan A hinged completely on Rendelf's support. Without the king, they would have to switch to Plan B, a violent takeover in which the Woodsman would have to fight the army and many of his fellow countrymen could be killed. But fortunately, Plan A was working. "Let's move on to the next step. Prepare the notices. Write to your contact. Tell him I will meet the king in eight days."

That would give him enough time to deliver Sorcha and the dragon shifter to the Eberoni border. He wanted to know that she was safe before he risked a clandestine meeting with the king. "Morghen will need to go with me. She knows the secret passageways into the palace."

"You'd better go sooner than that," Lord Daelen warned him. "You know how dangerous Jenetta is."

"The king will be safe from her for a while. She was with the army yesterday." The Woodsman took a sip of wine. "I believe she set up the ambush with Caladras. No doubt they intended to kidnap Gwennore and kill Silas."

"Damn." Lord Daelen curled his hands into fists. "I take it you thwarted her plans? Gwennore and her husband are all right?"

"Aye, they managed to escape. But after Caladras captured the Norveshki princess and dragon, he sent word to Silas that he would kill the prisoners if Silas didn't hand over Gwennore."

Lord Daelen snorted. "Caladras and Jenetta must have been furious when they discovered you ran off with their prisoners."

"I know. A search party could come here looking for them, so I'll move them to Haven as soon as possible."

Lord Daelen nodded. "I still say it's foolish not to use all the support we can get. Especially now, when King Silas already knows he is indebted to us."

The Woodsman sighed. This would not be a good time to let his uncle know that Sorcha had even better ties than he thought. Her adopted sisters were the queens of Eberon and Tourin. If he used her, he could gain the support of all three other countries on the mainland.

But the thought of using her turned his stomach. He couldn't do it. He wouldn't.

He changed the subject. "Is the production of the arrow launchers coming along?"

"Aye." Lord Daelen nodded. "We finished three more today. They're hidden with the others in the cave."

"So, we're up to forty-eight now? I'd like at least sixty. That would make three for each archer." The Woodsman had designed the arrow launcher himself. It was essentially a crossbow that could shoot five arrows at once. Since he had only twenty archers in his force, he was trying to give them a fighting chance against the hundred archers commanded by General Caladras. Of course, none of these weapons would be needed if Plan A was successful.

"We should reach sixty in less than two weeks. And remember, the Earl of Whistlyn is also gathering a small army for you." Lord Daelen picked up his goblet and took a sip. "Did Bronnie take good care of the princess?"

"Yes. Her name is Sorcha."

"I'd like to talk to her before you take her to Haven."

The Woodsman leaned forward. "She was captured by the elfin army yesterday when they tried to kill her brother. She has good reason to be suspicious of elves, but I think she trusts me. Let me deal with her."

Lord Daelen snorted. "You're sounding a little possessive."

The Woodsman shrugged and took a sip.

"Wait a minute." Lord Daelen sat forward, his eyes lit up. "Why don't you seduce her?"

The Woodsman choked as he swallowed his wine. "I just said I wasn't going to use her."

"It wouldn't be like that." Lord Daelen waved a dismissive hand. "You'd marry her, of course. And then we'd have her brother's support for sure. Caladras would piss in his breeches. And all the people of Woodwyn would praise you for ending the war once and for all."

"No." The Woodsman stood and set his goblet down with a clunk. "I already promised her that I would return her safely to her family. I gave my word to Gwennore, too."

"So, you'll let an opportunity like this slip right past you? Aren't you eager to avenge your father?"

"I am. But I intend to do it with honor." The Woodsman strode toward the door.

"Think it over," his uncle called after him. "You'll see that I'm right."

The Woodsman closed the door behind him. He usually listened to his uncle, but this time, he couldn't. Seduce Sorcha? Marry her? She'd probably slap him silly. No, he snorted. She'd knee him in the groin. And he would deserve it for using her that way.

He strode down the hallway. The only honorable solution was to keep his word and deliver her safely to her family.

But wait—what if she actually chose to stay? The thought made his heart pound. Would she, could she possibly choose to remain with him? She was the one who kept looking at his mouth. And she'd called him handsome, hadn't she? Hadn't he felt a sizzling energy in the air between them?

His groin tightened.

What the hell? He halted his steps. How could simply thinking about her cause him to react so strongly?

He wanted her. Even though she was completely wrong for him.

He still wanted her.

She didn't know whether to feel relieved or dejected. With a groan, Sorcha settled back in the tub of hot water. In spite of her exhaustion and aching muscles, her thoughts kept spinning, revolving again and again around one profound revelation.

The Woodsman was an elf. But not *the* elf. Not the one the Telling Stones had predicted.

Why hadn't she realized he was an elf? Her brief glimpse of his face when he'd blown out her flame had been enough to let her know he was beyond handsome. What man, other than an elf, could be that bloody beautiful and masculine at the same time?

And then there had been his cool and calm demeanor, so much like an elf. And his blasted self-assurance. She groaned again. How embarrassing that she'd actually messed up his hair. Hair that wasn't white!

She'd felt a surge of alarm when she'd realized his eyes were lavender. Lavender and white, that's what the Telling Stones had predicted. But no. The Woodsman's hair was reddish brown.

Relief had flooded her at first. She had not met the man fated for her after all. She was still free.

But then her heart had squeezed hard enough to take her breath away. The Woodsman was not the one.

In the tub, she pressed a hand against her chest. The dull ache was still there. Why? How could she be so affected by a man she'd met the day before? Was it simply because he had saved her and Aleksi?

Unfortunately, the ache in her heart made her suspect she was feeling more than gratitude. She'd been painfully aware of him. His every move. His every breath. The touch of his finger against her lips. His whisper-soft voice against her ear. She hadn't imagined the heat in the air between them.

Sorcha, do you mean to tempt me?

The ache in her heart spread down to her lower belly. Oh, dear goddesses. She dragged her hands down her face. It didn't matter that she felt drawn to him.

He wasn't the one.

She sat up, grabbed the soap from the nearby basket, and scrubbed herself clean. When she'd first arrived here with Bronwen, she'd found the bedchamber full of servants. They were bustling about, preparing the bath, setting a table with food, spreading fresh linens on the large bed, and laying out some clothing for her.

Sorcha had been too exhausted and emotionally drained to deal with all the servants. Fortunately, Bronwen had realized that and sent them away. She'd explained that the nightgowns and gowns were hers, but she would be happy to make some new clothes for Sorcha right away.

"That's very kind of you, but you needn't worry about me," Sorcha had replied. "I'll be going home soon."

Bronwen had actually looked disappointed. "I'll let you get some rest, then. If you need anything, please give the bellpull a tug."

Now Sorcha wondered if there was any harm in delaying her return. After all, Gwennore wouldn't worry too much since she'd had been told that Sorcha was safe. And didn't Aleksi need time to recover? If they stayed in Woodwyn for a while, she might become good friends with Bronwen. And the Woodsman.

Don't think about him. He's not the one.

She grabbed the nearby bucket of warm water and rinsed herself off. After drying herself with a towel edged with delicate white lace, she slipped on a nightgown that was beautifully embroidered. Was there some kind of law in Woodwyn that everything made here had to be beautiful?

A quick glance around the room seemed to confirm the notion. The silver forks, knives, and platters on the table boasted a pretty swirling design. The wine decanter and goblets were lovely, made of green glass. The rug on the smooth stone floor was thick and woven in shades of blue and green. The draperies at the balcony window and surrounding the large bed were blue silk, the embroidered coverlet blue satin. The furniture was a light ash, expertly carved.

She could spend hours admiring it all, but she was simply too tired. She climbed into bed and drew the covers up to her chin.

He's not the one.

Her eyes fluttered shut. Then why couldn't she stop thinking about him?

Chapter 11

In her sleep, Sorcha moaned and shook her head as panic set in. Aleksi was unconscious at her feet and the elfin army was closing in.

"Your Highness?" Lieutenant Kashenko rode up beside her.

"Help me!" She struggled to lift Aleksi, and the lieutenant leaped off his horse.

Another soldier stopped and dismounted.

"Guard us while I lift the captain," Lieutenant Kashenko told the other soldier as he leaned over to pick up Aleksi.

The soldier pulled his sword from its sheath, then plunged it into the lieutenant's back.

With a cry, Sorcha sat up in bed. Darkness surrounded her, and for a panicked moment, she wasn't sure where she was. But then she remembered they had arrived at Drudaelen Castle. She must have slept all day.

"Goddesses help me." She'd managed not to think about that horrendous scene since yesterday. But now that she was alone in the dark, the memory of that bloody sword kept stabbing at her mind, threatening to pierce her just as it had the poor lieutenant.

Stop thinking about it! She looked frantically about the dark room to make sure she was alone. Bronwen had told her that she was safe here at Drudaelen Castle, but how could she feel safe in Woodwyn?

The fire in the hearth had gone out, and only a little moonlight was filtering through the windowpanes of the doors to the balcony. The bloody sword slashed through her thoughts once again, and with a shudder, she buried her face in the satin comforter. But then, all she saw were the lieutenant's glassy dead eyes staring at her.

Don't think about it! She snapped her fingers to create a flame. It wavered in the dark, a sure sign that her hand was trembling. She lit the candlestick on the small bedside table, then blew out her flame.

Sitting on the edge of the bed, she took deep breaths to calm herself. It was only normal, after all, to be shaken by the lieutenant's murder. Who wouldn't have a nightmare after seeing that? This was entirely normal. In fact, it would be shameful of her if she had forgotten the lieutenant. The poor man had died trying to help her and Aleksi. Had his family been informed of his death? Had the elfin army even returned his body?

And what of that traitor? She recalled his sallow, pock-marked face, his thin lips curled with a smirk. That bastard needed to pay—

Of course! Why hadn't she thought of this earlier? She should ask the Woodsman to send Gwennore a message, explaining how Paxell had murdered the lieutenant. But where was the Woodsman? How late was it? She wasn't sure how long she'd slept.

She padded across the room and set the candlestick down on the table, still laden with food. After restarting the fire in the hearth, she headed toward the doors leading to the balcony. She peered outside and noted the twin moons were high in the sky. It had to be around midnight.

When she stepped onto the balcony, she winced at the cold stone pavement beneath her bare feet. But she didn't turn back, for the cool night air felt refreshing against her face. She took a deep breath and let the breeze sweep away all her nightmarish thoughts. It was cooler than she had expected for the middle of summer, but then this castle was in the foothills of the nearby mountains.

The scent of roasting meat came from the kitchen. Goodness, they must be slow-roasting it all night long. Her mouth watered, and she realized how hungry she was. She'd hardly eaten a thing for two days.

Had Aleksi been able to eat? She spotted the stone building next to the kitchen where he was being cared for. Had Morghen and Hallie successfully removed the arrowheads?

The door of the building opened, and Sorcha leaned against the balcony railing to see who was leaving. A man, dressed in green and brown with a cloak billowing behind him as he strode toward the keep.

The Woodsman. Her heart took a small leap. Had he been checking on Aleksi? If so, that had been kind of him. His long-legged stride was determined, but so graceful. His hood was down, and the stars and moons gleamed off his dark hair and pale face. So gorgeous. So appealing. So . . . wrong.

"He's not the one," she muttered, then stiffened with alarm when he came to a stop.

He glanced up at her.

Good goddesses! She stepped back from the railing and pressed herself into the shadows. He must have heard her with his superior elfin hearing. She waited in the shadows, her heart pounding; then after a few minutes, she ventured a peek over the railing. He was gone. Probably seeking his bed. After all, he had to be exhausted.

Dammit, she should have been more courageous. She should have asked him to come to her door, so she could tell him about the traitor. But she'd been embarrassed that he'd heard her. And seen her wearing only a thin nightgown.

With a resigned sigh, she slipped back into the bedchamber. She would just have to tell him first thing in the morning. After she was properly dressed.

A knock sounded at her door, and she froze. Who could that be? Surely not . . .

Another knock. "Sorcha. I know you're awake."

She gulped. It was the Woodsman. She would have to be more courageous after all.

What was Sorcha doing? The Woodsman heard some rustling noises as she scurried about the room. Once again, she had caught him by surprise. He hadn't expected to see her awake this late. He certainly hadn't expected to see her standing on a balcony, wearing only a nightgown. And he didn't know what to think about the words she had whispered.

He's not the one. What the hell did that mean?

Just as he raised his fist to knock a third time, the door was cracked open and Sorcha peered out at him. He was struck once again by how green her eyes were, how cherry pink her lips were, and how much he liked the few golden freckles scattered across her adorably turned-up nose. Her golden-red hair was loose and curling around her face. How could she look so innocent and so alluring at the same time?

Lord Daelen's words repeated in his mind. *Why don't you seduce her? No,* he reprimanded himself, but then her gaze lingered once again on his mouth, and heat rushed to his groin. Oh hell, now she was biting her bottom lip. Did it taste as sweet as it looked?

"I was hoping I would see you tonight," she whispered.

Holy Light. Was she trying to seduce him? He scoured his mind to come up with a pithy response. "Oh?" Damn, he wasn't usually this slow-witted.

"Of course. I didn't want to wait till morning." She motioned to his raised hand. "Why is your fist like that? Are you planning to punch me?"

With a start, he realized he'd remained frozen with his

hand about to knock. "No." He lowered his hand. Damn, he wasn't usually this unaware. "I saw you were awake and thought we could . . . talk." Oh hell, why had he paused like that? Now she would think he wanted to do more than talk. *Well, you do, don't you?* He mentally ordered a halt to those thoughts, but they still managed to reach his groin.

"Wonderful. I was wanting to talk, too." She swung the door wide open.

Holy crap. Did she make a habit of inviting men into her bedchamber? He quickly glanced around the hallway to make sure there were no witnesses. Then he stepped inside and shut the door.

"No one saw you, right? We do need to be careful." She adjusted a blue satin comforter around her shoulders, carefully clutching the ends together at her chest.

She'd taken the comforter off the bed, he realized, so she could cover her nightgown. That explained the rustling sounds he'd heard earlier. The comforter was much too long, though, and dragged on the floor behind her as she walked toward a table of food.

Doubt crept into his thoughts. If she was actually trying to seduce him, why would she cover herself up? And why would a princess want to seduce him? She didn't know who he really was. Earlier, when he'd joked about bedding her, she'd called it horrible. So, he had to be mistaken.

But then why had she invited him in? As he walked toward her, he glanced around the room, noting the fire in the hearth, the food on the table, and the bathtub still filled with water. Dammit, he should have washed up before coming here. His gaze landed on the bed with its rumpled sheets, and his breeches grew even tighter. Damn, he wasn't usually so lustful.

"Are you hungry?" she asked.

"Hell, yes." He stopped with a jerk. "Oh, you mean for food?"

"Excuse me?" She turned toward him, then gasped when the comforter suddenly fell off her shoulders.

He blinked. Holy Light, that was a gloriously thin nightgown. And she was beautiful. Was this part of her plan to seduce him? If so, it was definitely working. He took another step toward her.

"You're walking on it!" She hunched down to grab the comforter. "Get off!"

He glanced down. *Oh, shit!* He'd caused the comforter to fall off when he'd trodden on top of it. "Sorry!" He stepped back just as she gave the comforter a hard yank, making him lose his balance.

Bam. He fell on his rear.

"Ow." Damn, he wasn't usually this clumsy.

"Are . . . are you all right?" Her face blushed as she frantically wrapped the comforter around herself like a towel. Again and again.

He winced. The comforter was big enough to go around her three times. Was she that desperate to hide her nightgown? *Oh, shit.* He wasn't usually this big of a fool. "You really do just want to talk, don't you?"

She gave him a confused look. "Isn't that what I said?"

He rose to his feet. "I apologize."

"For what?"

He winced. For being a pig. "What did you need to tell me?"

"I was hoping you could pass another message on to Gwennore. I remembered something really important that she and Silas need to know." She drank some wine.

"What is it?"

She hesitated, then set the goblet down and handed him a plate. "You said you were hungry, right?"

"Yes." He accepted the plate, wondering why she seemed reluctant now to tell him what was so important. He piled some food on his plate. "I was checking on your friend earlier, and all they had to eat was bone broth and porridge. This looks much better."

"Is Aleksi all right?"

"Yes. They took the arrowheads out. He ate a little and took the tonic that Morghen makes for pain. When I left, he was fast asleep with Hallie watching over him." The Woodsman glanced at the bed. "I thought you would be asleep, too."

"I slept most of the afternoon." She placed a slice of cheese and ham on her plate. "Thank you for checking on Aleksi."

"I wanted to see if he could travel when the sun rises. If a search party heads this way, we'll have to move on to Haven."

"I see." She stared at her food, not eating.

"Sorcha," he said softly, and she glanced up at him with haunted eyes. "What did you want to tell Gwennore?"

She grabbed her goblet and gulped down more wine. "You have a way of talking about Gwen as if you know her."

"I've never met her," he hedged, then asked again, "What message did you want me to send?"

"It's about the ambush yesterday. After Aleksi was wounded, I wasn't able to lift him. Lieutenant Kashenko was—"

The balcony doors suddenly blew wide open.

"Oh!" She jumped, spilling wine on the table. The curtains on each side of the balcony door billowed as a strong gust of wind shot into the room. The flame on the candlestick flickered out.

"Good goddesses." She set her goblet down. "I didn't expect that."

He strode toward the doors to shut them, making sure the latch was firmly in place. A bolt of lightning flashed across the sky, brightening the room for a few seconds.

"This is not unusual," he said as he walked back to the table. "The weather in the mountains can change quickly."

"I see." She snapped her fingers to make a flame. As she

reached toward the candlestick, her hand trembled, causing the flame to flicker.

"Are you afraid of storms?"

"No, it's not that." She lit the candle.

He took hold of her wrist and lifted her enflamed fingers so he could see her face. "What is it, then?"

She leaned forward to blow out the flame just as he did the same. The flame disappeared, leaving their faces just a few inches apart.

He wasn't sure how long they stared at each other. When thunder sounded in the distance, she blinked and stepped back. He released his hold on her wrist. Damn, what was this woman doing to him?

And why the hell did she think he wasn't the one? Was it because she had something against elves? "Do you still think all elves are arrogant, two-faced bas—"

"Oh no!" she interrupted him, waving a frantic hand. "I-I'm so sorry I said that. I was thinking of General Caladras and his son—"

"Well, in that case, you were correct. They *are* a pair of arrogant, two-faced bastards."

Her face flushed pink. "I didn't mean you or Bronwen or anyone else around here. I was terribly wrong. Bronwen reminds me of Gwennore, and there's no one I love more in this world than Gwen. So please don't think poorly of me."

"Are you done wallowing in guilt?"

"Oh, I hope so."

His mouth twitched. "So, what is the important message you want me to send?"

Her face grew pale. "It . . . it's about Lieutenant Kashenko. He—I saw him . . ."

Lightning flashed outside, and she jumped. Another gust of wind rattled the balcony doors.

The Woodsman thought back to what he had witnessed that

afternoon. "Was the lieutenant the one who was stabbed to death?"

She drew in a sharp breath. "You saw it?"

"Yes." He should have realized sooner what was upsetting her. The man had been brutally murdered right in front of her. "Is that why you couldn't sleep?"

"If I close my eyes, I see it happen all over again."

His heart clenched at the sight of tears in her eyes. "I know it's hard. The first time I saw someone murdered, I had nightmares for months."

She blinked away her tears as she took a step closer. "Are you all right now?"

No. Not until he avenged his father's death. Thunder rumbled close by. He glanced at the balcony door as fat drops of rain pelted the glass. "It was a long time ago."

"How old were you?"

"Eleven."

She gasped. "That's terrible. I'm so sorry."

He gave her a small smile. "It wasn't your fault." And he shouldn't have brought it up. Why was he telling her secrets from his past? "Getting back to the lieutenant, it looked to me like he was killed by a Norveshki soldier."

"That's right." She nodded. "There's a traitor in the Norveshki army named Paxell. We should warn Gwen and Silas immediately."

"It's after midnight. If Gwennore is asleep, she may not hear the Kings of the Forest."

"If she's worried about me, she'll still be awake."

"She shouldn't be worried. As soon as we arrived at Drudaelen Castle, I sent a message to her that you were here safe."

Sorcha's eyes widened. "You did? You didn't tell me."

"Bronnie dragged you off before I could. But once I discovered you were awake, I thought you should know. That's why I knocked on your door. To tell you about the message and that we should be ready to leave at dawn." *Not because I wanted to be with you.*

"I see. Thank you for telling Gwen. Do you know if she received the message? Did she make a reply?"

He nodded. "She said that she and Silas were greatly relieved and they would send a message to Eberon and Tourin to let your other sisters know that you're safe. They'll start moving toward the Eberoni border so they can meet you there in a week."

Sorcha pressed a hand to her chest as she heaved a huge sigh. "Thank you so much! Did she have anything else to say?"

He shrugged. "They wanted to know who I am."

"What did you tell them?"

"I am the Woodsman."

She snorted. "Well, that didn't tell them much."

More wind rattled the balcony doors, and another flash of lightning brightened the room.

She hunched her shoulders. "I'm glad we're not still traveling."

"Aye." He glanced at the rain pouring down outside. "Well, you must be tired. I'll pass on the news about the traitor first thing in the morning." He grabbed his plate of food. "And I'll take this with me if you don't mind. You should get some sleep. Dawn will be here soon." He headed toward the door as a crack of thunder sounded close by.

"W-would you mind staying a bit longer? You could have more food. And wine."

He turned toward her. She was filling the two goblets with wine. "You're not tired?"

"I don't think I can sleep, what with the storm and the bad . . . memories." She set the two goblets on a small table between two chairs that sat in front of the hearth. "We could share a meal together."

Don't do it. Don't get any closer to her. "Why not?" Dammit, he didn't usually go against his better judgment.

He strode toward a chair, then sat down, placing his plate of food in his lap.

She grabbed her plate and settled into the chair beside him. "Thank you."

They ate in silence for a while, listening to the fire crackle in the hearth and the rain patter against the glass-paned doors.

Sorcha tugged at the comforter, unwrapping it till it was simply resting on top of her. "So Bronwen is your cousin?"

"Aye." He drained his glass, then fetched the pitcher from the table to refill their goblets. "My mother was Lord Daelen's younger sister."

"Was?"

He nodded. "She passed away."

"I'm sorry." Sorcha sighed. "My mother died when I was a babe, so I never knew her." She bit into a piece of ham. "Thank you for staying up with me. I'm used to having someone to talk to. Either Annika or one of my adopted sisters. Last night was my first night away from them all."

He sat back down in his chair. "So how did you and your sisters end up on the Isle of Moon?"

She gasped. "You know about that?"

He shrugged. "I know a lot of things."

"Know-it-all," she muttered.

"Now you're dangerously close to calling me arrogant."

She snorted. "You forgot two-faced."

"You forgot bastard."

Her mouth twitched. "Are you ever going to let me off the hook for that?"

"Not for a long time." They didn't have a long time, he realized. In a week, he would be handing her over to her brother at the Eberoni border. "You were going to tell me about your sisters?"

Sorcha nodded. "We always believed that we were sent to the island because we're Embraced. But that's only part of the story. In my case, my mother sent me away to save me from the plague and a curse. But everything's better now, thanks to Gwennore."

"I heard she is an excellent healer."

Sorcha gave him a wry look. "You hear a lot."

He merely shrugged. "And the other sisters?"

"Brigitta's father sent her to the Isle of Moon. He'd arranged her betrothal to Prince Ulfrid in order to lure the royal family into an ambush. Ulfrid survived, but his father was killed. Then, Brigitta's father wanted to be rid of her in case the betrothal caused any problems in the future."

The Woodsman took a sip of wine as he gazed at the fire. "And Ulfrid became the notorious pirate Rupert."

"You know that, too?" Sorcha narrowed her eyes. "You must have a network of spies."

He shrugged. "If I did, would I tell you?"

"Arrogant," she muttered.

"You forgot two-faced bastard."

Her mouth tilted up. "No, I didn't."

He snorted. So, she had thought the words. "I was surprised when Ulfrid married Brigitta. After all, her father killed his father."

Sorcha stiffened. "She was only a baby when the ambush happened. You can't blame her for that. Rupert doesn't. They're very happy together."

The Woodsman smiled. He liked how quickly Sorcha had jumped to her sister's defense. "And your eldest sister is now the queen of Eberon?"

Sorcha nodded. "Luciana was the first one to go to the Isle of Moon. Not only was she born Embraced, but she was a twin. Her father had to send her away in order to keep her and her sister from being killed."

"That sounds like what happened to Liz and Hallie."

Sorcha set her empty plate on the table and curled up in the chair. "How did they end up here? Is it all right to be Embraced in Woodwyn? I suppose it is, since you're Embraced. Or did the Church of Enlightenment want to kill you?"

"No." But others did. The Woodsman shifted the conversation away from himself. "Liz and his sister were born in the village of Mt. Baedan, which isn't too far from the Woodwyn border. When their mother died a few hours after giving birth, their father was convinced that the Embraced babies were cursed. He reported them to the local priest, who happened to be Father Kit. That was eighteen years ago, when Kit was newly ordained. The villagers were upset, for they believed the Embraced twins would bring misfortune to them all. So, Father Kit did as they asked and sent a message to Lord Morris."

Sorcha winced. "He probably wanted to kill the babes."

The Woodsman nodded. "A week later, the message came from Lord Morris, ordering Father Kit to deliver the babes to Morris in Ebton. Meanwhile, Father Kit had taken the babes into his house and had located a wet nurse for them. The little girl was close to dying, but Father Kit managed to save her. He was so happy that he named her Hallelujah."

Sorcha grinned. "Then Hallie is a nickname."

"Aye. And he named the little boy Halfric. When the message came to deliver the babes, Father Kit couldn't bring himself to do it. So, he packed up the babies and the wet nurse, and they made a run for the Woodwyn border."

Sorcha hugged the comforter to her chest. "What happened next?"

"They got lost in the Haunted Woods. The wet nurse was so frightened, she ran away, hoping to go back to Eberon."

"Oh, no! How did Father Kit manage?"

"He was struggling, and the babies were crying. That's when the Living Oaks called out for help. Morghen had just escaped from Wyndelas Palace. She was hiding in the

Haunted Woods, so she heard the trees and came to the rescue. She led them to Drudaelen Castle, where they would be safe."

"That's a great story." Sorcha leaned closer. "But why are the woods called haunted?"

"There was a time long ago when all elves could understand the words of the Living Oaks. But now, most hear only a whispering sound that makes no sense. They believe it is the murmuring of ghosts."

"I see." She shuddered. "And why did Morghen have to escape from Wyndelas Palace?"

The Woodsman shrugged. "That's another story for another night."

Sorcha wrinkled her nose at him. "I'm glad Lord Morris is no longer in power in Eberon. Twins are safe there now. And the Embraced." She suddenly sat up. "Oh, I just remembered something else you need to tell Gwen. Paxell said he was working for the Circle of Five, and that they were everywhere. I would never know whom I could trust."

A wary look crossed her face, and the Woodsman sighed. "You can trust me, Sorcha."

"Sorry." She gave him a sheepish smile. "I'm only suspicious because we don't know who the five members are. We suspect two people—Lord Morris and the Chameleon."

"That is correct. And you can add a third. General Caladras."

"Really? How do you know?"

He shrugged. "I know."

She snorted. "Know-it-all. Could you tell Gwen?"

"I will."

"Thank you." Sorcha bit her lip as she stared into the fire. "Gwen was so excited about finally seeing her mother. But I'm worried that her mother may not be the loving person Gwen hopes she is."

The Woodsman remained silent as he stacked his empty plate on top of Sorcha's.

"I'm afraid Gwen's mother may have taken part in the ambush." Sorcha leaned toward him. "You know, don't you? You seem to know everything."

"I would bet that Jenetta was in on it," he confessed. "She's been working with General Caladras for years."

"Then she wants to kill Silas and capture her own daughter?"

The Woodsman rested his head back on the chair. "It wouldn't be the first time she's committed murder."

Sorcha gasped. "Are you sure?"

His grip tightened on the arms of the chair. "I'm sure."

"Oh, no." Sorcha pressed a hand to her chest. "This is terrible. Poor Gwen."

"I would say your friend was lucky to have been raised far away from her mother."

"But it's going to break her heart when she learns the truth." Sorcha's eyes glistened with tears. "Gwen is the sweetest and kindest person I've ever known. She deserves better than this."

"You're truly upset for her."

"Of course." Sorcha wiped a tear from her cheek.

His heart squeezed. "She has received something she deserves. She has the love and loyalty of an excellent friend."

Sorcha smiled at him. "That's very sweet of you."

Then why wasn't he "the one"? Frustration tore at him as he rose to his feet. "I should let you get some sleep now."

"But I want to know more."

"You don't need to know more about Woodwyn. You're going home in a week." Dammit. There was no reason to speak so sharply. He winced at the injured look on her face. Now he did feel like an arrogant, two-faced bastard.

"I'll see you in the morning." He strode for the door. It was better this way, he told himself. Once he made his move, it would be too dangerous for anyone to get involved with him. Sorcha needed to go home, where she would be safe and happy with her family and friends.

He closed the door behind him. Yes, it was better this way. And it wasn't as if he was alone. He had his own family and friends. He had followers all over the country ready to risk their lives. So why did he suddenly feel so empty?

Chapter 12

The mountains were lovely, Sorcha thought, as she gazed about on their morning ride to Haven. Perhaps it was because of all the rain last night, but these mountains seemed much more green and lush than the ones back in Norveshka. Those had always seemed too steep and rocky for her taste. These were friendlier. Not quite as high, so they weren't capped with snow like in Norveshka.

She could hear a rushing stream to the right, but only caught a glimpse of it every now and then through a line of stately poplar trees. On either side of the path, wildflowers bloomed in shades of yellow and purple, bringing a smile to her face.

Ouch. Her smile turned into gritted teeth as the small horse cart bounced over another tree root. Her rump was quickly becoming sore from the constant jolting.

She was sitting on the driver's bench with Morghen, who held the reins. In the back, Hallie was watching over Aleksi, who was lying on his stomach on a pile of blankets in the wagon bed. Morghen had insisted it was too soon for him to be sitting on a horse, but every time their cart hit a rut or bounced over a root, Aleksi groaned.

Sorcha glanced back at him. "I'm worried this trip is too hard on him."

Morghen nodded. "No doubt it is, but we had no choice.

Shortly before dawn, we heard from the Living Oaks that a search party was on its way to the castle."

So we're still in danger. Sorcha cast a nervous glance over her shoulder, but there were too many trees blocking her view. They were only about ten miles west of Drudaelen Castle, and at the slow rate they were traveling, a search party could catch up with them. "What if some soldiers find this path? Won't it lead them straight to Haven?"

Father Kit glanced back at her. "This actually goes to Eberon. We'll cross a bridge soon and leave this path behind. Then we'll head into the Haunted Woods."

"Won't they still be able to track us?" Sorcha asked.

"Don't worry, lass," Morghen told her. "The Woodsman knows how to hide us."

"How?"

Morghen shrugged. "He has his ways."

Sorcha huffed. "That doesn't tell me much."

"So, are you interested in knowing more about him?" Morghen asked, her lavender eyes twinkling.

"No." Sorcha turned to study a cluster of aspen trees along the side of the road. "Not at all." Why should she even think about him? He hadn't said a word to her this morning in the courtyard. She'd given him a smile with her greeting, but he'd responded with only a curt nod. Then he'd proceeded to bark orders at everyone to get ready to go. Pushy know-it-all.

She glanced at him. He was riding in front, leading the way. Of course he was, since he always wanted to be in charge. He was sitting stiffly erect on his horse, so different from Father Kit and Liz, who slouched comfortably on their horses.

No wonder he was called the Woodsman. He had a wooden rod stuck up his backside. Her mouth twitched. It was a mean thought, but it served him right for ignoring her.

She'd really enjoyed sharing a meal with him the night before, but then, all of a sudden, it felt as if he'd slammed a door in her face. Why? Just because she was going to leave in a week? Was that any reason to be rude?

"You're glaring at him," Morghen whispered. "Are you sure you have no interest in him?"

"What?" Sorcha blinked. "No! I'm simply frowning because my rear end is sore from all the jostling."

"Ah." Morghen gave her a speculative look, then turned to Father Kit. "Weren't you telling me earlier about the different ways our enemies want to kill the Woodsman?"

"That's right!" The priest glanced back at her with a grin. "I thought chaining him to a lightning rod during a storm was rather inventive."

"Last night would have been perfect for that," Liz added with a smile. "They missed their chance."

Sorcha grimaced. "What are you talking about?"

"The soldiers have been laying bets on how General Caladras will execute the Woodsman if they ever catch him," Father Kit told her. "Drawing and quartering is in first place. Hanging in second."

"I liked the one where they coat him with honey and tie him to an iron stake close to a bear cave," Liz said.

"Why in the world—?" Sorcha began.

"So he would be mauled to death," Liz explained.

"I understand that!" Sorcha clenched her fists, wadding up the green velvet of her borrowed gown. "What I meant is, why would you jest about something so terrible? And you're doing it right next to him!" She gestured at the Woodsman, then lowered her hand and looked away when he glanced back at her.

"That was a rather strong reaction for someone who has no interest," Morghen said softly.

Sorcha's cheeks grew warm. She'd fallen headfirst into Morghen's trap.

"The men mean no disrespect," the wily old woman continued. "They make light of the danger because they face it together. If any of the Woodsman's followers are captured, they will be executed, too."

Sorcha winced. Why were these people leading a life that was so dangerous? And why would the Woodsman do this? He was Bronwen's cousin, so that meant he was from a noble family. Why had he taken on the role of a thief? Was he an outcast because he was Embraced? Or was there something else about him that kept him from living a normal life?

Secrets. If only Brigitta was here. She could use her gift to see what he was hiding.

Once again, Sorcha felt a pang of homesickness, not for Norveshka, but for the convent where she and her sisters had grown up. It still hurt whenever she dwelled on the sad truth that they would never live together again. At least now that the oldest were queens of Eberon, Tourin, and Norveshka, there could be peace among those countries.

The clattering noise of horse hooves clip-clopping across the wooden beams of the bridge brought Sorcha back to the present. She glanced at the water below as it rushed and foamed over rocks. Woodwyn was a beautiful country, but dangerous. The army was run by vicious thugs who destroyed villages and turned their own countrymen into refugees. And Princess Jenetta was no better. According to the Woodsman, she had a history of committing murder. What would happen when she inherited the throne? With her and General Caladras in power, the people would no doubt suffer.

Sorcha glanced at the Woodsman. Twice she'd heard mention of a rebellion. Was he planning to take over the country? She had an ominous feeling that she'd landed in the middle of something momentous. And life threatening.

They reached the other side of the bridge, where the path to Eberon continued along the valley, following the stream.

Morghen steered the horse cart off the path, following the rest of their party across a meadow.

Sorcha glanced back at the path, suddenly wishing for the safety that her eldest sister Luciana could provide. "Why can't we just go to Eberon now?"

Morghen shook her head. "It would take several days, and Aleksi isn't up to it. Besides, we can't risk being out in the open where search parties could find us."

Facing forward, Sorcha heaved a sigh.

"Are you homesick, lass?" Morghen asked her.

"A little." As much as she missed her sisters, Sorcha wasn't looking forward to telling Gwen that she had an evil mother. "I'll be fine, though. I don't want to do anything that would endanger you and your friends."

Morghen nodded. "All will work out well in the end, so don't worry."

Sorcha wondered if the older woman could actually see the future, or if she was merely offering a few words of comfort. She was about to ask, but stopped herself when she realized the horsemen in front of her were now lower. She could only see their heads. "What . . . ?"

"There's a gully ahead," Morghen explained as the cart approached the edge. "The stream we just crossed used to flow through this channel."

Sorcha noted the horsemen were already climbing the embankment on the other side. It was not a deep channel, but the recent rain had left a pit of mud in the middle.

Morghen flicked the reins, and the horses descended the gentle slope without a problem. But once the wheels of the horse cart reached the mud, the horses floundered, no longer able to move forward.

"We're stuck!" Morghen called out.

"I was afraid that would happen," Father Kit said as he and the other men dismounted.

"We should get out," Sorcha told Hallie. "We're extra weight."

Hallie nodded. "You stay put," she told Aleksi, then she jumped off the back of the cart to land on damp grass.

There was mud below the driver's bench, so Sorcha scrambled into the wagon bed. "Rest here," she told Aleksi, then joined Hallie on the grassy incline behind the cart.

Meanwhile, the Woodsman, Father Kit, and Liz had descended into the gully to analyze the situation.

"Liz, you grab hold of the horses," the Woodsman ordered. "Get them to move when I tell you. Father Kit, go to the back of the cart and be ready to push."

The two men did as they were told; then the Woodsman reached a hand toward the wheels.

"Now," he said as he rotated his hand to force the wooden wheels to turn. They did spin, but only in place, causing the cart to settle even deeper into the mud.

Sorcha shoved at the back of the cart, trying to help Father Kit. It wasn't easy since her borrowed shoes tended to slide on top of the slick grass.

"It's not working," Morghen announced.

"We'll have to do it the old-fashioned way." The Woodsman moved toward the back of the cart. "Step back," he told Sorcha as he planted his hands on the wooden beam. "You don't need to help."

Bossy man. He might be able to order everyone else around, but not her. She placed her hands back on the beam. "I'm going to do it."

He gave her an annoyed look, then said, "Everyone push on the count of three. One, two—"

Sorcha gasped when she spotted Aleksi. He was out of the cart and getting ready to push. "Aleksi! What are you—"

"Three!"

"—doing?" Sorcha yelled just as everyone pushed, and the

cart lurched forward. "Ack!" Her shoes slipped and, with her arms flailing, she fell forward, straight toward the pit of mud.

Suddenly, she was jerked back as strong arms pulled her hard against a solid chest.

"Umph." It had happened so fast, the air had been knocked from her lungs. As she caught her breath, she realized in an instant who was holding her from behind. After all, she'd felt these strong arms wrapped around her for hours during their long ride. She knew the soft sound of his breathing, the warmth of his broad chest. She knew his scent, as natural and comforting as the forest. She knew the feel of him, as if she had known him for years.

"Are you all right?" he asked softly, and the deep sound of his voice sent a tremor through her heart.

She turned halfway and found him watching her intently with his lavender eyes. She'd always thought Gwennore had the most beautiful eyes in the world, but the Woodsman had her beat. *Why can't he be the one?* Did it matter what the Telling Stones had predicted? Why should she let a few rocks decide her fate?

Aleksi cleared his throat, then spoke in Eberoni. "Let go of her, Tree Man. She's betrothed to me."

The Woodsman stiffened and released her immediately. Hallie gasped. And Sorcha spun toward Aleksi.

"That's not true," she said in Norveshki as she approached him. "Why would you say such a thing?"

He gazed around the meadow as if he were searching for a reason. "It would make your brother happy."

She gave him an incredulous look. "That's the best reason you can come up with?"

Aleksi scowled at her. "Fine. How about this? I need to protect you from that grabby elf."

"I don't need protection."

"Believe me, you do." Aleksi stepped toward her and lowered his voice. "I've seen the way he looks at you."

Her heart made a small leap. Did he? She glanced back at the Woodsman. He was standing stiffly, wearing his usual stoic expression as he watched them carefully. How much of this conversation could he understand?

"Is it true?" Hallie asked in Eberoni, her gaze lingering on Aleksi. "Are you betrothed?"

"Yes," Aleksi replied at the same time that Sorcha said, "No, of course not."

"Dammit," he grumbled in Norveshki. "You could have at least pretended until I got you home safely."

Hallie closed her eyes briefly as she heaved a sigh of relief. *She's falling for Aleksi,* Sorcha realized. But the silly man was oblivious and still glowering at her. "Don't be angry with me," she fussed in Eberoni. "Ye're the one in trouble. How dare ye push when ye're injured? Hallie, could ye take him back to the cart, please?"

"Of course." Hallie latched on to Aleksi's arm. "Come on. You need to lie down before you tear open your wounds."

"I'm a soldier," Aleksi grumbled as he skirted the mud pit with Hallie. "I can handle a little pain." He stopped at the back of the cart to cast one more threatening look at the Woodsman. "I'm watching you, Tree Man. I may not be able to fly at the moment, but I can still breathe fire."

Hallie's eyes grew wide. "Can you really? That's so awesome."

Aleksi shrugged. "It's no big deal." He climbed into the cart, seemingly unaware of the adoration gleaming in Hallie's eyes.

The Woodsman didn't look particularly impressed or intimidated, Sorcha thought, as he headed back to his horse. Did anything ever shake his annoyingly calm demeanor?

She followed him around the mud pit. "Thank you for catching me," she said in Elfish. "I would have hated to muddy this gown. Your cousin lent it to me. She said the green velvet was a perfect match for my eyes. It's very pretty, don't you think?"

No reply. He didn't even glance back.

She wrinkled her nose at him. "Do you mind if I walk alongside the horses for a while? I'm tired of sitting."

He continued his quick stride without looking back. "Suit yourself."

"Are you angry with me?" Did she imagine it, or did his back become even more stiff?

"I have no feelings." He mounted his horse and headed across the rest of the meadow.

She quickened her pace, but soon realized it wasn't necessary. He was keeping his horse at a slow gait. Very considerate for a man with no feelings.

They reached the end of the meadow, where a dense forest thick with underbrush rose up like an impenetrable wall. They followed the wall for a few minutes, then the Woodsman reined in his horse. Facing the forest, he lifted his hands together, then slowly separated them.

A tangle of branches unraveled and parted. The undergrowth flattened as if a giant had trod on top of it with enormous boots. And there, before them, lay a clear path into the forest.

Sorcha's mouth dropped open. So, this was how the Woodsman kept the location of Haven a secret. Father Kit and Liz rode through the opening; then Morghen took the horse cart through.

The Woodsman glanced at her. "Are you coming?"

"Yes." She walked alongside his horse as they entered the forest. Ahead of them, the rest of the party continued down the path.

The Woodsman dismounted and, facing the opening, he lifted his hands and brought them together. The underbrush rose back up. The branches moved together, interlacing until the thick wall was back in place.

"That's incredible," Sorcha said softly in the quiet stillness of the forest. "How do you do it?"

He gave her a wry look as he nabbed the reins of his horse. "Woodsman."

She rolled her eyes. *There he goes again.* "That doesn't explain anything. Why is your gift with wood?"

He shrugged, then headed down the path, leading his horse. "Why is your gift with fire?"

"In my case, it makes sense," she said as she walked beside him. "I come from a family of fire-breathing dragons."

"It makes sense for me, too. My mother was a Wood Elf."

"Then what was your father? A wood *elm*?"

His mouth twitched. "No."

Ah, she'd almost made him smile. No feelings, her ass. "Are you sure you're not part tree? Maybe you have a wooden leg?"

He gave her a bland look.

"Why do the trees do what you want? Do they relate to your wooden personality?"

He arched a brow at her.

"Or maybe it's because you have the sense of humor of a tree?"

His mouth twitched again. "Actually, the Living Oaks find you very amusing."

She cast a wary look at the forest. "You mean they're listening to us?"

"Maybe."

She narrowed her eyes. "You're jesting with me, aren't you?"

"How could I with this wooden personality?"

She lifted a hand to swat his shoulder, but he caught her by the wrist.

"Careful, you could get a splinter from my wooden arm."

She snorted, then grinned when the corners of his mouth curled up. He had a gorgeous smile. "You do have feelings. I knew it."

His smile faded, replaced by a look of fierce intensity. His grip tightened around her wrist for a few seconds; then he released her. "I promised to return you to your family."

A pang reverberated through her heart. Goddesses help her, she wasn't sure she wanted to leave Woodwyn. Or to be truly honest with herself, she wasn't eager to leave the Woodsman. "That doesn't mean we can't still be friends."

A hint of sadness glinted in his lavender eyes. "It could be dangerous to be around me."

She sauntered down the path. "It seems safe enough here in the woods. And Haven is safe, too, right?"

"Yes." He walked beside her, leading his horse. "We'll be safe as long as the army doesn't know our location."

The path twisted right and left, weaving its way through the woods and over the hills. The forest was filled with oaks that looked ancient to Sorcha, some with enormous branches as thick as tree trunks. Younger trees lined the path and cast a cool shade on them, and at times, the branches met overhead, forming a tunnel. Rays of sunshine shot through the branches, dappling the path and glistening off the drops of rain that still clung to tufts of grass.

Deeper in the forest, clumps of ferns grew around the base of trees. Moss and lichen covered the rocks and boulders, coloring them green and gold. The scent of summer and growing things mingled with the musty smell of rich earth. Birdsong trilled in the distance, and a soft breeze rustled the leaves, causing them to glimmer in the sunlight.

It was lovely, Sorcha thought. Green and full of life. "The woods don't seem haunted to me."

"The forest goes on for many miles, all the way to Eberon. Most people will not enter for fear of getting lost or attacked by a wild boar or wolf." He gave her a curious look. "It doesn't frighten you?"

"Why should it? I have the infamous Woodsman to protect me."

"So you trust me now?"

She glanced at him with a shy smile. "I suppose I do."

"Then why am I not the one?"

Her smile vanished as her heart gave a jolt. "You—you heard me last night."

His eyes glinted with an intensity that took her breath away. "I did. And ever since then, I've been wondering what you meant."

Why was he asking this? Did it mean he wanted to be the one? But then why did he keep distancing himself from her? "It doesn't mean anything. I was referring to a silly game that my sisters and I like to play."

"What sort of game?"

"The Game of Stones. We use it to predict the future. But it doesn't matter. As you said, I'm leaving soon."

He looked away, his normally smooth brow creased with a frown. An awkward silence hovered over them as they continued to walk. After a few more minutes, they emerged from a leafy tunnel, coming to a stop at the top of a hill.

"We have arrived," the Woodsman said. "This is Haven."

Chapter 13

Sorcha gasped at the sight before her. A green meadow, dotted with wildflowers, led down to a small lake. Cutting across the meadow was a narrow stream that tumbled over rocks to feed into the lake's crystalline blue water.

In the area around the lake, homes had been dug into the hillside. Footpaths wound about, connecting the homes and bisecting vegetable gardens. The gardens were completely haphazard. No straight furrows, but a jumble of different plants.

On the far side of the lake, a stand of tall conifers rose up, and in the boughs, she spotted more houses. Tree houses, connected by wood-and-rope bridges.

Down by the lake, Hallie was leading Aleksi into a hillside house. Father Kit and Liz took the horses and cart to a stable built into the side of another hill.

"What do you think?" The Woodsman watched her curiously.

"It's lovely. Incredibly lovely." She smiled as people emerged from houses and gardens to greet Father Kit and Liz. Many turned toward the Woodsman to give him a cheerful wave. "But how come people are living in the hills or trees? Did no one want to build a cottage of wood or stone?"

"In order to remain safe, Haven must remain hidden. From a distance, all that can be seen are hills or trees. Even the gardens will look like natural vegetation. If a dragon flies overhead, he won't see anything to draw his attention."

"That's clever. So do you live in one of the hills?"

"No." He pointed toward a tall fir tree. "That's my house there."

She snorted. Of course the Woodsman lived in a tree.

"The small house next door is vacant." He pointed to the conifer on the left. "Would you like to live in a tree for a few days?"

"Sure." She grinned. This was going to be fun.

"You're not afraid of heights?"

"No, not at all. Aleksi took me for a ride up in the sky one time, and we soared over mountains. I loved it!"

The Woodsman's brow creased as his frown returned.

Was he jealous? A small part of her hoped so. *Oh, be honest with yourself.* It was a large part.

"Welcome back!" A group of three middle-aged elfin women hurried toward them.

"Riona, Teresa, and Lauren," the Woodsman muttered. "They live under the false assumption that they're actually in charge here."

Sorcha smiled at how annoyed he sounded.

"Is it true, my lord?" one of them asked as she approached, her gaze slanting in curiosity toward Sorcha. "Father Kit said you brought a princess with you."

"Yes." The Woodsman motioned to Sorcha. "This is Princess Sorcha of Norveshka."

"Your Highness." They all curtsied.

"I'm delighted to meet you," she told them in Elfish. "Please call me Sorcha."

"She's speaks Elfish!" They exchanged grins, then all started talking to her at the same time.

"This is so exciting!"

"Goodness, your hair is very red, isn't it?"

"That is common in Norveshka, right?"

"You must let us show you around the village."

"Shh!" The eldest one hushed them up. "She'll be tired from the journey. First, she'll want to rest."

"And eat. She must be famished."

"Actually," Sorcha managed to cut in. "If you don't mind, I'd like to check on my injured friend first."

"Oh, of course!" The eldest latched on to her arm. "I'll take you straight to Morghen's house."

"And then we'll feed you," the second woman said. "We've been cooking since dawn to celebrate the return of the Woodsman."

"The feast will be ready soon, my lord," the third woman told the Woodsman.

"I look forward to it," he replied. "The princess has a parcel of clothes in the horse cart. Please have someone deliver it to the guest treehouse."

"Yes, of course, my lord," the eldest one said.

"Thank you." He bowed to Sorcha. "I will leave you in good hands for now." He strode down a path that skirted the lake.

Was he going to his tree house? Sorcha didn't have a chance to wonder, for the women were dragging her to Morghen's hillside cottage.

"Don't worry about your friend. Morghen is an excellent physician," the eldest woman said as she opened the front gate. "I'm Riona, by the way. And this is Teresa and Lauren."

"Thank you for welcoming me here."

"We're excited to have you." Teresa led them through a garden of flowers and herbs. "We hardly ever have visitors."

"Because no one knows we're here," Lauren added.

"Which is a good thing." Riona shuddered. "We can only pray that the army never finds us."

"Father Kit said you were captured by the army," Teresa

said. "You might have seen my son, Tarrant. He's a spy for the Woodsman."

Lauren huffed. "You shouldn't tell everybody that."

"I don't believe I met him," Sorcha said before the women could start talking again. She could see what the Woodsman meant now. When these three women teamed up, they were a force to be reckoned with.

"I'm afraid we'll have to leave you for a moment," Riona told her at the door to Morghen's house. "We need to check on the food."

"We'll fetch you when it's ready," Lauren added. "And I'll have your clothes taken to your tree house."

"Welcome to Haven!" They waved as they scurried out the garden gate.

Sorcha waved back, then took a deep breath to settle her nerves. As she looked about, she noted there was quite a bit of activity in the village. There were elves working in the gardens and fishing in the small lake. She hadn't noticed them earlier, for their green clothing and hats made them blend in with their surroundings. From across the lake, the sound of children's laughter wafted toward her. Some were playing hide-and-seek among the trees. Others were rolling like logs down a grassy hill.

It was a happy, peaceful place, she thought, not so different from any village in Eberon or Norveshka. But different from what she had expected. Like everyone else in the other mainland countries, Sorcha had always heard horror stories about how elves would stream unexpectedly across their borders to maim and murder. And then they would retreat just as suddenly without taking any plunder or prisoners. Since the elves didn't seem interested in gaining wealth or land, people believed they attacked because they simply enjoyed being cruel.

But Sorcha had not seen any cruelty at Drudaelen Castle.

Nor did she see it here. So why did the elfin army behave the way it did? Good goddesses, they even attacked other elfin villages. These people at Haven were refugees from their own army. And apparently, the men here were part of the Woodsman's band, risking their lives to help their countrymen.

She spotted him across the lake, climbing a ladder up to his tree house. Was he really going to lead a rebellion against those in power? If so, he had a dangerous road ahead of him. Was that why he kept behaving in a cold and distant manner? Was he rejecting her in order to protect her? Didn't that mean that he cared about her?

She hoped so. But according to the Telling Stones, he was not the one. So why did she want him to care? And how had she managed to fall for him so quickly?

With a sigh, she ducked her head under the low doorframe to enter Morghen's house. The parlor was a cozy place with books stacked haphazardly on tables and comfy chairs set around a blazing fire in a stone hearth. The flames of several lit candlesticks flickered around the room, gleaming off the glass jars and bottles that lined numerous shelves. The scent of crushed herbs filled the room. Voices drifted from an adjoining room, and it sounded like Morghen was fussing at Aleksi.

Sorcha caught a word or two. Apparently, one of Aleksi's wounds had started bleeding again, probably because he'd helped push the horse cart. While he was receiving a fresh bandage, she wandered over to a row of shelves to look at the neatly labeled bottles. Most were filled with different kinds of herbs and plants for making medicine. But then she spotted some green bottles with more unusual labels. *Hair Growth for Baldness. Fertility Enhancement. Hair Dye. Sleep Tonic. Love Potion. Erection Fortification.*

What on Aerthlan was erection fortification? The tablets looked blue in color. And what kind of physician made love potions?

"Oh, you're here." Hallie strode into the parlor, carrying a tray of discarded dressings.

Sorcha winced at the sight of the blood-soaked cloths. "Is Aleksi all right?"

Hallie nodded as she dropped the dressings into a copper tin. "The wound on his shoulder started bleeding again, but the stitches held." She bit her lip, frowning. "Is he always so grouchy?"

"Goodness, no. Aleksi is normally very easygoing."

Hallie exhaled in relief. "I was hoping that was the case, but right now, he's acting like a bear. Threatened to breathe fire and burn the house down if we gave him more porridge." She set the tray on a table as a worried look crossed her pretty face. "Actually, he's been a grouch ever since you lagged behind us on the path to walk with the Woodsman. Are you sure Aleksi is not your betrothed?"

"I'm sure. He's like a brother to me. An overprotective, grouchy brother."

Hallie smiled. "That's sweet of him. I'd better bring him some hearty food." When she opened the door, there was a girl lurking about the garden. "Oh, hello, Tara. Do you need some medication?"

Tara nodded, her pale cheeks blushing pink.

"Wait inside," Hallie instructed her. "Morghen will see you soon."

Tara slipped inside and slanted Sorcha a shy look. "Is it true what I heard? That you're a princess?"

"Yes. Please call me Sorcha." The girl looked about thirteen, Sorcha thought. Long-legged and skittish like a young colt, but in a few years, she would be a beauty.

Tara fiddled with the tasseled sash tied around her waist as her gaze shifted nervously about the room. "I-I guess a princess like you has a bunch of suitors."

"I've had a few," Sorcha admitted, surprised by the question. "But I wasn't interested in them."

Tara's eyes widened. "Why not? Were they not handsome?"

Sorcha shrugged. "They were all right. They just weren't right for me." The image of the Woodsman's gorgeous face crossed her mind, giving her a small start. *Why are you thinking about him now?* She shoved the image away.

Tara pressed a hand to her chest as her expression turned to one of abject horror. "Holy Light, are you saying you've never been in love?"

Immediately, the Woodsman leaped back into her mind. *Stop thinking about him!* Sorcha slapped herself mentally. "No, I haven't." What she felt had to be attraction, not love. She hardly knew the man.

"That is so tragic." Tears glistened in Tara's lavender-blue eyes. "How could a beautiful princess have no one to love her? How do you bear it?"

Sorcha stiffened. "I'm doing quite well, thank you."

"But I think everyone should experience love when they're young and beautiful, don't you?"

"I suppose that would be nice," Sorcha muttered.

"I'm sure you'll find someone worthy of you!" Tara gave her an encouraging smile. "I'll help you, if I can!"

"That's very kind of you, but I—"

"I think I'm in love!" Tara heaved a long sigh. "He's on my mind all the time. I can hardly sleep for thinking about him. Doesn't that mean I'm in love?"

Sorcha shifted her weight. Tara's description sounded uncomfortably familiar. "Well, it could be a . . . a temporary attraction." Surely, her feelings would return to normal once she was back home. Wouldn't they? But how could she forget the Woodsman?

"It has to be more than that," Tara insisted. "Whenever I see Colwyn, my heart beats so fast, I fear it will burst. And whenever he talks to me, the sound of his voice—" She closed her eyes briefly and sighed. "I don't even know how to explain it. It must be true love, don't you think?"

Sorcha swallowed hard. Didn't she react the same way? "I'm not really an expert." And neither was this girl, she reminded herself. So she shouldn't let this conversation unnerve her.

Tara pressed the back of her hand against her brow in a dramatic pose. "I think my heart will break if he doesn't love me back."

"Ah, Tara." Morghen bustled into the room. "What brings you here? Does Teresa need more sleep tonic?" She poured water into a basin and washed her hands.

"No, my mother is fine." Tara sidled up close to the shelf lined with unusual medications. "It . . . it's for me." Her face flushed a bright pink.

"What is ailing you, lass?" Morghen stepped close to her, giving her an assessing look. "Are your courses causing you too much pain?"

Tara shook her head, then pointed toward the bottle of love potion. "I would like some of this, please."

Morghen sighed. "You're a bit young to be needing that, lass."

"It's not for me!" Tara waved her hands. "I'm already in love. It's for Colwyn. Right now, he hardly even sees me. I just need a little help. Please." Her eyes gleamed with tears. "You have to help me. My heart is breaking!"

"Lass." Morghen gave her a sympathetic look. "That potion is not to be taken lightly. It's extremely potent, and the effect is irreversible. I never allow a couple to take it unless I know they are truly destined for each other."

Sorcha peered curiously at the green bottle. Was such a potion truly possible?

"But Colwyn *is* destined for me!" Tara cried.

"My dear, you do know that I'm able to glimpse into the

future when I touch someone, do you not?" Morghen asked gently as she took Tara's hand in her own.

Tara nodded, her chin trembling.

Morghen closed her eyes for a moment, then gave Tara's hand a pat before releasing it. "There is a good man in your future, my dear, but he is not Colwyn. I am sorry."

A tear rolled down Tara's cheek. "Why? If my name was Taren, would I be good enough for him then?"

Sorcha tilted her head, not understanding.

"Dry your tears, child." Morghen led her toward the door. "This will pass, and your heart will not break. I promise you, in the future you will be very happy."

Tara stepped outside, then gave Morghen a defiant look. "I won't give up on Colwyn. I love him too much!" With a sniffle, she ran to the garden gate.

Morghen sighed as she closed the door. "Perhaps I should create a tonic that can make a person forget."

"Does the love potion actually work?" Sorcha asked.

"Why do you ask?" Morghen's eyes crinkled as she smiled. "Do you have someone in mind?"

"No." Warmth crept up Sorcha's neck. "I was merely curious."

Morghen nodded as she fetched the kettle, which was warming by the hearth. "I've given the potion to five couples, and they all married within a month."

"Oh, my. It certainly sounds effective."

"It is." Morghen poured hot water into a teapot. "Of course it works mainly as a boost to spur on a couple that is already attracted to each other but too shy to admit to it. It inflames their carnal passions to the point they cannot resist each other."

"Oh, dear." That sounded dangerous. Sorcha turned her attention to the other green bottles on the shelf. *Hair Growth for Baldness. Fertility Enhancement. Hair Dye. Sleep Tonic.*

Erection Fortification. Did they all work? "Gwennore is an excellent healer, but she doesn't make potions like these."

Morghen readied two earthenware cups on a tray. "That's because Gwennore is not a witch. Would you like a cup of tea?"

Sorcha blinked. "You mean . . . ?" She gave the teapot a wary look.

Morghen chuckled as she filled the two cups. "Yes, I'm a witch. And no, there is nothing out of the ordinary in the tea." She handed Sorcha a cup, then took the second one and settled in one of the comfy chairs by the fire.

"Thank you." Sorcha sat next to Morghen. "Is that why you had to leave Wyndelas Palace? Did they not approve of your being a witch?"

"Ah, you've heard about my daring escape." Morghen drank some tea and stretched her legs toward the fire. "That must have been almost twenty years ago. By the Light, time passes too quickly. But how did you hear of it?"

"The Woodsman told me a little when he was sharing the story of Hallie and her brother."

Morghen slanted her an amused look. "So, have you been enjoying your time with the Woodsman?"

Sorcha drank some tea to keep from having to answer right away. Then, much to her relief, the door opened and Hallie returned with a tray of food.

"I'll take this to Mister Grumpy," she said as she strode across the room. "Riona says the feast will begin soon."

"Thank you." Morghen watched as Hallie entered the room where Aleksi was. "Love seems to be in the air these days," she whispered.

Sorcha leaned close and whispered back, "I don't think Aleksi is aware of Hallie's feelings."

"He will be soon enough." Morghen chuckled. "And he won't be needing the love potion."

"What did Tara mean when she asked about her name being Taren?"

"You don't know?" Morghen looked surprised. "But you speak Elfish so well. How did you learn it?"

"From transcribing books in Elfish. I grew up in the Convent of the Two Moons on the Isle of Moon, where the nuns transcribe books in all four languages."

"Ah, so you grew up with Gwennore." Morghen sipped some tea.

"Yes, I did. But what did Tara mean?"

"In Woodwyn, we worship the sun as our father, but we consider the Wyn River our mother, for it is there that the elfin people had their beginning many centuries ago. Since you learned Elfish from books, you're probably not aware that we pronounce the Wyn of Woodwyn like *when*. And since the Wyn River is sacred to us, we revere the sound of *Wyn* or anything that rhymes with it. Only those in the royal family are allowed to use the sound to begin their name. So, you have King Rendelf. Or his late sons, Kendelas and Brendelf." Morghen's eyes took on a pained look. "And the sons of Kendelas—Kendyl and Denys, who passed away too young."

Sorcha sensed that there was another story there. "Then Jenetta has a royal name."

Morghen's expression grew harsh. "Yes, she does."

"And Gwennore."

"Yes." Morghen gave her a wry look. "It should not have come as a surprise to you that Gwennore is an elfin princess. The truth was right there in her name."

"We didn't know."

Morgen took another sip of tea. "Nobles are allowed to use the sacred sound at the end of their names. So, you have Drudaelen Castle and Lord Bowen Daelen."

"And Bronwen, Aiden, and Helen?"

"Yes. Colwyn's name also signifies he is of noble stock, the second son of the Earl of Whistlyn, to be exact. Tara's name indicates she is a commoner." Morghen shrugged. "But Tara is mistaken. If Colwyn was the right man for her, he would not reject her because of her social rank."

Sorcha gave the witch a curious look. "Your name ends with the sacred sound, too."

Morghen nodded. "My father was a distant cousin to the current king."

"Then you must be a River Elf?"

"I am." Morghen motioned toward the shelf of unusual medications. "For years I had to use that hair dye to color my hair so I could blend in with the Wood Elves."

"Why did you have to hide here?"

Morghen ignored the question as her eyes narrowed on the bottle of hair dye. "It's almost empty. I'll need to mix up another batch tomorrow."

More hair dye? Sorcha glanced at the green bottle, then at the old woman's silver-gray hair. Obviously, Morghen was no longer using the dye. So who was?

A knock sounded on the door; then Tara trudged inside, a sullen look on her face. "Mother wanted me to tell you that the feast is ready."

"Ah, good." Morghen rose to her feet and motioned for Sorcha to follow her. "We left Drudaelen in such a hurry this morning, I never broke my fast. I'm starving." She paused next to Tara. "Will you tell Hallie to come, too?"

"Yes, my lady."

Morghen led Sorcha toward a large meadow by the lake. "There are too many of us in Haven to drag out enough tables and chairs, so we always have our feasts like a picnic." She pointed at a circle of colorful blankets. In front of each blanket, a large wooden tray had been placed, and on top of the tray, there were cups and eating utensils made of wood, along with a small basket of bread.

A table sat in the middle of the circle, its surface covered with platters of food, a large pot of soup, and stacks of wooden plates and bowls. Riona and Teresa were busy ladling soup into bowls, while Lauren was slicing a large ham.

Elfin families gathered around the different blankets, chatting excitedly to each other. When they noticed Sorcha's arrival, they all hushed and bowed to her.

Sorcha curtsied back. "Thank you for so generously taking care of me and my friend."

The whispers started. "Oh, she speaks Elfish so well!"

"She seems very nice."

"Goodness, her hair is very red, isn't it?"

"Are those freckles?"

"Hush! She can hear us!"

"Don't mind them." Morghen gave Sorcha a sympathetic look. "They've never met a Norveshki before. Here." She motioned to a coverlet made of embroidered blue silk. "They will expect you to sit on their best blanket."

"Thank you." When Sorcha sat down, most of the elves also settled on their blankets. Riona and Teresa rushed about handing out bowls of soup. Sorcha glanced around, but the Woodsman was nowhere in sight.

"Looking for someone?" Morghen smiled as she sat on the blanket to Sorcha's left.

"Wine for everyone!" Father Kit announced as he pulled a cart toward the circle. With the help of a few elfin men, brass pitchers of wine were deposited on each wooden tray.

Everyone filled their wooden cups with wine and buttered their bread. As soon as Father Kit blessed the food, they started eating.

"Be sure to try my soup," Riona told Sorcha as she set two steaming bowls on the tray in front of her. "I make it with fresh fish from the lake."

"Thank you." Sorcha smiled although she wondered why she was receiving two bowls.

"Am I late?" the Woodsman asked, and Sorcha glanced over her shoulder to see him walking toward her.

Once again, his long-legged stride caused her chest to grow tight. He'd changed his clothes and was now wearing a casual pair of brown linen breeches and soft leather shoes. His cream-colored linen shirt was only partially tucked in. And only partially buttoned. She swallowed hard at the sight of his upper chest, so firm and muscular. The shirt was tight enough across the torso to reveal more muscles, and the long column of his neck was both elegant and strong.

His long hair was still damp from a washing and tied back with a leather thong. He hadn't shaved, though, and she noticed that the whiskers along his jaw were black, the same color as his eyebrows. That seemed a bit odd since his hair was reddish-brown, but still, she found the combination quite stunning. Damn him.

"You *are* late," Father Kit grumbled as he sat next to Halfric on a blanket to Sorcha's right. "We started eating without you."

The Woodsman came to a stop at the edge of the priest's blanket. "I was talking to the Living Oaks. Some good news—the search party has left Drudaelen Castle."

"Without finding anything?" Father Kit whispered.

Sorcha looked away as if she wasn't listening in, but she had to wonder if the priest was referring to the weapons that were hidden in the catacombs.

"Everything is fine." The Woodsman kicked off his shoes before stepping onto her blanket. He dropped to his knees beside her. "Are we family today?"

She blinked at him. "Excuse me?"

"Each blanket is shared by a family," he explained as he sat cross-legged on the right side of her.

Her heart gave a lurch when his thigh brushed against hers. "You mean . . . ?"

His mouth curled up. "You're sitting on my blanket."

"Oh!" She glanced at Morghen, who ignored her as she ate her soup. "I was told to sit here, but I can move." She started to get up, but he grabbed her arm to stop her.

"Don't go. It's been tiresome always eating alone."

She settled back down. "You don't have any family here?" A quick glance around the circle, and she realized everyone was watching them curiously.

"A toast!" Father Kit announced with his booming voice. He filled his wooden cup with wine, then raised it in the air. "To another successful mission!"

Everyone gave a cheer, then drank some wine.

Sorcha was about to take a sip when Tara ran into the circle, carrying two brass goblets.

"Wait!" Tara knelt in front of the Woodsman and Sorcha. "You should use these. They're the best we have." She grabbed their pitcher of wine and quickly filled the goblets.

"What are you doing?" Tara's mother, Teresa, called from the table in the center, where she was helping Riona and Lauren fill plates with ham, cheese, and vegetables. "You know those goblets are only used for weddings and special occasions."

"This *is* a special occasion! We have a princess visiting us!" Tara handed the goblets to the Woodsman and Sorcha, then scrambled off to help her mother.

"To Princess Sorcha!" Father Kit yelled.

Everyone gave a cheer, then downed their wine. Sorcha took a sip and was surprised by how strong the wine was.

"To the Woodsman!" Father Kit shouted, and everyone drank some more.

Sorcha took a long drink, then noticed the Woodsman was holding his goblet in his left hand. "You're left-handed?"

"Mostly, but I'm adept with either hand."

She had a feeling he was adept at everything. A warm fuzzy feeling curled in her stomach as her gaze lingered once again on his beautiful mouth. How could a man be so absolutely gorgeous?

A corner of his mouth tilted up. "We should eat the soup before it gets cold."

"Oh, right." She reached for the bowl, but then got distracted by Hallie running toward Morghen.

"You're awfully late," Morghen told her. "Is something wrong with our patient?"

"No, he's fine. He insisted I bring him a second helping of ham." Hallie knelt beside the older woman and lowered her voice. "But I am concerned. I saw Tara take one of the green bottles."

Sorcha glanced at Tara and noted the bulge beneath her sash. Oh dear, it wasn't hard to guess which bottle the girl had stolen.

"Tara." Morghen motioned for her to draw near.

"Yes, my lady?" Tara inched toward them, her gaze darting about nervously.

"Is something wrong?" Teresa joined her daughter in front of Morghen's blanket.

"What have you done, child?" Morghen asked.

Tara fumbled with the tasseled end of her sash. "I . . ."

"Which bottle did you take?" Morghen asked softly.

Teresa gasped. "Tara, what have you done?"

The girl slanted a glance at Sorcha and the Woodsman. "I just wanted to see if it really works."

Sorcha gasped. *Good goddesses, no.*

The Woodsman turned away from his conversation with Father Kit to look at her. "Is something wrong?"

"I . . . maybe." She eyed her empty goblet as a feeling of doom crept over her. No wonder the wine had tasted so strong. Then she realized the Woodsman was taking another drink from his goblet. "Stop!" She grabbed his arm.

He frowned. "Something *is* wrong. What is it?"

With a wince, Sorcha motioned to the women beside her.

"Give it to me." Morghen reached a hand toward the girl, and Tara slowly retrieved the bottle from her sash and handed it over.

"I just gave them a little bit," Tara mumbled.

Morghen stiffened. "Good heavens, it's half gone! Didn't I warn you how potent this stuff is?"

Sorcha gulped. Oh, no! Would she start behaving strangely? Would the Woodsman?

"I'm sorry!" Tara wailed. "I just felt so sorry for the princess because she's never been in love before!"

Whispers spread like wildfire around the circle. "She's never been in love?"

Oh, goddesses, no! Heat burned Sorcha's face. This was too embarrassing.

The Woodsman raised a hand, and the crowd hushed. "What exactly is going on here?"

Tara fell to her knees. "I'm so sorry! I promised the princess I would help her find someone who was worthy. And no one is worthier than you! Please, forgive me."

"What did you do?" the Woodsman asked.

When the girl hesitated, Morghen showed him the bottle. "Sorcha and you have consumed half a bottle of love potion."

Chapter 14

*L*ove *potion?* The Woodsman gave the bottle a dubious glance, then realized everyone was watching him with an excited, expectant glint in their eyes. By the Light, did they think he would turn into a frantic, slobbering beast, ready to pounce on Sorcha at any second?

Or did they expect her to pounce on him? That last thought was rather appealing, actually, but one look at her mortified expression and he knew it was not going to happen.

He cleared his throat and addressed the crowd. "There's nothing to see here. Please continue to enjoy the feast." He smiled at Tara and her mother, who both had tears in their eyes. "No need to worry. We're perfectly fine. Please go on with what you were doing."

"Yes, my lord." Teresa curtsied and nudged her daughter to do the same. "Thank you, my lord." She rushed toward the center table and grabbed two plates of ham, carrots, and peas, then brought them to the Woodsman and Sorcha. "My apologies again. Please enjoy."

"Thank you." The Woodsman ignored the brass goblets and poured wine into the two wooden cups. "The wine is not tainted, I take it?" he asked Father Kit, who sat to his right.

"No, the wine is good. I filled the pitchers myself." The priest lowered his voice. "Are you feeling all right?"

"Of course." The Woodsman drank some wine. Why was

everyone still watching him? "Here. Have a drink." He offered a filled cup to Sorcha.

With her hands clutched tightly together, she gave him a wary look.

He leaned close to whisper. "I'm not going to succumb to beastlike urges and jump on you."

Her eyes widened. "Are you sure?"

"Are you disappointed?"

"Are you mad?" She ripped the cup from his hands and downed the contents.

He couldn't help but watch her. With her head tilted back, the graceful line of her neck was a beautiful sight. She was guzzling down the wine so quickly, though, that a drop escaped and rolled down her chin, a rich red claret against her pale skin. A sudden urge struck him hard, enticing him to lick the drop away.

His nerves tensed. Damn, was this a reaction to the love potion? No, he shook himself mentally. He refused to believe in such nonsense. The potion wasn't real. Unfortunately, he couldn't say the same for the stirring in his groin.

"Both of you should drink as much as you can," Morghen told them. "So you can dilute the effect."

"I will. Right away." Sorcha refilled their cups, then gulped down more wine.

Was she afraid of him? The Woodsman sighed. "Relax, Sorcha. Nothing is going to happen."

"How can you say that?" she whispered. "The facts are clear. We drank the potion. Quite a bit of it, and it's extremely potent. Morghen said so, and I don't doubt her abilities."

"When it comes to healing, I have complete confidence in her. But a love potion?" He shook his head. "It's not possible."

"It is!" She finished her cup, then refilled it. "The last five couples who took this potion all ended up married within a month."

Morghen interrupted, her eyes twinkling with mischief. "Shall I start planning a wedding?"

Sorcha gasped. "No!"

Did she have to look so appalled? He groaned inwardly. Was it because she thought he wasn't the one? *Dammit.* "There is no need for concern. I am acquainted with those couples, and I can assure you that they were already attracted to each other before they took the potion."

Morghen shrugged. "That is true."

"Oh, no!" Sorcha quickly downed another cup. "This is terrible."

"What is?" the Woodsman asked.

"I'm not sure I should tell you." She poured more wine but when her cup was only half full, the pitcher ran out. "Oh, no."

"Do you need more wine?" Father Kit asked.

"No," the Woodsman said at the same time Sorcha said, "Yes!"

With another silent groan, he turned toward Sorcha. "Will you stop drinking and tell me what's wrong?"

She gave him an exasperated look. "How can you remain so calm when we're doomed?"

He gritted his teeth. "We are not doomed."

"Well, maybe you're not, but I certainly am. You see . . ." She finished her half-full cup, then hiccupped. "I hate to admit this, but . . . I'm already attracted to you."

His heart lurched. "Oh?" *Wait, she hated to admit it?*

Her shoulders slumped. "So, that's why I'm doomed. The potion will work on me."

Did she have to look so damned depressed about it? "Sorcha, nothing will happen. I promise you, I will not allow a potion to dictate what I think or feel."

Her eyes widened as she sat up. "You're right!" She made a fist. "You must fight this. Don't you dare fall in love with me. And I promise, I will do my best never to love you."

"Wonderful," he grumbled, then turned to Father Kit. "I need more wine after all."

With a grin, the priest handed them a full pitcher.

The Woodsman filled their cups, but when Sorcha suddenly flinched beside him, he spilled some onto the wooden tray. "What is it now?"

She leaned toward him, her green eyes dancing with excitement. "I just had an idea. Obviously, the full effect of the potion hasn't hit us yet, so we might consider beating it to the punch."

"How?" He took a drink.

"We could have a quick affair."

He sputtered wine all over himself. "*What?*"

"We could beat the love potion to the punch—"

"There is no punch." He used a cloth napkin to dry off the wine that had run down his throat to his chest. Then he realized she was staring at the open neck of his shirt. Her gaze slowly lifted to linger on his mouth; then she licked her lips. Dammit, now he did want to jump on her like a beast. "Sorcha, stop looking at me like that."

Her eyes filled with horror. "Oh, no. I must have succumbed to the power of the potion."

"No, you haven't. You've been staring at my mouth since you first met me."

Her face turned pink. "I can't help it. You're just so disgustingly handsome."

"Was that a compliment?" he muttered.

She hiccupped. "It's true. I find you terribly attractive." Frowning, she picked up her cup. "Even though it makes no sense whatsoever."

He clenched his teeth. "I'm not that bad a catch."

"But you're all wrong." She drank some wine. "You're not the elf who was foretold by the Telling Stones."

"What?"

"Didn't I tell you about the Game of Stones that my sisters and I play together? Luciana has had unbelievable success predicting the man each of us will fall in love with. She was right about herself and Brigitta and Gwennore. When she picked the stones for me, she got the number five and the colors lavender and white. We figured the five refers to the Circle of Five. And the lavender—" Her blurry gaze met his. "Well, you do have lavender eyes. Damn you." She hiccupped.

He recalled her horrified reaction to his eyes the day before. "Most elves do."

"But thank the goddesses, your hair isn't white. So that means you're not—"

"I'm not the one," he grumbled. *Dammit.* So, this explained what she'd said on the balcony. "Am I understanding this correctly? You plan to choose your future husband by the color of his hair?"

She shrugged. "I wouldn't, but the stones did."

Then she would reject him because of this stupid game? He was too aggravated now to tell her that his hair was actually dyed. "Doesn't it seem ludicrous to you to choose a future mate based on the mandate of a few rocks?"

"Hmm. That is exactly what I thought." She tapped her temple with her forefinger, but then her hand slipped and bumped into her nose. "But no matter what we think, the truth remains that the predictions keep coming true. I know!" Her eyes lit up. "We could prove the Telling Stones are wrong by having a quick affair!"

He sat back. How come her solution for everything was a quick affair? He was tempted to agree, just to see if she would really go through with it. But why the hell did she keep saying "quick"? If he ever took Sorcha to his bed, being *quick* would be the last thing he wanted. "I think you'd better eat some food. You've obviously had too much to drink on an empty stomach."

She scoffed. "I'm not drunk."

Her glassy eyes told another story. "You're saying outrageous things."

She waved a dismissive hand as another hiccup escaped. "It runs in the family. My brother says naughty things all the time, and Gwennore loves it. But then, she doesn't have the sense of humor of a tree."

He hissed in a breath. "I am not a tree."

"Then why are you objecting to the idea of a quick affair?"

He balled his hands into fists in a vain attempt to remain calm. "Why are you willing to bed a man because of a few rocks?"

"Fine." She lifted her chin. "Since you obviously hate the idea of bedding me, I recant my offer. I wouldn't bed you if you were the last man on Aerthlan!"

He scowled at her. "What's wrong with me?"

"What?" She gave him an incredulous look. "First you're annoyed that I want to have an affair. Now you're annoyed that I don't. There's no pleasing you, is there?"

"No, I am not pleased."

She huffed. "Well, good. Because it would be a disaster if you did find me pleasing. Then we would never be able to fight off the effect of this potion."

"*There is no effect!*" he shouted, then looked away in frustration. To his shock, everyone in the circle was watching him and Sorcha.

"Don't stop now," Morghen said with a teasing smile.

Father Kit nodded. "Best entertainment we've had in ages."

With a groan, Sorcha covered her face.

The Woodsman jumped to his feet, and with great effort, he managed to sound calm. "If you will excuse us, we need to talk in private." He reached toward Sorcha, but she didn't see his hand since she was still cowering behind her own.

"Feel free to use my house," one of the elves called out. "I just had the bed re-stuffed."

Everyone chuckled, while Sorcha groaned.

The Woodsman took a deep breath. *You are these people's leader. Do not lose control in front of them.* "Please." He held up his hands. "Go on with the feast and talk amongst yourselves. I ask you to give the princess and me some privacy."

Everyone nodded and went back to eating and talking. Teresa, Lauren, and Riona rushed about, giving out second helpings.

"Sorcha." He held out his hand as she looked up at him.

With her face flushed bright pink, she shook her head. "We can't leave now."

"Why not?" He kneeled beside her.

She whispered, "They'll think we're . . ."

"Having a quick affair?" He gave her a wry look. "I wonder how they got that idea?"

She winced. "I can't believe I said that. It just seemed like a good idea at the time. I mean, I thought it might help me get over this unfortunate attraction for the wrong man."

Wrong man? Was she trying to shred away his last remnant of sanity? Dammit, but his control was slipping fast. He flopped down next to her on the blanket. "No matter what you might think, the fact remains that I will not allow a potion or a bunch of rocks to tell me what I feel."

She sighed. "I suppose that's true. After all, you've already told me that you have no feelings."

"That's not quite—"

"But it's for the best, isn't it?" She gave him a hopeful look. "We'll be fine because you have no feelings for me at all."

Ouch. "Sorcha—"

"So we're safe!" She heaved a sigh. "I always found it annoying before, but now I thank the goddesses that you're always so calm."

He gritted his teeth. "You think I'm calm?"

"Yes." She nodded. "Downright cold and wooden. You see, the potion is designed to inflame carnal passions, but since you obviously don't have any—"

"Enough!" He wrapped a hand around her neck to pull her toward him, then planted his mouth hard on hers. When she flinched with shock, he softened his kiss and cupped his other hand against her ear. Gently, he molded her lips against his own and, with his thumb, he stroked her soft cheek.

She didn't pull away! Yes! A thrill shot through him, burning a trail of heat straight to his groin. Yes, this was what he'd wanted since he'd first met her. The second he'd seen her snap her fingers to make a flame, a spark had ignited inside his heart. He wanted to feed the fire. He wanted her inflamed with fiery passion. And he wanted her to melt with it.

He sucked her lower lip into his mouth and gave it a slight tug as he ended the kiss. When he pulled back, her eyes flickered open with a dazed look.

A round of cheers and applause came from their audience, but he ignored them and took advantage of their noise to whisper words they wouldn't hear. He cradled Sorcha's face in his hands. "Do you still think I have no feelings?"

She blinked.

"I will accept your offer of a quick affair. But I'm warning you, there will be nothing quick about it."

She gasped; then her hand flew to cover her mouth as she scrambled to her feet. "I . . . I think I'm going to be sick!"

Chapter 15

Sorcha drew in a shaky breath and exhaled slowly. *Stay calm.* Oh, hell, how could she be calm? The butterflies that had fluttered in her stomach during that glorious kiss were now gathering into a violent swarm that threatened to lurch up her throat.

The Woodsman jumped to his feet. "Do you need to lie down? Morghen, is there something you can give her?"

Morghen nodded, then turned to Hallie. "Take her to my house and give her some nausea medicine mixed with hot tea and honey. Then let her rest in my bed. I'll bring her some bread and a bowl of soup in a little while."

"Yes, my lady." Hallie took hold of Sorcha's arm. "Let's go."

Sorcha didn't know which was worse—the nausea, the embarrassment, or the incredible shock. The Woodsman wanted to have a quick affair? *But I'm warning you, there will be nothing quick about it.* His words had nearly made her melt.

She stepped off the blanket, too embarrassed to look at him, much too mortified to look at the villagers of Haven. By the goddesses, they'd heard her suggest the affair! Twice!

It must have been a combination of too much wine and too much panic. Her sisters had always warned her that she was impetuous, and they were right. She'd known the man only three days! That was definitely too quick. *There will be nothing quick about it.*

Her stomach lurched again, and she hurried away with Hallie. But she could still hear the villagers gossiping amongst themselves.

"Has the princess taken ill?"

"The Woodsman kissed her, and it made her sick!"

"Is he that bad at kissing?"

"So, they won't be having an affair after all?"

Sorcha groaned. How could she ever look the Woodsman in the face again? Goddesses help her, she didn't know what to think.

Was his sudden wish for an affair simply a reaction to the love potion? Wouldn't that mean his desire was false? Then all the longing she felt for him would be for naught.

But what if his feelings were true? Goddesses help her, that was just as bad, for how could she possibly have a future with him? He was taking her to the Eberoni border in a week, and she might never see him again. And what if he was killed during the rebellion he was planning?

Either way, the relationship was doomed. And her worst nightmare might happen if she had to live with the terrible fear that a loved one was in danger and might not survive.

"I can't endure this," she whispered in Eberoni. "It will kill me."

"Now, now." Hallie patted her hand. "You just drank too much wine on an empty stomach. It won't kill you."

"Not that." Sorcha drew in a deep breath. "It's the Woodsman. I'm supposed to return to my family in a week. I might never see him again."

"Ah, that." Hallie sighed. "I know what you mean. I keep telling myself that I shouldn't have any feelings for Aleksi. I only met him last night, and he's going back home soon. But even so, I can't seem to stop myself."

Sorcha nodded. "That's it, exactly. There are moments, like right now, when it seems ridiculous that I could fall for a man so quickly. But then I see him again or hear his voice, and I know there is no point in denying the feelings that have already taken root in my heart."

Hallie gave her a sad smile. "We're a hopeless pair, aren't we? But in our defense, I have to say the men we have fallen for are extraordinary. Aleksi is such a brave, handsome, dependable"—she stopped with a jerk as they rounded the corner of Morghen's house—"irresponsible, stubborn arse. What on Aerthlan are you doing?"

Aleksi, barefoot and dressed only in a pair of breeches, was filling a bucket of water from the lake. His bare back was still covered with a white bandage. Muttering a curse, he turned toward them. "What are *you* doing here? I thought you would be gone longer than this." He stalked toward the house with the bucket of water.

"You shouldn't be carrying anything," Hallie fussed as she followed him inside.

"I thought ye were supposed to be in bed resting," Sorcha added from the open doorway.

"I decided to take a bath." He strode toward a huge brass tub set close to the fireplace, then glanced back at Hallie. "You're not washing me anymore. I'm sick of being treated like a child."

With a huff, she marched up to him. "There's a reason I've been giving you sponge baths. We can't get your wound wet."

"I'll be fine," he growled. "Come back in an hour."

Hallie motioned to the large brass tub. "Did you drag this in here from the storage closet?"

"I carried it."

"Aleksi, how many times do I have to tell you not to pick up anything heavy?" She reached for the water bucket. "Give that to me."

"No! I'll do it." He pulled the bucket back.

"Give it to me!" Hallie yanked hard at the bucket and water sloshed over the side and ran down her gown, completely soaking her white blouse. "Oh, oh, that's cold."

"Dammit, woman." He dropped the bucket on the floor and handed her a towel. His eyes widened at the sight of her breasts showing through the wet fabric.

"Oh!" She covered her breasts, giving him a startled look.

"Hallie," he whispered, his eyes boring into her.

"Aleksi," she whispered back, lowering her hands.

He pulled her into his arms and lowered his mouth against hers. With a groan, she wrapped her arms around his neck and dug her fingers into his long black hair.

Sorcha blinked. Goodness, that was quick. She backed out of the house and gently shut the door. A loud splash was followed by a squeal and a peal of laughter. What on Aerthlan were they doing? Had they fallen into the tub? She wasn't sure she wanted to know, although one thing was for certain: Aleksi had not been oblivious to Hallie.

Sorcha paced down the flagstone path to the front gate, then back to the door. How long should she wait? A few minutes? A few hours? At least they had some privacy, unlike the moment she'd shared with the Woodsman. Her cheeks burned with heat just thinking about that glorious kiss. It was every bit as thrilling as she had ever imagined a kiss could be.

Another feminine squeal emanated from the cottage, and Sorcha sighed. Perhaps it was for the best that her kiss had been in public. Otherwise, she might have easily ended up in the Woodsman's bed. And that would have been disastrous.

Although she had been the one to suggest an affair, she now understood what a terrible mistake she had made. Her overwhelming reaction to his kiss had proven that to her. There was simply no way she could have an affair with the Woodsman without falling completely in love with him.

She would have to reject him, she realized. It was the only way to safeguard her heart. With another sigh, she settled on the wooden bench beside the door. In the few days she had left here, she would need to avoid the Woodsman. Certainly, she couldn't go back to the feast. Everyone would want to know why she wasn't resting in Morghen's house.

She let her gaze wander about the cottage garden and the nearby lake. Bees were buzzing about the colorful flowers, and the sun sparkled off the blue water. This was a lovely, idyllic place. Safe and isolated from the rest of the world.

For a few seconds, she allowed herself to imagine what it would be like to live here with the Woodsman in his tree house. Making love high among the branches, serenaded by birdsong and the rustle of leaves.

Tears came to her eyes, along with a pang in her heart. What was the point in wishing for the impossible? She was going to leave this place. And the Woodsman would soon be risking his life. They were never meant to be.

He is not the one.

She closed her eyes and let the cool breeze sweep over her face. Coming to grips with reality had chased away the effect of too much wine, leaving her dismally sober.

A screech sounded overhead, and she glanced up to watch a large bird fly overhead. An eagle?

"I thought you would be inside resting." The Woodsman's deep voice caught her by surprise, and she turned on the bench to see him coming around the corner of Morghen's house.

Damn, so much for avoiding him. She watched him approach the front gate, a basket of food in his hand and, slung over his shoulder, the blue embroidered coverlet they had sat upon.

It was hard to look at him without remembering the glorious kiss. She shifted her gaze away from his beautiful mouth, focusing instead on his broad chest, but even that made her cheeks grow warm. His breeches? No, the way they clung to his muscular thighs was enough to make her heart race. The basket—that was safe to look at. "What do you have there?"

"Food." He opened the garden gate. "I was scolded by the villagers for frightening you off before you were able to eat. They claim that I'm single-handedly causing you to die from starvation."

She groaned inwardly. "It wasn't your fault. I drank too much too fast. But I'm feeling better now."

"That's good." He followed the flagstone path toward the front door. "You're lucky you left when you did. I just endured ten minutes of unsolicited advice on how to kiss a woman without making her physically ill."

She winced, too embarrassed to look him in the face. Should she admit she'd actually enjoyed the kiss? No, that would be dangerous.

"No comment?" With a sigh, he set the basket and blanket on the bench beside her. "I guess I need to work on my technique." He stepped toward the door. "How about a practice session after we eat?"

"No!" She jumped up to block the door. "We can't."

"We can't practice?"

"We can't go in." She lowered her voice. "Hallie and Aleksi are . . ."

"What?"

She bit her lip. "Practicing."

"The dragon is assaulting her?" The Woodsman reached around her for the doorknob. "How dare he—"

"No!" She placed her hands on the Woodsman's chest to stop him. "She . . . she's not being forced."

"Are you sure?"

"Yes. She's actively participating. And he—" Sorcha suddenly realized how wonderfully firm the Woodsman's chest was and removed her hands. "Well, he definitely didn't need any love potion."

The Woodsman's eyebrows shot up. "Are you saying I did?"

She gave him a frustrated look. "How else would I explain it? You told me you don't have any feelings, but then suddenly, you kissed me and said that you do. What changed, other than the fact that you drank some of the potion?"

With a groan, he turned and walked away a few steps. "I admit I've been . . . conflicted. But I can assure you that my feelings, no matter how confused, are my own. The potion had no effect on me. I've been tempted to kiss you ever since I first met you. That temptation has been steadily growing, but I was determined to ignore it. That's why I said I had no feelings. I . . . regret that now."

She bit her lip, recalling his muttered words. *I don't know whether to kidnap her or kiss her.* So his desire was real. He was attracted to her, just as she was to him. But he was fighting the temptation, just as she was.

"Then we are in agreement." She ignored the pain and forced herself to say the words. "We will . . . reject these feelings."

"What?" He turned toward her. "I didn't agree to that."

"It's for the best. Please forget that I ever suggested an affair."

"You suggested it twice."

"I was in shock because of the potion. And I drank too much." She slumped back onto the bench next to the basket. "I don't know how I can face the villagers again."

"Don't worry about them," he grumbled. "They heartily approved of your suggestion. I'm the one they're peeved at, since apparently I'm a lousy kisser."

"But you're not," she objected, then winced.

"Ah." He set the basket on the ground and sat beside her. "That is good news, but even so, you shouldn't be so quick to pass judgment." He gave her a wry smile. "The only way we can be sure is to give it another test."

She sat back. "I'm not kissing you. Never again."

His smile faded. "Why not?"

"Didn't you hear me? I am rejecting my feelings for you."

"Then you admit you have feelings. What are they?"

"It doesn't matter." She frowned at him. "You know that I'm leaving in a week."

"That doesn't mean we can never see each other again."

"We . . . we've known each other only two days."

He shrugged. "I knew the second I saw you that you were exceptional. Brave, beautiful—"

"Stop it." She lifted her hands. "I won't allow myself to fall in love. So stop saying nice things. And stop looking at me like that."

His brows pinched as he frowned. "Something is happening to us, Sorcha. I know you're fighting it. Hell, I've been fighting it, too. But it's still drawing us together. I can feel it pulling at my heart—"

"Stop it!" She jumped to her feet and ran to the front gate. How could she resist him when he was being so open? She turned toward him. He was still sitting on the bench, watching her. "I refuse to fall in love."

He stood and slowly walked toward her. "Why?"

"I-I'd rather not say."

"That's it?" His frown deepened. "How can I make a plan to solve the problem if I don't know what it is?"

She gazed out at the lake. "I made a vow to myself that I would never fall in love."

"Why?"

"I truly can't say."

"So you'll leave me hanging? Sorcha, I'm desperately clinging to the last remnant of my sanity."

She turned toward him. "You're not calm? You look calm."

"I am not."

She studied him closely. "There *is* a strange intensity to your eyes."

"Slipping fast, Sorcha."

"Oh. Well, in that case." She sighed. "I can't fall in love because I . . . I love too fiercely. And then, when my loved ones are in danger, and I'm not able to protect them, it nearly kills me. I'm not going through that again."

He shifted his weight, waited a moment, then finally said, "That's it?"

She lifted her chin. "Isn't that enough?"

"You don't want to love someone because you'll worry—"

"It's much more than worry! I become frantic. I can't eat or sleep. I really don't think I can endure it."

He nodded. "So you're afraid."

"More like terrified!"

His mouth twitched. "Because you love too fiercely."

"It's not amusing." She frowned at him. "It hurts like hell every time someone I love is in danger."

"I know." He frowned back. "Believe me, I know. Have you lost any of your loved ones?"

"My parents, but I never knew them—"

"I knew mine. When I was five, my mother died giving birth to my little sister. The baby died, too. Then when I was eleven, my father and his squire were murdered right in front of me."

Sorcha gasped. "I'm so sorry."

"We can't control the future, Sorcha. Danger can happen to anyone at any time."

"I know that. So the best thing to do is never fall in love."

He scoffed. "Are you going to stop living?"

She turned away, folding her arms across her chest.

"Fine." He strode back to the bench and picked up the blanket and basket. "You can at least eat with me. Come on. I know a nice spot." He marched through the front gate.

After a few seconds, she followed him. "All right. But only because I'm hungry."

He glanced back at her and gave her a wry smile while he waited for her to catch up. "I'm not the only one the villagers are giving a hard time."

"Are they upset with me?"

"No, they like you. It's Morghen. They claim to have doubts now that her medicine is any good."

Sorcha gasped. "Oh, that's terrible."

He nodded. "And all because we didn't pounce on each other like slobbering beasts."

"What?" She stopped with a huff. "Did they expect us to . . . right in front of everyone?"

"Apparently so." He shrugged. "And since the love potion didn't work, they're questioning Morghen's abilities."

"How can they say that it didn't work? You kissed me."

His mouth twitched. "And you suggested an affair. Twice."

She held up a hand. "I told you it's not going to happen."

He gave her an innocent look. "But it's the only way to save Morghen's reputation."

"Ha!" She swatted his shoulder, but when he started laughing, she joined in. "So you have a sense of humor after all."

"Are you sure? I might be quite serious about the affair."

She scoffed. "Then you'll have to come up with a better reason."

He stepped toward her, still smiling. "I'm sure I could think of something."

She gave him a shove. "I thought we were going to eat. I'm hungry."

"Me, too." He motioned toward a grove of trees. "This way."

Smiling, she walked beside him. What was the harm in enjoying his company for the few days they had left? *Because the more you see him, the more you'll fall for him.* Her smile faded. If she had any sense, she'd leave him now.

A loud squawk overhead drew her attention, and she spied an eagle swooping down toward them.

"What the . . . ?" The Woodsman pulled her to his chest when the eagle buzzed by them a few feet overhead.

Was that the same eagle she'd spotted before? It landed neatly on the ground next to an oak tree. As it hopped around to face her, she realized why it looked familiar. "Brody? Is that you?"

The bird gave another squawk, then began to shimmer.

"Brody!" She stepped toward him.

"Wait a minute." The Woodsman grabbed her arm. "You know this bird—what? Now he's a dog?"

"Roor-cha," Brody growled.

"A *talking* dog?" the Woodsman shouted.

"It's all right. It's Brody!" With a grin, Sorcha ran toward the shaggy black-and-white dog and threw her arms around his neck. "Oh, Brody," she said in Eberoni. "It's so good to see you!"

The dog gave a yelp, then licked her face.

"He's a shifter?" The Woodsman gave Brody a wary look as he approached.

"Yes." Sorcha patted the dog on the head. "Brody is really amazing. He can shift into any animal."

The Woodsman frowned. "He's like the Chameleon?"

Brody growled.

"Don't say that," Sorcha fussed. "Ye'll hurt his feelings. Brody doesn't take on the shapes of other people. Only animals. He's one of the good guys." She cradled his furry face in her hands. "Aren't ye a good boy, ye big sweetie?"

Brody barked, then trotted behind the oak tree.

"Oh, he wants to shift into human form." Sorcha snatched the blue embroidered blanket off the Woodsman's shoulder.

"You call him sweetie?" the Woodsman grumbled. "And let him lick your face?"

"Sure." She tossed the blanket toward the tree. "Everybody loves Brody."

"Including you?" the Woodsman mumbled.

Now in human form, Brody peered around the tree and

gave Sorcha a grin as he grabbed the blanket. "Was that ham I smelled? I'm starving."

"Oh, of course." Sorcha snatched the basket of food away from the Woodsman. "We should let Brody have this. He's hungry."

"Of course he is," the Woodsman muttered. "And what the hell, he's naked."

Chapter 16

"Yes, yes, I'm really all right," Sorcha muttered as she buttered a hunk of bread. "Just like I was the first five times ye asked that question." She had unloaded all the food from the basket, and now they were eating while sitting on the grass, since Brody had the blanket wrapped around his torso.

"Yes, but now you can answer honestly." He bit off another piece of ham and motioned toward the path that led around the lake, where the Woodsman was headed to his tree house. "Now that we're finally rid of the grouchy, pointy-eared elf."

"Shh, he might hear you." She glanced at the Woodsman, who was not that far away, and lowered her voice. "Is that why ye asked him to bring you some clothes?"

"Mmm-hmm," Brody mumbled with his mouth full. "Why am I not seeing Aleksi? Where is he?"

"He's . . . busy at the moment." Sorcha propped the butter knife on top of the crock of butter.

"How busy can he be? Isn't he injured?"

"He's healing quickly," she muttered, then gasped when Brody snatched the bread from her hand and bit into it. "Hey, that was mine."

"And it's delicious." Brody drank straight from the pitcher of wine, then wiped his mouth with the back of his hand.

Sorcha frowned at him. "Ye've spent too much time as a dog."

He shrugged. "Can't be helped."

She winced, regretting her words. Brody had no choice but to spend most of his life as a dog or some sort of animal. A witch had put a curse on him, so he was only able to take his human form for a few hours each day.

A sudden thought popped into her mind and she sat up. "Morghen is a witch!"

"What? Who?" Brody took another bite of bread.

"Morghen. She's the healer here. And a witch. Maybe she can undo the spell for you?"

Brody shook his head. "I learned a few years ago that only the same witch who put the curse on me can remove it."

"Oh. Do ye know which witch did it?"

"Which witch?" He snorted. "No. But it happened in the sea." His face grew grim. "I heard her voice, so I know it was a female. That bitch has a great deal to answer for."

What all had this witch done? Sorcha wondered. "Did she do more than curse you?"

Brody waved a dismissive hand. "I didn't come to talk about myself. I needed to make sure you're all right. Everyone is very worried—"

"But didn't the Kings of the Forest tell Gwennore that I'm fine?"

"They did, but since their message came from the mysterious Woodsman, we weren't sure it could be trusted."

Sorcha rolled her eyes. "Ye can trust the trees. The Woodsman told me they don't lie."

"But if he lied to the trees, they would pass it—"

"No! He wouldn't do that. He relies on the trees." They helped to keep him safe. She glanced at the nearby oak tree. Was it telling the Woodsman everything they said? Goodness, if trees all over Aerthlan were able to talk to the Woodsman, then he had the largest network of spies in the world! That certainly explained how he managed to know so much.

Brody jammed the rest of the bread into his mouth. "The Kings of the Forest said he was trustworthy—"

"He is."

Brody gave her a dubious look. "Silas heard a different opinion from Aleksi."

"What?" Sorcha sat up. "How?"

"Didn't you know the dragons can communicate telepathically with each other?"

Sorcha's mouth dropped open. Why had her brother kept that a secret from her? Aleksi, too. Dammit, even Annika probably knew. "So Aleksi has been talking to Silas?"

"Whenever he could." Brody took another bite of ham. "Unfortunately, the medicine he's been taking is causing him to sleep a lot. Even so, he warned Silas that you needed to be separated from the Woodsman as soon as possible."

Sorcha gasped. "Why that—he really should mind his own business."

"From what I could tell, Aleksi might have a point." Brody pointed a carrot stick at her. "I heard the Woodsman say that he kissed you. And you suggested an affair."

"Brody!"

"Twice." He bit off a piece of the carrot.

Sorcha huffed. "Were ye spying on me?"

"That's what I do." He tossed the rest of the carrot into his mouth.

"There's nothing going on," she declared, but when Brody just kept chewing and looking at her, she added, "It's a long story."

He snorted. "How long can the story be? You've known him three days."

She gritted her teeth. "I'm not going to get involved with him. I know I'm leaving soon."

Brody leaned toward her. "Who is he exactly?"

"The Woodsman."

"That doesn't tell me much."

"I know what ye mean." Sorcha sighed. How much should she say? She didn't want to cause any trouble for the Woodsman.

Brody adjusted the blanket that was looped around his waist. "Right after the elfin army took you prisoner, Silas sent a message by carrier pigeon to Leo and Luciana, requesting that they dispatch their army for a joint attack on Woodwyn. I immediately flew to Silas's army encampment, and that's when I learned that a message had come from the so-called Woodsman, claiming that he had rescued you."

Sorcha nodded. "He did. And he protected us from an army search party. Did he pass on my message about the spy, Paxell?"

"Yes, but when they were interrogating him, Paxell claimed that the Woodsman is an outlaw with a price on his head. You can see why Silas was worried. Gwen asked the Kings of the Forest about it, but they would only say that he's a good man."

"He *is* a good man."

"Then why does he live in hiding?" Brody frowned. "The trees seem to be protecting him. They refused to tell Gwen the location of this place."

"How did ye find us?"

"Aleksi told your brother."

Sorcha winced. "Aleksi talks too much."

Brody rummaged in the basket for more food. "Aleksi is simply doing his job. Protecting you."

"I don't need protecting. But Haven does. There are a lot of innocent people here. Aleksi should have never given away this location."

Brody pulled out a bowl of cherries. "The elves here are not really any of your concern."

"Of course they are! If the army finds this place, all these people could be killed."

Brody popped a cherry into his mouth. "If the people here are harboring a criminal, then they are guilty."

"He's not a criminal!"

"Paxell called him the most infamous outlaw of all Woodwyn."

She groaned. "Paxell murdered Lieutenant Kashenko. And he's working for the Circle of Five. Anything he says will be suspicious."

"He's not saying much anymore. He attempted an escape and was killed." Brody spit out the pit and helped himself to another cherry. "Tell me what you know about the Woodsman."

"Am I being interrogated now?"

Brody arched a brow. "Are you being defensive? If you truly believe the Woodsman is a good guy, then tell me why."

"He risked his life to rescue me and Aleksi. General Caladras and his son are the true enemies of the people of Woodwyn. Caladras has been sending the army to steal all the food from nearby villages, and if the villagers protest, their homes are burned to the ground. The Woodsman has been stealing the food the army takes and giving it back to the people. And those who are homeless are allowed to live here in Haven."

Brody's eyes widened. "So he's a folk hero?"

Sorcha smiled at the thought. "Yes, ye could call him that."

"Have you fallen for him? A man who lives in hiding with a price on his head?"

Her smile faded. "Nothing is going to happen."

Brody spit out another pit. "Silas will make sure of that. If you don't leave for the Eberoni border soon, he will fly here himself to pick you up. I'll be able to give him the location."

"That's not necessary. The Woodsman has given his word that he'll take me to the border."

Brody nodded. "Then we expect you to start the journey tomorrow."

Tomorrow? She glanced toward the woods and saw the Woodsman coming back, a parcel of clothing in his hands. How could her time with him end so quickly?

Brody leaned toward her. "Why don't you look happy at the thought of seeing your family again?"

"I'm not sure Aleksi is well enough for the journey," she hedged. "And I'm disappointed at how suspicious my brother is acting. He really should trust me more than that. The Woodsman and a few of his men risked their lives to rescue Aleksi and me. They have earned my trust. Silas should respect that."

"You like him."

She glanced at the Woodsman. His lavender eyes were focused on her as he approached. "I do like him." Was it her imagination or did his eyes suddenly flare with heat? He must have heard her.

"We leave for Eberon in the morning." Brody rose to his feet and turned toward the Woodsman. "Did you hear that?"

"I heard." The Woodsman frowned as he handed Brody the parcel of clothes. "I also heard that Aleksi told Silas the location of Haven. Who else knows?"

"Gwen and myself." Brody tilted his head, thinking. "I'm not sure about this, but I believe when a dragon sends out a message telepathically, all the dragons can hear it."

The Woodsman hissed in a breath. "Then there could be many."

Brody shrugged. "Perhaps, but no one will tell."

"You can't know that for sure," the Woodsman ground out. "There are traitors around Silas, and Caladras would pay dearly for that information. Do you understand how many innocent people here are now at risk?"

Brody winced. "I don't think Aleksi realized the danger. He was simply trying to protect Sorcha."

"I'll talk to Aleksi," Sorcha offered. "He can send another message, warning all the dragons that this place must be kept secret."

"And I'll ask the Kings of the Forest to pass on a message to Gwennore." The Woodsman sighed. "That is the best we can do for now. The Living Oaks will warn me and Morghen if any soldiers advance on Haven. The people here have been trained on how to handle an attack."

Sorcha hoped it wouldn't come to that. Haven was the last resort for these people. They had nowhere else to go. She knelt on the grass to load the empty dishes and cups back into the basket.

"Did you get enough to eat?" the Woodsman asked.

Sorcha nodded, and a sudden urge to cry swept over her. She was leaving tomorrow? If the trip took two days, then that would be all the time she had left with the Woodsman. She glanced up at Brody. "Are ye traveling with us to Eberon?"

"Yes." Brody slipped behind the large oak tree to get dressed. "I'll be watching over you two."

"Like a hawk," Sorcha grumbled.

"More like an eagle." He tossed the blue blanket toward her.

With a sigh, she picked up the blanket and started to fold it. Once again, tears threatened to overflow.

"What's wrong?" the Woodsman whispered.

She dropped the folded blanket on top of the basket. "I thought we would have more time."

"We will." The Woodsman took her hand. "Will you eat with me tonight?"

She looked at him and saw the desire burning like blue flames in his lavender eyes. How had she thought him so cold before? "Yes."

Brody cleared his throat as he stepped toward them, still

buttoning his shirt. Sorcha moved back a step, but the Woodsman kept his hold of her hand.

Brody frowned at them. "I'd like to rest now. I can sleep in canine form outside Sorcha's room."

"I don't need protecting," Sorcha muttered.

Brody ignored her and asked the Woodsman, "Where is she staying?"

"A tree house. This way." The Woodsman headed toward the path that circled the lake, still holding on to Sorcha. He smiled at her. "I hope you like it."

She smiled back. "I'm sure I will."

"I hope this isn't *your* tree house, Woodsman," Brody grumbled as he followed them.

"No, mine is next door." The Woodsman squeezed Sorcha's hand. "But there is a bridge connecting the two."

Brody snorted. "That's where I'll be taking my nap."

Sorcha loved her tree house. It was surprisingly comfortable, with gleaming hardwood floors and furnishings, a soft and cozy bed surrounded by white gauze to keep any insects at bay, and even a washbasin and small tub that were fed water from two rain barrels higher up in the tree.

Since she'd hardly slept at all the night before, she crawled into the bed and promptly fell asleep. The cool breeze that swept through the open windows was refreshing, and knowing that Brody and the Woodsman were nearby made her feel completely safe for the first time in days.

When she woke up, she washed and changed into another borrowed gown from Bronwen. She glanced out the window and saw Brody in dog form curled up on the bridge, still asleep. With the sun beginning to set, the air was becoming cool and crisp.

A movement caught her attention, and she spotted the Woodsman at a window in his tree house. He waved, then pointed down at the ground.

She nodded and headed for the ladder. As she descended, she glanced over at the Woodsman's tree house and saw him sliding down a rope. At the base of the rope, he'd left a basket filled with food.

She reached the ground. "Are we going on a picnic?"

He put a finger against his mouth as he glanced up at Brody on the bridge. "Shh, we don't want to wake up your guard dog."

"You're right," she whispered. "He would eat all of our food."

With a smile, the Woodsman picked up the basket. "Let's go."

She headed into the forest with him. As the sun made its descent, it shot rays through the trees, making the different shades of green grow brighter. "It's beautiful."

He nodded. "It is. I've always loved the forest."

She smiled to herself. Not surprising for a woodsman. "Do all of the trees talk to you?"

"Only the oaks and redwoods."

She brushed her hand against the rough bark of an oak tree. "They're your network of spies, aren't they?"

"I prefer to think of them as friends."

"Then you have more friends than anyone I know." She gathered up her courage and asked what she really wanted to know. "Are you planning to lead a rebellion against the elfin army?"

He stopped with a jerk, his expression turning wary. "You heard about that?"

She nodded. "Must you do it?"

"I'd rather not discuss it. I don't want you involved—"

"Must you do it?" she cried. "Don't you know how afraid I will be?"

"I can't leave my country in the hands of people like Jenetta and Caladras."

"I understand they're evil, but why you?" She stepped toward him. "Why do you have to risk your life?"

"It's my destiny."

She scoffed. "That sounds as ridiculous as the Telling Stones."

"No. This is not some random coincidence. I have to avenge my—" He stopped himself. "The responsibility is mine. And mine alone."

She blinked. For whom was he seeking vengeance? "Are you saying you have a claim to the throne?"

He started walking once again. "I didn't bring you here to talk about myself."

With a huff, she followed him. "You should be honest with me. And trust me. I have connections who could help—"

"No!" The Woodsman glanced back at her. "Don't worry about me, Sorcha. I have a plan already in place. If all goes well, there will be no violence."

"You . . . you're planning a peaceful takeover?"

"I have the king's support. That's all I can say for now." He stopped again and gave her a pleading look. "Please understand that I don't want you involved in this. If, for some reason, the plan goes awry, Woodwyn could become an extremely dangerous place. I will not be able to do what I must if I am worried about your safety."

"I'll be fine. It's you who—"

"You *will* be fine. For you will be safe with your family." He extended a hand toward her. "And when all is done and settled, I will come for you. If you will have me."

Tears stung her eyes. How could she resist this man? But the goddesses help her, her worst fear was coming true. She was going to be worried sick. "I will wait for you." She put her hand in his. "Can you at least tell me your real name?"

"Is it important? You know me, Sorcha."

"Yes, but—"

"I will tell you when I know for sure that the knowledge

will not endanger you." He gave her hand a tug, and they started walking once again.

How could knowing his name be dangerous? Sorcha contemplated that as she walked, and she recalled her conversation with Morghen. If the Woodsman's name carried the sacred sound, then it would signify he was a nobleman. But she already knew he was, since he was Lord Daelen's nephew.

Her breath caught. If the sacred sound began his name, it would mean he was a member of the royal family.

"Here we are." He led her into a clearing. "It's called the fairy glade."

"I don't see any fairies." She looked about the clearing. Bluebells dotted the green grass, and butterflies were flitting about. "But it does look magical."

She noted the blue embroidered blanket stretched out on the grass and a lantern placed nearby on a flat rock. "You were here before."

"Yes." He dropped the basket beside the blanket. "I wanted everything to be ready."

Ready for what? she wondered as she glanced at the blanket. Was he still thinking about a quick affair?

The last of the sunlight faded away, and she hugged herself as the air grew chilly. "I should have brought a shawl—" Her mouth dropped open as a thousand golden lights began to rise from the ground.

"This is what I wanted you to see," the Woodsman whispered.

She pivoted in a circle, watching as the golden lights rose higher and began to dance about. "How? Are these the fairies?"

"People call them fairies, but they're actually fireflies. They gather here each evening at dusk."

She smiled. "I feel as if we're floating in the heavens, surrounded by stars." The fireflies swirled around them, then slowly dispersed into the woods. "They're gone."

"Yes. It's a performance they put on every night for only a few minutes."

"I'm glad I saw it. Thank you." The stars and twin moons shone down on them, glinting on the grass and bluebells with a silver hue, and suddenly it felt as if she was exactly where she was supposed to be. She sent up a prayer of gratitude to the moon goddesses.

"We'll need some light in order to eat and find our way home." He picked up the lantern and opened the metal grate to reveal the candle inside. "Could you make a flame?"

"Of course." She snapped her fingers, then lit the candle. The flame flickered, illuminating the Woodsman's face with a golden glow. How could a man be so beautiful?

He set the lantern down as she blew out her flame. Then he took her hand in his and examined her fingers. "Still warm, but no sign of damage. I was so amazed when I first saw you make a fire to burn the ropes that were binding you."

"And you used your gift to slice through the cage that held me prisoner."

He smiled, lacing his fingers with hers. "And then you tried to knee me in the groin."

She winced. "You must have thought I was terribly ungrateful."

"I thought you were beautiful. But unpredictable like wildfire, a real threat to the calm and controlled existence I was accustomed to. But you ignited a spark in my heart, and the flame has been growing till I no longer want the calm. I want the fire. I want to burn with you."

Tears stung her eyes. Why couldn't this man be the one? Why was she letting the Telling Stones and her stupid fear of falling in love keep her from following her heart?

It has already happened, she realized with a start. While she had been fighting it in her mind, her heart had quietly surrendered on its own. She was already in love. "I don't want to leave in the morning. I don't want to be parted from you."

"This is not the end for us." He kissed her hand. "It is only the beginning."

A tear rolled down her cheek. She no longer cared what the stones said. "You *are* the one."

Chapter 17

Yes! The Woodsman placed a hand against her cheek, wiping away her tear as he leaned in for a kiss. He had intended to be gentle, for he was determined to take this slowly, but when Sorcha wrapped her arms around him, his control went up in flames.

With a growl, he pulled her tightly against him, his sweet kiss changing into a hungry, devouring one. A thrill shot through him as she melted against him and her mouth opened to him. He stroked her tongue with his, and by the Light, she was hot and eager with her response. His fiery Sorcha. A kiss would not be enough.

He trailed nibbling kisses across her cheek to her ear, then sucked her earlobe into his mouth. With a groan, she delved her fingers into his hair. When she stroked his ears, he gasped. "Sorcha."

"Yes?" She ran a finger along the pointed tip of one ear.

He hissed in a breath. "An elf's ears are extremely sensitive."

Her hand stopped. "Am I hurting you?"

"No. But it will cause a severe reaction."

"Really?" She studied his ears. "They look the same to me. Cute and—" She gasped when he grasped her hips and pulled her against his swollen groin. "What is that?"

"My reaction."

She glanced down at his breeches. "Is that normal?"

He snorted. "Since I met you, yes. It's been happening quite often."

"But I never touched your ears till now."

"Sorcha, I only have to look at you."

Her eyes widened. "Oh." She glanced down again. "That seems like a rather *large* reaction."

"It's no twig."

"More like a branch." Her mouth twitched. "Oh dear, you must be made of wood after all."

He moved his hands from her hips to her buttocks. "Are you going to set me on fire?"

"Shall I?" Her face grew serious. "Sometimes a flame can burn out very quickly."

"Not for us." He kissed her brow. "This will not be a quick affair, but a long one. One that should last as long as we live."

"I like that." She reached up and stroked his ear once more. "So are you going to talk all night or do something?"

Yes! He swept her up in his arms, then tumbled down onto the blanket with her. As she stretched out, her golden-red hair spread around her like sunshine, and her green eyes glittered in the moonlight.

"Do you know how beautiful you are?" He ran the tips of his fingers across her cheek, which was flushed pink with excitement.

"I feel beautiful when I'm with you." She skimmed her hand down his long hair, then gathered a lock of it and brushed the ends against the base of her neck.

He kissed her again, a thorough ravishing kiss that soon had her squirming beneath him, her hands clutching at his shirt, her legs rubbing against his. His groin grew harder and more desperate. With a groan, he cupped her breast in his hand.

She gasped against his mouth. "Yes."

That was all the encouragement he needed. He quickly unbuttoned the bodice of her gown, then unraveled the bow at the neck of her linen shift. Not to be outdone, Sorcha undid the buttons on his shirt. He yanked the shirt off and tossed it aside.

He paused for a moment, enjoying the feel of her hands as she dragged her fingers over his shoulders and down his chest. His skin pebbled with gooseflesh at the light, feathery touch.

"Sorcha, I want you to see you." He gave the shift's drawstring a tug, loosening the neckline so he could pull it down and uncover her breasts. Lovely round breasts.

She inhaled sharply, her hands growing still. Her rosy-pink nipples tightened into buds, and he winced, coming close to climaxing just at the sight. He stroked a finger along the soft white skin, then teased the hardened tip of her nipple.

Another gasp.

"You like that?" He gave her nipple a tweak, then leaned over to flick it with his tongue.

A groan. Her hands grabbed hold of his head.

He sucked one nipple into his mouth while teasing the other with his fingers.

"Woodsman," she moaned, starting to squirm beneath him.

"Do you want more?" he whispered.

"Yes!"

He reached down to gather the hem of her velvet skirt. Slowly he dragged the soft fabric up her legs.

"Faster." She kicked at her skirt, and her slip-on shoes went flying across the glade.

He grinned. She was still as impetuous as wildfire, but while that had worried him at first, he now loved it. He bunched her skirt up around her waist, then lifted her shift.

Red. The curls between her legs were as fiery as her mane of hair. "Beautiful," he whispered.

"Am I?" She bit her lip, gazing up at the moons. "I feel . . . strange. Chilled from the night air, but hot at the same time.

Frightened since I'm not sure what happens next, but so . . . so greedy for it. I want . . . but I'm not sure what I want."

"Do you want me to touch you?" He cupped her red curls.

With a gasp, she flinched. "I-I . . ."

He parted the folds and stroked her gently. Moisture had already coated the delicate pink skin.

"Oh, yes. I want that." She let her thighs drop open. "What else do I want?"

"This?" He rubbed against the nubbin there.

"Oh, yes!" She spread her legs wide. "What else?"

"This?" He inserted a finger inside her wet heat.

"Oh, goddesses, yes!" Her hands clutched at the blanket, and her eyes squeezed shut as he pumped his finger in and out. "Wha-what else?"

"Shall I taste you?"

Her eyes popped open with a look of alarm. "What?"

"Taste you." He moved between her legs.

"*What?*"

"Taste you. Lick you. Suck on you—"

"That sounds rather extreme, don't you—" She moaned when he parted her slick folds with his fingers. "I don't think . . ." She gasped when his tongue lapped at the folds. "But . . ."

He tickled the nubbin with the tip of his tongue.

"But don't let me stop you." She clutched his head with her hands.

He drew the nubbin into his mouth and sucked. Within seconds, she was squirming and moaning. Her hips lifted, then suddenly she stiffened, and he knew she was teetering on the edge of the cliff he'd brought her to.

He clasped her hips, holding her still while he devoured her. With a cry, she shattered against his face. He kept going, relishing each throb that shuddered through her body.

"I . . . what . . . I . . . dear goddesses." She managed a few words between pants. "That was . . ."

He sat up as the stiffness in his groin became increasingly hard to bear. She was so lovely with her hair tousled about and her cheeks flushed pink. And the taste of her was sweet on his lips. By the Light, he couldn't wait any longer. "Are you all right?" He pulled at the laces that fastened his breeches.

She pressed a hand against her chest as she continued to breathe hard. "That was . . . I had no idea."

Woodsman.

He glanced toward the forest. Why were the Living Oaks bothering him now? *Talk to me later. I'm busy.* He fumbled with the laces. "Are you ready for more?"

"More?" Sorcha's eyes widened as she looked at his breeches. "Oh, you mean—"

Woodsman.

"Hush!"

"What?" Sorcha sat up.

He winced. "Not you. The Living Oaks—"

Woodsman. One of your men has been captured.

He turned toward the forest. *What?*

A troop of soldiers has taken one of your men prisoner, a Living Oak explained.

He is being held just south of Whistler's Bog, three miles west of Whistlyn Castle, a second oak added.

The Woodsman recalled how Colwyn and Ronan had planned to lead the army into Whistler's Bog. *Who was captured? The tall, slender one, or the shorter one?*

Tall and slender.

Colwyn. With a wince, the Woodsman quickly retied his breeches. *And where is the other one?*

The one who calls himself Ronan is hiding in my branches. He is afraid to speak, for fear that the soldiers will hear him.

"What is it?" Sorcha asked. "Is the army coming our way?"

"No, we're safe here." The Woodsman pulled on his shirt and buttoned it. "Colwyn and Ronan had the job of luring the army away while my men took the goods to Drudaelen. But Colwyn has been captured. I have to rescue him. We never leave a man—"

"Of course." Sorcha jumped to her feet and quickly fixed her gown. "Colwyn? Isn't he the one Tara is smitten with?"

"Yes." The Woodsman located Sorcha's shoes and tossed them to her. "I need to leave tonight."

"You'll ride all night?" She slipped on the shoes.

"I'll be fine. I took a nap earlier." He gathered up the blanket and basket. "Can you get the lantern?"

"Yes." She picked it up and followed him back toward the tree houses. "Is Colwyn far away?"

"Close to Whistler's Bog. If we ride hard, we might reach him by tomorrow night." He stopped with a jerk. "I won't be able to take you to Eberon tomorrow."

"That's all right."

"No, it's not. I don't want your brother thinking I can't be trusted. I'll ask Morghen to take you. She knows the way through the Haunted Woods, and you'll have Brody and Aleksi to keep you safe."

"All right," she mumbled.

They would have to part ways in just a few minutes, he realized as they hurried through the woods. No wonder she sounded glum. But he had no choice. He had to reach Colwyn as quickly as possible. If the soldiers believed their prisoner knew the location of Haven and the Woodsman, they would torture him to get him to talk.

Colwyn's father, the Earl of Whistlyn, was one of the Woodsman's most trusted allies. Whistlyn was also good friends with King Rendelf, since he'd served a few years as chief counsel before retiring to his estate just south of Whistler's Bog. The earl loathed the fact that Princess Jenetta was the apparent heir to the throne. He, along with Lord Daelen, had secretly sent letters to the king, explaining the true identity of the Woodsman. The earl had also sent his second son, Colwyn, to aid and assist the Woodsman.

Colwyn had come to Haven with his Aunt Lauren and her husband and two children. With family living here, the young man would protect the location of Haven with his dying breath.

Is he injured? the Woodsman asked as he neared the edge of the forest.

Not badly, an oak told him. *A bloodied lip.*

He will be fine for a while, a second oak added. *The captain in charge has sent for someone to do the interrogation.*

I'll get there as fast as I can. He glanced at Sorcha. "I'm sorry we have to part like this."

"It's not your fault." She held up the lantern to illuminate the path as they neared the tree house. "But I'll miss you. And I'll worry about you."

"I'll worry about you, too."

"I'll be fine." She sighed. "I'll just be left wondering what other things you had planned to do this evening."

"The sudden change in plans was not pleasant for me, either," he grumbled. His groin was still objecting. "But we'll have the rest of our lives to make each other melt."

She stopped, and the look on her face made his imminent departure almost impossible to bear. He dropped the blanket and basket on the ground and touched her cheek.

"There you are," Brody yelled at them in Eberoni from the base of the Woodsman's tree house, and Sorcha stepped back.

With a sigh, the Woodsman glanced at the shifter, who was back in human form, wearing his clothes and stalking toward them with an annoyed look.

"I woke up and discovered you had snuck off—"

"And now we're back," the Woodsman told Brody as he passed by him on his way to the ladder. "I have to leave immediately. I'll fetch my weapons and be on my way."

"What?" Brody turned to follow him. "What's going on?"

"Sorcha can explain it to you," the Woodsman called down as he quickly ascended the ladder. Down by the lake, the bell began clanging, warning the villagers of danger. Morghen must have heard the Living Oaks, too, so she was gathering the people.

Inside his tree house, he exchanged his shoes for his riding boots, inserted a knife into each boot, fastened on his sword belt, grabbed his bow and quiver, and pulled on his gloves. When he headed back down the ladder, he heard Sorcha talking to Brody.

"He has to rescue Colwyn before the soldiers start torturing him," Sorcha explained. "So he can't take me to the Eberoni border tomorrow. He said Morghen could take me, but if she thinks Aleksi isn't up to traveling, I'm really all right with staying here in Haven."

Brody snorted. "Silas won't agree to that. If this Colwyn fellow tells the army about this place, then it will not be safe for you. Aleksi can go with you and Morghen tomorrow and provide all the protection you need."

"But what about you?" Sorcha sounded confused. "Aren't ye coming with us?"

"I'm going with the Woodsman," Brody whispered.

Sorcha gasped. "What? Why?"

Why, indeed. The Woodsman paused halfway down the ladder, looking at them.

Brody leaned close, lowering his voice. "Gwen asked me to find out what manner of man he is. Something to do with a prediction from the Telling Stones. Seeing him in action will tell me more than a conversation ever could."

So Gwennore was expecting Brody to spy on him. The Woodsman grabbed the nearby rope and slid down to land beside them. "This is not your fight, shifter."

"It never is," Brody replied dryly. "But I have helped three kings gain their thrones. Whoever you are and whatever you are up to, I want to see for myself."

"Brody can help you," Sorcha told the Woodsman, then turned to the shifter. "Please keep him safe for me."

With a snort, the Woodsman walked away. Did Sorcha think he needed a bodyguard? He could still hear them whispering to each other while they followed him around the lake.

As he approached Morghen's house, he saw the villagers crowded around her front gate. Many were holding lanterns, and a few had planted lit torches beside the lake. Hallie had brought Aleksi to the gate, and some of the villagers were demanding to know if he was really a dragon. Had he come to breathe fire on them and burn Haven down? Aleksi seemed unperturbed, though. Most probably, he couldn't understand their Elfish.

Morghen was trying to tell everyone what had happened, but the villagers were so agitated, they kept interrupting her. Ronan's mother, Riona, and Colwyn's aunt, Lauren, were clutching each other and crying. Meanwhile, Ronan's father, Dylan, was demanding to know which of the young men had been taken.

Father Kit held up his hands to quiet everyone down. "Now, now, remember, we are all in this together. If the army finds out the location of Haven, each and every one of us will be in danger."

The villagers jolted back with a cry of fear.

Morghen gave the priest an incredulous look. "That's how you calm everyone down?"

Father Kit winced. "Then let me assure everyone that there is no need to worry. The Woodsman will have a plan."

Liz smirked. "The Woodsman always has a plan."

The crowd gave the Woodsman an expectant, hopeful look as he came to a stop in front of them.

"So?" Father Kit turned toward him. "What's the plan?"

Hell if I know. The Woodsman removed his gloves and stuffed them under his belt while his mind raced. "I will leave immediately with a rescue party. We'll ride night and day till we reach Colwyn, then—"

Tara screamed and collapsed on the ground.

"It was Colwyn who was taken?" his uncle, Hadyn, asked.

"Aye," the Woodsman replied. "The Living Oaks have confirmed—"

Colwyn's aunt, Lauren, doubled over, her hand pressed to her mouth to muffle her cry.

Tara thrashed about on the ground. "Colwyn! My love!"

"Hush." Teresa hunched down beside her daughter and whispered, "This is no time for your dramatics!"

"But I love him!" Tara wailed. "And they're going to kill him!"

Lauren screamed and collapsed on the ground.

"Tara!" Morghen hissed at her. "Shut your mouth or I'll put a hex on you that will do it permanently."

Tara gulped, her eyes bulging.

"Everyone, calm down!" The Woodsman lifted his hands. "You know our motto: We never leave a man behind. I will bring Colwyn and Ronan back, I promise you. Liz, go and ready three horses. Father Kit, gather some supplies for the journey. The three of us will be leaving shortly."

Liz and Father Kit took off, running.

"Only three of you?" Hadyn asked. "How can that be enough? This is my nephew who is in danger. Let me go with you!"

"Me, too!"

"I want to go!"

Every man and even some of the women raised their hands, and the Woodsman's heart softened at the sight of their loyalty to one another and to him. Even a few youths under the age of fifteen moved forward, lifting their chins to try to look taller. By the Light, he would not let these people down.

"You are needed," he told them. "Each one of you is needed here in case the army marches on Haven. Take turns standing guard night and day. Stay alert and ready to protect your families. Do you all remember the defense plan?"

They nodded.

"Good. Practice it while I'm gone." The Woodsman took the lantern from Sorcha. "Although there are only three of us going on the rescue mission, we will have an advantage. Liz and I will use our Embraced powers."

"Actually, there will be four of you," Sorcha said in Elfish as she motioned to Brody. "He'll be going, too, and he's also Embraced."

"Where did he come from?" Dylan demanded, giving Brody a suspicious look.

Whispers spread among the villagers.

"Who is he?"

"I've never seen him before."

"He's not an Elf."

"How did he find Haven?"

"What's going on?" Brody whispered to Sorcha in Eberoni. "Why are they looking at me like that?"

He doesn't understand Elfish, the Woodsman thought. He turned toward the crowd. "Don't worry. This is Brody, a friend of Princess Sorcha. He's here to help us."

At the sound of his name, Brody smiled and waved at everyone.

Morghen's eyes narrowed. "You're a shifter?" she asked in Eberoni.

"I am," Brody replied with a smile. "You must be Morghen?"

"Yes." Morghen looked him over. "You've been cursed."

"Yes, my lady." Brody bowed his head.

"How did you find this place?" Hallie asked.

"King Silas told me."

Morghen and Hallie both gasped.

"How did King Silas know?" Morghen asked.

Brody motioned toward Aleksi. "The dragons can talk to one another telepathically."

With another gasp, Hallie turned toward Aleksi. "You told King Silas where Haven is?"

Aleksi shrugged. "Sorcha's brother has the right to know where she is. I didn't see anything wrong with—"

"This place is a secret!" Hallie cried.

"Silas isn't going to tell anyone," Aleksi grumbled.

"He told the shifter," Morghen muttered.

"What's going on?" the villagers asked in Elfish.

"You endangered us all," Hallie fumed at him. "After we saved your life? How dare you?"

Aleksi frowned at her. "I didn't do it to upset you. I was merely protecting the princess. That's my job."

Sorcha shook her head. "I don't think ye should have told Silas."

Aleksi scoffed. "He's your king, Sorcha. You don't keep secrets from him."

"He kept a secret from me!" Sorcha replied. "I didn't know the dragons could communicate mentally. If I had known, I would have asked you not to tell him anything. We don't have the right to put these villagers in danger."

Aleksi gave her a shocked look. "Are you siding with these people over your brother?"

"*These people*?" Hallie growled. "Is that all I am to you?" She shoved Aleksi in the chest. "I never want to speak to you again!" She stormed through the front gate, slamming it shut behind her.

"Hallie!" Aleksi reached for her.

She ran to the stables where her brother was saddling the

horses. Meanwhile, thanks to some hints from Father Kit, some of the villagers had figured out what had happened, and as they spread the word, they all turned to glare at Aleksi.

He stepped back. "Damn."

Morghen gave him a wry look. "Do you see how you have endangered us? Endangered Hallie?"

He winced. "Believe me, I meant no harm—"

"Then you should take responsibility for your mistake," Morghen declared. "How will you protect us if the army marches on Haven?"

Aleksi glanced over at Hallie. "I will remain here. And I will breathe fire on anyone who attacks this place."

Morghen nodded, then translated his decision to the villagers.

"We'll have a dragon to protect us?" the villagers whispered among themselves. Now they were smiling at Aleksi.

Ronan's father, Dylan, stepped toward Aleksi and extended his hand.

Aleksi shook it. "I won't let any harm come to you."

The Woodsman sighed. Even though he was relieved that Aleksi had taken on the role of protecting Haven and keeping his people safe, it meant the dragon would not be able to escort Sorcha. So now, she would not be safe. "Aleksi, you were supposed to take Sorcha to Eberon tomorrow."

He nodded. "I'll explain the situation to Silas." He turned to Sorcha. "Do you mind staying here for a while?"

Her face brightened. "No, not at all." She smiled at the Woodsman. "I'll be here, waiting for you."

He didn't know if he should be happy or worried. Both, he decided, as he took her hand. "Be safe."

Her smile faded. "You, too."

"I will come for you. No matter how long it takes." He kissed her hand, then dashed toward the stable where Liz and Father Kit were readying the horses.

Brody ran into the stable, then tossed out his clothes. "Pack these for me in case I need them later."

Father Kit stuffed them into a saddlebag, while Hallie gave her brother one last hug. The villagers gasped when Brody swooped out of the stable in eagle form, then soared up into the sky.

The Woodsman swung onto his horse. "Let's go."

Chapter 18

As they raced toward Drudaelen Castle, the Woodsman held up the lantern to light their way. Memories of making love to Sorcha kept invading his mind, but he pushed the thoughts aside. It would be too painful to ride all night if his groin remained swollen. And if he kept worrying about Sorcha's safety, he would lose the focus he so badly needed.

Soon, they spotted the battlements. Brightly lit with torches, the castle walls gleamed with a golden hue in the dark night. The Woodsman called out to the guards, and they rushed to open the gate. By the time he reined in his horse in the courtyard, Bronwen and her husband, Aiden, were there to meet him.

"We'll need three of your quickest horses," the Woodsman said as he dismounted. "And two of the arrow launchers."

"Right away." Aiden gave the order to a nearby guard.

"What has happened?" Bronwen asked, then gasped when an eagle landed in the courtyard and promptly turned into a black-and-white shaggy dog. "What on Aerthlan is that?"

"Brody," the Woodsman replied, then glanced at his men. "Grab something to eat. We'll be riding all night. Or flying," he added with a wry look at Brody.

"Let's go." Father Kit wrapped an arm around Liz's shoulders as they walked toward the kitchen. Brody gave a bark and trotted along beside them.

"Is Lord Daelen awake?" the Woodsman asked.

"Yes. He's still in the library." Aiden led them toward the keep. "What has happened?"

"I'll explain shortly." The Woodsman ran up the stairs into the Great Hall. Aiden and Bronwen followed him to the library.

Lord Bowen Daelen was sitting behind his desk, writing, and looked up when they entered. "Nephew." He dropped his quill. "What brings you here? Has something gone amiss?"

The Woodsman explained the situation. "So we must rescue Colwyn as quickly as possible."

Lord Daelen sat back in his chair, frowning as he rubbed his sore leg. "Lord Whistlyn is our strongest ally. We cannot let any harm come to his son."

"Oh, dear." Bronwen stepped close to the desk. "If the army suspects Colwyn of being one of the Woodsman's followers, they might also suspect his father. Caladras could have Lord Whistlyn arrested for treason."

The Woodsman winced. If he lost Whistlyn, he would lose an important witness who could confirm his true identity. He would also lose the small army Whistlyn had amassed for him.

Lord Daelen reached for his quill. "I must warn Whistlyn right away."

"I can do it," the Woodsman told him. "Whistlyn Castle is on the way."

"Do you need more men?" Aiden asked. "I could send Marius and some of my best soldiers with you."

The Woodsman shook his head. "We'll be fine. A larger, armed group would draw too much attention."

"But you have only two men," Aiden objected.

"And a dog," Bronwen muttered.

"A dog?" Lord Daelen asked.

"He'll be an eagle most of the time," the Woodsman explained, but when they all gave him a confused look, he waved it aside. "Don't worry about the shifter. He's on our side." *I hope.* "He's a friend of Princess Sorcha."

"How is she?" Bronwen asked.

"Is she still in Haven?" Lord Daelen asked.

"Yes." Unfortunately. The Woodsman winced. "She's still there, and the dragon is guarding the village."

"Excellent!" Lord Daelen beamed at him. "I knew you would come around. It only makes sense to use their support."

The Woodsman gritted his teeth. "I never intended to use them. As soon as I get back to Haven, I'll take Sorcha to Eberon. Her brother will be waiting for her there."

Lord Daelen shook his head. "There's no time to go back. You're meeting King Rendelf in seven days now."

Damn. The Woodsman swallowed hard. He'd been so intent on returning to Sorcha as soon as possible that he hadn't realized that he was now out of time. As soon as he rescued Colwyn, he would have to head to Wyndelas Palace. The takeover was happening. Now. And Sorcha was still in Woodwyn. "If something goes amiss, send some guards to Haven. Promise me you will get Sorcha back to her family."

"I promise." Bronwen touched his arm. "We won't let any harm come to her."

"Nothing will go wrong with the plan once the king announces you as his heir." Lord Daelen gave him a stern look. "Are you ready?"

The Woodsman nodded. "Yes. Did you prepare the notices?"

"Aye." Lord Daelen unlocked a wooden casket on his desk. "Over three hundred of them."

"I wrote half of them myself," Bronwyn boasted. "My handwriting is the best."

"That's true." Aiden smiled at his wife. "I'm better at wielding a sword than a quill."

Lord Daelen removed the stack of papers and set them on the desk. "Soon everyone will know you are alive."

The Woodsman picked up the notice on top. As he read it,

his heart started to race. Finally, all the years of planning and training would bear fruit. He would avenge his father and the rest of his family who had died to satisfy Jenetta's and Caladras's greed for power.

He turned to Aiden. "Post these tonight under the cover of darkness. Move in small groups so you can remain undetected. No uniforms. We don't want any witnesses who can point their fingers at Drudaelen. Once the army knows about me, they will already suspect Drudaelen." He glanced at his cousin. "You could end up in danger because of me."

Bronwen's eyes sparkled with tears as she smiled at him. "We've known that for years, you silly goose."

Aiden nudged her. "Is that any way to talk to your future king?"

The Woodsman handed the stack of notices to Aiden. "Post as many as you can tonight. Spread them all over Woodwyn."

"Every village will have a Church of Enlightenment," Lord Daelen suggested. "You could nail a notice on each door."

Aiden nodded. "We will."

"But some of the priests are working for Lord Morris," the Woodsman warned him. "They might tear the notice down before anyone sees it. You should also post the notices on the door of the village tavern."

"I understand." Aiden bowed his head. "I'll be on my way, then."

Bronwen quickly embraced her husband. "Be careful." She shifted her worried look to the Woodsman. "You be careful, too."

Aiden gave his wife a kiss, then rushed out the door with the Woodsman.

"Don't let any soldiers catch you," the Woodsman warned Aiden as they hurried toward the courtyard.

"I won't." Aiden gave him a worried look. "The next time I see you, you might be king."

The Woodsman nodded. The days ahead would be dangerous. Once the notices were posted and Caladras knew of his existence, the army would be searching high and low for him. Jenetta and the general would be eager to kill him.

And yet, he was more worried about Sorcha. How could she mean so much to him so quickly? He paused at the top of the stairs leading down to the courtyard. There was only one explanation.

He loved her.

"We're ready!" Father Kit yelled as he fastened two arrow launchers to his saddlebags.

"Let's go." The Woodsman dashed to his horse. His destiny was waiting. Sorcha was waiting. As he swung into the saddle, he realized the two were the same.

Sorcha slept late the next morning after tossing and turning most of the night. Her thoughts waffled between memories of the Woodsman's lovemaking and worries for his safety.

With a groan, she finally crawled out of bed and put on one of her borrowed gowns from Bronwen. She would need to do her laundry soon, she realized. Maybe she could do it at Morghen's house. She would need something to occupy her time, or she would go mad with worry.

She'd done it. Her worst fear had been realized. Now that she was in love, she had to deal with the terror of not knowing if the Woodsman was safe. She glanced out a window at his tree house. Oh goddesses, she missed him already.

His house was larger than hers. The shutters on the windows had been left open, and she narrowed her eyes, trying to catch a glimpse inside.

Who would ever know if she snuck over to his place and looked around? She slipped on her shoes and inched carefully across the bridge. It was suspended between the two trees on ropes, so it swayed gently with each step she took. Finally, with a sigh of relief, she reached his house.

He had a sitting room with a comfy-looking chair and

footrest. No fireplace, but then that would be dangerous in a tree house. Three piles of paper were neatly stacked on his desk. She smiled to herself. No surprise that the Woodsman was a tidy and orderly person. One stack held information on Haven, a list of the inhabitants and so forth. Another stack was drawings of different kinds of weapons. The third stack was blank paper.

She moved on into his bedroom. The sight of his bed made all the memories from last night come rushing back. The Woodsman kissing her, undressing her, making her melt. Oh, how she missed him!

Where was he? Was he tired after riding all night? He had to be. He had to be exhausted and hungry. She sat on the bed and smoothed her hand over his pillow. How could she have fallen in love so quickly? So thoroughly? And after she had promised herself that she wouldn't.

She lay down and nestled her cheek against his pillow, breathing in his scent. At least she was still here in Haven, and not on her way to Eberon. In a few days, she would see him again.

After wandering back into the sitting room, she was drawn once more to his desk. She eyed the blank sheets of paper. Surely he wouldn't miss one page.

She sat and centered a sheet on the desk before her, then opened the inkwell and selected a sharp quill. It was too bad she didn't have any paints with her, but she could still do a decent sketch with ink.

This will help me get through the days, she thought as she carefully drew the Woodsman's face. The long reddish-brown hair. The high, noble brow and finely-shaped black eyebrows. Eyes, slightly almond-shaped with thick lashes. Sharp cheekbones and a perfect jawline. A mouth that still made her stomach flutter. And made her face burn with heat when she remembered all the things he had done with that mouth.

Goodness, those thoughts were making her squirm in her

chair. "How soon can you come back?" she whispered to the sketch. "You said there was more."

With a sigh, she closed the inkwell and studied her completed sketch. Not bad. But could anything be as beautiful as he was in person?

"Your Highness!" a voice called from below. "Are you all right?"

Sorcha peered out a window and spotted Tara standing by the ladder to her tree house.

"Your Highness!" Tara yelled. "Morghen sent me to make sure you're all right. We haven't seen you all day."

Sorcha stepped out onto the Woodsman's front porch. "I'm fine."

"Oh!" Tara looked over at the Woodsman's tree house. "You're over there. My mother is making chicken soup if you'd like some."

"That sounds lovely." Sorcha retrieved her sketch, then started down the ladder. Unfortunately, the sketch slipped out of her hand and floated toward the ground. "Oh! Tara, can you catch that?"

Tara managed to nab the paper just before it touched the ground. "Oh, my! It looks just like the Woodsman! Did you do this?"

"Yes." Sorcha reached the ground. "I used one of the Woodsman's papers. I hope he won't mind."

"I'm sure he won't." Tara lifted up the sketch to admire it some more. "It's wonderful. I didn't know you were so talented."

"Thank you." Sorcha gave her a brief smile. She folded up the sketch, then started to wander slowly around the lake with Tara. "Is there any news about the Woodsman?"

"No." Tara shook her head. "I'm so terrified something awful will happen to Colwyn. I couldn't sleep at all last night."

"I know what you mean," Sorcha mumbled.

Tara stopped with a gasp. "Your Highness, could you draw a picture of Colwyn for me? I would love it so much, and it would help me as I suffer through this horrific ordeal!"

"I . . . I can't."

Tara's eyes filled with tears, and her bottom lip trembled. "You can't? Are you still mad at me for giving you the love potion?"

"No, I can't because I don't know what Colwyn looks like. I've never met him."

"Oh." Tara blinked away her tears. "Well, he's extremely handsome."

"That would describe most of the elves," Sorcha muttered as she resumed their walk.

Tara took a few steps, then stopped again with another gasp. "I know! You could draw a picture of me, and make it really beautiful. Then I could give it to Colwyn, and he could fold it up and keep it next to his heart!"

"I'm not sure he would—"

"Oh, please!" Tara clasped her hands together. "Please draw a picture of me."

"I don't have any more paper."

"I'll get some for you. I'll do anything for you!"

Sorcha thought about that for a while. "All right. There is something you can do."

"What?" Tara bounced up and down. "Tell me!"

"You could tell me everything you know about the Woodsman."

Tara's mouth fell open. "Oh. I-I'm not supposed to talk about him."

"But you gave us both the potion. Now we are destined for each other."

"True." Tara chewed on her bottom lip, then her face brightened up. "I would be your spy."

Sorcha blinked. "That's a bit extreme—"

"I've always wanted to be a spy!"

"But quite accurate," Sorcha added.

Tara grinned. "Spying runs in my family. My brother Tarrant is a spy for the Woodsman. He tells him everything that's going on with the army."

"Really?" So the Woodsman had some human spies after all, not just trees. "While I draw your picture, you can tell me more."

"Great!" Tara pointed to the field where the banquet had occurred the day before. The table was still sitting in the middle, and several chairs were arranged around it. "Just sit there, and I will bring you everything you need!"

Sorcha took a seat while Tara ran off.

Soon, Tara's mother brought her a bowl of soup and some bread and butter. "Is it true?" Teresa asked. "Tara says you are going to draw her portrait?"

"I'll give it a try." While Sorcha ate, Tara arranged the other end of the table with paper, inkwell, quills, and a penknife.

"Everything's ready!" Tara announced.

"Then sit here." Sorcha vacated her seat and moved to the chair on the opposite end of the table. "So." She sharpened the quills. "Tell me everything you know."

Tara nodded. "Well, the Woodsman is Lord Daelen's nephew."

"I already know that."

"Did you know Lord Daelen was injured saving the Woodsman's life when he was just a boy?"

"No. Tell me more." Sorcha studied Tara's face, then began to sketch.

"It happened a long time ago. When the Woodsman's father was killed, the bad guys tried to kill the Woodsman, too. But Lord Daelen saved him and brought him back to Drudaelen Castle."

"Who were the bad guys?"

Tara shrugged. "I'm not sure."

"Who was the Woodsman's father?"

Tara turned pale. "I-I think his mother was Lord Daelen's younger sister."

The girl was hedging, Sorcha thought. "You can't tell me who his father was?"

Tara shook her head. "It's a secret. The biggest secret in the world!"

Sorcha paused in her drawing. Tara tended to be overly dramatic, but in this case, Sorcha suspected her wild claim might be close to the truth.

"How is it going?" Teresa walked up to the table to remove the empty soup bowl and tray. She peeked over at the sketch and gasped. "Oh, that's lovely! Wait till I tell the others!" She ran toward the cottages.

Soon, there was a crowd around the table.

"Would you like some honey cakes?" one elfin woman asked as she set a plate on the table. "And when you're done with Tara's picture, could you draw my little boy?"

"I would be happy to," Sorcha said as she finished Tara's portrait.

By that afternoon, the table was full of delicious food and Sorcha was having a marvelous time snacking on elfin desserts and drinking delicious wine while drawing one elfin child after another.

The mothers whispered to each other. "Isn't she wonderful!"

"This is so kind of her!"

Sorcha smiled. The Woodsman would be impressed when he returned and discovered how well liked she was by the people of Haven. But she wasn't doing this simply to be popular, she realized. She wanted the elves to love her just as much as she wanted the Woodsman to love her.

Her smile faded. He'd said sweet words to her and he'd

made her melt, but he'd never confessed that he loved her. What if the Telling Stones were right and he wasn't the one? Could her destiny truly be with him?

If it was, she might never go home again. She would miss seeing Gwennore's baby being born. She would miss seeing all her sisters, for she would have to live in Woodwyn for the rest of her life.

Was that really what she wanted?

Chapter 19

By late that afternoon, Sorcha's hands were tired from drawing and she asked the elfin women to let her finish doing portraits the next day. They happily agreed, and she wandered off to Morghen's house to see how Aleksi was faring. She hadn't seen him all day, and she wanted to make sure he had let Silas know about the delay in their departure.

Inside, Hallie and Morghen were busy at the worktable. Hallie was grinding herbs with a wooden pestle in a stone mortar, while Morghen was mixing some sort of foul-smelling concoction in a bowl.

"It's good to see you." Morghen looked up with a smile. "I hear you've been busy."

"Yes." Sorcha peeked into the patient's room, but the bed was empty. "Where is Aleksi?"

With a huff, Hallie slammed her pestle against the stone.

Sorcha exchanged a look with Morghen. Apparently, Hallie was still angry at Aleksi.

Morghen's mouth twitched. "Aleksi is guarding the perimeter, as he calls it."

Hallie scoffed. "Fancy words for saying the silly man is marching around the boundary of Haven all day."

Sorcha wandered over to the table. "But shouldn't he be resting?"

"As if he ever listens to us," Hallie muttered as she tossed more herbs into the mortar.

"He's trying his best to protect us." Morghen poured the brownish concoction into a green bottle, then jammed a cork in it. "I think it's his way of apologizing for revealing our location."

Hallie slammed her pestle into the mortar. "He could try apologizing to me."

"I'm sure he's sorry," Sorcha said. "He just didn't understand the situation as well as I did, since he was asleep so much from the pain tonic and his knowledge of the elfin language is so limited. And, of course, he was being very protective of me. And very loyal to his king. Those are excellent virtues to have, don't you think?"

Hallie remained silent as she ground the herbs.

Morghen strode toward the hearth and picked up the kettle that was resting on a stone close to the fire. "Would you like some tea?" She poured hot water into the teapot.

"Yes, thank you." Sorcha picked up the green bottle to look at the label. *Hair Dye.* She recalled how Morghen had admitted to using it so she could blend in with the Wood Elves. Was there another River Elf at Haven who was blending in? "Who could be using this?" she asked softly.

"The Woo—why should I know?" Hallie winced, then dropped the pestle on the table with a noisy clatter. "That damned dragon has me too upset."

Had she been about to say the Woodsman? Sorcha wondered. Was he really a River Elf? Was his hair actually white? He did have black eyebrows like a River Elf. Her heart lurched. He might be the one the Telling Stones had predicted after all!

But no, he couldn't be. She'd told him about the stones and the colors she had selected. If he knew he was a perfect match for the prediction, he would have told her. Wouldn't he?

Dammit. She rubbed her brow. She'd had only three days with the Woodsman. It simply wasn't enough time. There was still so much she didn't know.

"I-I think I'll go get some fresh air," Hallie mumbled, then hurried out the door.

Was she going to find Aleksi? Sorcha hoped so.

"Come and have a seat by the fire." Morghen readied two cups on the table between the comfy chairs.

Sorcha's thoughts raced as she wandered toward the chairs and sat down. "Have you heard anything from the Living Oaks? Is the Woodsman all right? Has he reached Colwyn yet?"

"Yes, yes, and no." Morghen smiled as she took a seat. "They're still traveling. They've changed horses a few times. By tomorrow morning, they should reach Whistlyn Castle."

Sorcha swallowed hard. Would there be a battle in order to rescue Colwyn?

"You're worried about him."

"Of course." Sorcha shifted in her chair. "Aren't you?"

"He'll be fine." Morghen poured tea into the cups. "He's been through worse than this."

Sorcha leaned toward her. "You know who he is, don't you? Can you tell me?"

"It's up to him to tell you."

With a silent groan, Sorcha sat back. "I figured you'd say something like that."

"I can't tell you about him, but I could tell you about myself." Morghen handed her a cup. "If you'd like to hear my tale."

"Yes, of course." Sorcha took the cup and let the heat seep into her tired hands.

Morghen took a sip of tea, then set her cup down. "I grew up in Wyndelas Palace. My father was an excellent healer, and since he was cousin to the king, he became the royal physician. My mother died when I was young, so I followed my father around, learning from him. My Embraced gift of being able to foresee things helped me to make correct diagnoses, and so I became a healer myself by the age of fifteen."

"When did you become a witch?" Sorcha asked.

"Later. After I came here." Morghen waved a dismissive hand. "But back to my youth at Wyndelas. Princess Jenetta was about eighteen years younger than I, but instead of playing with the other children, she followed me around and claimed she wanted to be a healer, too. She was a sweet child, eager to please. When she was seventeen, she fell madly in love with the Norveshki envoy and married him in secret. When the king learned that she was pregnant, he had the envoy executed and Jenetta locked up in the white tower. I was there to help her when she gave birth."

"You delivered Gwennore?" Sorcha asked.

"Yes." Morghen took another sip of tea. "Unfortunately, the king had some guards take the infant away. I learned later that he'd shipped the babe to the Isle of Moon. As you can imagine, Jenetta was inconsolable. She'd lost her husband, her baby, and her freedom. At first, I tried to visit her whenever I could, but the king limited me to only a few hours every month."

Morghen sighed. "There was no stopping the damage that was taking place. At times Jenetta would act completely normal, but there were other times when I knew that her mind had twisted into something horrible."

Sorcha leaned forward. "What did she do?"

"After seven years, there was a plague that swept through the palace. King Rendelf's eldest son, Prince Kendelas, became ill, along with his wife and two sons. Many courtiers were sick. My father and I were hard pressed to take care of everyone. Then my father fell ill and died."

"Oh, no," Sorcha breathed.

Morghen's eyes glistened with tears. "It was a difficult time. So many were dying, and I felt so alone, struggling to keep everyone alive. I was at the point of exhaustion when Jenetta asked to be released from the tower so she could help me. The king was so afraid of losing his eldest son and two grandsons that he readily agreed."

Sorcha had a bad feeling about what was coming next. She gulped down some tea.

"I was taking care of Prince Kendelas," Morghen continued. "I had isolated him in a hunting lodge in hopes that would help, and it did. He began to recover. His wife had elected to remain with their two sons in the palace. I thought Kendyl and Denys were recovering. But then, after Jenetta started helping me, they both died."

Sorcha winced. "How terrible."

"I know." Morghen sighed. "The boys' mother was so distraught, she gave up fighting the illness and died a few days later. The whole palace was in despair."

"And you believe Jenetta . . . but how could she? Those boys were her nephews!"

"Exactly." Morghen's face grew grim. "I didn't want to believe it, but when I checked the medicine she'd given them, I realized it was laced with poison. Jenetta discovered me with the vial she'd used and realized I knew what she'd done. She said she would tell everyone that I was the one who had poisoned them."

"Oh, no." Sorcha sat forward. "What did you do?"

"I went to King Rendelf's office so I could tell him the truth, but before I could get an audience with him, Jenetta told her brother that I had murdered his sons. Kendelas believed her and sent his guards to arrest me. I realized he would never believe me. How could he believe that his own sister had murdered his sons? And so, I ran."

"You escaped?" Sorcha asked.

Morghen nodded. "I knew where the secret tunnels were, so I fled from the palace. Eventually, I ended up here."

Sorcha exhaled as she sat back. "I'm glad you made it out of there alive."

"So am I." Morghen sipped some tea.

"But Prince Kendelas survived the plague. How can Jenetta be the heir?"

"Ah." Morghen refilled her cup. "That's when General Caladras comes into the story. King Rendelf had two sons: Kendelas and Brendelf. After Kendelas had two sons, Brendelf knew he was fourth in line to the throne and not likely ever to be king, so he left the palace and made a life for himself. He married a Wood Elf, and they had a son. They were very happy. But after Kendelas's sons were poisoned, I met with Brendelf and told him what Jenetta had done. He sent a letter to his brother, warning him to be careful."

Sorcha sipped some tea. "So how does General Caladras fit in?"

"Jenetta convinced him to work for her."

"Ah." Sorcha nodded. "That's why the general's son, Griffin, says that Gwennore was promised to him."

"Yes," Morghen agreed. "Jenetta used her long-lost daughter as bait to get Caladras to help her. While I was hiding at Drudaelen Castle, we began to hear terrible stories about how Norveshka had attacked Woodwyn villages, killing every elf in sight."

"What?" Sorcha sat back.

"I don't believe it was true, but Caladras used that excuse to counterattack and start a war with Norveshka. He knew, and Jenetta knew, that Rendelf would send his son to lead the army. And once Kendelas was there, it wasn't long before he fell in battle."

Sorcha frowned. "You mean Caladras . . . ?"

Morghen nodded. "Brendelf went to collect his brother's body and discovered Kendelas had been stabbed in the back. Caladras claimed the prince had turned to run away during battle, but of course, Brendelf didn't believe it."

"So the war with Norveshka was nothing more than a ruse to lure Kendelas to his death?"

"Yes." Morghen nodded. "I'm afraid so."

Sorcha scoffed. "But so many Norveshki soldiers died! I'm sure elfin soldiers died, too."

"Mostly Wood Elves." Morghen grimaced. "The River Elves have a nasty habit of not caring how many Wood Elves are killed."

"That must make the Wood Elves furious."

"It does." Morghen sipped her tea. "That is why the Woodsman has so many followers among the Wood Elves. But back to my story: Brendelf suddenly found himself heir to the throne. His father asked him to come back to Wyndelas Palace, but Brendelf refused. He knew not to trust Jenetta, and he didn't want her anywhere near his son."

"Of course not." Sorcha refilled her cup with tea.

"Unfortunately, Caladras continued to keep the war going with Norveshka. The king ordered Brendelf to take charge, so the prince moved to the army camp. His wife had died in childbirth years earlier, so he took his son with him. And he took his wife's brother to keep watch over the boy. Brendelf accused Caladras of murdering his brother, and a fight erupted. Caladras and several soldiers ganged up on Brendelf, killing him and his squire. The brother-in-law was wounded, but managed to escape with Brendelf's son."

Sorcha sat back, her thoughts swirling so fast she heard a buzzing in her ears. "How . . . how old was the son when he saw his father murdered?"

"Eleven."

Her breath caught. Oh dear goddesses, all the pieces fit so perfectly. The Woodsman had told her he'd lost his mother when he was five. His mother was Lord Daelen's sister, so she'd been a Wood Elf. He'd seen his father murdered when he was eleven. And his uncle, Lord Daelen, had been injured saving his life. Now he lived in hiding.

Morghen finished her cup of tea and set it on the table. "And so, the lost prince is actually the heir to the throne. But in order to keep him safe, his mother's family spread the rumor that he had been killed along with his father."

The lost prince. A shiver ran down Sorcha's back. "How . . . how old would he be now?"

"Oh, about twenty-six."

"And what is his name?"

"Brennan."

Brennan. She drew in a shaky breath. Of course, the lost prince would have the sacred sound at the beginning of his name. And of course, he would not be able to tell anyone his name. "Would I happen to know him?"

"Ah." Morghen rose to her feet. "That would be for him to say."

Sorcha closed her eyes briefly. Dammit. She'd asked the Woodsman if he had a legitimate claim to the throne, but he hadn't answered. She'd offered to get support for him from her brother and her adopted sisters, but he'd refused. Why hadn't he told her the truth? Did he not trust her?

Did he not love her?

Chapter 20

That evening, Princess Jenetta returned to Wyndelas Palace. After a long and tiring voyage by land, she and her six guards had finally reached the Wyn River the evening before. There, she'd boarded the royal barge and slept comfortably all night while the vessel had meandered slowly down the river. During the day, she'd rested and enjoyed her meals while sailors had worked the oars.

Finally, they tied off at the pier of the village of Wyndemere. High above the village, Wyndelas Palace sat on a granite cliff, its white marble stone reflecting the golden rays of the setting sun. It was not a long walk to the palace, but it was mostly uphill, so she took the royal open-air carriage while her guards walked alongside her. If any of the villagers neglected to bow as she passed by, she had one of her guards remind them.

We know what you did.

Murderer.

Slayer of children.

The voices of the forest swept down from the nearby mountains.

Hush, she hissed mentally at them. "Hurry!" she yelled at the coachman.

He snapped his whip at the horses, and soon the carriage rolled through the gate and into the courtyard. Courtiers stopped and bowed as she strode to her suite of rooms in the north wing.

In her workroom, she prepared another small bottle of the special concoction that would supposedly heal the gout her father was suffering from. Now that the king could barely walk and was confined to his bed, she intended to nurse him night and day until the poison finally took him. About a week, that was all the time she wanted to spare the old wart. Just enough time for him to officially declare her the heir and put it in writing.

For some reason, the old man kept delaying. The first few times she'd hinted that he should write his will, he'd brushed her off and changed the subject. The last time she'd brought it up, he'd actually told her to leave his room before he had a guard remove her!

Such disrespect. Recalling how he had snarled at her still made her blood boil. The bastard had locked her up for seven long years. He should be begging for her forgiveness, not treating her like a piece of trash stuck to the bottom of his boot.

She rammed a cork into the bottle of poisoned medicine. *Your time is almost up, you old bastard.* She'd make sure she was there when he took his last breath, so she could whisper in his ear that she'd finally gotten her revenge. The mighty and all-powerful King Rendelf sent to his grave by the daughter he had held in disdain.

On the way to the king's suite of rooms in the south wing, she passed through the Great Hall and nodded her head regally at the courtiers, who had to stop and bow as she passed by. In a week, she would be their queen, so she made mental notes on what to do with each of them. The Earl of Gonlyn had made a crude jest about her behind her back. He would be whipped and stripped of his lands. Lady Marlyn was too pretty. She'd be sent back home. Or, perhaps, whisked off to a nunnery.

Jenetta smiled to herself as she ascended the marble staircase to the south wing. Down the hall, she spotted four guards outside her father's bedchamber.

"Open the door," she ordered as she approached them. "I have brought more medicine for my father."

They all bowed, not as deeply as she would have liked, and then one answered, "My apologies, Your Highness, but His Majesty is in conference with his chief counsel and does not wish to be disturbed."

Jenetta scoffed. "If it is about official business, I have every right to be present." She waved an imperious hand at the guard. "Now do as I say and open the door."

"No, Your Highness."

Her back stiffened. "You dare to deny me? Do you realize the risk you take?"

He gave her a stony look. "I am following orders from my king. Leave your medicine with me, and I will pass it on to his majesty."

She huffed. "I will not tolerate such disrespect. I am the future queen!"

The guard's lip curled up. "So you say."

She blinked. Did this man know something? Was her father delaying the writing of his will because he planned to disown her? Did he know she'd been slowly poisoning him over the last six months?

No, surely not. She'd always added enough honey to disguise the sour taste of the poison. This guard was simply being rude. Disrespectful, like so many others.

The guard held out a hand. "The medicine."

She slapped the glass bottle into his hand, then glared at all four guards. "I will remember your faces, and you will regret this." She pivoted on her heel, then marched away.

As she crossed the Great Hall, she spotted courtiers whispering in the corners. Were they talking about her? She'd make them all pay.

When she reached her suite of rooms in the north wing,

her guards were chatting excitedly to each other. "Has something happened?"

"Yes, Your Highness," Durban answered. "One of the palace guards was found murdered in the woods."

Her eyes widened. That was a crime punishable by death. "Was he robbed?"

"No." Durban shook his head. "He had a gold necklace that was left untouched. But his uniform was taken."

"All of his clothes were taken," a second guard added. "The poor sod was left naked."

Jenetta tensed. Had someone taken the guard's uniform in order to infiltrate the palace?

"A message for you, Your Highness," said a voice behind her, and she whirled about to see a guard striding down the hallway.

"Who are you?" Durban asked, his eyes narrowed. "I've never seen you before."

"I'm new. Just hired this morning." He bowed to Jenetta, then removed a folded piece of paper from his breastplate. "Your Highness, I was told to deliver this in person and to wait for a reply."

The guard's white-blond hair indicated he was a River Elf, but Jenetta's gaze lingered on the man's eyes. They appeared to be the usual elfin eye color of lavender-blue, but there was an odd silver glint to them.

The Chameleon. She inhaled sharply. "Come." She opened the door to her chambers. Once he was inside, she closed the door and whispered, "If you try anything, I'll have my guards cut you to shreds."

With a smirk, the Chameleon motioned to an open window. "They'll never catch me. I'll fly away as an eagle."

She stayed close to the door in case she needed her guards. "Is that how you arrived here at the palace? Was it you who killed the guard?"

He shrugged. "Can I help it that once I shift back to

human form, I have no clothes? I asked the guard nicely to hand over his uniform, but he refused."

With a huff, she motioned to his clothes. "That was worth killing a man?"

"Have you heard the saying 'Dead men tell no tales'?" The Chameleon sauntered over to the worktable where she made her medicines. "All the business of the Circle of Five must be kept strictly secret—you know that."

She extended a hand toward him. "The report. Give it to me."

He gave her a wry look. "Do you think I was able to carry a report while in eagle form?" He tossed the sheet of paper on the floor. "This is a silly love letter the guard was carrying."

"Then say what you have come to say." She crossed her arms over her chest. "And be quick about it. I have things to do."

He picked up a bottle of dried verna leaves. "Like making medicines that kill instead of heal?"

She scoffed. "Is that any business of yours?"

He set the bottle down with a clunk. "The next time you disapprove of my killing someone, you should remember what you are doing, Your Highness."

His cold, raspy voice sent a shiver down her spine. "What do you want?"

"Nothing." He sauntered over to the window. "Everything. All of Aerthlan." He glanced back at her. "Lord Morris asked me to come here. He has been questioning the priests who work for him. None of them know who the Woodsman really is or where he is hiding."

She rolled her eyes. "So he has accomplished nothing."

The Chameleon smirked. "I disguised myself as a traveling peddler and talked to villagers in their local taverns. The minute I mentioned the Woodsman, they all clammed up. Either they know nothing, or they are all loyal followers intent on protecting him."

Jenetta frowned. "How many followers does the Woodsman have?"

"There's no way of knowing. But Lord Morris and I suspect there could be hundreds."

"To what end?" Jenetta stepped toward the Chameleon. "Do you think the Woodsman plans to do more than thievery?" Surely he didn't intend to interfere with her taking the throne.

"Since I couldn't discover anything at the taverns, I changed into a mouse and sneaked into a few cottages to listen to the villagers."

"What did they say?"

"That soon it would be time for the Woodsman to rise, and they were ready to join him."

She gasped. "We have to find this Woodsman fast! We have to crush him before he—"

"There is another matter even more serious," the Chameleon interrupted, his face growing harsh. "This morning, there were hundreds of notices discovered on the doors of village churches and taverns. They all said the same thing: You are not the heir to the throne."

Jenetta gasped. "What? Who? Who would dare—?"

"The notices claim the true heir is the king's grandson, the lost prince."

"No!" Jenetta shook her head. "That's not possible!"

"The notices urge the people to rise in support of the lost prince."

Her heart raced so fast, she struggled to breathe. "No. It can't be true." She clenched her fists and screamed. "Lies! It's all lies!"

"Are you sure?" The Chameleon stepped toward her, his eyes glinting with anger. "Could there actually be a lost prince? The king's second son, Brendelf, had a son, did he not?"

"Yes, but he's dead. General Caladras killed Brendelf and his son. He swore to it!"

The Chameleon narrowed his eyes. "And the first son, Kendelas—he had two sons—"

"They're dead," Jenetta hissed. "They caught the plague, along with their mother, and I nursed them here at the palace. I swear to you, none of them survived."

"And no one suspected you?"

"I wasn't the court physician at the time. The blame was put on her, but she escaped before she could be executed." Jenetta waved a dismissive hand. "My point is, there is no way that any of the male heirs survived. If any man claims to be one of Rendelf's grandsons, he is simply a pretender."

"You had better hope that is the case." The Chameleon gave her a wry look. "Otherwise, you might cease to be useful."

She gulped. "I'm telling you it's nonsense. Lies. It's probably some scheme being played by the Woodsman to cause trouble."

The Chameleon scoffed. "Has it not occurred to you that the Woodsman might be the lost prince?"

She gasped. "Tha-that's ridiculous!"

"If the people of Woodwyn believe it, it will not be ridiculous. I ask you once again, is it possible that the Woodsman could be the son of Brendelf?"

"No." She shook her head. "No, he couldn't."

"Who was Brendelf's wife?"

"A Wood Elf. The daughter of an earl of no importance. She died years ago."

"Where was she from?"

Jenetta frowned as she tried to recall. "I was young at the time, so I didn't pay much attention. I remember Father was not pleased with the match. He didn't want our bloodline mixed with the Wood Elves. But of course, Brendelf wasn't punished for it. Not like me, locked away for seven years for marrying a Norveshki."

"Where was she from?" the Chameleon repeated with gritted teeth.

"Somewhere north and west of here, close to the Haunted Woods."

The Chameleon stiffened. "Drudaelen Castle? Lord Daelen's estate?"

"Yes." She nodded. "That sounds right. Why?"

"The general recently stole food supplies from Drudaelen, the same food supplies that the Woodsman stole back. And when the general sent a search party to Drudaelen, no foodstuffs could be found. But the people there were clearly not starving."

"You think the Woodsman helped them out?"

"If he is Brendelf's son, then his mother is from Drudaelen, and he would be related to the current lord. He could be hiding close by. Perhaps in the Haunted Woods."

Jenetta swallowed hard. "He can't be Brendelf's son. The general swore that he killed him."

"I'll look into it." The Chameleon strode to the window as he removed his breastplate and shirt. "Keep these clothes here in case I need to return. Now I know which window to fly into." He shifted into an eagle, hopped out of the breeches that had fallen to the floor, then flew out the window.

Jenetta's knees gave out and she crumpled onto the floor. Could it be true? Had the general made a mistake and not killed Brendelf's son? She covered her mouth to stifle the cry that escaped. If the prince had survived, then she was no longer the true heir to the throne.

Oh, dear Light, no! Was that why the king had delayed naming her the heir? Was that why the guard had disrespected her? Were all her plans coming to naught?

We know what you did.

Murderer.

Slayer of innocent children.

Jenetta covered her ears and screamed.

Chapter 21

The next morning, Sorcha slept late again. She'd tossed and turned most of the night, putting together the puzzle pieces over and over in her mind until she was exhausted.

But she was also convinced that she was right. The Woodsman had to be the lost prince. Brennan, son of Brendelf, grandson of King Rendelf.

With a groan, she sat up. He should have told her. He should have trusted her. If he was half River Elf and his hair was actually white-blond, he should have told her that he matched the prediction of the Telling Stones. He shouldn't have left her wondering and struggling with an attraction that she had feared was a mistake.

A part of her wanted to be angry with him, but she was too damned worried for his safety. Why wouldn't he accept help from Silas or Leo or Rupert? The man was so aggravating!

Quickly, she washed herself and put on one of Bronwen's gowns. She bundled up the shifts she'd worn before to take to Morghen's house to launder them there. After dropping the clothes over the railing, she descended the ladder.

With the bundle in hand, she strode toward Morghen's cottage. A shadow passed over the ground, and she glanced up to see an eagle flying by. Brody? It landed on a branch of a nearby oak tree. No, it was too brown. Brody usually had black and white feathers with a white head. Still, this eagle reminded her that she didn't know how the Woodsman and Brody were faring.

She hurried to Morghen's cottage. "Good morning."

"Ah, there you are." Morghen was at the hearth, stirring something in a cauldron. She motioned to a nearby pot. "I kept some oatmeal warm for you."

"Thank you." Sorcha peeked into Aleksi's room. Empty. "Is he guarding the perimeter again?"

"Yes." Morghen smiled as she spooned some oatmeal into a wooden bowl. "But today, Hallie is keeping him company."

Sorcha snorted. "I doubt they'll get much guarding done."

Morghen nodded as she brought the bowl over to the table. "It's all right. The Living Oaks will tell me if any soldiers are headed our way."

"What do the oaks say about the Woodsman? Has he reached Colwyn yet?"

"He arrived at Whistlyn Castle last night. They rested a few hours, then set off to find Ronan." Morghen stiffened suddenly.

"What is it?" Sorcha asked, but Morghen lifted a hand to hush her. While Sorcha waited, she grew increasingly tense. Had the battle begun?

After a moment, Morghen lowered her hand, then gave Sorcha a worried look. "The Living Oaks have spoken. The Woodsman and his men are about to rescue Colwyn."

"Everyone understands the plan?" the Woodsman whispered.

After the Living Oaks had guided him to where Ronan was hiding, the young man had taken them straight to the clearing where Colwyn was being held prisoner.

On the way, Ronan had shared what he knew. "I've been hiding in nearby trees, watching the soldiers. They sent for a lord who's apparently important, though I don't know why.

He's not even an elf. He arrived last night, but insisted on sleeping before starting the torture. He said torturing people was exhausting, and he needed to be well rested."

"Sounds like a creepy bastard," Father Kit muttered.

Ronan nodded. "I think he just said that to make Colwyn stay up all night in fear."

"Aye," Liz agreed. "They want him exhausted and terrified."

During the long journey from Haven, the Woodsman had come up with a plan, so he explained it to the men in Elfish. Brody, the sneaky rascal, had admitted the day before that he actually understood Elfish.

Now, they were hiding behind some thick bushes, close to the clearing. Brody and Liz had stripped down to their small clothes. Between some leaves, the Woodsman spotted Colwyn. He was sitting against an elm tree with a rope bound around him several times. Bruises spotted his face, and blood oozed from a cut lip. One of his eyes was blackened and swollen shut.

There were ten soldiers, all Wood Elves—six standing around Colwyn while the other four busied themselves around a campfire. They'd obviously killed a few rabbits, for the meat was skewered and roasting over the fire.

A man wearing a hooded, velvet robe was sitting by the fire. He reached his hands out to warm them, and the firelight glittered off his numerous jeweled rings. This had to be the lord Ronan had talked about.

A soldier picked up a bucket and splashed some water onto Colwyn's face. "Don't fall asleep on us, asshole. Why were you leading the army on a wild-goose chase?"

"There was no chase," Colwyn replied wearily. "I told you. I'm the Earl of Whistlyn's son. I live nearby in Whistlyn Castle. I was going into the bog to hunt pheasant. All you have to do is ask my father, and he will verify—"

The soldier slapped him.

"Enough." The man in the hooded, velvet robe rose to his feet. "The man's story has not changed since I arrived."

"Because it's the truth," Colwyn growled.

"No. Because you haven't been properly motivated." The man removed his robe, revealing the black robes of a priest.

Hunched beside the Woodsman, Brody stiffened. "Lord Morris," he whispered.

From the Circle of Five? The Woodsman took a deep breath and noticed that Father Kit was turning red with anger.

Lord Morris picked up a spear, then held the metal tip in the fire.

One of the soldiers snickered. "That's going to hurt."

The priest nodded. "If the boy is wise, he will tell us what he knows of the Woodsman." He pulled a sheet of paper from his robe. "And you will tell us what you know of this!" He tossed the paper at Colwyn.

It was one of the notices that had been posted, the Woodsman realized. Colwyn would know nothing about them.

Lord Morris stabbed the red-hot spearhead into the notice, and it burned to ash. "What do you know of the lost prince?"

Colwyn lifted his chin. "Never heard of him."

Lord Morris pointed the spear at him and took a step forward. "You have only a few seconds to change your mind."

"Now," the Woodsman whispered.

Brody changed into a dog and dashed into the clearing. Barking, he ran around the campfire.

As expected, all the soldiers turned to look at their canine invader. Liz took on the colors of the forest, becoming invisible, and with a knife in hand, he darted to a position behind the tree where Colwyn was tied. While he sawed through the ropes, Brody snapped his jaws around the skewer and pulled the roasting rabbits into the fire.

"What are you doing?" a soldier shouted as he ran after Brody.

"Save our dinner!" Lord Morris ordered, and a few soldiers tried to fish the rabbits out of the fire.

Brody scampered about while the other soldiers chased after him. He jumped at one man, put his front paws on the man's shoulders, and licked his face.

"He's yours?" one of the soldiers yelled. "Why did you bring your dog here?"

"I've never seen him before!" The soldier pushed Brody aside.

Brody dashed off, making the soldiers run in circles.

Meanwhile, the Woodsman stood and aimed an arrow launcher at the sky. *Zing.* Five arrows shot up. And since they were made of wood, the Woodsman controlled where each one of them landed. *Thud.* Each arrow pierced a soldier in the thigh. All five men collapsed in pain.

"We're under attack!" Lord Morris cried, and the five remaining soldiers drew their swords.

Ronan handed the Woodsman the second arrow launcher, fully loaded. *Zing.* Five more arrows and the last five soldiers fell to the ground, wounded.

Liz ran into the clearing to collect the swords, but since he was invisible, it looked like the swords were rising by themselves.

"Witchcraft! Sorcery!" The wounded soldiers cowered on the ground in fear.

"You fools!" Lord Morris yelled at them. He reached down to pick up a fallen sword, but Father Kit ran into the clearing and kicked it out of the lord's hand.

"So you're Lord Morris," Father Kit growled. "Murderer of Embraced children."

Liz dropped his pile of swords as he took on human form. "This is the priest who wanted to kill me and Hallie?"

"Aye." Father Kit drew his sword and pointed it at Lord Morris. "He's the one."

Liz picked up a sword. "How many Embraced babies has he killed?"

Now free from his bindings, Colwyn scrambled to his feet and picked up the spear that Lord Morris had threatened to use on him. "The tables have turned, priest."

Lord Morris stumbled back as Colwyn, Father Kit, and Liz all advanced toward him. "Soldiers, attack these men!"

A few of the soldiers attempted to stand and limp toward Lord Morris.

"Stand down," the Woodsman ordered as he strode into the clearing. "If you attempt to help Lord Morris, the next arrow I shoot will go straight through your heart."

"Who—?" Lord Morris retreated, glancing wildly about as all the soldiers collapsed on the ground in surrender. "Who are you?" His back bumped into a tree.

With a flick of his hand, the Woodsman moved the tree's branches. They wrapped themselves around the priest, pinning him to the tree.

"The Woodsman," the soldiers whispered.

"I am Brennan, son of Brendelf, grandson of King Rendelf. The rightful heir to the throne." He looked the soldiers over. "I spared your lives because you are my countrymen. If you wish to be on the side of righteousness, you will follow me. I'll take you to Whistlyn Castle, where your wounds will be tended. Then you will join my army there."

The soldiers bowed their heads. "Yes, Your Highness."

"You fools!" Lord Morris yelled. "He's given you no proof of who he is!"

"He's a Wood Elf like us," one of the soldiers mumbled.

"I am half Wood Elf," the Woodsman clarified. "But I have lived among the Wood Elves all my life. I give you my word, there will be no more discrimination. No more useless wars where the Wood Elves are treated as if they were expendable."

The soldiers exchanged excited looks.

"Fools," Lord Morris growled as he struggled against the branches that held him tight. "Traitors."

Brody shifted into human form and, grabbing a sword, he advanced on Lord Morris. "It's your turn to talk, Morris. Who are the last two members of the Circle of Five?"

"Ah." Morris sneered at him. "So you're the dog who keeps running about like an errand boy."

Brody swung the sword, stopping the blade right at Morris's throat.

Morris gulped. "I have nothing against you, shifter."

"Yes, you do." Father Kit stepped closer. "He's Embraced, and you hate all the Embraced. You were the one who ordered me to turn over this boy to you."

"And my sister," Liz growled.

"Ah." Lord Morris nodded. "You're the silly fool who ran off to Woodwyn with the Embraced twins."

"He kept us alive!" Liz shouted. "You were going to kill us!"

"Idiot!" Morris hissed at Liz. "You really think I was killing all the Embraced babies? When this fool ran off with you, he denied you the chance of being in the greatest army ever to exist on Aerthlan!"

"Army?" Brody asked.

"Yes." Morris smirked. "Why would I kill children with supernatural powers when I can use them to take over the world?"

"The children are alive?" Father Kit jabbed the point of his sword against Morris's chest. "Where? What have you done with them?"

"They've been trained to do whatever the Circle of Five orders them to do." Morris's mouth twisted with a smirk. "Imagine. An army where every soldier has a magical power."

"Why should we believe you?" the Woodsman demanded. "If you have such an army, why haven't you used it?"

"They're young." Morris glanced at Liz. "The oldest are about his age. They're almost ready." He laughed. "You think you are undefeatable because a few of you are Embraced. You will be no match for an entire army."

"Where are they?" Brody demanded.

Morris snorted. "As if I would tell you."

Brody glanced at the Woodsman. "I don't think they could be in Eberon, Tourin, or Norveshka. Those kings would know about it. Could they be in Woodwyn? Perhaps to the south?"

The Woodsman shook his head. "The Living Oaks would have told me." He glared at Lord Morris. "We'll take him to Whistlyn Castle. After a few days of starvation in the dungeon, he'll be ready to talk."

Morris's face turned pale.

"Oh, so you've lost your smirk now," Colwyn taunted him. "After my father sees how you treated me, he'll be eager to return the favor."

Morris gulped. "I—my rings are worth a fortune. Take them and let me go."

"Not happening," the Woodsman replied.

Morris took a few deep breaths, then grew still. "I have a map that will show you where the Embraced army is located. Release my arms and I will show it to you."

"Just tell us," Brody growled.

"I-I need my hands free," Morris insisted. "I can't get to the map the way you have me tied up."

"Watch him." The Woodsman loosened the branches around the priest while the other men held their weapons pointed at him.

Morris reached inside his robe and fumbled about. "May the Light be with me," he whispered, then quickly withdrew a vial and put it up to his mouth.

"Stop him!" the Woodsman yelled, and Brody knocked the vial from Morris's hand.

Morris licked his lips, trying to ingest what poison he could. When he smiled, blood was coating his teeth. "You'll never find the army. But they will find you, and then, you will all die." He coughed, and more blood oozed out. His body suddenly spasmed, then he fell forward, hanging over the branches that were loosely wrapped around him.

"Damn," Colwyn muttered.

Brody dropped his sword and pressed a hand against Morris's neck to check for a pulse. "He's gone. Now it's a circle of four."

"An army of Embraced children." Father Kit shook his head, frowning. "Stolen babies raised to become killers? If the man wasn't already dead, I'd kill him myself."

"I'll check into it." Brody glanced up at the sky. "Tonight the moons will be full. I'll miss seeing her, but it can't be helped. I need answers."

"Seeing whom?" the Woodsman asked.

Brody stepped back. "Good luck to you, Woodsman. Be good to Sorcha." He shifted into an eagle and flew off.

The shifter was a secretive fellow. The Woodsman took a deep breath. "We'll take these soldiers to Whistlyn Castle and ready the army there. In the morning, we march to Wyndelas Palace. Once we're there, the king will announce I am his heir."

Chapter 22

The next morning, Sorcha hurried to Morghen's house to hear if the Living Oaks had said anything new about the Woodsman. The day before, Morghen had told everyone about the success of Colwyn's rescue, and the entire village had spent the rest of the day celebrating. Sorcha also learned that one of the Circle of Five, Lord Morris, had died.

"Any news?" she asked as she entered Morghen's house. "Are they on their way back to Haven?"

Standing by the hearth, Morghen poured two cups of tea. "I'm afraid it will be a while before you see him again."

"Why?" Sorcha grew tense. "Has something happened to him? Was he injured?"

"He's fine." Morghen motioned to one of the comfy chairs. "Come and relax by the fire."

"Tell me." Sorcha strode toward her. "I'm worried sick as it is. I have to know what's happening."

Morghen took a seat. "The Earl of Whistlyn has gathered a small army in support of the lost prince. The Woodsman is leading the army to Wyndelas Pal—"

"Because he is the lost prince," Sorcha finished for her. "Are you telling me the rebellion has begun?"

Morghen nodded. "Yes."

Sorcha's chest tightened as panic threatened to engulf her. "Why does he need an army? He told me the takeover would be peaceful. He said there would be no danger."

"There is always danger. The army is for his protection. You must know that Jenetta and General Caladras will be trying to kill him."

Sorcha's knees buckled and she collapsed in the chair. Oh goddesses, she was so afraid. "I have—I have to do something." She jumped to her feet. "Aleksi! He could send a message to my brother. Silas could fly here. And Dimitri."

Morghen stood. "Aleksi went to the stables to feed the horses."

"I'm going!" Sorcha ran out the door. At least now, she had a plan. A pang shot through her heart as she recalled the Woodsman's words: *It is imperative to always have a plan.*

"Please be safe, Woodsman," she whispered as she strode to the stables. *Please be safe, Brennan.*

It was almost noon when a sudden loud banging on Princess Jenetta's door startled her and made her spill a drop of wine onto her blue velvet gown. "Damn." She used a lace handkerchief to dab at her bodice.

"Your Highness!" Durban shouted.

"What on Aerthlan could be so important?" she muttered as she wandered to the door. "This had better be good," she yelled at her head guard as she opened the door.

"Your Highness." Durban and her other guards executed a quick bow. "The news has just arrived. The Earl of Whistlyn's army is marching this way!"

"What?" Jenetta scoffed. "Has the fool gone mad? General Caladras will destroy him."

"Caladras and his army are still by the Norveshki border. They won't be able to catch Whistlyn's army before it arrives here." Durban exchanged a worried look with his fellow guards. "And there's more. The king's scouts have reported that the lost prince is leading the army."

Jenetta stumbled back a step. "No. That can't be."

"It's Prince Brennan. At every village he goes through, the people are cheering for him!"

"No!" Jenetta shook her head. "He's a pretender. It's that damned Woodsman." She rubbed her brow. "Go. Go see if you can find out when they are expected to arrive."

"Yes, Your Highness." Durban sent one of the guards.

"Stay vigilant," Jenetta ordered. "Guard me with your lives."

"Yes, Your Highness," Durban replied, and they all bowed.

She slammed the door shut and shot the bolt. The lost prince! She paced across the floor. Could it be true? Had Prince Brennan survived?

"That damned Caladras!" she hissed. Had he lied to her? Had the fool made a mistake?

What should she do? She paced toward the window and looked out at the forested mountains. How long would it take before the lost prince arrived? Was the king going to acknowledge him as the heir?

We know what you did.

Murderer.

Slayer of innocent children.

"Shut up!" she screamed, then turned away from the window. Yes, murderer. That was what she needed to do. The king had to die before Prince Brennan arrived.

She grabbed a vial of poison from her worktable and slipped it up her sleeve. Just as she strode toward the door, an eagle shot into her room.

The Chameleon! She grabbed the uniform he'd left and tossed it to him as he changed into the guise of a River Elf. "Did you hear what's happening? The lost prince has an army and he's headed this way!"

"Yes, we know. He killed Lord Morris yesterday." The Chameleon turned his back to her as he pulled on a pair of breeches. "He must have sold off the priest's jewelry, for he's tossing coins to the villagers as he passes by."

Jenetta scoffed. "No wonder they're cheering for him. So do you have news? It had better be good."

"It is good." He turned to face her. "I have discovered the Woodsman's hideout."

"What good is that?" Jenetta screeched. "He's not there! He's pretending to be Prince Brennan, and he's coming here!"

"Not for long." The Chameleon smirked. "I just came from General Caladras. He's taking the army to attack Drudaelen Castle and Haven. Once the Woodsman realizes his family and friends are in danger, he will hurry home."

Jenetta took a deep breath. "That is good. Caladras can defeat him there. I want the Woodsman dead! Kill him and all of his followers!"

The Chameleon nodded. "Of course. But Caladras wants to make sure you do your part, too. The king cannot be allowed to name Prince Brennan his heir."

"I know that." Jenetta lifted her chin. "I don't need you telling me what to do. I'm taking care of the problem today."

The silver glint in the Chameleon's eyes sparkled. "See that you do." He changed back into an eagle, hopped out of the breeches, and flew out the window.

Jenetta took a deep breath and steeled her nerves.

Murderer.

Slayer of innocent children.

Watch me, she hissed mentally at the trees while she slid the bolt free. She opened the door and told her five remaining guards, "Follow me."

When she reached the king's quarters in the south wing, she glared at his two guards. "Open the door. I wish to see the king."

"He is resting and doesn't wish to be disturbed," one of the guards replied.

She glanced at Durban. "Make sure I get in."

"Yes, Your Highness." Durban drew a sword, and his guards jumped the two personal guards of the king.

"What the hell?" the king's guard shouted as he was pinned against the wall. "This is treason!"

"Not for long." Jenetta strode into the room and shut the door behind her.

The king looked up from his desk, and his eyes widened. "What are you doing here?"

"What are *you* doing?" Jenetta walked toward him. "I thought you would be in bed resting."

"I'm feeling better these days." He quickly gathered the papers on his desk and shoved them into a drawer. "Guards! Remove her!"

"Your guards will not be coming." Jenetta came to a stop in front of his desk. He *was* looking better than he had a month ago. Damn him. His eyes were sharper, his skin clearer and less gray, and his silver-white hair gleamed in the light of the candles on his desk.

He locked the drawer. "I will ask you to leave."

"No."

He scoffed. "Why? Do you expect me take more of your poison?"

Her breath caught.

Her father rose to his feet. "I didn't want to believe it. I wanted to trust you."

"Then you never should have locked me up for seven years! Or killed my husband. Or taken my baby away—"

"I regretted it!" Tears glimmered in her father's eyes. "But in the end, you proved that I was right, that you could never be trusted." He walked over to a screen and pulled it aside.

"You see this?" He motioned to a large potted plant that was brown, withered and dying. "When I first received the letters that claimed you were a murderer, that you had poisoned my grandsons and were most probably poisoning me, I didn't believe it. How could you do something so heinous to your own family! But Nolen, my chief counsel, convinced me that I should check the medicine you'd been giving me. And so, I started watering this plant with it."

"No." Jenetta shook her head. "Any medicine for a human would have a bad effect on a plant. You can't call that proof."

He fisted his hands. "You are a monster. I never should have let you out of your cage."

"You did this to me!" she screamed. "It was your fault! You've always hated me!"

"You fool! If I hated you, I would have had you executed weeks ago!" He strode toward the door. "But it's not too late to take care of that now."

He was going to have her killed? Jenetta grabbed a candlestick off his desk and ran after him. With a vicious swing, she clobbered him on the back of his head.

He crumpled to the floor, blood seeping from the wound. Reaching a hand toward her, he groaned.

He was still alive. She looked frantically about. After setting the candlestick back on the desk, she grabbed a pillow off his bed, then kneeled beside him. "I've had to wait too long for you die. I will be queen, and I will dance on your grave."

When he moaned again, she placed the pillow over his face and pressed down. He struggled but was too weak to stop her. Soon, he was still.

She waited a moment longer while her heart thundered in her ears. She'd done it.

He was dead.

And she was finally free.

She dug through his pocket for his keyring, then hurried to his desk to unlock the drawer. She fumbled through the papers. All letters—some from the Earl of Whistlyn, others from Lord Daelen, claiming that Prince Brennan was alive and well. There was even an old letter on yellowing parchment that Prince Brendelf had written before he died. It was folded up in a letter from Lord Daelen, sent to the king three weeks ago. In the letter, her late brother explained how she and Caladras had murdered Prince Kendelas and his sons.

"Whistlyn. Daelen," she muttered. "I'll make you pay for this." She gathered up the letters and threw them in the fire.

Shouts outside made her jump. She took a deep breath and walked toward the door. Nolen, the king's chief counsel, was insisting that he be let inside.

She pinched herself hard till there were tears in her eyes, then flung the door open. "Help! The king fell down and injured his head!" She ran into the hallway. "Guards, fetch the physician. Hurry!"

Nolen dashed into the room. "Your Majesty!"

"Do you think he'll be all right?" Jenetta asked from the doorway.

The chief counsel looked around the room, his gaze pausing on the bloody candlestick holder on the desk and the open drawer. He ran to the desk to peer inside the drawer, then looked at Jenetta. "What have you done? You murdering bitch!"

"Guards! Arrest him!" Jenetta lifted her chin. "I am the queen now, and anyone who speaks ill of me will die!"

We know what you did.

Murderer.

Slayer of innocent—

He wasn't innocent! Jenetta hissed at the trees. *He got what he deserved.*

Then you killed him? Your own father?

So what if I did? She clenched her fists. *Leave me alone, or I will destroy you, too.*

Chapter 23

The sun was high in the sky. Almost noon, the Woodsman thought. He'd been traveling with Whistlyn's army since dawn. The men would need a break soon and a light meal. He didn't dare stop for very long, though.

Soon, he would meet his grandfather for the first time and be formally acknowledged as the heir. All the years of hiding would finally come to an end. It had been fifteen years since he'd even used his real name.

Woodsman.

The Living Oaks interrupted his thoughts. *Yes?*

The king is dead.

What? He reined in his horse. *Are you sure?*

Beside him, Lord Whistlyn raised a hand to halt the army. "What is it?"

"It must be news from the Living Oaks." Father Kit maneuvered his horse next to the Woodsman. "What's going on?"

King Rendelf is dead.

Murdered.

Princess Jenetta killed him.

The Woodsman inhaled sharply. *She killed her own father?*

Yes. She admitted it to us.

The Woodsman clenched his reins tight. That murdering bitch! Did she have to kill everyone in his family?

"Your Highness, what's wrong?" Lord Whistlyn leaned closer. "Do you need to rest?"

"No." He rubbed his brow. "The king is dead."

"What?" Whistlyn sat back.

"Jenetta killed him."

"Damn," Liz whispered.

"She killed her own father?" Colwyn yelled.

"Are you sure of this?" Whistlyn asked.

The Woodsman nodded. "The trees don't lie. The king is dead." And he would never meet his grandfather.

"Ah, Rendelf." Whistlyn slumped in his saddle, shaking his head. "My old friend."

Whispers filled the air as the news spread down the ranks of the army.

"Bloody hell," Father Kit grumbled. "Then the king can't name you his heir. The plan has fallen apart."

"What do we do?" Colwyn asked. "Will we have to attack Wyndelas Palace?"

"No." Whistlyn sat up. "All is not lost, Your Majesty."

The Woodsman flinched inwardly. Dammit, he'd barely gotten used to being called "your highness." But now, he had a new title. He was king.

"There are several letters that prove your identity," Whistlyn continued. "Our man in the palace was Rendelf's chief counsel. Nolen will have kept the letters safe."

"Unless Jenetta finds them," Father Kit grumbled. "Then she'll destroy them for sure."

"You still have witnesses," Whistlyn insisted. "Lord Daelen and myself. We were close friends to Prince Brendelf. And we've known you, Your Majesty, since you were born."

"Every Wood Elf wants you to be king," Colwyn added. "Most of the River Elves will, too. No one likes the princess."

The Woodsman nodded. "We have three hundred men. There are only a hundred soldiers guarding Wyndelas. Most of the soldiers are up north with Caladras. We can reach

Wyndelas before the general does. We'll convince them to accept me. By the time Caladras arrives, we will—"

Woodsman!

What is it now? he asked the Living Oaks.

Caladras and his army are marching to Drudaelen.

The Woodsman stiffened. *Are you sure?*

He will reach the castle some time tonight.

"What is it?" Father Kit asked.

"We have to go to Drudaelen." The Woodsman pulled his horse's reins and headed west at a fast trot. "This way!"

"What?" Whistlyn spurred his horse forward to catch up with him. "Why?"

"Caladras is taking his army there," the Woodsman shouted as he urged his horse into a gallop. "He has eight hundred men. Lord Daelen has only a hundred and fifty."

"And we have three." Father Kit rode beside him. "Even if we make it in time, we will still be outnumbered. Almost two to one!"

"It's a trap!" Whistlyn shouted. "Caladras is trying to lure you in so he can kill you! You should still go to Wyndelas first and establish yourself as king."

"And sacrifice everyone in Drudaelen?" the Woodsman yelled back. "My own family and friends? What kind of king would I be if I ignored the people I am sworn to protect?"

Whistlyn sighed. "You're right. I just hate being manipulated."

"We'll work this to our advantage. Once Caladras has been defeated, there will be no one to stop us." *Jenetta could be a problem, but she didn't have an armed force or very much support.* The Woodsman held up a hand and shouted, "To Drudaelen! We fight!"

The soldiers behind him gave a cheer.

As he charged across the countryside, the Woodsman sent up a prayer that his family there would be safe. At least Sorcha was safe in Haven. *Living Oaks, please pass a message on to Morghen. Tell her that Sorcha must stay in Haven where she will be safe.*

We will, the oaks replied. *Good luck to you, Woodsman.*

He urged his horse to go faster. Soon, he would be able to avenge his father. After fifteen years, he would finally kill Caladras with his own hands.

Sorcha was in Morghen's house, eating lunch with her and Hallie, when Morghen suddenly jumped to her feet, her bowl of soup clattering onto the floor.

"The army is marching on Drudaelen Castle!"

With a gasp, Sorcha scrambled to her feet. "Th-the entire army?"

"Yes!" Morghen dashed to the front door.

"But Caladras has hundreds of men." Sorcha followed her.

"Eight hundred," Hallie said as she ran beside her.

Morghen reached the bell close to the front gate and began clanging it.

As the villagers came running, Sorcha yelled over the noise of the bell, "How many soldiers does Lord Daelen have?"

"A hundred and fifty." Morghen dropped the rope and held up her hand for quiet. "The oaks have more to say."

While Morghen listened, the villagers began to arrive, shouting and demanding answers.

"Quiet!" Sorcha cried. "Morghen has to hear the trees." She spotted Aleksi running from the farthest boundary of Haven. Was he well enough to shift into a dragon?

"All right." Morghen stepped up onto a stone so everyone could see her. "The Living Oaks have told me that the army is on its way to attack Drudaelen Castle."

Shouts and cries spread among the villagers.

"Listen to me!" Morghen lifted her hands. "Someone must go immediately to warn Lord Daelen so he can prepare for battle. And he'll want to evacuate the women and children and send them here."

"I'll go!" Ronan's father, Dylan, raised his hand.

"Me, too!" Colwyn's uncle, Hadyn, turned to face the crowd. "If Drudaelen falls, we could be next! Every man here should help them fight. Who is with me?"

Most of the men raised their hands.

"No!" Lauren grabbed hold of her husband's arm. "Fighting would be suicidal. The army is too big!"

"We must go," Hadyn told her.

"It is not as hopeless as it seems," Morghen declared. "The Woodsman is with Lord Whistlyn's army. They are coming as quickly as they can."

Sorcha gulped. The Woodsman was going to battle?

"They will still be terribly outnumbered," Lauren whined.

"Oh, my poor Colwyn!" Tara screeched. "Are they all going to die?"

"Hush!" Morghen yelled. "The Woodsman will have a plan. He will not let Caladras defeat him."

"That's right!" Dylan shouted. "The Woodsman has never let us down. We should fight!"

The men cheered.

"Who will be here to guard us?" Teresa cried, holding her daughter tight while Tara whimpered.

"We're not helpless!" Sorcha shouted. "We can protect ourselves. For now, the Woodsman and Lord Daelen need all the help we can give them."

"Exactly." Morghen gave Sorcha an approving nod. "Men, prepare yourselves to go. The rest of you, you know the defense plan. We can do it by ourselves if we have to."

As the men ran off to gather their weapons, Sorcha grabbed Aleksi by the sleeve. "Are you able to shift?"

"I can, but I'm not sure if I can fly."

"Can you ask Silas to come? And Dimitri?"

Aleksi frowned. "This is not their battle."

"It is *my* battle. My future lies with the Woodsman. He's Prince Brennan, the rightful heir to the throne."

Aleksi's eyes widened. "Why didn't you tell me this?"

"Because I haven't seen you. You're either gone, guarding the perimeter, or you're off somewhere with Hallie."

Aleksi ducked his head. "I-I had to apologize."

Sorcha snorted. "I'm sure you did. Numerous times."

Aleksi blushed.

"The Living Oaks had more to tell me," Morghen said as she approached them. "The Woodsman has sent a message for you, Sorcha. He insists you stay here where you will be safe."

Her shoulders slumped. "That's it?" The man could die in battle soon and he wouldn't tell her if he loved her?

"There is more," Morghen admitted.

"Ah, good." Sorcha perked up.

"King Rendelf is dead," Morghen announced.

Sorcha blinked. "What?"

"The Woodsman is in even more danger now," Morghen added. "Caladras and Jenetta know who he is, and they'll be determined to stop him."

By killing him. Sorcha groaned. "Aleksi, please ask Silas to help him."

"All right." He nodded. "I will."

She clenched her hands together. Dammit, she hated doing nothing while the man she loved was in deadly peril. "There has to be something I can do, or I will go mad."

"There is something," Morghen told her. "As soon as the men reach Drudaelen, Lord Daelen will send the women and children here. I will need your help teaching them our defense plan."

Sorcha frowned. "Do you think we could be in danger here?"

Morghen sighed. "I don't know, but we should be prepared for the worst, don't you think?"

Sorcha nodded. "If the army comes, we'll be ready for them."

* * *

By mid-morning the next day, the Woodsman arrived at Drudaelen with the cavalry. They'd ridden hard all night and were exhausted, but when they saw the castle was already under attack, they rallied what energy they had left.

They stopped on a ridge overlooking the valley. The castle was on the other side, perched on a higher ridge. It was an excellent position for defense, so even though Caladras had a much greater force, he was not making any headway.

Up on the battlements of Drudaelen, the archers were using the arrow launchers the Woodsman had designed, shooting five arrows at once. Caladras's front line was having trouble advancing to the wall. His men were falling, while Lord Daelen's men remained safe behind the stone ramparts.

"What is the plan?" Lord Whistlyn asked.

"First we let our horses rest." The Woodsman dismounted and led his horse back a few yards to a grassy clearing in the forest.

"We're doing nothing?" Colwyn asked as he dismounted. "Why don't we attack from the rear?"

"There are only fifty of us." Father Kit led his horse to the clearing. "We need to wait for the foot soldiers to catch up."

"But we rushed here to help," Colwyn grumbled.

"We will help." The Woodsman pivoted in a circle, so he could see all the cavalrymen who were standing next to their horses. Among them were Liz, Father Kit, Ronan, Colwyn, and Colwyn's father, Lord Whistlyn. "Once I start using my powers, Caladras will realize I'm here. He'll send troops to attack us. Hide behind the line of trees along the ridge and have your arrows nocked and ready."

"Aye, Your Majesty." The men grabbed their weapons and headed back to the ridge.

The Woodsman laid a hand on Father Kit's shoulder. "You

and Liz have been riding for days. Stay here to watch the horses and get some rest."

His old friend frowned at him. "You haven't had much sleep, either."

"I'll be fine." The Woodsman headed back to the ridge. Not much had changed at Drudaelen. Caladras was clearly getting frustrated, for he was sending men with ladders to approach the outer wall, but the men were getting shot down, five at a time.

Lord Whistlyn snorted. "By the time our foot soldiers arrive, Caladras's army will be down to seven hundred."

Two groups with ladders made it to the wall by holding their metal shields over their heads. They planted the ladders against the outer curtain wall. But as the soldiers began to climb, they were picked off with arrows.

Four more ladders were successfully lodged against the wall, and while the archers busied themselves shooting at the climbers, Caladras's front line began to advance.

The Woodsman spotted Caladras and his son, Griffin. They were at the back, readying a trebuchet. With it, they could possibly knock a hole in the castle wall.

"It's time," the Woodsman warned his men. "Be ready." He stepped out onto the ridge, and, with a slice of his hand, he broke all the wooden ladders. The men who were climbing fell, some of them landing on the spears of their comrades below.

The front line had readied their bows and arrows, and with one swipe, the Woodsman broke all their bows. Then he snapped the trebuchet in two.

Chaos ensued for a few minutes on the battlefield until Caladras managed to rally the men. The Woodsman saw Griffin pointing at him and shouting. He gave them a friendly wave, then ducked behind a tree. Soon a troop of horsemen was racing toward them.

"Wait for it," the Woodsman warned his men.

They remained hidden behind the trees. The Woodsman quickly nocked five arrows in his arrow launcher, while Ronan readied the second one for him.

Once the horsemen were close enough, the Woodsman yelled, "Now!"

A barrage of arrows took out most of the troop. The Woodsman shot his weapon, then using his powers, he made sure his arrows landed in five of the surviving men. Ronan handed him the second arrow launcher, and with that he eliminated the last of the troop.

Caladras retaliated by sending three troops to attack them. Most were killed with arrows, but a few men managed to make it to the ridge with their swords drawn. There, they found themselves outnumbered and were quickly cut down.

On and on the cycle repeated. The Woodsman was either shooting arrows or breaking ladders and weapons that Caladras's army was using.

"We're running out of arrows!" Colwyn yelled.

"Then we fight with swords," his father shouted.

His men were growing tired, the Woodsman realized. He could hear the weariness in their voices. They'd ridden all day and night to get here.

He winced when he saw what had to be five troops charging toward them. A hundred men. This time, he and his men would be outnumbered two to one.

Suddenly, a burst of fire shot down from the sky, and he glanced up. A dragon! Was it Aleksi? No, there were three of them!

The dragons made a trail of fire between the oncoming troops and the ridge where the Woodsman and his men were located. Then they flew toward the castle and breathed fire on the front line that was attacking the outer wall.

Caladras's men fell back and found themselves sandwiched between the two trails of fire.

Father Kit ran up to the Woodsman. "The foot soldiers are here!"

"Everyone, gather around!" the Woodsman yelled, and his cavalrymen surrounded him. "We mount up. I'll take half the army. Lord Whistlyn, you take the other half. We will skirt around the fire and attack Caladras from both sides. Understand?"

Liz grinned. "The Woodsman always has a plan."

They mounted up and soon they were descending the ridge through the forest and coming up on Caladras's army from each side.

"We fight!" The Woodsman drew his sword and charged forward. The earl attacked from the other side.

Caught by surprise, Caladras's men were mowed down with slashing swords and stabbing spears. The dragons circled overhead, watching.

A horn sounded in Drudaelen Castle; then the gate opened and the castle troops rode out, led by Lord Daelen. They charged across the burnt grass, headed for Caladras's army. They collided with the enemy in the center, close to the general and his son.

As the Woodsman slashed his way toward Caladras, he realized his uncle would reach the bastard first. Lord Daelen was still a formidable warrior on horseback, and he was cutting a path straight for the general. No doubt he also wanted to avenge his dear friend and brother-in-law, Prince Brendelf.

The Woodsman fought more viciously in an attempt to beat his uncle to their prey. But as soldiers fell around him, he grew increasingly sick of it. These were elves, his own countrymen.

"Caladras!" Lord Daelen bellowed as he drew near to the general. Their swords clashed.

Lord Daelen succeeded in cutting the general's arm. In a desperate and cowardly move, Caladras stabbed Daelen's horse, causing it to fall and Daelen to tumble to the ground.

The Woodsman winced. With his uncle's bad leg, he would have trouble fighting on foot. He charged toward his uncle.

While Daelen struggled to stand, the general lifted his sword overhead, ready to make a killing blow. But as the sword came down, Daelen rolled to the side and pierced the general with an upward thrust into his gut.

Caladras's sword slipped from his hands as he collapsed to his knees.

"For Prince Brendelf!" Daelen shouted as he swiped his sword across the general's neck. Blood gushed out.

Yes! The Woodsman enjoyed a sudden spurt of satisfaction, but then he saw Griffin coming up behind his uncle. "No!"

Griffin roared as he plunged his sword through the back of Lord Daelen's neck. He spotted the Woodsman coming at him and jumped on his horse. With a group of soldiers, they dashed for the forest.

"Coward!" the Woodsman shouted at him, then slid off his horse to kneel beside Lord Daelen. "Uncle!"

It was too late. He was gone. With a groan, the Woodsman leaned over the man who had been a father to him since the age of eleven. The man who had saved his life and spent the last fifteen years training him for the day he would take the crown.

"Woodsman!" Father Kit yelled as he deflected a blow that would have wounded him while he kneeled. "Come to your senses!"

The Woodsman rose to his feet. He'd had enough of the killing. "Your general is dead!" he bellowed as loudly as he could. "King Rendelf is dead! I am your king! I am Brennan, son of Brendelf, grandson of King Rendelf! Drop your weapons now, and I will grant you clemency!"

His shout was taken up by his men. "Surrender to your new king!"

As Caladras's army realized their leader was gone and his son had run away, they began to drop their weapons and kneel.

Lord Whistlyn raised his sword in the air. "Victory is ours!"

The Woodsman's army gave a cheer. "Long live King Brennan!"

It wasn't over yet, the Woodsman thought as he looked over the sea of kneeling men, mostly Wood Elves. He still had to take over Wyndelas Palace and convince the River Elves that he was their new king. And he still had to deal with Griffin Caladras and his murderous aunt, Jenetta.

Woodsman!

What is it? he asked the Living Oaks.

A group of soldiers have hacked through the forest barrier and are headed toward Haven!

The Woodsman flinched. It had to be Griffin, that bastard. *How does he know where Haven is?*

He is following an eagle.

The Chameleon. The Woodsman sheathed his sword and leaped on his horse.

Father Kit and Liz ran toward him. Colwyn's uncle, Hadyn, gave Colwyn a slap on the shoulder, while Ronan and his father embraced. The Woodsman realized that most of the men from Haven were here. They must have come to fight with Lord Daelen. But damn, that left the women and children of Haven unprotected.

"Griffin has taken his men to attack Haven," he told them. "Ready your weapons and mount up. Lord Whistlyn, I will leave you in charge here."

The earl nodded. "Be careful."

The Woodsman and his men raced toward Haven.

Liz rode beside him. "Why? Why is Griffin attacking women and children?"

"He wants Sorcha," the Woodsman growled. The bastard must be thinking that if he captured Sorcha, he could make the new king submit to his demands.

He gripped the reins hard. Unfortunately, the bastard was right.

Chapter 24

Everyone in Haven was at the banquet field, sitting on the grass and listening to Morghen as she stood in front of the table, reporting to them what the Living Oaks were telling her about the battle. Meanwhile, Sorcha paced around the edge of the field, too nervous to sit on the grass like the others. Did they think this was story time?

She breathed a great sigh of relief when she heard there were three dragons in the sky. Thank the goddesses! Silas and Dimitri had answered Aleksi's plea and come to help. But when she heard that the battle had disintegrated into hand-to-hand combat, she found it hard to breathe at all.

Morghen suddenly went quiet. A pained look crossed her face, and her gaze slowly drifted to Bronwen, who was sitting close by with her daughter, Helen. Bronwen turned pale.

Oh, goddesses, no. Sorcha pressed a hand to her mouth.

Morghen took a step toward Bronwen, then stopped and looked at everyone. "It's over! Caladras is dead, and his army has surrendered."

"We won!" The women jumped to their feet and hugged each other, then hugged their children. Some of the younger girls danced about, no doubt hoping to gain the attention of the boys who were standing to the side with sullen looks. Aged eleven to fifteen, the boys had been deemed too young to go to Drudaelen and fight. They had been sorely disappointed to be left behind with a bunch of women and children. Even now, with everyone celebrating the victory, the boys were grumbling that they had missed taking part in it.

Morghen wasn't smiling, either, Sorcha realized. The older woman approached Bronwen with tears in her eyes, and Bronwen stumbled to her feet.

"Who?" Bronwen asked with a shaky voice. "My husband? My father?"

Morghen touched her shoulder. "Your husband is fine."

"Papa?" Bronwen covered her mouth to stifle a cry as tears ran down her face.

"Mama?" Helen grabbed her mother's skirt. "Mama, what's wrong? Is Papa hurt?"

"Your daddy is fine." Morghen drew the little girl into her arms and hugged her.

Sorcha pulled Bronwen into her arms. "I'm so sorry." While Bronwen cried on her shoulder, Sorcha asked Morghen, "What happened?"

"Lord Daelen killed Caladras," Morghen explained. "But then the general's son . . . took revenge."

Griffin, that asshole. "I hope someone took care of him," Sorcha muttered.

Morghen stiffened with a gasp. "Oh, holy Light." She released Helen and turned toward the crowd. "Quiet! There are soldiers headed this way!"

"What?" Sorcha asked. "They're coming to Haven?"

"Yes." Morghen nodded. "Griffin and a troop of soldiers have hacked through the forest and found the path to Haven."

Sorcha looked over the crowd, noting all the different reactions. Some were crying, some of the mothers had fallen to their knees, grabbing their children, while others were completely motionless, frozen in shock. The girls who had been dancing now huddled together, whimpering. And the boys looked excited.

"How did he know how to find us?" Hallie asked.

"They're following an eagle," Morghen replied.

"The Chameleon," Sorcha whispered, mentally slapping herself. That had been the eagle she'd spotted the other day.

"We're all going to die!" Tara wailed.

"No!" Sorcha yelled. "We're going to defeat them. We practiced for this. We're ready for them." She made a fist. "We can do this!"

Everyone turned to face her.

"You know your parts," Sorcha continued. "Boys, get in position. Make sure they chase you, but don't get caught!"

With excited looks, they scampered off to the piers on the south side of the lake.

"Bronwen, can you take the women and children to the tree houses?" Sorcha asked, and Bronwen nodded, wiping her face. "Once you're safe in the houses, pull the ladders up."

"Come along!" Bronwen motioned for the women and children to follow her. "Hurry!" They skirted around the lake to the north, headed to the row of tree houses, which included the Woodsman's house and Sorcha's.

There were a total of five tree houses, and earlier they had made sure each one was stocked with food and extra clothing in case the people hiding there had to stay for several days.

"Hallie." Sorcha turned to the young woman. "Can you use your Embraced gift to slow Griffin down?"

"Sure." Hallie closed her eyes and concentrated. The air grew thicker; then a mist began to form. With a push of her hands, she shoved the mist into the forest where the invaders were coming.

They would have trouble seeing where they were going, Sorcha thought with satisfaction. "All right. Let's go to my tree house."

As they circled the lake, Morghen reached out to pat her shoulder. "You make a good leader. A perfect match for the Woodsman."

Sorcha snorted. "Are you saying I'm pushy?" Was it only a

week ago that she'd fussed at the Woodsman for being that way? "I'm not sure how good a leader I am. I'm only trying to control things because I'm scared to death."

"Aren't we all?" Hallie muttered.

Was that why the Woodsman acted that way? Sorcha wondered. Was it simply his way of handling fear? "Does he know what's happening?"

"Yes," Morghen replied. "He's coming as fast as he can."

"Good," Sorcha said as they passed by the Woodsman's tree house. His rope ladder had already been pulled up. Up on the front porch, Riona and Lauren waved at her.

At Sorcha's tree house, she waited for Morghen and Hallie to climb the ladder, then took her turn. Once she made it to the front porch, she pulled up the rope ladder. Inside the tree house, she discovered Bronwen, Helen, Teresa, Tara, and a young mother with a month-old infant.

"We'll be fine," she assured them, then went back onto the front porch so she could see what was happening. Hallie joined her, prepared to use her gift of calling down the mist. Right now, she was keeping the mist in the forest, where Griffin and his men were.

After what seemed an eternity, ten horsemen emerged from the mist and slowly entered Haven. Sorcha spotted one with a golden helmet. That had to be Griffin. He pointed at the stable, then Morghen's house. His men dismounted and checked out the cottages built into the hillsides. Meanwhile, Hallie shrouded the ground just below the tree houses with mist. Anyone passing by would not be able to see them.

After finding no one in the hillside houses, Griffin looked frantically about.

The boys on the pier stood up and shouted, "Oh, no! They found us!" They turned and ran, headed into the southern pasture.

"Catch them!" Griffin ordered, and seven of his men mounted their horses to give chase.

While the boys ran, Hallie gathered some mist on the southern pasture. Soon, it was impossible to even see the boys, but Sorcha knew from their practice runs what the boys were doing. They would divide up and each group would run into the forest; there, they would climb up rope ladders to emergency shelters in the trees. Once they pulled up the ladders, they could remain hidden for days. Each shelter was stocked with food and water.

Meanwhile, the seven horsemen would keep charging forward till they met a rude surprise. A large ditch, ten feet deep, had been dug into the ground and covered with a few flimsy branches and leaves.

When Sorcha heard the crying whinnies of their horses and the shouts of the men, she knew it had happened. They'd fallen into the trap.

Behind her in the tree house, the baby started crying. The young mother quickly put the baby to her breast. "I'm so sorry!" she whispered.

"Mama, I want to go home!" Helen wailed.

"Hush." Bronwen pulled her daughter against her skirts. "We have to be quiet."

"But I'm scared," Helen whimpered.

"We're going to be all right," Sorcha told her, but when she glanced at Griffin, he and his last two men were headed around the lake. They'd heard the noise.

"They're coming," Hallie whispered.

"Are we going to die?" Tara cried.

"Hush," Teresa scolded her daughter.

Next door, in the third tree house, a young child started crying. They managed to hush him up, but now Griffin and his companions were running toward them.

Hallie thickened the mist, so they couldn't see. But unfortunately, Sorcha couldn't see them, either.

"We know you're hiding nearby," Griffin shouted, his

voice echoing eerily in the mist. "Give us Princess Sorcha, and we will leave in peace."

Sorcha winced. So they had come for her?

"I think they're hiding in the trees," one of the soldiers said.

"We'll burn the trees down if you don't hand over the princess!" Griffin yelled, then in a lower voice, he asked his men, "Does one of you have a flint?"

"Aye, my lord."

Sorcha glanced at the tree houses on either side. There were too many women and children counting on her. "Quickly," she whispered to the women in her house. "Go across the bridge to the Woodsman's house. Now!"

"What are you planning?" Bronwen asked. "Surely you're not giving yourself up?"

"No." Sorcha hustled the women toward the bridge. "Quickly." The mother and infant went, then Bronwen and Helen.

When Teresa started across, Sorcha grabbed Tara. "I need you for just a few seconds."

"Me?" Tara's eyes widened. "What can I do?"

"You can be very dramatic, right?"

"I-I suppose."

Sorcha explained what she wanted, then headed back to the front porch. "Hallie, can you clear the mist just around this tree house? They need to be able to see this porch."

"All right." Hallie spread her hands and the mist separated, slowly making their tree house visible.

Sorcha and Hallie slipped just inside the door, where Tara was waiting.

"Hallie, head across the bridge," Sorcha ordered. As Hallie hurried away, she turned to Tara. "Do it. Give them the performance of a lifetime."

Tara nodded, her eyes sparkling with excitement. She ran

onto the front porch. "Oh please, don't kill me! I'll do whatever you want." She fell to her knees. "Please spare me. I'm too afraid to die!"

"Where is Princess Sorcha?" Griffin called up.

"She's hiding in there," Tara whispered loudly as she pointed at the door.

"Lower the ladder, so we can take her," Griffin said softly.

"Of course." Tara threw the rope ladder over the ledge. "You won't hurt me, will you?"

"Of course not," Griffin replied.

A moment passed, then Tara slipped inside the door. "He's sending his last two soldiers," she whispered.

"Good." Sorcha motioned to the bridge. "Hurry and go across. Oh, and Tara—" Sorcha stopped her with a hand on her shoulder. "You did a fantastic job."

Tara blushed. "Did I?"

"Yes. Now go." Sorcha gave her a little push, and the girl ran quickly across the bridge into her mother's waiting arms.

Sorcha waited close to the bridge, and when the two soldiers rushed into the house, their swords drawn, she gave a small cry. "Oh, no! Don't hurt me!" She hurried on to the bridge. Halfway across, the bridge swayed suddenly as the two soldiers jumped onto the bridge to follow her.

She winced, working her way across as fast as she could. On the other side, she quickly snapped her fingers, making flames with both hands. Then she held the flames to the ropes. The ropes were burning, but not fast enough!

Bronwen reached around her and jiggled the bridge, making it sway back and forth. The guards stopped and grabbed the ropes to steady themselves.

Snap! Sorcha's flames burned through two of the ropes on one side. The bridge collapsed, and the soldiers cried out as they plummeted all the way to the ground.

"My leg!" one of them moaned.

The other whimpered. "I think my ribs are cracked."

"My leg! I think it's broken."

"Dammit," Griffin muttered.

The sound of horse hooves thundered in the distance.

"Where are you, Griffin?" the Woodsman shouted.

Sorcha's heart leaped up her throat. The Woodsman had come!

"Bloody hell." Griffin mounted his horse and spurred it into a gallop.

"Dammit," Sorcha muttered. "He's escaping."

Hallie quickly lifted the mist, but there was no sign of Griffin. He'd disappeared into the forest. But Sorcha could see the Woodsman and a group of men on horseback, racing around the lake to the tree houses.

"Sorcha!" the Woodsman yelled. "Are you here?"

With a grin, she dropped the ladder and hurried down. Women and children were descending from all the tree houses. When they reached the ground, they hugged one another, laughing. The fathers who had gone to Drudaelen ran to their families to hug them.

Her heart leaped when she saw the Woodsman approaching.

"Sorcha!" He slid off his horse and pulled her into his arms. "Thank the Light. I was so worried about you."

She held him tight. "I was terrified." She leaned back to look him over. He was just as beautiful as ever. "You weren't injured in any way?"

"I'm injured," the fallen soldier moaned. "My leg."

The Woodsman gave him a quick glance. "What happened to him?"

Sorcha snorted. "He was defeated by some women and children."

The Woodsman looked at the villagers, who were still laughing and hugging one another. "Sorcha, you're amazing." He gave her a quick kiss. "Thank you."

"Thank you for not getting yourself killed." She touched his cheek. "Did I tell you how terrified I was?"

"Yes." He pulled her close once again.

"But I've been a bit angry, too."

He pulled back to look at her. "Why? Because I was gone so long?"

"No, because you had three days when you could have told me who you really are." She gave his chest a small push. "You should have been honest with me. You should have trusted me."

"Sorcha—"

"And you should have let me ask my brother to help."

"We did help," Silas said in Norveshki as he marched forward with Dimitri and Aleksi. They were in human form and someone had given them each a pair of breeches.

"Silas!" She ran to hug her brother. "Thank you! Thank you, Dimitri."

Dimitri merely nodded as he gave the Woodsman a suspicious look.

"Your Majesty," the Woodsman said in Eberoni as he bowed his head. "Thank you for coming to our aid in battle."

"Aleksi assured us it was for a good cause," Silas answered in Eberoni as he looked the Woodsman over. "And we owed you our thanks for rescuing him and Sorcha."

The Woodsman nodded. "You're welcome."

Silas wrapped an arm around Sorcha's shoulders. "Now that it's over, we'll be taking her home with us."

Sorcha jumped back. "B-but I'm not ready to go."

Silas frowned at her. "You've spent enough time in enemy territory. We want you home safe."

"The elves are not our enemy," Sorcha insisted.

"There will be no more attacks from Woodwyn," the Woodsman pledged. "I plan to be at peace with all my neighbors."

Sorcha nodded. "And when the Woodsman plans something, it happens."

He smiled at her. "Thank you."

She smiled back. "Ye're welcome."

Silas hissed in a breath, then muttered to Aleksi, "I see what you mean. She needs to be separated from this man."

"I do not!" Sorcha huffed.

"It's not as bad as I thought," Aleksi grumbled. "At first, I thought she'd fallen for a thief—a popular one, but still a thief."

"Aleksi!" Sorcha glared at him.

"But the more I got to know him, the more I realized he's a good man," Aleksi continued. "And, actually, he's a prince!"

"Actually, he's a king," Sorcha corrected him.

"Can I talk for myself?" the Woodsman muttered.

"You're a king?" Silas asked. "How is that? What happened to King Rendelf?"

"King Rendelf was my grandfather," the Woodsman explained. "He was murdered yesterday by Princess Jenetta."

Sorcha winced. "Ye have one crazy aunt."

"Tell me about it," the Woodsman grumbled.

Silas held up a hand. "Gwen's mother is a murderer?"

Sorcha nodded. "I'm afraid so. She also killed two of the royal princes when they were young."

"Gwen is fortunate to have been raised away from her," the Woodsman said.

Silas narrowed his eyes. "You speak as if you're familiar with my wife."

The Woodsman smiled. "She's my cousin."

Dimitri stiffened. "No. She's *my* cousin."

The Woodsman's brows lifted. "She is?"

"Dimitri's uncle was Lord Tolenko, Gwennore's father," Sorcha explained.

"Ah." The Woodsman smiled at Dimitri. "Nice to meet you."

Dimitri grunted. "Are we leaving yet?"

"Not until Sorcha agrees to come with us," Silas muttered.

Sorcha crossed her arms over her chest. "I'm not ready to leave."

Silas glowered at her. "This country is in turmoil. Why would you want to stay?"

"Your Majesty." The Woodsman stepped toward Silas. "This may not be the ideal time, but I would like to ask you for Sorcha's hand in marriage."

Her heart lurched up her throat. He wanted to marry her? But wait, he'd never told her if he loved her.

Silas frowned at the Woodsman. "You've known her about a week. How can you be sure you want to marry her?"

"I'm sure." The Woodsman turned to Sorcha. "I'm sure because I love her."

Sorcha gasped. "Ye do?"

"Of course I do." He took her hands in his. "You didn't doubt me, did you?"

She winced. "Well, ye didn't seem to trust me—"

"I didn't want to endanger you with information that could get you killed. Sorcha, marry me."

She snorted. "Pushy as always."

"You mean decisive."

She laughed. "I will."

Silas cleared his throat. "I don't recall agreeing to this."

"Silas!" Sorcha shot him an annoyed look.

He groaned. "This has happened too fast."

"Didn't you fall for Gwennore really fast?" Sorcha asked.

"Of course I did, but Gwen is exceptional—"

Sorcha cleared her throat.

"And you are, too," Silas mumbled. "But you realize, don't you, that if you marry this man, you will be living in Woodwyn for the rest of your life?"

Sorcha glanced at all the villagers, who were smiling at her, since Father Kit was translating everything into Elfish. She'd drawn portraits of most of the children, and their mothers had praised her and given her sweets and handmade gifts. And when they had been in danger, they had listened to her and believed in her.

Bronwen gave her a sad smile. As the Woodsman's cousin, Bronwen and her family would become Sorcha's family here in Woodwyn.

"I hope you will stay," Colwyn said in Elfish, and his family agreed.

"Colwyn, my love!" Tara clasped her hands together as she gave him an adoring look.

He glanced over at her. "Who is that?"

Tara huffed. "You don't know me? If it wasn't for me, we wouldn't have been able to kill those soldiers over there!" She pointed at the men who had fallen from the bridge. "I can take care of myself, so who needs you!" She flipped her hair over her shoulder as she turned and stalked away.

Sorcha smiled to herself. *Good for you, Tara.*

"We're not dead," one of the soldiers whimpered.

"I think my ribs are broken," the other one moaned.

"My leg. I broke my leg."

Morghen walked over to them and gave them an assessing look. "You'll live. Stop your whining."

Riona shook a finger at them. "That's what you get for trying to hurt our princess."

Our princess? Sorcha's heart filled with joy, and she turned to her brother. "Yes, I would be happy to live in Woodwyn."

The villagers of Haven gave her a cheer, and the Woodsman squeezed her hands once more.

Silas took a deep breath. "It pains me to be separated from you, but I do want you to be happy." He shifted his weight. "Very well. I will give you my blessing."

Sorcha grinned. The Woodsman gave her a quick kiss, and the crowd cheered once more.

Morghen laughed. "Didn't I tell you that every couple who drinks the love potion ends up married within a month?"

"So I expect the wedding will be soon?" Silas asked.

The Woodsman nodded, then gave his cousin Bronwen a sympathetic look. "Yes, but first, we must have a funeral."

Chapter 25

L ater that afternoon, Aiden arrived in Haven with a wagon carrying the body of Lord Daelen. The captain of the guard, Marius, had come, along with a troop of soldiers and many people who had lived and worked in the castle.

When Aiden dismounted, Bronwen ran into his arms, and he embraced her and their daughter, Helen.

The Woodsman took Sorcha by the hand, and as they walked among the people of Drudaelen, he introduced her to everyone and extended his condolences.

"Are you going to be our queen?" one of the women asked Sorcha.

She glanced at the Woodsman. "I hope so." Then she turned back to the castle folk. "Would you be able to accept me?"

"We will if the Woodsman wants you," the woman replied.

"The Woodsman wants her very much," he said, giving Sorcha a heated look that made her blush and the women giggle.

While the women gathered around Sorcha, plying her with questions, he stepped over to Aiden. "So you are now the new lord of Drudaelen Castle."

"And you're the new king." Aiden bowed. "Your Majesty."

"Enough of that," the Woodsman muttered, clapping his old friend on the shoulder. "What is happening at Drudaelen? Does Lord Whistlyn have everything under control?"

"Yes." Aiden nodded. "The wounded are being cared for. And everyone has pledged fealty to you."

"Good." The Woodsman gave the wagon a sad look. "The cost of our victory was too high." He pulled Bronwen in for a quick hug. "I'm so sorry I didn't reach him in time."

"It's not your fault." She wiped away a tear. "Did you see who did it? Who killed my father?"

"Griffin Caladras," the Woodsman told her. "Sorcha told me he escaped, but I'll find him and avenge your father."

Bronwen nodded. "Thank you."

"We have some special guests." The Woodsman motioned to the dragon shifters, who were now fully clothed after raiding the Woodsman's closet. "My uncle would be pleased to know that his funeral is being attended by the king of Norveshka and two of his war dragons."

The Woodsman introduced his family to Silas, then took Sorcha's hand and led everyone into the forest. Marius and five of his soldiers carried Lord Daelen on a stretcher made of wood and leather. His body had been wrapped in white linen.

After a short walk, the Woodsman stopped in front of a great oak tree. The soldiers set the stretcher on the ground, and everyone gathered around.

"Lord Bowen Daelen was loved greatly by his family and his people," the Woodsman began. "He was an excellent father to Bronwen, a father to me for the last fifteen years, a close friend to my father, Prince Brendelf, and a loyal follower of the late king."

He rested a hand on the tree beside him. "This is the oak that agreed to take Lord Daelen when we first built Haven. It is here where he will spend eternity as one of the Living Oaks."

It is time, the Woodsman told the tree. *Are you ready to accept the body and spirit of Lord Daelen?*

The trunk of the tree split wide open, revealing a space in

the center. While the elves were not surprised, Sorcha and the dragon shifters stiffened in shock. Marius and his five soldiers lifted Lord Daelen's body and set it inside the tree.

Bronwen burst into tears. "Papa," she whispered as the trunk closed up, sealing her father inside.

Sorcha gasped.

The Woodsman laid a hand on the trunk once more. *Uncle, are you there?*

There was a pause, and then he heard the voice of Lord Daelen. *I am here, Woodsman.*

We are here, the rest of the Living Oaks spoke in chorus. *We are one.*

The Woodsman gave Bronwen a tearful look. "He has become one with the Living Oaks. May his spirit last throughout the ages."

With tears running down her cheeks, Bronwen smoothed her hands over the oak tree's rough bark. Then with a cry, she rested her cheek against the tree.

The crowd slowly dispersed, leaving Bronwen alone with the Living Oak that had melded with her father.

Silas strode up to the Woodsman and asked him in Eberoni, "What was that?"

Sorcha joined them. "I've never seen anything like that before."

The Woodsman nodded. "I am glad you were here to witness it." He had told Silas earlier why Caladras had kept attacking Norveshka over the years, simply to give him a chance to kill Prince Kendelas and Prince Brendelf. Now, there was more to explain. "The elves have a special relationship with the sentient oak trees of Woodwyn. When we die, our bodies and spirits become one with a chosen tree. That, in turn, causes the tree to become one of the Living Oaks."

"And they're able to talk to each other and to you?" Silas asked.

"Yes." As the Woodsman led them back toward the lake,

he pointed to one Living Oak after another. "There are thousands of Living Oaks, since elves have been melding with the oaks for centuries. The Living Oaks are more than trees. They are the spirits of our ancestors." He glanced at Silas. "That is why our forests are so vast compared to a country like Eberon. The Living Oaks are sacred and will never be cut down."

"So the woods are sacred to you, along with the Wyn River," Sorcha said softly. "No wonder ye call this country Woodwyn."

"Exactly," the Woodsman agreed. "And when someone from Norveshka or Eberon crosses the border and chops down a Living Oak, it is the same as murdering one of our people."

Silas's eyes widened. "Is that why the elves make those raids across the border? For revenge?"

"Yes." The Woodsman nodded. "I would appreciate it if you could explain the situation to King Leo of Eberon. We do have some trees that are not sentient, elms and ashes and so forth. If the Norveshki and Eberoni are in need of wood, we could arrange a trade. I don't want any more violence between our peoples."

"Agreed." Silas shook hands with the Woodsman. "We will be on our way now. Our wives will be worried about us."

"Give Gwen and Annika a hug from me," Sorcha told her brother and Dimitri.

"Aleksi has volunteered to remain here," Silas said. "He will stay in communication with us and let us know when it is time to come to the wedding."

"Good-bye for now." Sorcha hugged her brother.

Silas and Dimitri disappeared into the woods to shift and fly away, while Aleksi went with them to collect their discarded clothes.

"Alone at last," the Woodsman said in Elfish as he took Sorcha's hand and led her toward his tree house.

"We're not really alone." She motioned to all the people

gathering in the banquet field to have a drink and reminisce about Lord Daelen. "Would you like to join them?"

"No. I haven't seen you in days."

She sighed. "I missed you something terrible."

"You were always in my thoughts," he confessed. "So much so that I had trouble focusing on the matters at hand. That's when I realized how much I love you."

She smiled. "I was hoping for days to hear you say that."

He waited, then gave her an exasperated look. "Isn't there something you would like to tell me?"

She thought for a while. "Have you been using hair dye? Is your hair actually white?"

He groaned inwardly. "Yes."

"You should have told me! White and lavender—those were the colors I picked in the Game of Stones. You're an exact match. Why didn't you tell me?"

"Because I don't believe in your silly stones. And I wanted you to choose me without any outside influence, no matter what color my hair is."

She huffed. "But all this time I was wondering if I was making a great mistake, falling in love with the wrong man."

He stopped with a jerk. "In love?"

"Of course. Didn't you know I love you?"

"You do?"

She scoffed. "Would I have let you make love to me if I didn't?"

"Speaking of which . . ." He stopped by the ladder to his tree house. "We have unfinished business."

She blinked. "You mean . . . ?"

"Yes." He pointed up to his house.

"Now?"

"Yes."

"It's not even dark."

"Sorcha, I want you. I've wanted you since I first met you." He leaned close and whispered, "I haven't had much sleep the last few days, but whenever I lie down, I think about kissing you and touching you till you scream and shatter in my arms."

"Oh." Her cheeks grew pink.

"Hurry. Up the ladder with you."

"Pushy." She gave him a flirtatious smile. "But we'll have to be careful."

"Why?"

She started up the ladder. "So we don't burn your house down."

At first, Sorcha was a bit nervous and shy, undressing in daylight in front of the Woodsman. But he was throwing off his clothes so quickly she paused, still dressed in her shift, to watch him. The muscles in his arms tightened while he moved, and the muscles in his back and chest rippled so curiously. But his skin was no longer perfect. She winced at the bruises and cuts along his arms and shoulders. There was even some swelling around his ribs.

"Are you in pain?"

"Not yet, but I will be if I don't bed you soon."

"What?"

He dropped his breeches and she gasped at the sight of his manhood, nestled in black curls. That wasn't so surprising, given the fact that his eyebrows and whiskers were also black. No, what gave her a start was how swollen and stiff he was.

"W-were you injured there?" She pointed at his groin.

"No, not at all." He kicked off his breeches, then headed for the washroom.

She followed him. "But the swelling looks really bad."

He pulled the lever and water splashed down on him from the tank overhead. "Oh, so cold."

"Maybe that will bring the swelling down."

He snorted, then lathered up his body with some soap. "Would you like to join me?"

Her mouth fell open. "You want to bathe together?"

He crooked his fingers at her. "I won't be so cold if you warm me up."

"Well." She hesitated. "I would hate for you to catch a cold."

"I feel a sneeze coming on."

She scoffed, then stepped into the small room.

"Brace yourself." He pulled the lever and another gush of cold water splashed over them.

"Oh!" She crossed her arms and shivered. He looked magnificent, the way the soap was running down his chest in rivulets. His manhood jutted out, growing larger and stiffer. And suddenly, she no longer felt quite so cold.

He brushed her wet hair out of her face, then leaned in for a slow, lingering kiss. "Feeling warmer?"

"Yes." Even though she was standing there in a wet shift, she was beginning to feel downright hot.

He kissed a trail to her ear while his hands smoothed down her back to grasp her rump. "Sorcha," he whispered in her ear.

"Yes."

"I want you naked." He pulled her forward till the tip of his manhood pressed against her stomach.

All the shyness and nervousness she'd felt before vanished. She pulled off her shift and wrapped her arms around his neck. "Can you do all the things you did that night under the stars?"

"That much and more." He swung her up in his arms and carried her to his bed.

"We'll get your sheets wet."

"I don't care." He dumped her on the bed and jumped on top, straddling her. "I love you, Sorcha."

"I love you—" Her words were cut short when he dove in for a ravishing kiss.

Her heart pounded, and goodness, she felt like she was burning for him.

"Your skin is hot," he murmured as he kissed his way to her breasts.

"I know." Somehow he managed to touch the inner fire inside her. "I-I hope I don't burn you."

"I will gladly go up in flames with you." He latched on to her nipple and suckled.

Oh, this was every bit as good as she remembered. She clutched his shoulders, then dragged her hands into his long, wet hair. The heat inside her seeped down to her womanhood, making her ache for his touch. "Woodsman," she breathed. "Brennan."

He glanced up and smiled. "I like the way you say my name."

"Brennan." She slid a hand down to his hip. "May I touch you?"

"Hell, yes." He lifted himself up so she could slide her hand to his groin.

"It's even more swollen." She curled her fingers around him. "And, dare I say, wooden?"

He snorted, then groaned when she gave him a squeeze. "You're killing me, Sorcha. I'm dying to take you."

"Then do it." She released him. "Take me, Brennan."

His eyebrows lifted. "Are you being pushy?"

"Decisive."

His mouth twitched as he wrapped her legs around him. "Brace yourself."

"Is it going to hurt?"

"I hope not." He stroked her with his fingers.

"Oh." She squirmed beneath him. "I like that."

"I can tell." He slipped a finger inside her. "You're so wet and hot."

"And you're so wooden."

He laughed, then winced. "Don't make me laugh. I'm barely in control."

"Lose it." She cradled his face in her hands. "Burn with me."

"Sorcha, you fiery vixen." He eased himself inside her slowly.

She moaned.

He stopped. "Am I hurting you?"

"No," she whispered, her eyes flickering shut. "Do it."

He plunged inside her, and she let out a cry. "Sorcha."

"More." She clung to him. The fire he'd ignited inside her was greedy for more heat.

He moved inside her, then with a hoarse shout, he quickened his pace, thrusting in and out.

Fire, she was on fire. She felt the flames growing with each thrust. The friction was searing her womanhood with a delicious heat. And still the fire grew, enveloping her, coiling inside her, pushing her toward an eruption.

She cried out as she shattered. As her body shuddered, he pumped into her even harder, then with a shout, he emptied his seed inside her.

He collapsed next to her, and they both breathed heavily for a while, holding each other.

"Sorcha," he whispered. "I'll never get enough of you."

She liked the sound of that. Turning toward him, she stroked his damp hair. "I can see some white along your scalp. Are you going to use that hair dye again?"

"Mmm." He shook his head, his eyes shut.

"We certainly don't need any more of the love potion."

"Mmm." He shook his head again.

"There is some erection fortification—"

"What?" His eyes flew open. "I don't need that!"

She grinned. "I wasn't sure what it was for, but now I have an idea."

"I don't need it," he grumbled, closing his eyes.

"No, you certainly don't."

"I need sleep."

"I know." She watched him as he fell into slumber. After a short while, she snuggled up beside him and fell asleep, too.

Hours later, she woke up and noticed it had grown dark outside. She was hungry and chilled, so she got up and lit a candle. There was plenty of food in the tree house, but she didn't want to put on her damp shift and dirty clothes. She would have to go next door to fetch some clean clothes. She found a velvet robe and wrapped it around her, then headed down the ladder.

The grass was cool under her bare feet. It was a shame there was no longer a bridge between the two houses. The injured men had been taken away, probably to Morghen's house.

Music and laughter drifted across the lake from the banquet field. The villagers were still there, drinking and making merry.

"Sorcha!"

A loud whisper caught her attention. She blinked, trying to peer through the dark. Was that Silas calling to her? He was naked and peering at her from behind a tree in the forest. "Silas? What are you doing?"

"I just flew here. Gwen was so worried about us that she became ill. I'm afraid she'll lose the baby. She wants to see you. Hurry!"

"Gwen is sick?" Sorcha moved toward him.

Something dark jumped out from behind a tree and before she could see what it was, a hard object clobbered her on the head. Pain shot through her, and then everything turned black.

Chapter 26

Shortly before sunrise, the Woodsman woke to the sound of the Living Oaks.

Woodsman! Wake up!

Sorcha has been taken!

He sat up with a jerk. *What?* He looked at the empty place beside him in bed. Sorcha was gone. He jumped out of bed, his heart racing. *What happened?*

She was taken during the night.

A dragon flew off with her.

Her brother? the Woodsman asked.

No. It was the Chameleon. Griffin Caladras knocked her out. Then the Chameleon took him and Sorcha to Wyndelas Palace.

"Dammit!" The Woodsman threw on some breeches and a shirt, then ran for the ladder. He stopped himself, then went back to pull on his boots and insert his knives. By the Light, he was so frantic, he wasn't thinking straight.

He buckled on his sword belt, put on his gloves, then grabbed his bow and quiver of arrows and slung them over his shoulder before sliding down the rope.

As he ran for the stables, he realized a horse wouldn't be fast enough. It would take at least two days to reach Wyndelas on horseback. He needed to get there the same way Sorcha had—by dragon.

He slammed into Morghen's house. "Aleksi!" He barged

into Aleksi's room and found him asleep next to Hallie.
"Dammit, Aleksi, wake up!"

"What the hell?" Aleksi grumbled as he sat up. Hallie
gasped and pulled the sheet over her head.

"The Chameleon and Griffin have taken Sorcha!" the
Woodsman shouted.

"What?" Aleksi jumped out of bed and reached for his
breeches. "How?"

"The Chameleon took the shape of a dragon and flew
them to Wyndelas Palace." The Woodsman snatched Aleksi's
breeches from his hand and threw them across the room.
"Don't bother getting dressed. I need you to shift and take
me to Wyndelas right now!"

Hallie sat up with the sheet gathered under her chin.
"You're going to Wyndelas alone? Isn't that dangerous?"

"What is going on?" Morghen called from the sitting
room.

The Woodsman stepped into the sitting room and quickly
explained.

"You're right. You must go quickly." Morghen pulled on a
robe over her nightgown. "I'll send Father Kit and Liz to
Drudaelen Castle to tell them what has happened."

"Thank you." The Woodsman realized he might need the
army if he ran into problems at Wyndelas. "Have them tell
Lord Whistlyn to gather the army and march on Wyndelas.
I'll expect them there in two days."

"I understand. Good luck to you." Morghen dashed out
the front door.

"Come on!" the Woodsman yelled at Aleksi, and the
shifter followed him outside.

"I don't know the way to Wyndelas," Aleksi grumbled.

"I've never ridden on a dragon." The Woodsman opened
the front gate and strode onto the meadow. "We'll go south
and east until you see the Wyn River. Then you just follow
the river south. Wyndelas Palace is huge. You can't miss it."

Aleksi nodded. "You'll climb onto my back at the base of my neck. Hold on tight, for we'll be going fast."

"Good luck!" Hallie called from the garden, her body wrapped in a blanket. She blew Aleksi a kiss.

He smiled at her, then shifted into a beast with gleaming black scales and enormous wings.

"Amazing," Hallie breathed.

The Woodsman climbed onto Aleksi's back and grabbed hold of his neck.

With a whoosh, Aleksi took off.

We're coming for you, Sorcha, the Woodsman thought as he hung on tight and the wind pelted his face. Would he be able to take over Wyndelas Palace without the army?

Sorcha woke up on a cot in a plain, white room. She sat up quickly, then winced at the pain that shot from the back of her head. Damn. She gingerly examined her head and was relieved not to find any blood.

Where was she? And how had she gotten here? She was still wearing the voluminous velvet robe she'd borrowed from the Woodsman. Did he know she was missing yet? Was he frantically looking for her?

She rose slowly to her feet as she looked about. The room was circular and made of stone. Ah, a window!

She dashed over to it and peered outside. Forested mountains to one side, a wide river to the other. She was up high, so most probably this was a castle tower. And the castle was probably in Woodwyn. Her sisters were the queens of the other three mainland countries, so no one would take her to those places. Was that the Wyn River? Was she in Wyndelas Palace?

The door was across the room. She wandered over to it, noting with dismay that it was made of metal. If it had been wood, the Woodsman could simply break it in half. She listened at the door and heard male voices outside. Her guards?

She gave the latch a try, but wasn't surprised to find the door locked.

"She's awake."

She heard one of the guards talking in Elfish.

"Go tell Her Majesty."

A queen? Did they mean Princess Jenetta? After killing her father, Jenetta would consider herself queen. Sorcha swallowed hard. How long had she been here? Was the Woodsman on his way? Brennan, she corrected herself. She needed to start calling him by his real name.

She went back to the window. As far as she could tell, it was close to noon.

The door behind her creaked open, and a beautiful elfin woman strode inside. A servant came in behind her, carrying a tray of bread and cheese.

"There." The elfin woman motioned to the cot, and the servant set the tray down, then dashed out of the room as if she wanted to get away from the woman as quickly as possible. An armed guard swung the door shut with a bang.

The elfin woman looked Sorcha over, then smoothed her hands down her red velvet skirt. Numerous rings sparkled on her fingers. "You must be wondering why you are here."

Sorcha propped an elbow on the windowsill. "I suppose you're Gwen's mother. There is a bit of a resemblance, although Gwen's much younger. And prettier."

The woman's eyes flashed. "I am Queen Jenetta, and you would do well to remember you are my prisoner."

Sorcha shrugged. "For the time being."

Jenetta scoffed. "You put up a brave front. I wonder how long it will last?" She waved her hand around the room. "Would you still be courageous after seven years in here?"

"Is this where you stayed?" Sorcha asked.

"This is where I was *imprisoned*," Jenetta corrected her. "Here in the White Tower. For seven long years."

"And how did you get me here?"

Jenetta waved a dismissive hand. "If you must know, Griffin knocked you out, and the Chameleon became a dragon to bring you both here."

"Why?"

Jenetta's eyes flashed again with anger. "You are impertinent with all your questions."

Sorcha snorted. "I'm impertinent? You're the crazy one who murdered her own father."

"Lies," Jenetta hissed.

"And now you've kidnapped me? What can you possibly hope to achieve by taking me? Caladras is dead. His army has been taken over by Prince Brennan. No one is on your side—"

"Shut up!" Jenetta's face flushed almost as red as her gown. "If I have you, I can force the Pretender Brennan and the King of Norveshka to do my will. They will give me Gwennore in order to keep you alive."

"And you would use Gwennore like that? What are you planning to do with her? Marry her to Griffin against her will? Are you going to kill her baby?" Sorcha's voice rose to a shout. "How can you treat your own daughter like that?"

"She owes me!" Jenetta screeched as she paced toward Sorcha. "If I hadn't gotten pregnant with her, my father would never have known that I had secretly married. I wouldn't have lost my husband or been locked up here for seven years!"

"You're blaming Gwennore for that?" Sorcha gave her an incredulous look. "You're a crazy, murdering bitch!"

Jenetta slapped her hard. "You're my prisoner. Remember that if you want to stay alive." She strode to the door. "Guards!"

They opened the door to let her out.

Holding a hand against her sore jaw, Sorcha peered out the door. A total of three guards. The door slammed shut, and she was alone once more.

With a sigh, she sat on the cot. A stone room. A metal

door. A window too high to climb out. Her Embraced gift of fire was not going to help her here.

She ate her food to keep her strength up.

Surely the Woodsman would come for her.

That afternoon, the Woodsman and Aleksi arrived at Wyndelas Palace. Aleksi flew over it a few times, so the Woodsman could see what the defenses were. The outer wall was guarded by a few soldiers and the massive wooden gate was closed and barred. The inner courtyard was mostly empty; just a few servants going about their work could be seen. No courtiers in sight. They had either fled the palace or were staying in their rooms. No doubt everyone was afraid of angering Jenetta.

Aleksi landed about a hundred yards from the front gate and the Woodsman slipped off his back.

"Stay behind me," the Woodsman told him. "If they try to kill me, breathe fire on them."

Aleksi nodded and lumbered slowly behind the Woodsman as he approached the front gate. The guards gathered on the battlements, readying their bows and arrows.

The captain of the guard yelled at the Woodsman, "Who are you to dare approach us with a dragon? Be gone before we attack!"

"I am Prince Brennan, son of Brendelf, grandson of King Rendelf. I have come to claim the throne and my bride. You are holding Princess Sorcha of Norveshka a prisoner. This dragon is sworn to protect her and myself." He motioned to Aleksi, who glared at the soldiers with red glowing eyes.

The guards talked amongst themselves; then the captain asked, "What proof do you have? Queen Jenetta has told us you are a false pretender to the throne."

"The Earl of Whistlyn is on his way with the army. He knew my father and has known me my entire life. He will swear to my identity."

"Caladras is on his way, too," the captain shouted. "He also claims you are a false pretender."

So Jenetta was keeping these guards in the dark, the Woodsman realized. Otherwise, these men would not be obeying her. "General Caladras is dead. His army has sworn fealty to me."

"You would have us believe that you defeated Caladras and his army?" The captain scoffed. "How did you manage that?"

With a swipe of his hand, the Woodsman split the massive gate in half. Then he broke the bows of every soldier on the battlements.

"He has magical powers!" the guards exclaimed. "And he has a dragon!"

"I am your rightful king," the Woodsman told them. "I suggest you surrender to me before the army arrives. They outnumber you four to one."

Behind him, Aleksi snorted and smoke bellowed from his nostrils.

The guards exchanged looks.

"Do you really want Jenetta for your queen?" the Woodsman shouted.

"We'll follow you!" the guards yelled.

"Come on in, Your Majesty!" The captain ordered the guards below to open what was left of the gate.

While the Woodsman and Aleksi walked into the court-yard, the guards and servants gave a cheer.

The captain ran down the stairs to meet him. "I am Captain Villard, Your Majesty." He bowed.

Behind him, the other guards bowed.

"Thank you for your fealty," the Woodsman said. "Now, where is Princess Sorcha?"

Chapter 27

Jenetta was in her suite of rooms when her head guard, Durban, banged on the door. "Your Majesty!"

"What?" She opened the door.

"Prince Brennan has arrived—"

"I told you not to call him that," she hissed. "He's not a prince!"

"Yes, Your Majesty." Durban bowed. "The Pretender has arrived with a dragon! And he's taken over the palace. Captain Villard and all the castle guards are swearing fealty to him in the courtyard!"

"What?" Jenetta clenched her fists. "That traitor! He swore allegiance to me yesterday!"

"He didn't know that Caladras had been defeated," Durban muttered.

"You have to take the palace back!" Jenetta ordered.

Durban's mouth fell open. "Your Majesty, there are only six of us."

"And you swore to die for me!"

"Your Majesty!" Another one of her guards ran up to them. "The new king is sending armed guards to arrest you! He released Rendelf's chief counsel from the dungeon, and they're saying you murdered King Rendelf!"

"Lies!" Jenetta's heart raced. "You have to stop them."

"They outnumber us," Durban said helplessly.

"Then die for me!"

Durban scoffed. "And once we're dead, what will stop them? If you want to stay alive, you'd better leave the palace now."

Leave? Jenetta stepped back.

In the distance, she heard the tromping of booted feet. The soldiers were coming for her.

"Go!" Durban shoved her into her room and slammed the door shut.

Leave? Jenetta paced across the room. How could she leave?

An eagle flew into her room and shifted into the guise of a River Elf.

"Chameleon! You have to help me!"

He gave her a look of disdain. "Woodwyn is lost. I only came to tell you that I'm leaving."

"What? How can you give up? You coward!"

He scoffed. "I haven't given up. Aerthlan will still be mine. Fortunately, I won't have to share it with you." He changed back into an eagle and flew out the window.

"No!" She ran to the window. Bloody hell. This couldn't be happening to her. She was the queen! Would this Pretender have her executed for killing her father? How would he even know what she'd done?

We know what you did.

Murderer.

Slayer of innocent children.

Shut up! she mentally screamed at the trees.

We told the Woodsman what you did.

He is the rightful king.

Jenetta fought a surge of panic. Soldiers were coming for her. She had to flee!

She gathered up her jewelry and stuffed it down her bodice. Then she took a lit candlestick and opened the hidden door to the secret passageway. Quickly, she descended the stairs, all the way down to the cellar. From there, she opened another door that led to the secret tunnel. It was pitch black inside, but she made her way as fast as she could, shielding the flame of her candle with her hand.

At last she saw sunlight! She hurried up a flight of stone steps, then opened a grate and stepped into the forest. A breeze swept by her and the flame flickered out. She dropped the candle and ran down the forest path.

If she could make it to the Wyn River, she could buy passage on a boat going south to Wynport. Then she could leave the country. But where could she go?

We know what you did.

Murderer.

Slayer of innocent children.

"Shut up!" she screamed but the forest was all around her. So many voices.

We know what you did.

You killed your own father.

A root suddenly erupted from the ground, causing her to trip and land on her face.

We know what you did.

Murderer.

"Shut up!" She grabbed some of the jewelry that had fallen out of her bodice and stuffed it back in.

You killed your own father.

You killed your two nephews.

"Stop it!" She scrambled to her feet. "Leave me alone, or I will burn you all to the ground!"

As she ran down the path, the branches on either side thrashed back and forth.

You must pay for your crimes.

Another root erupted from the ground, tripping her again. This time as she fell, she watched in horror as a root lifted toward her, its end pointed like a sword.

She screamed as she collided with it and it pierced her through. The last thing she saw was her jewelry tumbling out onto the ground. And her blood mingling with the diamonds and rubies.

As the Woodsman hurried toward the White Tower, he came to a screeching halt on the battlements. Griffin Caladras was there, holding Sorcha in a tight grip, a knife against her throat.

The Woodsman drew his sword. "Release her!"

"You will do as I say," Griffin yelled. "Or I slit her throat!"

The Woodsman eased toward them. "What is it that you want?"

"Drop that sword."

The Woodsman dropped it with a clatter.

"I want safe passage out of the country," Griffin said.

"That can be arranged." *Over my dead body.* The Woodsman glanced at Sorcha. To his relief, she looked more angry than frightened. "Anything else?"

Suddenly Sorcha snapped her fingers.

A flame sprang up, burning Griffin's hand. With a yelp, he dropped the knife.

Sorcha stomped on his foot, then whirled around to stab her fingers in his eyes.

"Ow!" Griffin stumbled back.

She slammed her knee into his groin. With a strangled cry, he fell forward onto his knees.

"Sorcha!" The Woodsman ran up to her and pulled her into his arms.

"I did it!" Her eyes sparkled with excitement.

"You sure did." He glanced over at the groaning man who was crawling away on all fours. Griffin deserved more than that for killing Lord Daelen.

"How did you get here so fast?" she asked.

"Aleksi brought me." He noticed Griffin had managed to find the sword he had dropped. Of course his sword had a wooden handle. "Excuse me." As he strode toward Griffin, he flicked his hand and the sword flew out of Griffin's hand and over the parapet.

"It's over," the Woodsman said as he whipped a knife out of his boot. "Don't make me use this."

Griffin pressed against the stone parapet, a frantic look on his face. "I can't surrender to you. You'll just have me executed."

The Woodsman paused, his knife pointed at the colonel. Griffin was right. Even if he were tried in court, the judges would come to the same conclusion. He would have to pay for his crimes.

Griffin shook his head. "I won't let you decide how I die. Damn you, you won't have that kind of power over me!" He turned and flung himself off the ramparts.

"No!" The Woodsman leaped toward him but was too late. Griffin hit the stone surface of the courtyard with a thud. Blood pooled around his head.

Sorcha rushed toward the Woodsman, but he grabbed her by the shoulders and turned her away so she couldn't see. "He's gone."

She grimaced. "Then it's over? We're safe now?"

Safe? There were still three members of the Circle of Five. And there was the army of Embraced soldiers that Lord Morris had told them about. "I'm not sure we can ever be entirely safe." He brushed her hair back from her brow. "But that doesn't mean we can't be happy."

She rested a palm against his cheek. "Then we should plan always to be happy."

"You're right." He smiled. "It's imperative to always have a plan."

Epilogue

Three weeks later . . .

"You made a beautiful bride," Luciana said as the five adopted sisters retired to Sorcha's sitting room in Wyndelas Palace.

"Thank you." Sorcha removed the golden crown from her head and placed it on the table. It was a simple design, but like everything the elves did, it boasted exquisite craftsmanship. Gold filigree wires were braided to make the circlet and adorned with golden leaves shaped like the leaves of the Living Oaks.

"And ye make a beautiful queen," Gwennore added.

Sorcha snorted. "Takes one to know one."

The five sisters laughed.

"Can ye believe that four of us are queens?" Brigitta collapsed on a blue velvet settee. "Who would have believed that when we were growing up in the convent?"

"Help yerselves to some food." Sorcha loaded a plate with roast beef, cheese, and some of the elfin pastries that she loved. "The ceremony lasted so long, I'm starving."

Luciana eyed her suspiciously. "You seem to have a much greater appetite these days."

Sorcha bit into a pastry. "How would ye know? Ye've been here only three days."

"I noticed that, too." Gwennore tapped a finger against her mouth as she studied Sorcha.

"Hmm." Brigitta narrowed her eyes. "The wedding was today, but I take it the wedding night has already happened?"

Sorcha snorted. "About fifty times."

"Fifty?" Luciana's eyes widened.

Sorcha shrugged and popped another pastry in her mouth. Her older sisters all exchanged glances.

Gwennore patted her own belly, which was starting to swell. "Could it be ye're eating for two?"

Sorcha gulped. "What?" Could it be possible?

"You've obviously done what is needed," Luciana told her as she filled a plate with food.

"About fifty times," Maeve grumbled.

Sorcha looked over at her younger sister. Maeve had been very quiet all through the wedding and coronation. "Are ye all right?"

Maeve plopped down on the settee next to Brigitta. "None of you noticed that someone was missing today?"

"Missing?" Luciana helped herself to a piece of cheese. "We're all here at Wyndelas. And our husbands are, too."

"Brody!" Maeve exclaimed.

Brigitta gasped. "Oh, ye're right. It's not like Brody to miss a wedding."

"That's true," Gwennore agreed. "I thought he would be here. After all, I asked him to come originally to investigate the Woodsman."

"That was weeks ago." Sorcha took a sip of wine. "When he left, I figured he must have gone back to Eberon."

Luciana shook her head. "No, he never came back."

Sorcha set her goblet down. Where on Aerthlan had Brody gone? Brennan had told her about the encounter with Lord Morris and how the priest had claimed that there was a hidden army of Embraced children. Had Brody gone off in search of it?

"He missed seeing me when the moons were full," Maeve mumbled. "He's never missed that before."

"I'm sure he'll come back," Brigitta assured their youngest sister.

"Speaking of shifters"—Sorcha sat in a chair next to the settee—"I hope ye can all stay for four more days. That's when Aleksi is getting married."

"Oh, how wonderful!" Gwennore clasped her hands together. "Is he marrying Hallie?"

"Yes." Sorcha smiled. Gwen had taken a special liking to Hallie since they were both healers. "And they're going to live here in the palace. Hallie will be the royal physician, along with Morghen. And Aleksi will be in charge of security here at the castle."

"That sounds perfect." Luciana sipped some wine.

"It is," Sorcha agreed. "Aleksi can also keep in touch with my brother, so I'll know immediately when Gwen goes into labor. And then Aleksi can fly me to Norveshka, so I can help."

"And so everything is settled," Brigitta announced, then shifted on the settee to look at Maeve. "Except for you. Isn't it yer turn to play the Game of Stones?"

Maeve shook her head. "I don't want to play."

"Oh, don't be such a sourpuss." Brigitta jumped up and rummaged through a trunk of clothes. "Here they are!" She brought the linen bag over, then poured the stones into a golden chalice.

"Pick!" She handed the chalice to Maeve. "It's the chalice from the palace!"

Everyone but Maeve laughed.

Frowning, Maeve stared down at the stones.

"Ye're not supposed to look," Sorcha told her.

"I can't do it." Maeve reached forward to set the chalice back on the table, but caught the bottom of the goblet on the edge of the table. The chalice fell over and three stones tumbled out onto the table.

Green, purple, and the number three.

The five sisters stared at them.

"Could these be the Telling Stones for Maeve?" Gwennore asked.

Maeve shook her head. "I don't want them."

"Don't worry, my dear." Luciana sat beside their youngest sister. "All of our fates have turned out well. I'm sure yours will, too."

"How could anything bad happen to you?" Brigitta asked. "All of the mainland countries are at peace."

But there were still three members of the Circle of Five. Sorcha glanced at the stone painted with the number three. And then there was the army of Embraced soldiers that Brennan had told her about.

"Maeve, we won't let anything bad happen to you," Gwennore insisted.

"Right," Luciana agreed. "And we can do it, since the rest of us are queens."

With a smile, Sorcha looked at her sisters. "It's good to be queen."

Read on for an excerpt from the next novel in
Kerrelyn Sparks's Embraced by Magic series,
THE SIREN AND
THE DEEP BLUE
SEA!

Chapter 1

Maeve glanced at her two eldest sisters as a startling realization popped into her mind. Luciana and Brigitta had everything a woman could wish for. They were queens. They were powerful, smart, and beautiful. They had lovely children and handsome husbands who were admirable rulers. So how on Aerthlan had they become so incredibly boring? Good goddesses, she was tempted to scream!

For the last two hours, Luciana and Brigitta had talked about nothing but babies. Feeding a baby, weaning a baby, bathing a baby, dressing a baby. Weren't there more important things to discuss? For example, where the hell was their friend Brody? He'd been missing for almost two months. Why hadn't he let anyone know where he was going?

It was so aggravating! The blasted man had a history of keeping secrets. At first, he'd led everyone to believe he was simply a dog shifter. But then they'd learned he could shift into any animal he liked. And recently, they'd discovered he was able to talk while in canine form. What other secrets was he hiding?

Unfortunately, all her thinking and worrying had not yielded any results, other than to make her tired and weary. In frustration, she let her gaze wander aimlessly about the elegant cabin of the Eberoni royal barge. It was decorated in the country's official colors of red and black: a thick red carpet and big, comfy chairs and footstools upholstered in red velvet; a carved black table laden with cold meats, fruit, and pastries. It was the most comfortable way for her pregnant sisters and their young children to travel. The mothers' soft droning voices and the gentle sway of the barge had caused the little ones to fall asleep on cushioned pallets.

Maeve stifled a yawn. After leaving Wyndelas Palace, they had traveled for three days to reach the town of Vorushka, where they had said good-bye to Gwennore. Then they had crossed into Eberon so they could board this barge on the Ebe River. Maeve was exhausted but far too worried about Brody to take a nap.

Luciana and Brigitta's conversation took a sudden turn for the worse as they delved into the pitfalls of training a child to use a chamber pot. With a groan, Maeve lurched to her feet. *I can't bear it any longer!*

"Sweetie, are you all right?" Luciana asked.

"Ye look a bit flushed," Brigitta added.

"I'm fine." Maeve wandered over to the table, but nothing looked appealing to her. She'd hardly eaten at all the last few days.

"You'll feel better once we're back home at Ebton Palace," Luciana announced. "No doubt there will be a dozen suitors waiting for you at the pier."

Maeve winced. Why were her sisters so eager for her to marry?

Luciana leaned close to Brigitta and whispered in a voice loud enough to be heard, "Maeve has become extremely popular of late."

"I'm not surprised," Brigitta whispered back. "She's grown into such a beauty."

Maeve rolled her eyes. Right. As if all those suitors were interested only in her appearance, not the fact that all four of her sisters were now queens.

"I know of at least one duke, three earls, and a dozen or so barons who claim to be smitten with her," Luciana continued.

"Oh, my!" Brigitta clasped her hands together. "A duke would be perfect!"

Maeve sighed. She didn't want a duke. She wanted a dog.

Luciana chuckled. "I wonder if the duke will be dressed in purple or green?"

Maeve stiffened at the reference to the Telling Stones. The number three; the colors purple and green. Those were the stones that had predicted her future.

And she hated it. She hadn't wanted to play the Game of Stones. In fact, the stones had only fallen out of the chalice because of her refusal to play. So maybe they didn't count?

But the pebble marked with the number three seemed too fitting to discount. There were only three members left in the Circle of Five, a murderous group intent on taking over the world. No one knew who the first two members were, but no doubt the Chameleon was the third. And three also matched the number of kings the evil shifter had killed: Frederic of Eberon, Gunther of Tourin, and Petras of Norveshka.

The Chameleon had caused trouble in Woodwyn, too, shifting into a dragon to kidnap Sorcha. Whoever he was, he had proven impossible to catch since no one knew what he really looked like. Only Brody could identify him through his scent.

But what had happened to Brody?

"Excuse me." Maeve headed toward the door. "I think I'll take a turn on the deck."

"No doubt the fresh air will do you some good," Luciana said as Maeve slipped out the door on the barge's port side.

Closing her eyes, she lifted her face to the warm sun and took a deep breath. A summer breeze feathered her cheeks and brought several scents to her nose—the sweat of hardworking sailors, the earthy smell of nearby farmland, and most importantly, the familiar scent of the Ebe River.

All her life, she'd felt a strange connection to bodies of water. She'd always known whenever a storm was brewing over the Great Western Ocean. And she'd been able to communicate with seals and other creatures of the sea.

Now that she was able to actually shift into a seal, she was even more attuned to water. With just a sniff, she knew which ocean, which river, which lake, even which well a sample of water came from. More than that, water had become a second home to her, as comforting as her bedchamber at Ebton Palace.

The river called to her, inviting her to jump in and shift. Let the water carry her weight, buoy her burdens, and wash away her worries. *Not now.* She opened her eyes and glanced up at the sun. It was high in the sky, so it had to be almost noon.

She wandered toward the bow of the barge, passing by the sailors who stood at the railing, using poles to keep the vessel floating down the deepest channel of the Ebe River. Eberoni soldiers, under the command of Colonel Nevis Harden, stood watch every few feet. Nevis and his troop had met the women and children this morning in Vorushka and would see them safely down the river. Once they arrived at Ebton, a troop of Tourinian soldiers would be waiting to escort Brigitta north to the capital of Tourin, where she ruled with her husband.

For the last three years, Maeve had been living at Ebton Palace. Although she was happy to be with her eldest sister, she always missed the other three something terrible. And so, she'd been delighted when they had all been reunited for three weeks at Wyndelas Palace in the elfin kingdom of Woodwyn. There, the fourth sister, Sorcha, had married the elfin king and become his queen. The eldest three sisters had stayed for the entire three weeks, but their husbands had returned to their countries and royal duties after a few days. It hadn't taken long for Luciana, Brigitta, and Gwennore to complain about how much they missed their mates.

But did no one miss Brody? Maeve stopped at the bow of the barge and searched the sky. Sometimes, Brody took the shape of an eagle. But not today. The sky was clear.

She shifted her gaze to the river to see if she could spot any otters. While living at Ebton Palace, she'd used this river as her place to shift into a seal, and every month on the night of the full moons, a river otter had come to play with her. It was Brody, of course, although the fool had never realized that she knew. She'd kept waiting for him to admit what he was doing, but he never did. It was another one of his blasted secrets.

Even when she'd shifted for the first few times on the Isle of Moon, he had come to keep her company in the form of a seal. He'd always been there for her. Every month.

Except the last two. Where the hell was he?

And why was this stupid barge going so terribly slowly? She needed to do something to find Brody. But what?

Once again the water called to her, and she was tempted to shift. If she swam really fast, she could beat the barge to Ebton Palace. Wouldn't that give her sisters a shock! They thought she could shift only when the moons were full.

It had bothered her for years that Brody could shift whenever he wanted while she couldn't. So, in the privacy of her bedchamber, she'd used her bath time every evening to train herself. For the first week, she'd only succeeded in getting her feet to morph into flippers, but now she could become a seal whenever and wherever she wanted.

She hadn't told anyone yet. She had wanted Brody to be the first to know.

With a groan, she turned and paced toward the back of the barge. Why had the purple and green stones tumbled from the chalice when it had tipped over? Those colors meant nothing to her. Now a blue stone—that she would have liked.

Brody had the prettiest blue eyes she'd ever seen. Or at least she could have picked black and white, since he spent most of his time as a furry black-and-white dog with a black patch surrounding his left eye.

She stopped at the rear end of the barge and planted her hands on the railing. Instead of worrying over a few silly stones, she should deal with reality and figure out what to do. She wasn't a child anymore, in spite of what her sisters thought. In a few months, at the Autumn Embrace, she would be twenty years old.

Something bumped against her skirt, and with a jump she glanced down at the furry black-and-white cat rubbing against her legs.

"Oh, you gave me a start." Her eyes narrowed on the cat's face as it looked up at her. Blue eyes. Just like Brody. Her heart leaped up her throat. "Brody, is that you?"

"It's called a cat," a wry voice announced, and she glanced up to see Colonel Nevis Harden approaching. He smiled at her. "The sailors keep her onboard to catch mice."

"I see." To hide her embarrassment, Maeve leaned down to rub the cat behind its ears.

"I heard something interesting this morning." Nevis stopped beside her at the railing. "Apparently, on the way to Vorushka, you asked several farm animals if they were Brody."

Maeve straightened, her face growing warm. "I had good reason to suspect the cow. He was black and white spotted."

Nevis's mouth twitched. "So are a lot of cows. I take it the pig was black and white, too?"

She gritted her teeth. "Yes. But I fail to see why this is so amusing. Brody has been missing for almost two months, and no one seems the least bit concerned."

Nevis's smile faded. "We are concerned."

"Then do something!"

"Such as?" Nevis gave her a frustrated look. "Brody can

shift into a bird or beast. He can fly over mountains and swim across oceans. How on Aerthlan would we ever find him?"

"But he could be in trouble. He might need help."

"If he's in trouble, he can shift into some sort of creature and escape." Nevis folded his arms as he leaned against the railing. "Try not to worry so much. I've known Brody a long time, about nine years now. It's not uncommon for him to disappear for a few months at a time."

"But he—" Maeve stopped herself before saying that he'd always made time to see her on the night of the full moons. That was their secret time together, and she didn't want anyone else to know.

"But he always comes back," Nevis finished her sentence. "And he usually has some important information. He's simply doing his job as a spy and investigator."

Maeve knew what Brody did for a living, but not much more than that. "Do you know where he came from?"

"Not sure where he grew up." Nevis dragged a hand through his hair, and for a few seconds the scar on his forehead was visible, one he'd received years ago from his best friend Leo's lightning power. "Brody told me once that he has a mother and a sister, but I don't know where they live."

"How did you meet him?"

"Hmm." Nevis's eyes narrowed as he thought back. "It was the summer of the year 691. Brody was sixteen. Leo and I, twenty-one. There was a severe drought that summer, and with no lightning storms, Leo's power was completely depleted, leaving him vulnerable to attack. My father and I were extremely worried about him. Then, one day, this scraggly dog wandered into camp, looking half-starved. I gave him a bone from the commissary. Then he followed me into my tent and shifted. Scared the crap out of—oh, no offense, my lady."

"Go on," Maeve urged.

"He said his name was Brody, and that he'd just spent a

month at Ebton Palace, listening in on King Frederic's secret meetings. You know who that was?"

"Yes." Maeve nodded. King Frederic had been Leo's uncle, and he had feared Leo because of his Embraced powers. Feared him enough that he had tried his best to get his nephew killed. And when Luciana had been betrothed to Leo, she'd also become a target.

"So I gave Brody some clothes and took him to see Leo and my father, the general," Nevis continued. "They hired him on the spot, and he's been working hard ever since. Not just helping Leo, but the other kings on the mainland, too."

"I knew about that last part." As far as Maeve was concerned, Brody was the unsung hero of all the changes that had happened over the last few years. "It upsets me that no one seems to realize how valuable he is."

Nevis scoffed. "If you value him so much, why do you keep calling him Julia whenever he's a dog?"

She winced. It had been an honest mistake to begin with. Brody made such a pretty dog with his long, silky fur and bright blue eyes, that she had assumed he was female. But later, after she knew the truth, she'd continued to call him Julia. For deep down inside, she'd wanted to annoy him.

The blasted man had a rude habit of ignoring her. Whenever there was a ball, he'd dance with her sisters but not her. He hardly even talked to her. She would have thought that he hated her, except for the fact that he always showed up on the night of the full moons as a seal or otter to play with her. That had to mean he liked her, didn't it? So why did he avoid her when he was human?

"You seem to have lost most of your island accent," Nevis observed.

She nodded. "While I was living at Ebton Palace, Luciana encouraged me to improve my diction." No doubt so she could attract a noble suitor. "Where do you think Brody could be?"

Nevis shrugged. "My guess is he's investigating the secret Embraced army that Lord Morris talked about before he died."

She stiffened. "*What?* An Embraced army?"

Nevis's mouth dropped open. "Oh. Oh, shit. I—I thought you knew. All your sisters know. I thought they . . ."

"No." Maeve gripped the railing hard. "They didn't tell me."

Nevis winced. "Sorry."

"What is this Embraced army?"

"I—I don't think it's my place to say anything." He stepped back and made a quick bow. "I should check on my soldiers. Good day, my lady." He strode away, disappearing around the side of the cabin.

With a groan, Maeve propped her elbows on the railing. Of course her sisters hadn't told her. She wasn't a queen like they were. During the few days when all four kings and their queens had been in Wyndelas Palace, they had closeted themselves in the royal privy chamber for private discussions. Maeve hadn't been invited. After all, she didn't have a country to protect. She understood that, but even so, it was aggravating to feel left out.

It was a feeling she'd struggled with since childhood. Not that she was ignored. Her sisters had doted on her as the baby of the group. But it had always been clear that the eldest two, Luciana and Brigitta, were the best of friends. And the next two, Gwennore and Sorcha, were equally close to each other. Maeve was always the baby. The fifth wheel.

And now she felt even more left out. Her sisters and their husbands had become an exclusive group she could never join. There was only one kingdom left on Aerthlan, the island kingdom of Moon and Mist, and it already had a queen and an heir. So Maeve would never be a queen like her sisters.

She closed her eyes briefly. *There's no point in feeling sorry for yourself.* Being a queen didn't matter to her. What was important was that Nevis had given her a big clue. An Embraced army?

When she opened her eyes, she noticed the ripples coming from the barge and undulating their way to the riverbanks. Cause and effect. Lord Morris had claimed there was an Embraced army, and Brody disappeared searching for it. Since he hadn't returned, it seemed likely that he hadn't found the army yet. Had Lord Morris been speaking the truth, or had he taunted them with lies before dying?

She recalled everything she knew about Lord Morris. Before Leo had become king, when King Frederic ruled Eberon, Morris was his chief counsel and the head of the Church of Enlightenment. In those days, the kings on the mainland feared anyone who was born Embraced, so they had them hunted down and killed as infants. That way, the Embraced children could never grow up and use their magical powers to usurp the royal thrones. In Eberon, it had been Morris's job to eliminate the children.

But once Morris had become a member of the Circle of Five, had he realized that keeping the Embraced children alive could help the circle take over the world? Had he secreted the children away to train them as an army? Was the widely believed story that the Embraced children had all been murdered actually a lie?

It wouldn't be the first time that Maeve and her sisters had come across a falsehood. Growing up in the convent on the Isle of Moon, they had always believed that they'd been hidden away because they were Embraced. But in the last few years, they'd learned that this was only partially true. There had been other reasons. Luciana had been sent away because she was a twin. Brigitta's father had gotten rid of her to make everyone believe she was dead. Gwennore had been taken away to punish her mother for giving birth to a half-breed, and Sorcha's mother had been trying to keep her safe from the plague.

At the convent, Mother Ginessa had told the five young girls that they were orphans. For her elder sisters that had also proven to be a lie. What other falsehoods would they discover?

As she did every day, Maeve wondered if she would ever know the truth about herself. She had no idea where she had come from. The nuns at the convent had estimated that she was nearly a year old when she'd been left in a basket by the front gate. That had been midsummer, so from then on, the nuns had celebrated her birthday in late summer. But no one knew why she had been abandoned, so they had assumed she was Embraced like her adopted sisters, and that her actual birthday had to be when the moons embraced in autumn. That theory had proven correct when, at a young age, Maeve had displayed the odd gift of being able to communicate with the seals that lounged about on the nearby beach. Then, at the age of sixteen, she'd shifted for the first time into a seal.

This was one of the reasons she'd always felt a closeness to Brody. His past was mysterious, too, and he was also an Embraced shifter. Because of a witch's curse, he could maintain human form for only two hours each day, and unfortunately, he spent most of that time in secret conferences with Leo or whichever king he was currently helping. So it was only on rare occasions that Maeve saw him as a human. When he wasn't looking, she would study him intently, memorizing every bit of his handsome face and lean, strong body, so she could keep the image in her mind until she saw him again.

She wandered slowly back to the cabin and stopped by the door. When she'd left, the door hadn't latched properly, and now the gentle sway of the boat had caused it to swing halfway open.

"I don't think the Embraced army could be in Eberon." Luciana's soft voice filtered across the cabin. "The land is all cultivated. There would be no place to hide."

"Rupert is having the mountains in northern Tourin

checked," Brigitta said, referring to her husband by his pirate name. "But I don't think anyone could be hiding there. The lords in the highlands are very loyal, and they would have reported anything odd to us."

"I suspect there are vast areas of wilderness in Norveshka," Luciana continued. "But Silas is having his dragons survey every inch. And Aleksi is scanning the remote areas in Woodwyn."

Maeve sighed. Her sisters were no longer discussing babies. Had they been waiting for her to leave so they could discuss business matters?

She leaned against the cabin wall, thinking. If she had to hide somewhere, where would she go? The mainland kings would know if an army was hiding in their countries. Was there somewhere else? When Brigitta's husband had been a pirate, he'd hidden on a secret isle he'd named after himself. Could there be other islands in the Great Western Ocean?

A faint memory stirred in her mind. Over a year ago, while searching for something new to read in the library at Ebton Palace, she'd come across an extremely old book using a form of the Eberoni language that was so archaic, it had taken her about an hour to decipher it. But once she'd started to understand it, she'd become fascinated with the story it told.

According to the old book, an ancient continent had existed in the Great Western Ocean and the culture there had flourished long before the primitive people of Eberon had learned to even count the years. It had been the year 699 when she'd found this book, so she figured that this ancient land had to date back over seven hundred years.

The continent, Aerland, had been a place of magic with sorcerers so powerful that the rest of Aerthlan had quaked in fear of them. The ancient race had worshipped the twin moon goddesses and that had made the sun god, the Light, seethe with anger and jealousy. In a fit of rage, the Light had struck several volcanoes on the continent, causing them to erupt all at once in a massive explosion. Earthquakes had joined the devastation and after a few days, most of the ancient continent had collapsed far below the sea, and most of the people had perished.

There had been a map in the book, and after studying it, Maeve had suspected that the Isles of Moon and Mist were all that was left of the ancient continent of Aerland.

Could there be other islands? As soon as she arrived back at Ebton Palace, she would search the library for this book. And then, tomorrow, she would travel to the Isle of Moon. The nuns at the convent transcribed books, so they had a huge library. She might find more information there. And she could ask the seals at the nearby beach if they knew of any other islands.

Her breath caught. She could also go to the Isle of Mist and ask the Seer if he knew where the Embraced army was hiding. He might even know where Brody was.

Finally. She took a deep, satisfying breath. Finally, she had a course of action to pursue. It was so much better than sitting around worrying.

She strode into the cabin.

Luciana spotted her. "Oh, the air must have done you good. You look much better."

"I am better." Maeve stopped by the table of food and began loading a plate. Now that she had a plan, her appetite had returned.

"Ye should try the cherry tarts," Brigitta suggested. "We were just talking about how yummy there are."

"I know what you were talking about." Maeve gave them an annoyed look. "You should have told me about the Embraced army. And that Brody is gone because he's looking for them."

Luciana's and Brigitta's mouths fell open.

"Well . . ." Luciana winced. "We didn't want you to worry—"

"I'll worry more if I'm kept in the dark!" Maeve set her plate down with a thud. "Did it never occur to you that I hate being left out?"

Luciana and Brigitta exchanged looks, then turned to her with apologetic expressions on their faces.

"I know I'm not a queen, and I never will be," Maeve continued. "But that doesn't mean I don't care about you or your countries. I want to help."

Luciana sighed. "I'm afraid there's not much we can do."

Brigitta nodded. "It's frustrating for us, too."

"I believe there is something I can do." Maeve put a cherry tart on her plate. "I want to go back to the convent. Can you arrange passage for me to leave tomorrow morning?"

Luciana sat back with a shocked look. "Why? Are you not happy at Ebton Palace?"

Brigitta winced. "Are ye angry with us for not telling you everything?"

Luciana rose to her feet. "I was thinking of hosting a ball for you. And having my seamstresses make you a beautiful new gown. A sea-green color that would match your lovely eyes."

"Chee-ana." Maeve used her nickname for her eldest sister. "I don't need a ball. Or a new gown. And I'm not angry." She was determined. If the Embraced army was hiding somewhere in the Great Western Ocean, then there was no one better suited than she to track them down. She could finally put her Embraced gift of seal shifting to a good purpose.

And with any luck, she might find Brody, too.